Moonfire

Anne Clarke

Hard Shell Word Factory

To my husband for his unwavering support
and unfaltering belief.

© 2001 Anne Clarke
ISBN: 0-7599-0534-7
Trade Paperback
Published March 2002

eBook: ISBN: 0-7599-0249-6
Published February 2002

Hard Shell Word Factory
PO Box 161
Amherst Jct. WI 54407
books@hardshell.com
http://www.hardshell.com
Cover art © 2001 Dirk A. Wolf

Chapter 1

HOW THE HELL had she gotten herself into such a ridiculous predicament anyway?

From her gently rotating position in mid-air, Joanna Chase unhappily surveyed the brightly checkered floor just out of reach below her, then surreptitiously glanced around the room again. It was empty, unusual for this place where one normally had to book a time slot at least a day ahead. But then she was here at an odd time, having been driven to work off a morning's worth of frustration and stress from the latest debacle at the Taragon negotiating table.

She was relieved that no one was present to witness her highly embarrassing condition but, on the other hand, how by the star pits of Balien was she supposed to get down? She couldn't quite reach the release clip attached to the back of her harness, nor did she want to use the emergency transmitter clipped to a belt at her waist. Not yet, anyway. There had to be another way out of this.

She swung her legs again, trying to build momentum to reach the closest of the multi-layered, pitted walls of the climbing gym, and groaned in frustration when her efforts brought her nowhere near her goal. She glanced up. Just how *had* she ended up in mid-air in the middle of the room? The obvious answer, of course, was that a clasp on her harness equipment had been defective and had given way when she had slipped at the top of her climb. But she had a sneaking suspicion that in her earlier impatient and angry frame of mind, she hadn't attached it properly.

"Need some help?"

She squeaked in startled dismay at the deep voice coming from behind her and frantically spun around. Arms and legs flew ungracefully in four different directions.

The sight that met her eyes produced another yelp, this time of fright. The man was closer than she had expected, his face at a level only slightly below hers. And all she could see of his features were a pair of brilliant pale blue eyes and a small portion of his mouth. He was covered entirely in a form-molding, black water exercise suit that revealed every superb, hard contour of a tall, lean body. Even though she had the slight advantage of looking down on him, he exuded an aura that was wholly intimidating, mysterious, formidable.

Joanna licked her lips against a sudden dryness as her gaze skimmed over a heavily muscled chest, flat belly, and strong, powerful thighs.

"Well?" There was lazy amusement in the tone. "Do you need any help coming down from there, or would you prefer to look some more?" He finished snapping on a pair of black gloves and fisted his hands expectantly on his hips.

"Yes! No! I mean, of course, I don't need any help. I do this all the time," she lied, cringing as her voice squeaked with nervousness. "I can get myself down." She felt a wave of heat cross her face as he studied her intently. The expression in the blue eyes was unreadable, but she got the distinctly uncomfortable impression he didn't believe her.

Then he shrugged slightly, regretfully. "Whatever you say." His eyes flickered to the transmitter on her belt. "Just for your information, the mecattendant was occupied with a group in the other hall when I came in, and I'll be about a half hour in the water tunnel." His gaze swept the deserted room before coming back to rest on her face. "Not that you need any help, of course."

Joanna's mouth fell open as she watched him walk away toward the arched opening on the opposite side of the hall. How dare he? He *knew* she needed help, despite her denial, and he was leaving anyway. What an inconsiderate, arrogant—

Suddenly realizing her most immediate source of assistance was about to exit the hall, she cried, "Wait! Please— maybe I do need a little help to get down."

The dark form paused and turned slowly. "Maybe?"

"Oh, all right, I'm stuck," she snapped. "I've tried. I can't get down by myself."

He sauntered back toward her, every movement of muscle clearly defined. "Was that so hard to admit?"

The amusement in the deep, rich tones and the obvious provocation triggered her volatile temper. God, the man was downright obnoxious. "Oh, go away. I've decided I don't need *your* help after all," she declared rudely, and spun away. Instantly, she wished she hadn't since he now had a clear view of her vulnerable posterior, and the strangled guttural sound she heard was clearly one of approval.

Abruptly, a strong hand flattened against her rib cage raising her slightly, while an arm reached over and his other hand wrestled with the harness clasp. "Well, whether you want it or not, I'm bringing you down. I don't have time for games," came the infuriatingly calm response.

As the clasp released, her body came down across his shoulder. Hands caught her about her waist and slid her down against his length until her feet touched the ground.

"Thank you," she mumbled grudgingly. "I..." She looked up and the words died in her throat.

Pale blue had deepened to dark sapphire, and the message in his eyes was unmistakable. Knowing she should break the contact, she seemed to have completely her lost her will to do so, and could only watch in utter fascination as his face drew closer. His hands were burning holes in her clothes. The shakiness in her legs had nothing to do with being returned to solid ground.

Then his lips touched hers, gentle as the breath of a breeze, and she was lost. She sagged against him, her legs refusing to support her. Fire and ice raced through her body. The pressure of his mouth increased slightly, and she felt the startlingly warm brush of his tongue across her lips. Someone moaned, and a corner of her mind was shocked to recognize that the sound had come from her own throat.

The next instant, he had drawn back. She blinked dazedly, unwilling to relinquish the promise he had offered, strangely bereft without his body heat.

"That was quite a 'thank you'." The words were murmured huskily. A thumb brushed across her lower lip.

The spell was broken. Reality returned with shocking abruptness along with the realization that his other thumb was stroking the underside of one breast.

"Get your hands off me!" She flung up her arms breaking the hold he had on her, but held her ground. "How dare you?"

His eyes narrowed. "How dare I what?" he asked softly, dangerously.

"How dare you do that—take advantage of me like that?" Damn, but she wished she could see his face. The mask effectively concealed his every expression, and his strange eyes had lightened again, become blankly opaque.

"I believe it's called 'kissing', and you enjoyed it as much as I did."

"You still had no right!" she spluttered.

He towered over her, but she refused to let him see how much his sheer height intimidated her. Then he leaned closer, forcing her this time to take a step backwards. "You, lady, have absolutely no concept of what my 'rights' are. But I'll be glad to continue this debate later. Meet me at the Second Lentali tonight after the evening meal." His voice deepened, washing over her like a caress. "Although I do think we have far more interesting things to discuss."

"Hah!" Joanna's knees were threatening to betray her again. She sniffed and wrinkled her nose. "*I* think you probably have a very inflated opinion of yourself, and I wouldn't—"

A hard arm snaked out, wrapped around her waist and jerked her against him. This time his mouth came down on hers with crushing force but was just as quickly gone, leaving her gasping for breath.

And when her head had stopped spinning and she finally gathered her wits again, she was quite alone in the hall.

WHO WAS SHE?

He had been instantly attracted to her, this creature with the flashing green eyes and ivory skin that flushed such an interesting shade of pink. Her red-gold hair had been pulled back carelessly into some sort of a binding at the back of her head, but several strands had escaped and he could tell it must be quite long. The face that it framed was nothing short of stunning. He had been no less enchanted by the front view of the intriguing creature as he had been by the sight of her gently rounded posterior when he had first walked into the exercise hall. The sudden excitement that had raced through his blood had nothing at all to do with the anticipation of a strenuous workout.

And the two kisses he had permitted himself, as quick as they had been, had had him on the verge of losing control. He had ached for so much more, wanting to sweep her back into his arms, kiss her senseless, hear that sexy little moan again before laying her down on the floor to thoroughly explore all the delights her slender body promised.

It had been a long time since he had reacted so strongly and instantly to a woman.

And he couldn't afford this distraction. Not now!

As his body battled the churning thrust of the water, the image of bright hair and angry emerald eyes remained engraved on his mind. His hands still felt the slender shape of her. His torso still tingled at every point of contact. He wondered if she would show up that evening, and thought there was an even chance she might, if only to continue the battle she so obviously relished.

He guessed her heritage to be that of Earth. There was a small community here on the sixth substation in the Neutral Realm, a fragmented asteroid colony in the Crestar System. It should be easy enough to find out more about her but, with an unexpected sense of loss, he knew he wasn't going to pursue it. He couldn't even afford the time to meet with her. He had information to seek out, preparations to make. The instructions he had received were unequivocal and, as much as he disagreed with them and believed the substance of them to be founded in rumor and misinformation, he couldn't ignore them. The slightest possibility of truth could bring a fragile alliance to its knees, and crush the life from the peace initiative before it had a chance to breathe.

His body was beginning to tire, and thoughts of the delightful encounter faded as his mind turned to the business at hand. This mission could be dangerous, or could be nothing at all. But it could also have a tremendous impact on an entire star system, and be a turning point in a conflict that had raged for generations and taken a terrible toll.

He would need all his wits about him.

There was no latitude to consider his personal desires.

Chapter 2

FIVE MONTHS later, Alex Mariltar, Commander of the Seventh Fleet, impatiently paced the small captain's meeting room of the warrior vessel, *Astran*. His body ached with tiredness. His eyes felt gritty from lack of sleep.

Where *was* Jason? His second-in-command had requested this meeting, said there was urgent news to convey. Just what was so urgent, after his five month absence, that it couldn't wait until he had grabbed a few hours of sleep? He ran a hand through his dark hair, and swung around again, coming to a stop in front of the large curved window.

Far in the distance, he could see the yellow moon that orbited his home planet, Mariltar, and its neighbor, Soron. The planets themselves were already out of sight, but something about the shape of the moon caught his attention, and he studied it more closely, finally identifying the shadow that curved around its lower edge.

A giant fist squeezed at his gut.

An eclipse!

The fifth in the moon's recorded history and, some would say, an omen of major significance.

What could it portend this time? Many believed this rare and irregular phenomenon foretold of momentous change in the Crestar System. Previous occurrences had been linked to the implosion of a small planet, the arrival of strangers in the System and the creation of a nation, as well as a war so prolonged that most had difficulty remembering its origin.

Or was it merely a confirmation of events already set in motion? Because, unknown to most of its inhabitants, a birth was taking place in the Crestar System. Even as their people continued to battle, the leaders of nine great nations had come together to form a Coalition. The Coalition's simple vision was one of peace, a quest for harmony, an end to the Conflicts that had wreaked a terrible destruction on their worlds and families.

As the moon vanished completely from sight, swallowed into the blackness of space, Alex sighed and turned away. Pushing his hands into the pockets of his breeches, he avoided the comfortable padded bench across from the information console, and walked instead to stand in front of a three dimensional holographic image suspended in the corner of the room.

The planet, Treaine. Beautiful, ancient and steeped in mystery.

Here would be the genesis of the Vision. Treaine, on the outer boundary of the Crestar System and virtually abandoned for years, would nurture a small colony peopled by men and women from each of the nations and colonies of the Crestar System. Carefully screened and chosen for their dedication to the peace initiative, the vastly diverse populace would be expected to coexist and intermarry. They would craft common laws to be implemented throughout the System, and build learning institutions to incorporate the values of all the nations. Trade agreements would be revived and re-negotiated, and technologies integrated.

The challenge, he knew, was great but not insurmountable. The Vision had a basis in the distant past. Before the Conflicts, forged from greed for the rich and varied natural resources on each other's planets, had torn the Crestar System apart, the great clans had traded peacefully and occasionally entered into marriage partnerships. Those alliances would be formed again on Treaine. And there were relative newcomers to the System. Traders, scholars, engineers and others from distant worlds, who had been drawn to the Crestar System despite the Conflicts, would also have a place in the new colony.

As the holograph revolved slowly in front of him, Alex's tired mind refused to erase the image of that ominous shadow. Not superstitious by nature, he nevertheless couldn't help but wonder what its appearance meant at this precise point in time.

Success or failure for Treaine?

Destruction or survival for the Crestar System?

"ALEX, YOU'RE going to have to make a decision. You can't postpone it any longer. You're the last of the ambassadors to enter into a marriage partnership."

Alex allowed the irritated drum of his fingers on the metal table to be, for the moment, Jason Trion's only answer. The blond captain of the *Astran*, his striking looks given a slightly rakish air by a small faint scar which broke the smooth curve of his mouth, was studying him warily. Eyes narrowed to mere slits, Alex deliberately forced his tall form, stretched out on the bench, to appear relaxed even though he felt anything but. He waited. Jason undoubtedly had more to say.

"Sagar's sacred crystals, Alex," Jason said with a touch of

impatience, "I sympathize with you. I really do. But you knew marriage was a condition of your appointment as Ambassador to Treaine. I'm frankly surprised the Coalition hasn't demanded an answer before now."

Alex cracked one eye slightly wider for a better look at his subordinate and close friend. A corner of his mouth curled in bleak amusement. "When you send a man on a diplomatic mission to every forsaken star pit in the System, Jason, it's a little difficult to keep track of him, let alone pin him down." A huge yawn took him by surprise. He bent forward and cupped his head in his hands, saying with annoyance, "Blood of Cor, I thought I had more time. I can barely think."

Groaning, he rose tiredly to his feet, jabbed his hands into the pockets of his breeches and walked to the window. *This* was the issue that was so urgent. It was something he had avoided, hadn't wanted to think about. Now he was out of time. He turned. "I can't accept the choices of the Coalition, Jason. There must be other alternatives!"

Jason Trion grimaced and shook his well-groomed head. He swung around in his seat to glance briefly at the information console behind him. "There are, but they don't look promising. The Coalition is deeply disappointed by your refusal to make a selection from the women they've identified. Obviously, political objectives would be satisfied and strengthened by an alliance with any one of them. But, because of your reluctance, they did give permission just this morning for the Match Key to be used more extensively."

"And?"

His question was greeted with a shrug. "We've searched the Match Key data banks of all the eligible nations and colonies. Only two colonies have yet to report back, including the Earth colony whose files are not complete. There were no close matches with the others."

Alex shook his head in frustration. "How long for the search to be completed?"

"Another several hours, at least."

"Then I'll wait until all possible search avenues are exhausted. Blood of Cor, this is my life we're—"

"Captain Trion?" The query came loudly over the communicator cube.

"Yes," Jason snapped, "What is it? We were not to be disturbed."

"My apologies, sir. We're being hailed by the *Claxiarten*, a Coalition vessel. She was forced to stop for repairs at the last substation, and was left behind by the pod in which she was traveling.

There's an ambassador and several negotiators aboard, sir. She's requesting permission to join our pod."

"Permission granted."

Alex saw Jason become absorbed in the data on the information console again, data that could change his life. He sighed and turned to look out the window into the depths of space and swirling star debris. Certainly the answers were out there somewhere. But where? Not for the first time, he wondered if he had chosen the right path by accepting his election as an ambassador to the Coalition colony of Treaine. But he hadn't really had a choice. As the third son of the ruling High Lord of Mariltar, the expectations were clear and how could he have denied the Coalition?

Behind him, he heard Jason's chair creak as it swung around, and then his footsteps as he crossed the room to stand beside him. "You're in a tough position, Alex," Jason said sympathetically, clapping him hard on the back. "But you have the luck of Pormiam with women. Isn't there anyone from all those, ah, relationships you've had over the years you could tolerate as a mate? What about Cerata? She has the added benefit of being a Coalition choice."

Alex snorted in disgust and tiredly wiped a hand across his face. *Women!* Yes, there had been many. But none he could even remotely imagine as a marriage partner. Except—with blinding clarity, a vision rose in his mind of red-gold hair, flashing green eyes and a lushly rounded bottom that just begged to be cupped by a man's hands. She hadn't shown up to meet him that night five months ago, and he hadn't had time to investigate her, nor had he had opportunity to return to the Neutral Realm.

But he hadn't been able to forget her either during those excruciatingly long months of chasing phantoms, of following trails that led nowhere, of dissecting rumors that ended up being nothing at all. And time hadn't diminished the memory of the strength of his attraction to her. The thought was outrageous anyway. He had been in her company for barely five minutes. How could he even think of her in the context of wife material? The matter was moot in any event. She was most certainly out of reach, even if he had the luxury of pursuing the standard mating negotiation ritual.

Raking a hand through his hair, he turned to Jason. "Cerata is an extraordinary distraction, but far from having the qualities I would want in a mate. That goes for the rest of the Coalition's choices as well. I've been intimately acquainted with several of those women and not one of them appeals to me as a marriage partner."

He slumped into a nearby chair and stared darkly at the ceiling, then back at Jason, and said accusingly, "I can't believe the Match Key hasn't found a single woman who is truly compatible. It shouldn't be *that* difficult to find one female in the whole of the Crestar System who would be a suitable match."

He saw Jason struggle to hide a grin and knew with disgust what he was thinking. All his captains had joked about it loudly and often enough in his hearing. Mariltar men were typically large and well-built, but Alex, as they were so gleeful to point out when it suited them, was a particularly fine specimen. Dedication to strenuous exercise had honed and hardened his body, and the sculptured, aristocratic features of his face and confident, come-hither smile had been known to cause more than a few female hearts to beat a little harder. As a son of the ruling clan on Mariltar, he had never had the slightest difficulty in securing female companionship, and suspected there were women who would quite possibly commit mayhem for an offer to become his life mate for the privilege of rank alone. Even he might find the situation darkly amusing if it were not so time-sensitive and serious.

"It does seem peculiar," Jason admitted, losing the battle to control his features. "But the Match Key is nothing if not thorough." With some ruthlessness, he reminded Alex, "You *have* turned down suitable women already, Alex, and you accepted that a marriage partnership was a condition of your election as an ambassador to Treaine. You knew you'd have to make a choice sooner, rather than later."

"I know. *I know.*" Feeling his frustration level soar, Alex swiveled to stare out the window again. An unfamiliar vessel had appeared in the window's opening. Even as he watched, it passed through a moisture veil causing a momentary but spectacular pale green halo to appear. Excitement, unexplained and unexpected, suddenly gripped him and he said, "The *Claxiarten* is carrying colonists, is she not? Perform a search of her personal data banks!"

Jason's mouth dropped open in astonishment. "Alex you're being unreasonable. The chances that the *Claxiarten* is carrying a compatible partner are infinitesimal and—"

"But still, there's a chance," Alex interrupted, "and what is there to lose? With your training, you can access her data banks undetected and be out of there before anyone is any wiser." His gaze fixed on the strange vessel, he added softly, "That *is* a direct order."

Jason hesitated, then turned with obvious reluctance back to the console. Alex went back to staring out the window. How he wished this business was over. The thought of taking a life mate still rankled. He had too many other responsibilities, ones he had willingly sought. He didn't want this one—not yet anyway.

"Great Sagar!"

Alex swung quickly around at the astonishment in his senior captain's voice. "What is it?"

His gaze glued to the screen, Jason whistled softly under his breath. "Look at this!"

In a few long strides, Alex stood behind him. His brows shot up and his eyes focused intently as data rolled across the screen. His glance flicked over the name which held no meaning for him. *Joanna Chase.* "Can you pull in an image?"

Jason touched a key. A digitized image of a woman's face popped up that held both men spellbound. Reddish gold hair the color of a malan prism fell smoothly past her shoulders. It framed a face remarkable for high, delicate cheekbones and sparkling green eyes. Her mouth was curved in an impish smile revealing a deep dimple in her cheek.

"Sagar's sacred crystals, Alex, she's stunning!"

Yes, she was. And exactly as he remembered her, except the hair was smoothly in place, and the face was a serene translucent ivory, not flushed with frustration and fury. Excitement roared through his blood. She had haunted his dreams for months, and now she was just a star vessel away.

Jason pressed another key. The image shrank and data continued to roll across the screen. "She's a senior negotiator for the Coalition—from the Earth colony, a member of Ambassador Kromon's team. Great Sagar, Alex! She's matched up in almost every aspect with your key. She's the closest match so far. It's a pity she's an Earth colonist."

Alex straightened up still staring at the screen, then dragged his gaze away and started to pace restlessly around the room deep in thought. She was here! An extraordinary coincidence. Not out of reach, after all, in the Neutral Realm. But marriage? To an Earth colonist? Why not? If their first encounter was any indication, there was much to look forward to and the Match Key had provided the ultimate sanction. Certainly, the alternatives had zero appeal.

Abruptly, he said, "She'll do! The Coalition shall have its marriage partnership. Arrange a conference with the captain of the *Claxiarten* and Ambassador Kromon. There's no reason to delay and every reason to get this accomplished quickly."

Turning swiftly to face Alex, Jason swore loudly as his elbow cracked against the corner of the console. "Don't you think you should give this a little more thought. Balls of Sortor, Alex, she's an Earth colonist. It's an unpredictable race, at best; certainly not an ideal choice in the eyes of the Coalition."

"They included Earth colonists in eligibility criteria, didn't they?"

"Yes, but—"

"She's the best match by far, not in every aspect, but certainly close enough to satisfy requirements. I want her. And I want this business settled as soon as possible. We have far more important concerns to deal with."

Jason rubbed his elbow and shrugged in helpless resignation. "I suppose your mind's made up and nothing will change it, as usual, but shouldn't you seek the Coalition's approval first?"

"Cor's blood, Jason, I've made my decision. The Coalition should accept the partnership. After all, she *is* from one of the eligible colonies. And, as you pointed out so correctly not too long ago, I'm running out of time. She's a negotiator with the Coalition and presumably aware that partnerships are being formed at the direction of the Coalition. I have to assume that she'll be receptive to this proposition, but I *don't* have time for lengthy discussions. If she's as compatible with me as the Match Key indicates, there shouldn't be a problem."

Alex saw with irritation that unconcealed amusement was back on Jason's face. "I hope your confidence about this decision isn't misplaced, Alex. Earth colonists follow customs and practices that are quite different from ours, and most of the Crestar System's for that matter. She may not be as receptive to this partnership as you might hope. Are you sure you don't want to complete the search of the personal data banks of the other colony?"

His mouth twisted in a grimace, Alex's eyes sought the *Claxiarten* again. Jason's words had reminded him of how very feisty and uncooperative this female could be. But, even with the thought, his determination grew along with his sense of urgency. "No! Suspend it. If there is any reluctance, I'll deal with it. But I don't believe there will be much resistance. Any of the nations of the Crestar System would be anxious to enter into a marriage alliance with the Clan of Mariltar. The colonists shouldn't be any different. The arrangement offers nothing but advantages to her."

Alex spoke without boasting, but with the complete confidence and assurance of the position to which he had been born. In all honesty, he *couldn't* imagine why any woman, even an independent spirit with green eyes, would turn away an alliance with the Clan of Mariltar. He could tell that Jason wasn't so convinced, and knew his friend was concerned about the lady's race. Earth colonists *were* known for somewhat unpredictable behavior. The strongest objections, of course, despite what he had told Jason earlier, might come from the Coalition who would not view an Earth colonist as the preferred mate for a High Lord of Mariltar. But they *had* given their permission to extend the search to the colonists, and the results of the Match Key offered powerful persuasion.

Jason sat down and reached for the communication cube. "A conference within the hour then?"

"Yes. I'm going to get some rest. Call me when it's time." Alex yawned and rolled his aching shoulders, then headed for the door as Jason opened a communication relay. "Let's get this business out of the way. I'll need all of the captains for a briefing later. We have some vital issues to discuss."

As he plodded tiredly down the *Astran*'s corridor, Alex reflected with some amusement that his captains were going to have plenty to speculate about before they met as a group. His thoughts turned serious. Even with the men he trusted more than any others, he would have to be very careful not to reveal too much about his five-month long journey, thinly disguised as a diplomatic mission. The Coalition's Vision had to be protected at all costs and would not be well-served by distrust and suspicion born of rumor.

Chapter 3

THE MESSAGE was delivered to Joanna Chase at mid-morning, interrupting a negotiating session.

That was the first surprise. Once the doors were shut, the negotiators were normally left alone with only occasional visits from Ambassador Kromon. Surprise turned to concern at the request for her to report immediately to the captain's private meeting room for a conference with both the captain and the ambassador.

As she hurried down the corridor, Joanna's mind was wildly seeking an explanation for the summons. Everything had been going all right, hadn't it? Kromon had told her only yesterday he had thought her suggestion to resolve a petty issue raised by the Sorons was particularly creative. Never mind that, in the end, it hadn't been implemented.

She reached the entrance to the room and paused to smooth her hair and collect herself. The serious faces both men turned toward her as she entered the room caused her sense of misgiving to mushroom. Kromon's warm greeting and the slight stretching of his pale blue lips, which for him passed as a smile, did little to relieve her anxiety.

He waved her to a chair then, hands behind his back, fell into contemplation of the floor and nervously cleared his throat. Joanna squirmed unhappily in her seat and glanced at the silent captain. His gaze immediately slid away from hers. She looked back at the Merlon. His ridged brow was deeply furrowed and he was darting little assessing glances at her. She was used to these disconcerting habits by now, and sometimes wondered if Kromon employed them deliberately to disarm his audience, since he truly was a master negotiator. But it was definitely nerve wracking to have them turned on her. She took a deep breath and opened her mouth to ask the reason for her summons just as the Merlon launched into an explanation.

"Joanna, I apologize for calling you out of a session, but what we have to convey is urgent and of extreme importance." He cleared his throat again. "We received a message this morning, a proposal actually, from the *Astran*. It, ah, requires a response from you. The *Astran* also transports an ambassador to Treaine. Ambassador Mariltar has not yet entered into a marriage partnership as all the ambassadors to Treaine are required to do. He has, apparently, rejected the Coalition's choices and has made his own decision."

He paused, clearly uncomfortable, his pallid features looking more drawn and unhappy than usual. Joanna felt a chill of foreboding slide down her spine, and gave an involuntary shiver. Just what did any of this have to do with her? Kromon drew himself up, folded his long hands inside the sleeves of his robe and raised speculative eyes to hers. "Ambassador Mariltar is offering the honor of a marriage partnership to you, Joanna. Furthermore, he has suggested that the, ah, mating ceremony take place without delay."

Stunned into speechlessness, Joanna could only stare at the Merlon. Surely, she hadn't heard him correctly. This was too bizarre. A proposal of marriage? From a man she'd never heard of? Not even delivered in person? A strangled noise that could have been a giggle and sounded slightly hysterical to her own ears burst from her throat. Out of the corner of her eye, she saw the captain tug nervously at an ear.

Kromon continued on hastily, "Before you answer, think carefully about this, Joanna. You would not only be marrying an ambassador to Treaine, but a son of the ruling clan on Mariltar, a very powerful and influential family. Any one of the leading clans in the Crestar System would be honored to make such an alliance. The fact that he has rejected the Coalition's choices and chosen outside of a ruling clan, and, indeed, has chosen from outside of the Crestar System itself, should be highly respected and given strong consideration."

Understanding dawned, and she sat forward on the edge of her seat. There could be no other explanation. "This is someone's idea of a joke, right? You're all getting back at me for extending the negotiation session yesterday."

"No!" If his emphatic denial wasn't enough, the shocked expression on the ambassador's face was enough to convince her he was perfectly serious. Star pits!

"Who is this man? Oh, I know, I know." She waved her hands. "You've already told me. He's some lord from the Mariltar clan. What I meant was, *I* don't know who *he* is, so how could he possibly be proposing to me? And why isn't he doing it himself?"

"It's Mariltar custom to make the offer through a third party, and I believe—"

"Well, it's not Earth custom," Joanna interrupted, anger starting to surface as the gravity of the situation began sinking in. "No! Absolutely not! This is too ridiculous. I will not consider this. I contracted to be a negotiator for Treaine, not a wife. I don't care *who* this man is. I have absolutely no desire to enter into a marriage partnership"

She saw Kromon sigh heavily and draw his robes more closely around himself. He glanced at the *Claxiarten's* captain as if for support, but the captain, Joanna noticed, had apparently decided to distance himself from the discussion and was engrossed with his information console. Kromon turned his attention back to her. This time, the expression in his eyes made her dig her fingers painfully into her thighs as a stab of pure panic rushed through her. "Joanna, I'll be candid. I've known you for some time and I cannot say I didn't anticipate this response." His mouth twisted unexpectedly with humor. "Certainly, I didn't think this task would be easy. I empathize with your position, but there is far more at stake here than just your feelings on the subject. You know the Coalition is requiring some mixed marriage partnerships at the highest of levels to solidify alliances and strengthen the peace accord. My own partnership is a result of that. You are one of my best negotiators. And with your skills and experience, you would undoubtedly perform the official duties of an ambassador's wife to perfection. Your role in the peace process would be greatly enhanced if you agreed to this arrangement."

"I think the peace process would be better served if he chose a partner from Taragon or Soron," Joanna snapped. An overwhelming sensation of helplessness was making her dizzy. He was so concerned about the public side of this marriage. But what about the private side? She had to get out of here before she panicked completely. "Please tell him I am most definitely *not* interested."

Kromon took a step forward, as intense and serious as she had ever seen him. "Joanna, take some time to think about it! Alex Mariltar is a well-respected leader. This proposal *deserves* the appropriate consideration. He's requested a visual conference with you later in the day."

"It's a little late for *that*," she said stubbornly, rising to her feet. "I've made my decision and I won't change my mind, so I don't see the purpose for a conference. You know I have no time today anyway and I need to get back to the session. May I be excused?" She struggled to keep her tone polite, and her features composed, but she knew neither man was likely to miss the anger that was making her cheeks burn. Nor did she really care. Her legs were threatening to collapse underneath her and it would take all of her concentration to get out of the room before she embarrassed herself. Without waiting for permission, she left.

"ALEX MARILTAR is not going to take 'no' for an answer." The captain finally stirred, breaking a thick, heavy silence. He reached for his private supply of tagvar wine and poured himself a healthy drink. It didn't cross his mind to offer a goblet to his distinguished companion.

Ambassador Kromon shook his head, clearly frustrated. "He's going to have to. I think I know that young lady well enough by now to believe she *won't* change her mind, but I wish she could have been more open-minded to the proposal. I think it would have been an excellent marriage partnership." He turned to leave. "Will you contact the *Astran*, and convey the message?"

The captain of the *Claxiarten* drained his goblet in one gulp as he watched him go. He reluctantly reached out to activate the communication cube. He knew Alex Mariltar by reputation, and was convinced beyond a doubt that relaying the message would not be the end of the matter. Briefly, he thought of taking steps to shield his now vulnerable passenger, but quickly rejected the idea. It was none of his business. He had only been hired to transport colonists. He most certainly did not want a confrontation with Alex Mariltar or, for that matter, the most elite warrior force in the whole of the Crestar System which served him.

Chapter 4

LATER THAT SAME day, as the pod of vessels continued to navigate through the Crestar System toward the planet, Treaine, the captains of the Seventh Fleet of Mariltar, summoned by their commanding officer, began gathering in the *Astran's* large conference room. The five men were of similar age and had served together under Alex Mariltar for most of their warrior careers. They had sworn allegiance to the House of Mariltar as soon as they were old enough to take up the weapons of war, and had pledged to protect its son with their lives. Their loyalty to their commander was unquestioned.

The Seventh Fleet had been chosen by the Coalition to secure the peace in the multi-ethnic infant colony of Treaine. As defenders rather than aggressors in the great Conflicts, the Mariltar fleet, nevertheless, had won a formidable reputation. The most neutral of all the nations, its elite warrior force commanded sufficient respect and confidence from its former enemies to handle the sensitive task ahead.

The atmosphere in the room was one of subdued anticipation. Every man knew that there had been a greater purpose behind Alex's so-called diplomatic mission, and they were anxious for the debriefing. As they obtained drinks for themselves from the dispensing unit, Eric Stromi, the captain who had accompanied the commander, was peppered with questions. He dodged each one adroitly, as they had known he would, unaware that even he was not fully cognizant of the true purpose of the mission.

In the midst of growing boisterousness, the door slid open and Jason entered the room. He was not alone. The man by his side was well-known to the group, and his appearance momentarily surprised and silenced them. Tall and well-built, there his physical similarity to the other Mariltar males ended. His thick, blond hair fell unbound to the middle of his back, and a simple metallic-colored robe covered him from neck to toe. Advisor Barok, a spiritual counselor, had never attended a warrior debriefing before, and his presence only served to heighten each man's anticipation.

As greetings were exchanged, Jason moved over to the information console and began to enter a series of commands. He studied the results then turned to survey the group. Rocking slightly on his feet, hands behind his back, he savored the moment. His announcement would produce some interesting reactions.

This group had been as close as brothers. Raised in the shadow of conflict, trained to take up leadership roles at an early age, they were an elite group of warriors. Not only would they protect the House of Mariltar with all the formidable skills at their disposal, but they would support and defend each other to the death. Treaine offered a lifestyle that was so foreign to their upbringing, he only hoped they could all adapt.

And the first significant change was about to occur.

He cleared his throat. "Gentlemen, Alex will join us in a few minutes. We will finally hear about this farce of a diplomatic mission-" Hoots and hollers greeted this pronouncement, and he grinned and waved his hand carelessly for silence. "—but, before that happens, he has a small task for us."

A heartfelt groan was heard. Sebastian Asteril, the acknowledged rebel of the group, slumped dramatically in his chair. "Not again. Balls of Sortor, the last time Alex had a 'small task', I got sprayed with corft fire by an angry husband." He squirmed in his seat. "I swear I still have shards embedded in my flesh."

Jason took a swallow of the Mariltar ambrosia someone had thrust at him, and waited patiently for the chuckles and rude comments to die down. "Well, this does involve a woman and a husband, but I think I can guarantee you the corft fire will be kept out of it. Alex has finally made his decision about a marriage partner. She—"

"It's about time!"

"Who is she?"

"Anyone we know?"

Raising his voice to be heard over the chorus of voices, Jason continued, "She was identified through the Match Key this morning. She's an Earth colonist, a senior negotiator assigned to Treaine."

Mark Oberan, the strategy maker, serious and scholarly, spoke up doubtfully. "An Earth colonist? For the House of Mariltar?"

"Why not?"

Speculation and argument broke out around the room as each man voiced his opinion on the choice of their commander's future mate.

Once again, Jason raised his voice. "I would remind you that the Match Key has sanctioned the partnership, and we all know its success is extraordinary. More importantly, Alex himself has no objections. He seems quite anxious, in fact, to settle the issue and move on."

"So, when do we get to meet her?" Sebastian asked. Half

seriously, he added, "As Alex's personal guard, seems we should have the right to inspect the lady before he makes an irrevocable commitment."

Jason set down his goblet and clasped his hands behind his back. A small frown furrowed his brow. He still wasn't entirely comfortable with Alex's decision. "You'll meet her shortly. We're porting her over from the Claxiarten. I should warn you though, Alex is unyielding on this decision." He nodded toward Advisor Barok. "He's requested that the advisor perform the mating ceremony without further delay, and that's where your task comes in."

The stunned expressions on five faces were eminently satisfying.

"Yesterday he was complaining that he couldn't *make* a decision with the choices he had, and now he's getting *married? Tonight?*" said Eric Stromi. "Care to enlighten us?"

Jason shrugged his shoulders and spread his hands. "Once he'd made up his mind, Alex saw no reason to delay. Unfortunately, the lady is, uh, less than receptive to the idea. She's refused to even talk to Alex about his proposal."

And Alex's reaction had been interesting to say the least. He hadn't seemed a bit surprised that he had been so quickly and thoroughly rejected. But her refusal to respond to repeated requests for a visual conference had produced cold anger and impatience. Even now, Jason still winced inwardly at the ruthless solution Alex had proposed. If what he wanted couldn't be obtained willingly, then he would simply take what he wanted and make sure he kept it. Within the next hour, an unsuspecting Joanna Chase would be ported to the *Astran.*

Into the silence created by this revelation, someone dared to ask the question, "Then what changed her mind about coming here this evening?"

"She didn't. We've secured her signal, and have coded and shielded the port."

Mark Oberan's jaw dropped. "Balls of Sortor, we're kidnapping her? Alex is testing the limits of convention on this one. What does the Coalition have to say?"

Jason swung around as a beep came from the information console. Over his shoulder, he said, "The Coalition doesn't know yet. Alex will inform them after the mating ceremony. He was concerned that they might not be entirely pleased with his choice of an Earth colonist, which is partly why the ceremony takes place tonight. They'll have to accept his choice once the marriage partnership has been legalized.

He's too valuable for them to do otherwise."

Sebastian Asteril threw his head back and gave a shout of laughter. "Act now, and deal with the consequences later. That's so typical of Alex. I almost feel sorry for the poor woman—or maybe I should feel sorry for Alex. I'd sooner go into battle than face an angry woman," he finished, his tone filled with admiration.

Uneasy laughter rippled around the meeting room, until Jason squelched it with a gesture. "The reason you're here, besides being Alex's friends and his personal guard is that the marriage, of course, requires a quorum. In the absence of Alex's family, you'll all be asked for your consent before the marriage can be legalized. And it *must* be legal. The Coalition cannot have any opportunity to break the bond. Alex is adamant about that. After the Advisor—"

The door opened and the subject of the discussion strode into the room. The room immediately erupted into a cacophony of whistles, cheers and claps.

Alex, in the formal dress uniform of a warrior commander of Mariltar, paused and made a half bow with a grim smile on his face. "Thank you, all. I assume you've all been briefed and I'll interpret this unruly display as a sign of support. I'll expect better manners in front of the lady."

Sebastian strolled over and pounded him on the back. "Congratulations, sir. You continue to provide us with exemplary leadership in everything you do. And although, I, for one, am not anxious to follow where you're leading this time, I expect I will learn and benefit from your experience."

"And *I* predict, that before the year is up on Treaine, more than half this group will have entered into marriage partnerships." Alex took the goblet Eric offered him and raised it in mock salute, before setting it down untouched. Clearly unmoved by the spate of vociferous denials his words had inspired, he moved off to talk with Advisor Barok, leaving the group to argue good-naturedly about who would fall prey to his prediction.

Suddenly, a series of insistent beeps erupted from the information console, and Jason leapt to examine the screen. Straightening again, he turned a serious face to the now silent room. "It's time, Alex. If you're going to proceed with this, it needs to be done now. She's isolated in a corridor."

The Mariltar commander's eyes locked with Jason's. Jason saw his brow quirk as if in silent query, and knew his own doubts were still reflected on his face. Then Alex gave a curt nod. As Jason issued commands into the central computer, all eyes turned to the port tube in the corner of the room.

JOANNA HURRIED along the corridor in the *Claxiarten*, heading for her private quarters. Tiredly she plucked at the white scarf around her throat and undid the top fastener of her jewel-green tunic suit. Damn, but that last meeting with Kromon had been grueling! Fifteen and a half very intense hours had passed since the senior negotiators had started the day's session. Although the team wouldn't be complete until they were on Treaine, some of the prioritizing was already in progress.

Muttering to herself, she rounded a corner. If someone handed her the choice right now, she would be very tempted to return to trade negotiations in the Neutral Realm. But then she had known when she signed up that there would be days like this. Trying to marry philosophies and agendas of nine very different cultures so recently at war would be considered by some to be downright impossible. But these nations had coexisted peacefully before and would again. And she had to remember to remind herself of that in the days ahead. She had no doubt that today's squabbles and disagreements would seem tame by comparison when the real negotiating started.

And then there had been that outrageous marriage proposal. And all those requests for a meeting. Four of them. Whoever the man was, he was certainly persistent and she had to admit to some curiosity about him. If she hadn't been so annoyed at being interrupted during a particularly tricky moment that last time, she might have agreed to the visual conference, just to have the satisfaction of telling him 'no' to his face.

Now she was exhausted and looking forward to crawling into bed. Her thoughts shifted longingly to images of a steaming hot bath filled with silky, fragrant bubbles, and she sighed. How she hated the hand-held cleansing equipment on these star vessels. While they were practical and more than adequately performed their function, she never really *felt* clean after using one. She hoped the accommodations on Treaine, primitive though they were purported to be, would at least have proper bathing facilities. It would still be some time before the highly efficient living units designed to accommodate the Earth colonists were completed.

Suddenly, she sensed a strange sucking sensation, and felt as if she had run into an invisible barrier. Her movements slowed involuntarily, and then ceased altogether. She watched in horror with heightened consciousness as her body was enfolded and squeezed into a rectangular column of light, which spun straight through the walls of the vessel and out into space. Seconds of swirling helplessness and numbing, undefined fear followed. Her mind was screaming in terror, her vision blurred by the speed at which she was traveling. It was several minutes before the pressure eased and the column of light released her body.

She put out a hand to steady herself and raised her eyes to find herself in an unfamiliar room filled with strange men all studying her with varying degrees of curiosity. She immediately recognized the dull gray uniforms of Mariltar warriors. Exhaustion and fear battled in her mind erasing all other thought. God, what was happening? She closed her eyes tightly hoping frantically that the familiar corridor of the *Claxiarten* would be there when she opened them again.

Unfortunately, it wasn't. Eight pairs of eyes still stared at her in fascination. She was beginning to have a glimmer of understanding as to where she might be, but her exhausted mind refused to acknowledge the reason. It *had* to be a mistake and she would find herself back in her quarters in her bed very soon.

A very tall, dark-haired man with commander's insignia on his clothing moved in front of her. Pale blue eyes studied her intently from a face she supposed many would describe as handsome. His expression seemed faintly expectant. On his right temple, a three-quarter crescent pulsed the same blue color as his eyes and she remembered that Mariltar males were all marked with such symbols, an identifying feature of their clan.

He smiled slightly and stretched out his hand.

She ignored it, and swiveled her hips to step out of the port tube by herself. The action brought her to within an arm's length of the Mariltar commander, and she was forced to tip her head back to look up at him. Immediately she wished she hadn't. His brilliant eyes caught and held hers captive. Unable to tear her gaze away, she watched in fascination as the blue of his eyes and the pulse in his temple deepened to dark sapphire. A memory, elusive and gone in an instant, teased her mind and left behind entirely unwelcome shivers of sensation curling through her belly.

This was too insane! Whatever was happening, she wished desperately it would stop.

"Welcome to the warrior vessel, *Astran*, my lady." His voice was deep and husky. The quivering in her stomach intensified. She knew with absolute certainty who this man was. "I'm Lord Alex Mariltar, Commander of the Seventh Fleet. These are my captains, Jason Trion,

Eric Stromi, Sebastian Asteril, Mark Oberan, Bavin Moresol, Justin Emil and—this is Advisor Barok." As he turned back to her from identifying each of the men, she interrupted before he could continue.

"What am I doing here?"

Dark brows lifted slightly at her abrupt tone. His eyes narrowed dangerously. "If you will remember, I requested a conference—several times—to discuss the proposal I put before you earlier in the day."

Panic started to claw upwards from Joanna's belly almost paralyzing her ability to think. Hadn't her messages been conveyed? "I thought my answer was clear." Behind the dark-haired man, she noticed that the others had moved to the far end of the room to give them privacy.

"Your answer was perfectly clear. I simply couldn't accept it." He was watching her closely, too closely. She was beginning to feel trapped, claustrophobic. Fury started to mix with panic.

"I don't want to discuss this," she said shortly. "My answer won't change. I'm tired and I don't want to be here. I don't know what you're up to, but I do know that even a Mariltar warrior," she emphasized with some sarcasm, "can't just...just remove someone from another vessel without their consent. Send me back! Now!"

Her own words and tone shocked her. She sounded like a rude, petulant child. But then why should she care? This man had abducted her. The situation was beyond outrageous. She was rapidly developing a headache, and *he* was provoking the strangest feelings in her. Feelings she most certainly didn't want to examine too closely.

The commander's lips thinned and a determined expression entered his eyes. "I'm afraid I can't do that," he said, impatience creeping into his voice. "And it's obvious there's no point in trying to discuss this further right now. You are my choice for a mate. As soon as the partnership has been formalized, you can rest in my—our quarters. You'll remain on the *Astran* for the duration of the voyage to Treaine. Ambassador Kromon will understand since marriage partners, in most cultures, tend to cohabit. I'm sure that special arrangements can be made for any negotiations in which you need to be included."

As the implications of what he was saying crashed through her mind, Joanna felt the blood drain from her face. "What are you talking about," she whispered.

"You're here for our mating ceremony!" He reached out a large hand to steady her, alarm showing briefly in his face as she swayed slightly on her feet.

"Don't touch me!" Her hands swept up to fend him off and she stumbled back a few steps. "*You* are a complete lunatic! What makes you think, even for a second, that I'll give my consent to this? And why me?"

"I don't need your consent." He spoke through gritted teeth. It was obvious he was struggling to hold on to the remnants of his patience. Nor had she missed the flash of anger in his eyes. "The Match Key results and the Coalition's mandate that I marry give me all the authority I need to establish this partnership. Besides—" His tone softened slightly, his voice lowered so that she alone could hear his words, and his strange sapphire eyes swept her body intimately. She felt as if she had been stripped of her clothes and left completely exposed and vulnerable in a room full of warriors. "I like what I see and I think—"

Whap!

Of its own accord, her hand reached out and smacked him hard across the face.

Someone swore. In her peripheral vision she saw a man move as if to defend his commander. The action was stayed at a brief warning motion from another. The room froze. Only the soft sound of breathing broke the silence.

Alex's hand briefly touched the side of his face. His gaze, disbelieving and ice-cold, raked over her. Despite herself, she shuddered.

"Don't ever, *ever* try that again," he said softly, "or, believe me, you will *not* enjoy the consequences."

He stretched out his hand, grabbed her arm and yanked her none to gently in front of him, subduing her struggles easily, before turning them both to face the room. "Let's get this over with," he ground out. "Advisor?"

Advisor Barok cleared his throat and moved in front of the couple as the captains hastily arranged themselves in a semi-circle around them. Joanna barely heard the ancient words of the Mariltar mating ceremony, and wouldn't have understood them if she had been paying attention. Her thoughts were whirling uncontrollably but, foremost of all, were the words screaming through her mind that *this couldn't be happening.*

She was jerked back to awareness as Alex took her right hand and spread her fingers across the cold, smooth surface of a black triangular box. His left hand held hers clamped against the box while the fingers of his right meshed with hers from the other side. She watched in fascination as a strange glow lit the inside of the box, and a thin, blue, glittering streak of light rose up, curled around and embedded itself in the flesh of their middle fingers.

Advisor Barok paused, then began polling each of the captains in turn, asking for their consent to the mating ceremony. With each man's consent given, the Advisor carefully slid the box out from under the meshed fingers and gently separated them. Identical bands of blue glowed brightly from the two hands.

"It is done!"

Joanna felt a rush of warm air against the top of her head as the Mariltar commander exhaled. His body was still pressed uncomfortably against her side. She felt ill. Squeezing her eyes closed, she desperately tried to channel her thoughts in another direction to calm her heaving stomach.

She heard Alex quietly thank the advisor and the other men. "I'll return shortly. I will see my..." he stumbled over the word "...wife settled first in our quarters."

The word caused another surge of panic. Her head was pounding. Pain bit deeply behind her eyes. She just needed to lie down, she thought frantically. She would be all right if only she could lie down. Once she got rid of this hellish headache and got some rest, she would be able to handle anything. A tiny spark of hope still flared that this was truly all a nightmare, and she would wake up in her own bed.

She felt his body shift slightly and a curiously gentle touch on her arm. She opened her eyes reluctantly to see him looking at her, his brow furrowed in concern. Then a large hand on her back was urging her toward the door.

AS THE DOOR slid shut behind the couple, Sebastian Asteril was the first to break the tense silence. "Balls of Sortor! Poor Alex! She's going to have him groveling to fulfill her every desire before we reach Treaine."

".Don't be so sure about that," Mark Oberan muttered. "Alex has the luck of Pormiam with women though. She's gorgeous."

Justin Emil chuckled. "Any woman who has the courage to call Alex crazy and strikes him *and* gets away with it in the space of a few minutes deserves a lot of credit and respect from *my* perspective."

"Who says she's gotten away with anything? Alex wasn't exactly happy with her behavior and the evening isn't over yet."

The noisy discussion and speculation degenerated into good natured bet-taking. Most were convinced that Alex would claim his usual victory, but Jason and Sebastian were equally sure that their commanding officer might finally have met a woman who wouldn't be so easily swayed by his charm and power.

Chapter 5

FAR AWAY, in the serene quiet of a meadow surrounded and guarded by Treaine's vast forests, the soft whisper of a breeze curled and twisted through the branches of the saralin tree. It lightly kissed the tree's crimson petals, encouraging them to release their delicate hold. They danced briefly in the warm air before drifting down to settle gently on the shape resting under the tree's sheltering branches. There was a slight shudder, and the great, noble head slowly lifted. The breeze's soft fingers played across his face, teasing the shaggy mane of hair.

He sniffed.

Sharp and sweet and distinctive, the scent of change, cradled in the currents of air, filled his senses. He sniffed again.

At last!

There was no mistake! It had been too long in coming, but he recognized the elements.

A deep sigh shook the massive body. These soaring forests which had sheltered him for a generation, these deep waters which had nurtured his soul, this spectacular, dazzling beauty of a land which had revived and strengthened his spirit would soon be shared with others.

And he welcomed, indeed had longed for, the change. The few who were already here, and rarely ventured beyond the settled area, were insignificant. It was those who were yet to come who would lay the foundation and build the frame of the Vision.

The path had been set many memories ago. He and his kind had been hitchhikers, travelers, observers, always seeking the right time, the right place, the right minds in which to plant the seed of the Vision.

Now the seed had been sown, the Vision about to become reality. Soon the Chosen Ones would arrive. Slowly the mists of darkness that had blanketed and smothered the Crestar System, and brought the Conflicts generations ago, were lifting. Peace was spreading silent, yet often hesitant, wings to the furthest boundaries of the System, desperately trying to reach even the darkest nations.

But peace demanded a price and, as he tested the warm, sweet air again, he detected a trace of corruptness. Faint still, yet stronger than before, it would fester and swell daily, he knew, feeding its power until it was ready to act.

And he had to ensure that the price would not be too great.

Chapter 6

ALEX HURRIED her down a short, deserted corridor and onto a lift tube. The ride was over in seconds and, just as quickly, they were standing outside another door which slid open at his touch. The room they entered was spartan, with little more than an information console, a low couch, a couple of hard chairs and an eating recess. A huge porthole dominated the room and framed a spectacular view of space, while an archway announced the entrance to a narrow sleeping chamber. Alex led her into the latter and indicated the concealed cleansing unit on one side.

"Please, make yourself comfortable," he said stiffly. "I'll be back after I've made arrangements to communicate our marriage partnership to the Coalition." He turned to leave, changed his mind and reached out to tip her chin up. She refused to meet his eyes, but felt his intent examination, felt her face start to burn in response. "Are you all right?"

The question, for some reason, brought a fresh surge of anger. No, she wasn't all right and wouldn't be until she was rid of *him*. She squelched a childish impulse to kick him in the shins, swallowed hard and nodded instead.

Apparently satisfied, he released her.

Joanna watched him leave in relief, and then collapsed on the bed. She shot up almost immediately into a sitting position as, through the pain of her headache, an unwelcome thought entered her mind. Surely he wasn't expecting to sleep—have sex with her tonight, was he? Her stomach clenched again in panic. This was all so utterly bizarre.

She left the sleeping area and wandered around the main room. The configuration of the information console was unfamiliar to her. But, desperate to contact the *Claxiarten*, she poked at it half-heartedly. It remained distressingly silent. She resumed her wandering, exhaustion making her stumble once or twice, before she finally settled on the cushioned bench under the porthole.

She wanted nothing more than to remove her clothes and stretch out, but would rather die than give *that man* the satisfaction of finding her undressed and in his bed. She leaned her head back and sighed, trying to will away the pain in her head. There must be a medication dispenser in the room somewhere, but she didn't know where to look for it, or what to look for. The lights streaking by the porthole were mesmerizing. She resisted as long as she could, but eventually her eyelids drooped closed, and she slept.

JASON WAS ISSUING instructions to a new crew shift when Alex entered the private meeting room some time later. He dropped into a chair and stretched out his long legs while he waited for his senior captain to finish. A few minutes later, when Jason closed the channel, he asked in a deceptively bored tone, "So, what are the bets?"

The captain hesitated and Alex laughed shortly. "Come on, Jason. I know these men. They wouldn't hesitate to pass up an opportunity to place bets on my relationship with my wife, especially after her behavior tonight! I'd do the same if I were in their position."

Jason swung around in his chair, and crossed his hands behind his head. He grinned. "Well, some of them thought you'd have her tamed by the time we reach Treaine."

"And the rest?"

"Thought she'd have *you* tamed by the time we reach Treaine!"

Alex laughed. "Yes, well, there's the challenge. It's certainly one that promises to be somewhat, if not wholly, pleasurable." He contemplated his boots with a half smile on his face as the vision of angry green eyes and a mouth made for kisses flashed into his mind. Feisty and uncooperative, and utterly desirable. The memory he had carried for all those long months had not been deceiving. When she had stepped out of that port tube, he had felt like someone had punched him in his gut. Cor's blood, but she was even more beautiful than he had remembered and her physical presence had the same blood-churning, spine-tingling impact it had had five months ago.

And now she was his!

Jason cleared his throat and said dryly, "I hate to disturb your thoughts, Alex, but you do have an obligation to notify the Coalition. I've already spoken with the Captain of the Claxiarten. He'd been alerted to the port and traced Joanna's signal here. To say the least, he's not happy, but he knows he's hardly in a position to object or take action. Someone will pack up her belongings and transfer them over in the next few hours. We agreed that Ambassador Kromon should not be disturbed since he's already retired for the evening. A message has been left that you will speak with him in the morning."

"Good! Send the transmission to the Coalition. Tell them the partnership has been forged by my choice, and that the marriage is irrevocably bound under Mariltar law and confirmed by a quorum.

Send them the Match Key statistics. Any questions will be addressed in the morning."

"Alex, wait!"

In the process of rising, Alex looked up surprised at the tone of Jason's voice. The concerned expression on his second-in-command's face had him lowering himself back into his chair.

Clasping his hands on the table in front of him, Jason leaned forward and said carefully, "I sensed you weren't telling us everything in the debriefing tonight. Is there anything else we should know?"

Alex swore softly. "Was it that obvious?"

"No, I doubt the others noticed."

"Cor's blood, Jason, I—" Alex bit off what he was about to say, and turned his head away. He trusted Jason with his life, but how much should he reveal at this point? The doubts and suspicions he harbored were festering inside of him. His report to select members of the Coalition, as inconclusive as it had been, had produced a surprising lack of reaction, and no further instructions.

"Alex, our fealty is first and foremost to you, and then to our task on Treaine. If there is anything at all that threatens you, we need to know about it."

He swung quickly around. "What makes you think the threat is to me?"

"So there is one?"

"I didn't say that." Swearing, he pushed himself to his feet and began to pace the room. "You're not going to let this go, are you? Cor's blood, Jason, you're as irritatingly tenacious as a noil vine and twice as hard to get rid of when you get an idea about something. All right, but this goes no further until and if it's necessary for the others to know. I need your word on it."

Jason gave a cautious nod of agreement. "You have it, of course."

Alex came to a stop in front of the holographic image of Treaine. "As I explained tonight, the diplomatic mission was also an effort to identify pockets of resistance to the peace initiative. There were many and they'll be dealt with. But certain members of the Coalition had approached me in strictest confidence to ask me to investigate another matter."

He turned his back on the holograph. "This came out of pure rumor and speculation, Jason. I didn't give it much credence to begin with, but the more I dug, the harder I looked, the more convinced I became that there might be some truth to it. And yet, I have nothing at all of any substance."

"And what was the rumor?"

"That there is a well-organized movement to destroy the peace initiative, to infiltrate the colony on Treaine and disrupt the negotiations. It goes so far as to suggest that the colony itself could be in mortal danger."

"Who or what is rumored to be behind it?"

Alex dug his hands in his pockets, and rocked back and forth on his feet. Gritting his teeth, he reluctantly ground out, "A clan of Soron."

"Balls of Sortor, Alex," Jason exploded, coming to his feet in a rush. "Rumor or not, this is deadly serious, and you have an obligation to keep us fully informed. This will significantly affect security procedures on Treaine."

"No!" Alex shot back. "It is just that as far as I've been able to determine. Pure rumor. And our obligation is to protect the colonists which we will do without implementing unnecessarily tight security. The peace initiative will not be held hostage to rumor. And we never had this conversation."

Jason sucked in a deep breath, clearly struggling to calm himself. "If it's true, you and yours are at greatest risk."

"I know." Alex grinned with little humor. "And I suspect my wife is going to present the security team with some challenges."

"Undoubtedly!"

Alex glanced sideways at his friend. "I'm glad you know, Jason. But nothing changes. We proceed as planned."

"For the record, I still have strong concerns."

"So noted." Alex nodded and turned to leave. "And now, I'm going to bed—with my wife, and I don't wish to be disturbed."

LEFT TO HIMSELF, Jason shook his head. Alex was so blasted sure of himself with women. And not without good reason. His aristocratic dark looks, lean, powerfully muscled body and natural air of authority, not to mention considerable charm when he chose to exercise it, drew women like magnets to his bed. But Joanna seemed so different from the women to whom Alex was usually attracted. He hoped his friend wasn't going to regret his choice.

Jason sighed and rubbed tired neck muscles. The events of the day, and especially this most recent revelation, had provided serious food for thought. Despite what Alex had said, some plans would change. But all that could wait. He rose to his feet, and went off in search of company, confident that the other captains hadn't yet left for their respective vessels.

ALEX WALKED Into the narrow sleeping chamber and stopped short.
She wasn't there! Where in Cor's name was she? He stepped back into
the main room and saw her slumped on the bench under the porthole.
She was fast asleep and still fully clothed right down to the ridiculous
dainty shoes. As he walked past the information console, he noticed a
tiny orange light flashing, an indication of an unauthorized access
attempt. His lips twitched. So, she had tried. He would have been
disappointed with anything less.

He stopped in front of her, taking in every minute detail of the
thick, long lashes sweeping her cheeks, the straight little nose, the
softly curved mouth. Her body was petite and small-boned, but the cut
and style of the clothing hinted at a figure that was gently rounded in
all the right places. The narrow skirt of her suit ended at mid-thigh
revealing an expanse of slender, curving legs and delicate ankles. She
was different from most of the women he had known who tended to be
taller and larger proportioned. He had a brief moment of doubt when he
wondered if she would breed less easily because of her daintier size,
but set it aside quickly. She *was* the right one.

She slept so soundly, he decided against shaking her awake. The
memory of her pale face, all color drained from it, and listless response
when he had left her earlier still concerned him. She had looked ill, in
pain, and it was more than just reaction to what he had put her through.
Instead, he lifted her easily into his arms and took her through to the
sleeping chamber. She stirred only slightly as he sat her on the bed
propped against his side while he unbuttoned and removed her tunic
jacket and scarf. Laying her back on the bed, he slid off her shoes and,
unable to resist, ran his hand caressingly over the curves of an arched
foot and ankle. His fingers rose to hover over the front of her undervest
before falling away. No, he decided, he wanted her fully conscious
when he undressed her completely for the first time.

Alex pulled a cover over her, then stripped off his own clothes,
used the cleansing unit, and stretched out beside her under the cover on
the bed. Her faint breathing tickled his ear, and the light, spicy scent of
her hair teased his nostrils. Images flickered through his mind of what
could, and would, happen in this bed.

He shifted uncomfortably, resigned to a restless night.

Chapter 7

JOANNA STRUGGLED through suffocating waves of fog. As consciousness slowly returned, a niggling discomfort told her that her headache hadn't disappeared while she slept. She opened her eyes and lay quietly in the semi-darkened sleeping chamber, realizing that someone, undoubtedly the Mariltar commander, had put her to bed.

At least she was alone and still fully dressed—almost. She replayed the events of the previous evening in her mind, and cringed when she remembered her own behavior. She had never, *never* lost control like that in front of anyone before, let alone a roomful of men. But then she had never felt so helpless, so powerless to change the course of events impacting her own life.

Ambassador Kromon. She must be allowed to get a message to him. There was no doubt in her mind that he would settle this whole outlandish situation, and she would soon be back on the *Claxiarten* where she belonged.

As she sat up, a wave of pain crashed through her temples, and she whimpered. Her hands were rubbing the side of her head trying to ease the intensity of it, when a quiet voice asked, "What's the matter?"

Joanna's head jerked up causing her more distress. The Mariltar commander was standing propped against the wall near the entrance to the chamber watching her. Even in repose, he gave off an aura of barely restrained power and energy which, this morning, she found particularly annoying.

"Nothing," she said shortly, willing him to go away.

He moved swiftly, with lethal grace. She felt the bed shift as it accepted his weight, and he grasped her wrists, forcing her to meet his eyes. "Don't lie to me. You're obviously in pain."

And he was most definitely the cause of it. She scowled at him, tempted to tell him so, but the pounding in her head was making her feel slightly sick. "I-I have a headache," she finally whispered.

"Bad, isn't it?" he asked.

She nodded, wincing at even the brief movement.

"Stay there!"

Where the hell did he think she would she go, she thought resentfully as he left the chamber? He returned minutes later, settling himself on the bed beside her. "Lie down and turn your head to the wall."

She noticed a narrow cylinder in his hand, as she leaned back. "What's that?"

"A pain neutralizer from the *Astran's* medical officer. Turn your head."

Joanna hesitantly obeyed, reluctant to trust him, but desperate for relief, and felt him gently brush her hair aside. Her skin burned where he had touched her. The next moment, she felt a tiny pinch behind her ear, and an immediate lessening of the pounding pain. Within seconds, it was completely gone.

Alex nodded at her quiet word of grudging thanks. "You had this last night, didn't you? Next time, say something!" He reached past her and handed her a cup of liquid. "Here is some nourishment. Later, I'll show you how to use the food dispenser. For now, you have five minutes to do whatever women need to do after waking up. Ambassador Kromon wants to speak with you."

Joanna experienced a tingle of excitement and hope as she watched Alex saunter out of the chamber. She hadn't expected it to be this easy to get in touch with Kromon. Despite the ambassador's encouragement to her yesterday to consider the Mariltar's proposal, she knew he wouldn't support what had happened since.

She pushed the cup aside untouched. The glitter of blue across her hand caught her attention and, once again, fingers of panic cramped her stomach. She forced herself to breathe deeply for a few seconds then rose and stepped across the chamber into the cleansing unit.

Three minutes later, with her hair brushed into place and her clothes tidier, if a little rumpled, she walked into the main room where Alex was sitting before the information console.

HE NODDED AT her. "It'll be a minute." He turned his attention back to examining some data on the screen.

Joanna wandered over to the porthole. As she stared out at the vessel riding next to the *Astran* and then back to Alex, she felt the beginning twinges of alarm. He seemed so unconcerned. Why wasn't he at all disturbed about letting her communicate with Ambassador Kromon? She started at his voice.

"Come have a seat, Joanna. He'll be on the screen momentarily." He pushed his chair to one side of the console where he would have a good view of the screen and be able to observe her at the same time.

Ambassador Kromon's familiar pale image appeared on the

screen. "Good day, Joanna, Ambassador."

"Ambassador." Alex grinned and nodded.

Kromon turned his full attention to Joanna. "How are you this morning, my dear?"

How did he think she was, she thought in pure frustration. She felt like screaming. Unleashing her temper. Venting her frustration and helplessness. But respect for her superior made her respond in a politely controlled voice, "Terrible, as a matter of fact! I assume a mistake has been made and that this whole ludicrous situation can be remedied immediately. I'd like to come back to the *Claxiarten* right away, sir."

The ambassador's gaze shifted slightly before refocusing on her. "Joanna, Alex has explained the events of last evening and provided me with the Match Key data. The same information has been reviewed by the Coalition."

He sighed gloomily and continued. "I know you're not going to like hearing this, but the marriage partnership *is* legally binding under Mariltar law. Further, although the Coalition had not previously considered an Earth colonist as a possible partner for Alex Mariltar, after looking at the Match Key data and weighing all the aspects of your respective positions and cultures, they consider the match to be an excellent one."

Joanna felt the blood drain from her face. Stunned, she whispered, "What? You can't possibly condone what he's done! He *abducted* me and forced me into a marriage! I'm on this vessel against my will, and you're not going to help me?"

Ambassador Kromon shook his head. "I don't approve of his methods. As a matter of fact, Alex and I have had a long talk about that." He frowned in the commander's direction. The frown deepened at the unconcerned smile that was directed back to him. "While the ability to assess a given circumstance and make instant decisions might serve a warrior well on occasion, he will need to develop some restraint in his new position. He should have used persuasion rather than force. I will allow, however, that he was faced with time constraints, and I cannot disagree with his or the Coalition's conclusions. I've known Alex Mariltar a long time, my dear. I've been acquainted with you only a short while, but feel I've come to know you quite well, too. While your cultures differ in many ways, your personal values are very similar. The Match Key recognized that. Once some of your initial feelings of hostility over Alex's, er, methods and the marriage partnership have subsided and you've had time to get to know one another, I think you'll find that the arrangement will be quite pleasant and rewarding."

Pleasant? Rewarding? He was talking about the rest of her life! Joanna bit down hard on her lips as the urge to erupt like a howling banshee swept over her. A glance at the source of her distress didn't help. Alex was watching her warily, but the telltale twitch at the corner of his mouth raised her temper a few notches. Struggling to stay calm as she sorted through all that Kromon had said, Joanna grasped at one point and asked, "How did my personal data get into the Match Key anyway, sir? I never signed up."

Once again, Kromon's gaze flickered and he looked over at the Mariltar commander before he answered. "The *Astran* made an unauthorized scan of the personal data files of the *Claxiarten*."

Joanna surged to her feet. Her hand slammed down on the console. "I cannot believe this! I just cannot believe it. I'm losing control of my life," she choked out. She stabbed an accusing finger in Alex's direction. "*He* makes an unauthorized access into another vessel's data banks, and no one thinks anything of it. You're telling me that you *and* the Coalition endorse this marriage? That I have to submit to it? That I have to stay with *him?*"

She threw a furious glance at Alex, who was stretched out in his chair now with a carefully blank expression on his face. Whirling back to Kromon, she demanded, "Why does everyone have so much faith in this Match Key, anyway? How can a computer possibly decide whether or not two people are suited to each other? A computer can't define emotion, or...or what attracts one person to another."

"Perhaps not," Kromon soothed. "But the Match Key has been extremely successful over the generations it has been in existence and for those who have chosen to use it. For most of the nations in the Crestar System, once a partnership is forged, that partnership is for life. You Earth colonists, by contrast, will often have two to three partners, perhaps because many of you bond through extremely volatile emotions early on in a relationship rather than first establishing a strong basis of mutual respect, shared values and common interests. Long-term commitment to your relationships is often lacking."

Joanna made an impatient movement, but he held up his hand and continued before she could speak, "You must give this marriage a chance. This partnership and others similar to it are the very foundation of the Coalition's mandate on Treaine which, as you are very well aware, is to bring the many nations and colonies of the Crestar System into harmony and unity."

He smiled, instantly transforming his habitually sad expression, and concluded, "You and your husband need to talk, my dear. I'll give you a day to settle in. Tomorrow, I'll need you in the negotiation sessions. Good day, Joanna. Ambassador."

The screen faded out.

Joanna sat shaking with anger and fear in her chair. Her life *was* completely out of control, a spinning vortex of confusion and events manipulated by someone other than her. All her plans and dreams had vanished in an instant. She had been sucked into a nightmare. Absorbed in her misery, she jumped when she felt the Mariltar's hands on her shoulders massaging her tense muscles. Instinctively, she tried to jerk away but he held her firmly in place.

His not unsympathetic voice said, "We do need to talk, but I think you need some time to consider what Ambassador Kromon has said, and I have some other obligations to which I must attend. Your belongings are here." He indicated some containers in the corner of the room that she hadn't previously noticed. "And there's sufficient room to store them with mine. You also now have access to the information console for certain functions. That does not include off-vessel transmissions unless they're initiated by Ambassador Kromon. The yellow pad on the console will give you some direction if you have difficulty finding what you require."

The weight of his hands was removed from her shoulders. Strolling to the door, he added, "By the way, as wife to a High Lord of Mariltar, your position is now somewhat elevated above that of Ambassador Kromon's. You no longer need to address him as 'sir'. 'Ambassador' is more appropriate."

Before she could stop herself, Joanna said nastily, "Oh, and what do I call you? Your Exalted Lordship?"

To her deep chagrin, he seemed to think that was funny. Grinning, he raised his dark brows and said provocatively, "Anything you like, as long as it's polite. A simple 'beloved' would be acceptable, but Alex might be better when we're in public."

He nodded at her and left the room whistling.

Chapter 8

JOANNA PACED the room, her mind frantically seeking a way out of a trap with no obvious exits. She finally decided the only thing she could do was appeal to the Mariltar commander. Maybe she just hadn't expressed her feelings clearly enough. Surely, he wouldn't want a wife who was so vehemently opposed to the partnership. And she would have neither the time nor the inclination to fulfill the duties undoubtedly required of such a prominent position in the new colony.

The decision brought a measure of relief, and she looked with renewed interest at her surroundings. The man certainly hadn't done anything to personalize his space, she thought in disgust. Bare walls and functional furniture lacked any personal items and offered no clues to his tastes. The narrow sleeping chamber she had left so hastily earlier that morning yielded the same results.

With nothing else to do, she decided to explore the information console. It was easily mastered with the assistance of a self-help guide. As she scrolled through the vast data bank of the *Astran*, she caught a reference to Treaine and paused. This was probably as good an opportunity as any to learn more about her new home. She was lost in the planet's history when Alex returned some time later.

"Fascinating, isn't it?" His warm breath tickled her ear.

She jumped with fright and her hands flew to her face to muffle an involuntary squeal. The look she threw at him was indignant. "Did you have to sneak up on me?" He was too close to her. Again. And the tingling sensations racing over her skin bothered her.

Alex straightened and chuckled. "I wasn't aware I *was* sneaking. But next time, I'll make a point of loudly announcing my presence."

"Or just stay away altogether," she muttered.

He laughed outright at that. "*That* would produce some interesting conversations in the officer's quarters." His glance fell on the containers of her belongings still stacked against the wall. A brow lifted arrogantly above a darkened sapphire eye. "Testing my patience already, my dear? I wouldn't recommend it."

Before she could anticipate it, he had grasped her chin in a firm hold. The light brush of his thumb across her lips left them feeling swollen and aching with a nameless need. His voice, deep and husky, and infinitely seductive said, "I should warn you, one way or another, I *always* get my own way." He released her and stepped back, his gaze lingering for a moment longer on her parted lips. His eyes lifted to hers, and he smiled slowly, then turned and walked across to the eating recess.

The man was insufferable, Joanna fumed. One minute he was laughing at her, and the next he was delivering what sounded very much like a threat wrapped in velvet touches and seductive, molten glances. Once again, she felt a niggling sense of familiarity. But she would have remembered meeting him before. She was convinced of that. His commanding presence and dark good looks, even without the distinctive mark at his temple, would be hard to forget. Not that he was the type she normally found appealing. And she had never met anyone before who provoked her so easily into such uncharacteristically rude and snappish behavior.

"Would you like something to eat?"

His question reminded her that she hadn't had anything to eat all day. The cup he had brought her that morning remained untouched in the sleeping chamber. Suddenly, she was starving. Still, she hesitated, common sense battling with the overwhelming urge to be contrary and resist him at every opportunity. A practical streak in her finally won as she instinctively recognized that, if she was to get what she wanted, the negotiation process had to start somewhere.

"Yes, please." The meekness of her response earned her a sharp look, but she gazed back at him innocently, and rose to follow him over to eating recess. He showed her how to make a selection from the mostly unfamiliar foods on the menu bar and retrieve the packaged product from the food tube.

As they sat down, he said, "The food selection in the private quarters is unexciting, but nourishing. The *Astran's* dining chambers have a far more varied menu. Tonight, we'll eat with the vessel's officers and the captains of the Mariltar fleet."

Joanna promptly lost her appetite. Star pits! Why not just stick a pin in her and mount her in a glass case? She cringed inwardly at the memory of her very public loss of control the previous evening. She had never before slapped anyone, and still couldn't quite believe she had attacked this man, no matter how much he had deserved it. And she hadn't even been in his presence five minutes! She certainly wasn't anxious to face the group that had witnessed her humiliation.

She took a deep breath and concentrated desperately on redirecting her thoughts. She had an ultimate goal, after all. But as she nibbled at her food and tried to quell the nervous flutters in her stomach, she knew that achieving it wasn't going to be as simple as she had thought. His mere presence was disturbing, and the little speech she had planned to deliver to gain her freedom had completely flown out of her mind.

SENSING HER discomfort, and wishing he could see more of the beautiful face partially hidden behind a shining fall of bright hair, Alex deliberately continued speaking in a conversational tone. He explained that the officers and captains of the Seventh Fleet of Mariltar also represented his personal guard and had the same duty and obligation to protect and serve his wife.

When this information produced no reaction, he sighed and decided to move onto another topic until they had finished their meal. At some point, and soon, she would have to understand that her movements would no longer be as free as she had been accustomed to previously. Rank brought privilege, but it also introduced a certain amount of risk to personal safety. And, under the circumstances, she could be at tremendous risk.

"What prompted you to sign up for Treaine?"

"What?" She looked up startled, and he wondered if she had listened to anything he had said. Not accustomed to being ignored, he nevertheless patiently repeated the question.

"Oh. I, ah, was working as a trade negotiator in the Neutral Realm and had done some work for Ambassador Kromon. When the Coalition was asking the ambassadors to form their teams, he asked if I would join his. I knew some Earth colonists who had already been accepted as part of the first group to populate the planet, so I agreed."

Alex made a mental note to have Mark Oberan pay special attention to checking the records of the Earth colonists on Treaine. The more he knew about her, the better equipped he would be to deal with her. He finished his meal and glanced at her. She had gone back to contemplating her half-eaten food and was distractedly pushing around a large chunk of bread in the rapidly congealing stew.

Trying to decide on the best way to prompt her to speak her mind, he asked, "Did you learn much about Treaine from the data banks this morning?"

She nodded her head hesitantly, refusing to meet his eyes. "Yes, there was some information." He grunted encouragingly and with obvious reluctance, she added, "I also found an intriguing reference to the City of Sarach."

The City of Sarach. The seat of the most advanced civilization in the Crestar System until the planet was mysteriously abandoned. He leaned back in his chair, wondering what she had found in the records to interest her. Treaine certainly had had a turbulent history and it also had its secrets. It's physical features were wildly beautiful in parts, with soaring mountain peaks, vast forests and deep lakes. Five moons orbited it producing sometimes unpredictable and violent weather. The tiny trading colony, which would be expanded into the new settlement, had been established there generations ago, well after the mysterious disappearance of the planet's ancient civilization.

Again she seemed disinclined to elaborate on her answer. Impatiently, Alex pushed back his chair. Better to get this over with. He doubted she was going to like what he had to say, but he saw no sense in putting it off any longer. Inquiring politely if she had finished her meal, he rose and filled two cups from the liquid dispensing unit in the recess, then showed her the waste disposal tube. When the remains of the meal had been disposed of, he gestured to the couch. It was barely large enough to accommodate the two of them and, from the way she shifted and drew away from him, he knew with a twinge of irritation that she was uncomfortable with his proximity. That would change soon enough, he vowed silently. She nervously took a sip from the cup he handed her and he saw her shudder slightly at the almost bitter, unusual flavor.

"It's seeka, a favorite beverage of the Mariltar. I suppose it is an acquired taste." He studied her closely through narrowed eyes, trying to anticipate how she would react. "Joanna, give me your hand."

She froze, gazing at him with wide puzzled eyes over the rim of her cup.

"Give me your hand."

There was a strange expression on her face but she didn't resist when he removed the cup from her hands, nor when he took one in his own and traced the glowing blue band with a gentle finger.

He considered her carefully and said with deep seriousness, "Joanna, I know this is difficult for you. Your life has been turned upside down in the last twenty-four hours. I think I can even understand your initial resistance to this arrangement, and I will do what I can to make the transition easier for you. But it's important that you understand from the outset what will be expected of you. You will, of course, have official duties as my wife, ranging from acting as hostess at various functions, to representing the Ambassadors' Council in the community, to entertaining visiting dignitaries."

He reached out a finger to tilt her chin, forcing her to meet his gaze. "This position offers you many advantages. You may pursue whatever interests, including work, you wish, as long as you understand that your duties as my wife, both public and private, come first."

He teased the softness of her lip again with his thumb and held her eyes captive, probing the enchanting green depths. Taking a deep breath, he altered his tone, speaking more softly and gently. "I expect commitment, support and companionship and, eventually of course, children. And I have no doubt that you will give me extraordinary pleasure in bed." He was surprised to see a wave of color wash over the delicate features. He was convinced and encouraged that she was not indifferent to him, especially when he thought about that encounter so long ago, but he was beginning to wonder about her sexual experience level. It was an intriguing thought, the journey of discovery to be greatly anticipated. His fingers tightened when she made a feeble attempt to jerk her chin out his hand. Failing to free herself, she met his eyes defiantly, nostrils flaring.

Ignoring the signs of the gathering storm, Alex continued firmly, determined to make sure that she understood her position. "Mariltar custom dictates that, once married, women refrain from intimate associations with other men until they have borne children to the marriage partnership. Then they are free to form other attachments, if they choose, as long as they continue to support the marriage partnership. Our men are not bound by that custom. I expect you to observe it, just as I expect you to respect my wishes and support me in every way."

He paused. This was not going well, but then he hadn't really expected it to. Something in particular he had said had disturbed her. Her eyes had narrowed to mere slits and her whole body had become rigid. She was furious. Her hands were clasped so tightly in her lap that the knuckles were white.

She jerked her chin and this time he released her. Jumping to her feet, she walked the short distance to the window, and stood with her back resolutely turned to him. Drawing a deep breath, she said shakily, "You expect a lot, and it's more than I can give. This was your choice, not mine. If you wanted a willing partner, you should have chosen someone else. I didn't sign up with the Coalition to be forced into a partnership. I don't want to be married. I chose not to be a part of the Match Key program. I cannot be an ambassador's wife and I will not be *your* wife." Turning finally to face him, she said with an obvious attempt at humility even though the green eyes were still clouded with anger, "Please— let me go."

Alex studied the slender figure outlined against the blackness of space, and settled back in his seat. The strength of her emotions only heightened her appeal and he felt desire, hot and painful in its intensity, rush through him. "No!" he said with finality. "I will not release you. This marriage is legal in every respect, and the Match Key hasn't failed yet. If you support the Coalition's Vision, then you must support this marriage which is the very essence of that Vision. All the other ambassadors have taken partners from nations or colonies other than their own. You are my choice. The sooner you start to accept the reality of this partnership, the sooner we can both concentrate on our assigned tasks on Treaine."

Desperately she flung at him, "This situation is just so...so *loathsome* to me. How *can* you want a partner who doesn't want *you*. You may call me your wife, but I won't acknowledge that I am and I *won't* sleep with you—willingly."

He surged to his feet in one powerful movement and stood in front of her. His hands grabbed her shoulders as she would have turned away, holding her still. "You may not acknowledge our marriage partnership, Joanna, but the community will. That mark on your finger is *my* mark and everyone in this Star System will recognize it as such. Few men will be willing to touch you when they see it, at least until you have performed your duty and produced some children under this partnership. And," he continued softly and with deep conviction, "whether you want to recognize it or not, the fact is there is an extraordinary attraction between us that promises untold pleasures. Don't fight me, Joanna. The course is set and this is a battle you cannot win!"

She shook her head in vehement denial and squeezed her eyes shut against his intent gaze.

"Look at me!" he commanded gently. Her eyes fluttered open again with obvious reluctance. He was taken aback to see them glittering with tears. "You need time to adjust to all this. We can delay any intimate activities until you're more comfortable with me and have grown accustomed to what's expected of you. But," he said huskily, "don't make me wait too long, Joanna. I want you, and I am not a patient man."

He frowned slightly as a tear welled out of a large green eye and spilled down her cheek. His thumb brushed it gently away. Deciding she needed time to herself, he reminded her of the captain's dinner in a few hours and left her alone.

JOANNA WAS once again absorbed in the history of Treaine when Alex returned to their quarters at the appointed time. Her calm demeanor revealed nothing of the battle that had taken place in her mind in the interim. She was disgusted with herself for her failure to communicate adequately with him. But she couldn't think when he was so close, couldn't formulate the logical arguments that made her such a skilled negotiator. Nor could she remember ever feeling quite this helpless and angry. The vortex was sweeping her away, and she was powerless against it.

Insufferable and obnoxious didn't begin to describe this man. A tiny corner of her mind acknowledged that he hadn't made the rules, that he was following the Coalition's orders. She supposed she should be grateful that he had made an attempt to explain his nation's customs to her. This, after all, was the whole purpose and reason behind the creation of a new colony on Treaine, a place where different nations and colonies would learn to live in unity, respect each others' customs and values, and perhaps even share them. But, as far as she could tell, he wasn't exactly giving any consideration to the customs and values of her people, nor had he given her any choice in accepting his. And why did he have to choose her in the first place?

Her instincts screamed at her to put as much distance as possible between them. Accepting the impossibility of that until she could enlist some assistance, she clung to his concession that he would have no immediate expectation for the fulfillment of the intimate duties of marriage. And she would work on convincing him at every opportunity that she had no interest in taking on the other duties either. And, she vowed to herself, she would seek every opportunity to escape the partnership, even if it meant leaving Treaine.

With several days of the journey left, and deciding not to test the limits of his patience over such a minor issue, she occupied part of the afternoon by unpacking her belongings and had taken vicious satisfaction from jamming his clothes into the corners of the storage units to make room for her own.

Now, she glanced around guiltily at his appearance and apologized sweetly for having lost track of time. He simply smiled, his eyes watchful, and gestured her before him into the sleeping chamber to choose her clothes for the evening. While she was occupied with that task, she heard the soft rustle of fabric and rip of a fastener and turned in time to see him reach for the waist of his breeches. Heat washed across her face and she couldn't prevent a soft "oh" of embarrassment from escaping her lips as her gaze fell on a hard, muscular chest liberally sprinkled with dark hair. She looked hurriedly away as he finished removing his breeches, and tried to sidle past him with the intention of dressing in the other room. A hard arm shot out blocking her path.

"Joanna." The word washed over her like a caress and she closed her eyes tightly, wishing she could close her ears as well. When he used that tone, all her intentions feebly crumbled into nothing. "Stay right here. I only meant we would forego any sexual activities for a while. I didn't mean that we would avoid any of the other normal intimacies of marriage."

In splendid male nakedness, feet spread wide apart and arms crossed, he seemed unconcerned by her embarrassment. She tried to find somewhere, anywhere to look but at him, to avoid the sapphire gaze that saw far too much. Heat was radiating from his bare skin in waves, and she felt a corresponding rise in her own body temperature. Then, abruptly, he appeared to take pity on her, and disappeared into the cleansing unit.

She was nervously waiting for him in the main room when he emerged again. His gaze swept over her in approval, the pulse in his temple deepening in color as his eyes lingered on the expanse of legs revealed by the short skirt of her dress. A hungry, possessive expression crossed his face.

"I wish," he said, as he took her arm and led her to the door, "that we could spend the evening alone, but I have a group of captains who are very anxious to meet you again. And if you're uncomfortable over that prospect, they are doubly so. You will dazzle them."

Thrown into confusion, yet somewhat reassured by his words, the evening went better than Joanna had expected. The captains were on their best behavior, and seemed determined to put her at her ease. They rivaled one another in telling fantastic stories of their travels in the Crestar System and beyond. As the tales became more exaggerated, she forgot her nervousness and even found herself laughing at the more outrageous of their tales.

Alex appeared content to let them entertain her. By the time he called an end to the evening, Joanna realized that she had actually enjoyed herself. Exhausted from all the emotional upheavals of the day, she was relieved when, as they entered their quarters, Alex gently pushed her toward the sleeping chamber and went off in the direction of the information console.

Chapter 9

THE NEXT THREE days before they reached Treaine went by quickly. Alex, who didn't seem to require much sleep, left their bed and usually their quarters before she even awoke and stayed away much of the day. Joanna was kept busy working with Ambassador Kromon and her team on various priority issues identified by the Coalition. In her spare time, she continued to explore the data bank files to locate information on Treaine.

The opportunity to escape the *Astran* never presented itself. She tried talking to Ambassador Kromon once more but, while he expressed some sympathy, he refused to assist her since the Coalition had endorsed the partnership.

She toured the *Astran* with Jason and was surprised to discover several children on the warrior vessel. Jason explained that most of the crew had been permanently assigned to Treaine, and the few crew members that had families had, of course, brought them along. And, several times, with Alex's encouragement, she went to the officers' lounge where once the *Astran's* senior medical officer and a Striker pilot tried unsuccessfully to teach her a Mariltar mind skills game.

The evenings were different. Alex always returned to their quarters to eat the evening meal with her. As her initial discomfort and hostility toward him began to fade and he refrained from making any sexual overtures, she began to enjoy their discussions, many of which centered around what they expected to find on Treaine, and the challenges that lay ahead. Both avoided any mention of family and their personal pasts. Joanna was afraid that any such discussions would bring them much closer to the intimacy she wanted to avoid.

Occasionally, at odd moments, she did find herself wondering what making love with Alex would be like, but her mind always skittered quickly away from pursuing those thoughts. He was just not the type of man to whom she was normally attracted. Although, when she was honest with herself, she supposed he was handsome enough and acknowledged that other women might find him so.

Her determination to find a way out of the partnership remained undiminished, despite her suspicion that she was beginning to like him a little.

ON THE FOURTH day, they reached Treaine.

Joanna was rudely awakened that morning by a stinging smack on her bottom, and Alex demanding in a disgustingly cheerful voice that she get dressed immediately. She rolled away to protect her vulnerable posterior and mumbled, "Oh, go away and bother someone else!"

"Very well," came the amused response, "I just thought you might like your first glimpse of Treaine from space before the *Astran* prepares to land."

She shot up in bed. "We're there? I thought we weren't supposed to arrive until later today?"

"We, ah, saved time by not stopping at the last substation..." Alex's response was distracted, and she realized belatedly that his gaze was focused intently on her chest. Glancing down, she saw with horror that the thin shirt she had worn to bed left little to the imagination, clearly outlining the curve of her breasts and hardened peaks in their center. She yanked the cover up and glared at him.

He looked at her a little dazedly, his strange eyes and the pulse at his temple glowing a deep sapphire. Then he smiled slowly, a smile filled with the promise of a thousand pleasures, and it stole her breath. For a single horrifying instant, she knew, if he had reached for her then, she wouldn't have been able to resist.

But, instead, he rose abruptly to his feet and stretched, treating her, intentionally she was sure, to a rippling display of muscle. "If you hurry up, I'll take you into the Command Center with me. The best view is from there." He disappeared into the main room and then stuck his head back around the corner.

"I take that back. The *second* best view is from there."

A well aimed pillow sent hurtling in his direction produced an echo of unrepentant laughter.

Joanna took barely ten minutes to dress. She was trembling with excitement. Treaine at last! She was so looking forward to stepping onto solid ground once again after almost two years on space vessels or substations.   She was concentrating on a particularly stubborn fastening on her dress when she hurried around the corner and bumped into Alex. His arm reached out to steady her, pulling her close against his side.

"Are you all right?" His hand swept down her back and lingered on her bottom.

Joanna's voice was muffled against his chest. "Yes, you can let me go now!"

"I was just bringing you some nourishment."

His arm fell away, and Joanna stepped back to peer doubtfully at the strange yellow liquid streaked with orange he had offered her the first morning.

"Go on, drink it! It's good for you," Alex encouraged her.

Taking a tentative sip, she discovered she liked the unusual taste. She watched Alex walk over to the information console and begin shutting it down. Her body was still tingling from the contact moments before, and a thread of panic clawed at her. If a look and a touch could reduce her to this state, how would she react if he tried to kiss her? She could not—would not—fall under this spell he wove. The life he offered held no appeal whatsoever. With a start, she realized he was waiting patiently, propped against the information console, arms folded, for her to finish. His gaze was taking in every detail of her appearance.

Joanna shifted uncomfortably and frowned. "Don't stare at me like that," she complained.

"Just enjoying an exceptionally lovely morning." His smile sent more unwelcome tremors through her body. "Ready to go?"

AS THEY ENTERED the Command Center, a voice snapped out, "Commander present!" The crew came to attention. Alex's quick nod of acknowledgment sent them back to their duties and he and Joanna joined Jason on the captain's podium.

Jason greeted Joanna with a brief smile. "We'll be coming around in just a minute to begin our landing approach. Treaine will be in sight just about...now!"

"Oh..." Joanna whispered in stunned awe. Nothing had prepared her for this. "It's absolutely spectacular!"

A section of the planet had appeared in the wide, curved viewing bubble. It was covered by a transparent, shimmering lavender haze. As the vessel moved rapidly closer and the planet filled the bubble, its geological features became apparent. Treaine was dotted with small lakes, although most of the planet's water was contained in huge reservoirs deep under the planet's surface. The side of the planet that the *Astran* was approaching was blanketed with dense forest pierced every now and then by a multitude of thinly sculptured, silver mountain spires. As the warrior vessel moved even closer, a wide, relatively flat area on the edge of a lake came into view. A smallish settlement nestled on a spit of land between forest and lake.

Joanna was enchanted.

"Ready to enter the atmosphere, sir!"

Jason acknowledged his navigator's statement and opened the *Astran's* internal relay. "This is the captain. All personnel, prepare to land. Strap in securely, people. It could be a rough ride."

As the *Astran's* warning chimes sounded throughout the vessel, Alex guided Joanna to a seat next to him, and pressed a button triggering a strap which wrapped itself securely over her shoulders and around her waist.

Jason waited, then nodded at his navigation crew, "Take her down slowly and gently, Control. It's been years since this lady was last grounded. She's likely to object."

Joanna squeezed her eyes shut as the *Astran* entered Treaine's atmosphere and began to shudder violently. She felt Alex's hand cover hers and was grateful for the small comfort. The vessel continued to buck wildly as it fought against external pressures. Gradually the shuddering lessened and then ceased altogether as a curious gliding sensation took its place. There was a gentle bump, and then the sound of the crew cheering filled the Command Center.

"Welcome to Treaine, Joanna," Alex said softly into her ear.

Chapter 10

AT MID-DAY, Joanna and Alex walked down the ramp of the *Astran*. They were followed closely by her captain and officers. The *Claxiarten* had also landed, and Ambassador Kromon had disembarked with his wife and own small party. The remaining vessels in the pod still rode high above them.

Advancing across the landing platform was a reception committee led by a tall, slender man dressed in a long-sleeved tunic which fell to mid-calf. His head was bald, except for three thick bands of black hair, each of which was drawn back and bound with strings of small colored pebbles, then allowed to hang down his back to his knees.

"Ambassador Mariltar, Ambassador Kromon." He raised a six-fingered hand in greeting, his expression calm and unsmiling.

"Ambassador Soron." As Alex and Kromon returned the greeting, Joanna saw her husband and the Soron eye each other warily. Alex had told her only yesterday that the last time he and this man had met, they had faced each other in a battle neither had won. Both sons of the ruling clan on their respective planets, there were generations of warfare and a bitter enmity between their two nations which had created a chasm that soon would have to be bridged. Alex's glance slid over the Soron ambassador's shoulder and she felt a strange tension radiating from him as he surveyed the large party comprised mostly of Sorons.

"I was assigned to head the advance party on Treaine," the Soron continued. "We've been here a month, readying the settlement for the colonists and supervising the robotic construction of the new city. There are quarters for you and your senior officers and staff in the settlement. The remainder of your people will have to stay on your vessels until more of the settlement's living units are habitable and some of the construction is completed, which should be very soon. We're expecting the next pod of vessels in a few days, and want to have yours docked at the new facility and all your personnel settled by then. Would you care for a tour?"

Alex and Kromon both agreed enthusiastically. Alex reached behind him and drew Joanna forward. "Ambassador Soron, I'd like to introduce my wife, Joanna."

The Soron smiled for the first time, raised his hand in greeting and said with more warmth than he had previously displayed, "Welcome to Treaine, my lady." He turned to his own party, and took the hand of a tiny woman with a greenish cast to her skin. She was obviously pregnant. "Allow me to introduce *my* wife, Kara of Liarte."

With a bright smile of welcome, Kara smoothly took over the introductions. But as Joanna tried to concentrate on the confusing parade of people and names, she heard the Soron ambassador say in an undertone to Alex, "I had received news that you had entered into a marriage partnership with an Earth colonist. My sister was very disappointed. She had high expectations that, as a Coalition choice, and because of her previous association with you, you might select her."

Out of the corner of her eye, she saw Alex's expression turn even more wary at this disclosure. The Soron seemed to find his reaction amusing and actually chuckled. "You must not concern yourself. I, myself, am a strong believer in the Match Key and would never dispute its power. I want to make it very clear that my sister received no support from me in her demand that the Coalition dissolve your marriage, but I also wanted to let you know that I'm not sure she has accepted their decision."

Alex's response was lost as Kara urged Joanna forward to greet another group. Joanna gave up trying to remember names and barely heard the rest of the introductions, even as she desperately tried to appear as if she was paying attention. Her excitement and euphoria over Treaine's beauty and exotic scents had vanished abruptly with the Soron's statements to Alex, leaving her with a peculiar feeling of emptiness and coldness, despite the warmth of the day. She mentally shook herself. Well, what could she expect? Of course other women wanted him. So, why should she care? He had set out to charm her in the last couple of days, and had succeeded well enough that she had started to let down her guard. Now she had received another warning, loud and clear, and her defenses were back in place even stronger than before. She would not become another statistic in a long line of women, never mind that he had chosen to legalize their arrangement. She avoided his hand and ignored his look of surprise as they walked to where several land cruisers were waiting to transport them to the settlement.

The tour of the settlement took less than an hour. Mostly a trading post, the main attraction was the large Marketplace which was open on this warm day but could be covered with a transparent dome in severe weather. Vendors from several star systems displayed a large variety of wares. Ambassador Soron explained that the Marketplace never shut down completely, remaining busy even during the night hours.

Off to one side and in caverns underneath the Marketplace, entertainment houses offered a host of recreational activities from the bizarre to the familiar. Kara leaned over to whisper in Joanna's ear that she thought someone should investigate exactly what went on in some of those places. There were some ugly rumors circulating and no one in her husband's party had had the time to look into them. Since the Mariltar contingent was responsible for security, among other things, she expressed a hope that something would be done soon.

As the tour drew to a close, the land cruisers dispersed to take their occupants to their respective quarters. Joanna hadn't been paying attention to the discussion between the Soron and Alex, and was surprised but relieved when Alex told her he wanted to look over the construction site, leaving her to enter their new quarters on her own. Kara left the land cruiser as well and walked with her to the entrance of the unit chatting happily about trivialities and pointing out several exotic species of flowers peeping from the dense lush growth of greenery edging the pathway. Their heavy scent filled the air, and Joanna breathed deeply, trying to recall some of her earlier excitement.

Kara touched her arm when they reached the entrance. "I hope we can be friends," she said. "The units have been well stocked with supplies. If you need anything at all, we're in the next one over."

Joanna summoned a smile, wondering how this woman would react if she begged for her assistance to escape this intolerable arrangement that had been thrust upon her. Somehow, entering the permanent living quarters she would share with Alex made the marriage seem much more real, and with that came the just as frightening reality of the host of duties she would be expected to fulfill. She glanced back at the empty pathway behind them and, for a brief instant, considered simply walking away. Instead, she turned back to Kara. "Thank you," she said softly. Then she gestured and added shyly, "When is your baby due?"

"In two more months. The gestation period for a Liarte is relatively short. But you probably want to settle in. We'll talk again, soon." She waved cheerfully and disappeared down a narrow pathway.

Feeling a strange mixture of reluctance and anticipation, Joanna walked through the door and into a large, light-filled great room with a low ceiling. One wall was entirely of glass and faced out onto a dramatic view of an overgrown garden which gave way to a rose-colored beach and the deep, aqua waters of the lake. She spent several minutes reveling in the sight before turning to inspect the rest of the room.

It was comfortably if not imaginatively appointed, and designed to hold a number of people in several distinct sitting areas. One corner housed an extensive work area and contained an information console with multiple screens. Directly opposite, a narrow counter curved out into the room, behind which was some equipment which Joanna could only guess represented a food preparation area. She noticed a short, shallow flight of stairs in the far corner and, upon investigating, discovered it led to a sleeping chamber which shared the great room's view. The bed itself was huge, taking up an inordinate amount of space, but she felt only relief that she would have little difficulty keeping her distance from her husband.

An archway opened into a fully appointed bath chamber. Joanna exclaimed in delight at the oversized bath sunk deeply into the middle of the room, and ran over to push the controls. Steaming water bubbled into the bath. Further exploration of the room revealed toweling cloths hidden behind sliding panels and a variety of colored bottles. Wondering who was responsible for placing them there, she selected a pale green, deliciously scented liquid and poured it into the water. A mound of fat bubbles appeared instantly.

She hurriedly stripped off her clothes, bundled her hair on top of her head and sank blissfully into the water. As she relaxed, her thoughts turned to Alex and the marriage she so desperately wanted to escape before it was too late. Under other circumstances, she might have enjoyed getting to know him. She might even have allowed herself to be a little attracted to him, but would never have chosen him as a life mate or a lover. He was too sure of himself and he overwhelmed her and aroused her anger too easily. On top of that, the Mariltar marriage custom with its standards applied differently to husband and wife was simply too hard to accept given her own cultural heritage.

As soon as she could, she would locate some Earth colonists she knew had arrived with the first group and seek assistance. Treaine intrigued her, and she hated to think of leaving without a chance to explore. She also felt guilty at the thought of giving up her position with Kromon, but he would find another negotiator. And she could return to negotiating trade deals in the Neutral Realm. That option, as unexciting as it sounded now, was far preferable to a marriage partnership she didn't want.

With her eyes closed and her thoughts whirling over the events of the last few days and her predicament, Joanna paid no attention to a slight disturbance in the water. But when something rough and unyielding brushed against the outside of her leg, she yelped in fright and shot up to a sitting position. Her eyes flew open in shock just as a masculine voice murmured huskily, "This looks so, ah, enjoyable. Mind if I join you?"

Alex was sitting against the opposite end of the bath. His arms were draped along the ledge. A smile twitched at the corners of his mouth. He looked very relaxed, very satisfied and far too pleased with himself. The smile became fixed, his eyes narrowed as his gaze lowered to her chest and a peculiar rumble issued from his throat.

This time, she realized with a spurt of fury and resentment at this invasion of her privacy, there was no shirt to lend her a false sense of modesty. Her breasts, covered with a thin, completely transparent layer of bubbles, were exposed to his hungry eyes. She promptly sank back under the water.

"Yes, I *do* mind," she snapped. "Go away!"

"Oh, I will— eventually," Alex assured her, quite undeterred by her tone. He leaned his head back and closed his eyes. "I'd forgotten how relaxing this could be." His leg brushed against hers again.

In rising panic, Joanna looked frantically around to see where she had left her clothes and towel. They were too far out of reach for her to safely get to them and preserve her modesty. She glared back at Alex who now looked like he was ignoring her entirely. She felt horribly vulnerable. Nor was she convinced that she could trust him to keep his word. This was, after all, the most intimate circumstance he had forced her into so far, and she had seen that particular look of hunger in his eyes more and more frequently lately, especially when he thought she wasn't looking. Well, all she could do was wait until he left. He couldn't stay there forever.

She moved as far away from him as she could get. All the pleasure had gone out of the bath, and now she wished desperately for it to be over. But wishing didn't seem to help at all. Alex gave no appearance of being in any hurry. After a few minutes, he sat up lazily and reached for a small cloth on the ledge of the bath to scrub himself. Joanna closed her eyes and tried to ignore the sounds. This was so embarrassing!

"Wash my back?" Her eyes opened to find a cloth dangling in front of her face and Alex, eyebrow raised, looking at her expectantly. She thought briefly of refusing, but decided complying with the request might get rid of him sooner. Reluctantly, she took the cloth from him and he shifted around in the water presenting a broad hard back.

Joanna swallowed. That tingling sensation was back in her lower belly, and the water temperature seemed to be rising. She swished the cloth lightly over his back several times and handed it back to him. "Here, I'm done."

He twisted around, his leg once again brushing against the outside of hers. His smile was nothing short of suggestive, his eyes a deep glowing sapphire. "Your turn. Turn around!"

"What?" This little game of his was getting far too intimate for her comfort level. "My back doesn't need to be washed."

"Turn around anyway," Alex commanded softly.

He was sitting too close to her, her thoughts were in a muddle, and she desperately needed to put some distance between them. She turned her back unwillingly, thinking if he touched her anywhere else she would be out of the bath in a flash, modesty be damned! But Alex simply washed her back in a seemingly detached manner, then announced he was getting out. Her irritation soared as he took an unreasonably long time drying off, whistling all the while.

She had her back turned and was studying the curious ceiling pattern when he came up behind her, leaned his hands on the ledge and said in her ear, "You'd better get out before your skin resembles a puri leaf. Your belongings have arrived from the *Astran*, and some other containers from the storage hold of the *Claxiarten*. They're all in the sleeping chamber."

Chapter 11

ALEX STRODE from the bath chamber. Despite a body aching with arousal, he couldn't stop grinning. He felt ridiculously pleased with himself.

When he had first discovered her in the bath chamber, he had leant against the wall for several minutes observing her, wishing the bubbles didn't hide all but her lovely face framed by damp tendrils of hair. He wondered what she was thinking about. She looked more relaxed and contented than he had yet seen her.

He had just decided to leave her to her thoughts when he changed his mind. It was time to advance this game of seduction a step further. And he wasn't displeased with the results. He had expected her anger and resentment. He knew her well enough by now to believe she wouldn't give in so easily. But his reward had been that delightful glimpse of perfectly rounded ivory breasts crowned by tempting rosy peaks, and a chance to explore the slender territory of her back. And he had noticed a distinct tremble in her hand when she had handed the cloth back to him. Progress indeed!

As he pulled on a pair of thin black pants, he couldn't help but wonder what her reaction would have been if she had opened her eyes while he was drying himself. He had deliberately taken his time, allowing plenty of opportunity for her considerable curiosity to assert itself and discover his heavily aroused body. His disappointment when she didn't was short-lived. There would be other opportunities in the evening that lay ahead.

He was busy in the utility area when she entered the room some time later. Even at this distance, he saw her roll her eyes exaggeratedly as they fastened on his bare chest. He turned his head to hide a grin. He had intentionally left off his shirt, wanting to keep her off balance and as a gentle reminder of the relationship he wanted. She started to head for the opposite end of the room.

But he had other ideas. He looked up as she passed, and asked mildly, "Are you familiar with these cooking appliances?"

"No. Why?"

He laughed. "Don't be so suspicious. I'm not going to add meal preparation to your list of duties. We'll have a mechaide for that. I merely thought you might like to see how some of this equipment operates."

"Oh!" She was clearly put out that he had read her reaction so easily, and wandered over reluctantly. But she watched closely as he quickly prepared a meal with little fuss, and agreed readily enough when he suggested they eat outside.

"It's so beautiful here, so perfect," she remarked, looking around as they sat down on a padded bench.

"It seems so," Alex agreed, "but there's much we don't know about this planet. So much of it is unexplored." He smiled lightly at her. "I'll reserve judgment about the 'perfect' part until we've had an opportunity to thoroughly explore at least the area in the immediate vicinity of this settlement."

"What do you expect to find?" Joanna asked.

Alex shrugged. "Not much beyond what we know to expect. Perhaps nothing. The planet has some indigenous non-human life forms, and some that were brought here from other systems and have adapted. There will eventually be teams sent to explore all parts of the planet to make a thorough study of what is here. Our first priority is to secure this area. Tomorrow, we're establishing a security perimeter around the settlement and the construction site, so we'll know exactly who or what enters and leaves. Security is going to be extremely tight for a while until the peace accord is well established in the Crestar System."

And the greatest threat could be as close as the neighboring living unit. Any one of the Sorons in the welcoming party today could have been hiding a destructive agenda behind the facade of unity they had presented, but the leading clans of Mariltar and Soron, in particular, had a long history of conflict. As Jason had pointed out, his wife could be the one most at risk. What better way to destroy the fragile peace initiative than for the House of Soron to attack the House of Mariltar at one of its most vulnerable points? He hid his worry as he watched her eat, glad once again that he had confided in Jason.

They ate in companionable silence. A light breeze blew gently around them, lifting and playing with Joanna's bright hair. Out on the lake, the water shifted and shimmered, and whispered softly on the sand a short distance away. Overhead, the large, silver, plate-like leaves of a barniian tree swayed in supple movement, setting pale shadows to dancing around them.

Alex finished his meal and set aside his plate. He was reluctant to disturb the tranquil mood, but knew he couldn't put off discussion of her personal safety any longer. This wasn't going to be easy, but it was also one issue on which he refused to compromise. He reached over to tuck a wayward strand of hair behind her ear, earning himself a wide-eyed, startled look. Excellent. He had her attention. "Joanna, it should be safe enough for you to move freely within the settlement during the daylight hours, but I must insist that you arrange with Jason for an escort if you have to be out after dark. I also cannot permit you to go outside the perimeter for any reason. All colonists in key positions will be issued wrist communicators within the next few days, and will be asked to wear them whenever they leave their private quarters. These may seem like excessive precautions, but we feel they are necessary for now."

The vociferous objections he had expected were never uttered. To the contrary, there was not a flicker of reaction. Joanna sat quietly staring out at the lake. He wished once again he could read her thoughts. In the last several days, she had made very clear her aversion to having certain boundaries imposed. These were major restrictions on her freedom and he hadn't even told her everything. A security detail had also been assigned to follow her wherever she went outside of their living unit. His conscience pricked him for holding his silence. She had a right to know. And he would tell her—eventually—he promised himself but, for now, he had given her enough to think about and come to terms with.

A strong gust of air flattened the thin fabric of her tunic against her chest and molded it to the swell of her breasts. He was reminded forcefully of his earlier plan to advance his seduction of her a little further. He shifted uncomfortably and swore under his breath, switching his gaze back to her expressionless face. Just what *was* going on in that mind of hers? Her lack of response bothered him more than he cared to admit and raised all sorts of suspicions and doubts. Well, he decided impatiently, short of a mind probe, it didn't look like she was going to reveal her feelings and he was curiously reluctant to ask her directly. Besides, he had another agenda to pursue which would certainly command her full attention and pull it back from whatever place his words had sent it to.

Just thinking about how he would make his first approach heated his blood to boiling. Suddenly, urgently, everything else could wait. He couldn't. He had been patient too long.

She was so intent on her thoughts that she jumped when he brushed his hand over hers and relieved her of her empty plate. Her expression of surprise turned to shock as he put an arm around her waist and pulled her onto his lap.

"I would give a gir sarion to see what's going on inside that lovely head of yours," he murmured in her ear. "You have no idea what you do to me, do you? No! Just sit still and be quiet." The order was delivered gently, but still she objected and tried to wriggle away. "Joanna," he whispered, nuzzling her ear, "don't fight me, Meira. All I want to do is hold you. You must admit, I've exercised a great deal of restraint and patience." With a surging sense of satisfaction, he felt her cease to struggle, although her body still trembled in his arms.

"You promised you w—"

"Shh! I know. And I'll keep that promise." Even if it killed him which it was likely to do. It seemed as if he ached from every pore. His hand cupped her chin and he studied her face intently, making her squirm again in his lap. Their clothing was no barrier, and he knew from the startled look on her face she could feel every hard curve and swell of his flesh. He closed his eyes briefly and groaned. "You're a mystery, Meira, but one I will take a great deal of pleasure in unraveling."

He rubbed his hand up and down her back in slow circles, content for the moment to just hold and stroke her. Gradually, he felt her relax against him. Her breath warmed his skin where it fanned against his chest. Slowly, he bent his head and nuzzled gently at her ear and neck again. When she didn't object, his lips moved to touch the sensitive place under her ear, then roamed softly across her cheek to her mouth. He brushed his tongue across lips which tasted faintly of the spiced food they had eaten, and probed insistently for entrance. Her head fell back and her mouth opened under his assault in complete surrender. Her tiny moan stoked the fire raging through his body as he deepened the kiss and claimed the lush contours of her mouth for his own. She was quivering delightfully in his arms and arched into his touch as he stroked his hand slowly and purposefully down her chest and closed it over one perfect mound of flesh. His thumb found her nipple immediately and teased it into hardness under the light fabric.

Just as he was about to move on to explore other delights, he felt her stiffen with shocking suddenness. A hand flattened against his chest, she jerked her mouth away from his and stared him full in the face. Fury lit the green eyes. She tumbled off his lap with a strangled sound.

On her feet, she stabbed a finger at him. "You!" she said accusingly. "It was you, all those months ago in the gym on the substation. *Wasn't* it?"

He leaned back warily and crossed his arms. "I was wondering if you were going to remember. I wasn't sure you ever would."

"How dare you?" she yelped. Her hands slashed the air angrily, green eyes flashed fire, her body tensed and trembled with outrage. "Why didn't you *tell* me? How could you mislead me all this time. How could you pretend we'd never met? Do you think I'm a fool? How could you *treat* me like this?"

Stunned by the attack, Alex shook his head a little dazedly. This was the reaction he had expected over restricting her movements, not over something that had happened months ago. "I never pretended we hadn't met. I was curious to see if you would make the connection. Joanna, it's not *that* important. It was a long time ago and a very brief incident. Now come back here."

A curious expression very much like pain crossed her face. "Leave me alone," she shot back. "Go find someone else to play with. Someone who wants you." She turned and all but ran into the living unit.

Alex sat staring blankly at the lake, breathing deeply, forcing himself to calm his own temper, willing the aching pressure in his groin to ease. What by the blood of Cor had just happened? Why had she been so upset? She had melted under his touch, as he had known—hoped—she would, and then had erupted like a veliari steam vent. Over an incident from long ago! He shook his head in bewilderment. Now he had to figure out what had gone wrong, and chart a course of seduction all over again. Jason's warnings sounded mockingly in his mind. But at the same time, the memory of her response just a few minutes ago caused his body to tighten once more. By Pormiam, she was so sweet, and she affected him as no other woman had!

Chapter 12

LATE THE NEXT morning, Joanna was helping to organize the conference and work space assigned to Ambassador Kromon's team in a building near the Marketplace. She was tired and definitely out of sorts. Sleep had come only from sheer exhaustion in the early hours of the morning. She had lain awake, angry, tense and expectant for most of the night, half convinced she would have to fend off more advances from her husband. And then, when he had failed to make an appearance at all, had become increasingly disturbed.

She remembered the exact moment when the vague sense of familiarity about him that had been haunting her became a clear, sharp memory. The touch of his lips against hers and the feel of his hand on her breast had inspired the same head-spinning, soul-numbing, heart-pounding sensation she had experienced only once before several months earlier. And she knew without a doubt that it was the same man at the precise instant she realized he had been deceiving her for the better part of a week.

How could she not have recognized him? The fact that his features had been almost entirely obscured at that first meeting was no excuse. No one else moved with such lethal grace, or dominated the space around them in quite the same way. And, if nothing else, she should have made the connection from those devastating eyes alone. She had allowed her anger to erupt as a self-defense, to hide a curious sense of betrayal she had felt that he hadn't chosen to voluntarily reveal himself. Yet fury had turned swiftly to a strangely piercing pain when he had discounted the importance of that first meeting.

Now, unexpectedly, she felt the sting of tears behind her eyes. Not important? Not important to him maybe. But she had fantasized about that brief encounter ever since. Variations on that kiss had disturbed many a dream and then she had experienced the reality again. And the worst part was, she wanted more and could never admit that to him. The depth of utter longing he had aroused in her shocked her and made her furious with herself. How could she have let it go that far? And just where *had* he spent the night?

She slammed a communication cube down onto her work table then, immediately contrite, picked the fragile instrument up again to examine it for damage. She didn't really care where he had spent the night, did she? But he could have had the consideration to let her know he was leaving.

A tapping sound attracted her attention and she looked up to see a familiar face smiling at her from outside the room's sliding glass panels.

"Melissa!" Delighted, she hurried over to open the panels. The two women embraced affectionately. "I'm so glad to see you. How *are* you, and how are things going here?"

"I'm glad to see you, too. I'm just great, and things are going very well." Melissa laughed and stepped back, holding Joanna at arms' length. "But I'm more interested in hearing all the juicy details of what's been happening to *you* since I last saw you. The rumors have been absolutely *sizzling*! Can you get away for a while?"

Joanna wrinkled her nose, mortified by the knowledge that she and Alex were food for the gossip mills. "Only if you can promise me a shoulder to cry on. Let me see what I can do."

She excused herself from the team members still in the room, and walked quickly back to Melissa. "Where are we going?"

"To the Marketplace. They actually have some decent Earth cuisine there."

As the two women made their way to the Marketplace, Melissa chattered happily about her experiences on Treaine. Distracted by her problems, Joanna listened with half an ear but, even in her preoccupation, became increasingly aware of the attention they were generating from the male sector of the population.

She slid a sideways glance at Melissa, who seemed completely oblivious to the bold stares. Of course, Melissa had to be used to attention like this. Her appearance demanded such a tribute, if that's what it could be called. Melissa was nothing if not a contradiction. A melange of clothing styles in clashing colors draped over a tall, slender frame, wide innocent eyes and long, silky blond hair styled into a rather fantastic and improbable arrangement all contributed to an image of irresistible mystery and surprisingly seductive appeal. Appearances aside, Melissa had a brilliant mind and was a well respected scholar. She chose to focus her considerable talents on designing learning programs for children and adolescents whom she genuinely adored. Her assignment on Treaine was to establish and manage a multi-ethnic learning environment for young students.

Her other love was men in every size, shape and form. She went after them with a passion, and few refused her invitation to her bed.

None, from Joanna's observation, ever seemed to enjoy her affections for longer than one or two months.

They had selected their food and were seating themselves in a quiet area when Melissa pounced. "Enough about me. I'm about to *die* of curiosity. Tell me about this marriage. Where did you meet? What's he like—and, most importantly, how's your sex life?"

Joanna blinked. Trust Melissa to get right to the heart of what she wanted to know. And how much should she reveal? She and Melissa had formed a strong bond in the short time they had known each other in the Neutral Realm, and if she couldn't trust her, who could she trust? She had to find help somewhere. She swallowed against a sudden tightness in her throat, lowered her eyes to her tightly clasped hands and said carefully, and not altogether truthfully, "Well, sex is non-existent, I don't think I like the man, and we met when he forced me into marriage after abducting me."

The short silence was broken by a peal of laughter that had Joanna cringing and peering around to see if they had attracted attention. "Very funny. You almost had me convinced. You—oh, Lord, you're not joking, are you?"

Joanna shook her head and surreptitiously wiped away the tear trickling down one cheek. She struggled to hold back the flood and maintain an appearance of composure, when what she really felt like doing was bawling like a baby.

"You're really serious. Lord, Joanna. Stuff like this just doesn't *happen* to you. No." She waved a hand carelessly at Joanna's choke of denial. "I didn't mean it that way. It's just you're not the type to—oh, never mind. *How* did it happen?"

WITH HEADS CLOSE together and absorbed in their discussion, the two women seemed unaware of the many admiring glances directed their way by other diners. One, in particular, watched with avid curiosity from a table deep in the shadows, noting the tall Mariltar warrior poorly disguised by everyday dress who had seated himself not too far away from the two women. Diners came and went, but still the Mariltar stayed, toying with a single cup, carefully observing without seeming to the activity in the immediate vicinity. The watcher in the shadows shifted his feet, and drew his rich, dark robe more closely around him. So, the new wife to the High Lord of Mariltar had a bodyguard. The discovery wasn't cause for concern. One man was no barrier. He would still take her when he wanted her. The entire Mariltar force couldn't prevent it. This was his destiny.

He turned his attention back to the woman. She was a pretty thing with that bright hair and delicate body. So easy to break. But he wasn't interested in her body. It was her mind he wanted. She was different, he sensed, so different from the others, and he wasn't sure why. Excitement heated his veins. It had been a long time since he had felt this particular surge of energy, a prelude, he knew, to that next level, that next step, of the only thing that mattered.

Power.

"MELISSA, YOU have to help me. I can't stay in this marriage." Joanna was on the verge of tears again. *Damn!* She hated crying in front of others, and wished they had picked a less public place for this discussion.

Appearing a little stunned by the story she had heard, Melissa dug in one of her many pockets and handed her a handkerchief. "What do you want to do?"

"I don't know. Get away from him. I don't want to leave Treaine. I really looked forward to coming here. But I just can't see staying, now." She blew her nose and concentrated on folding the square of cloth neatly. "I suppose I'll go back to the Neutral Realm."

"He won't let you go? He knows how you feel?"

"Of course he does. He just keeps quoting Match Key statistics until I want to throw up, and keeps reminding me of all these 'duties' I have to perform that apparently are supposed to take precedence over my work. I really want out of this marriage, Melissa."

"All right. All right. Let me think." Melissa leaned back in her chair and glanced idly around the increasingly busy area. Joanna saw her gaze linger for a moment on the tall man seated a short distance away them. The chagrined expression on Melissa's face when he refused to meet her eyes would have been amusing if Joanna hadn't been so upset. "If that's what you want, and it's not what *he* wants, I think it's pretty obvious you can't stay here. I'll inquire in the Earth community about transportation. But even if you did find a vessel returning to the Neutral Realm, and a captain willing to transport you, its going to be tough getting you past the new security procedures. Since the Mariltar group arrived, they're watching all arrivals and departures very closely for some reason."

"I know. But I have to try." Otherwise, she might not survive what she feared Alex wanted her to become. She stared blindly into the shadows. One, darker and denser than the rest, seemed to move and grow, then blended into the others. An icy chill touched the back of her neck and a deep sense of dread seized her. She blinked and looked again, but there was nothing to cause alarm in the scene before her. Now she was imagining things! She sighed and turned back to Melissa.

Melissa looked at her, hesitated, then asked gently, "Are you sure you want to leave so soon without giving this more of a chance? I have the same reservations about the Match Key you do, but there must be something to it with so many seemingly successful marriage partnerships as a result of it."

"Melissa!" Indignant and hurt, Joanna's voice was louder than she had intended. She lowered it and hissed, "My life is a living nightmare. This is *not* what I wanted or expected. I *want* to be a negotiator, not a wife married to a control freak, an *ambassador*, for God's sake, who has his own ideas about what I should be doing with my time."

"All right. But, tell me—" Melissa began, and leaned closer, forcing Joanna to meet her eyes, "—how did he make you feel when he tried to make to love to you?"

Chin propped in hand, Joanna scowled at her. "I don't know. Confused...angry..."

"Dizzy with passion, desperate for his kisses, burning for his touch, ready to spread your legs and—?"

Joanna reared back. "No, of course not. Well, I wouldn't have put it quite that way."

"Hah!" Melissa pointed an azure tipped finger at her. "Forgive me for being so blunt, but I have *never* seen you in such an emotional stew over *any* man before. Even what's-his-name, who dumped you for that dancer, apparently wasn't worth this much effort."

"That was different. I wasn't married to him."

Melissa frowned and shook her head vigorously, putting her hairstyle in imminent danger of collapsing. "What's marriage got to do with how you feel about him?"

"Everything! He can take lovers, but I can't. I'm not free to move around as I please. He wants to control how I spend my time. He—"

"That still has nothing to do with how you really *feel* about him," Melissa interrupted ruthlessly. "And besides, none of those are real issues. You're a negotiator. You could easily overcome any one of them if you wanted to."

Joanna's fingers tightened around her cup. Her eyes narrowed. "You don't know Alex. Are you saying now you won't help me?"

"No, no," Melissa replied hastily, "I just think you ought to think about it some more. You've married into one of the ruling families of this star system, *and* you're an ambassador's wife. He's handed you position, rank and privilege. If things don't work out between you, you'll be free to do what you want after one or two children."

"Yes, I have all the privileges of breeding stock," Joanna muttered furiously. The bustling scene before her shifted and blurred as panic gripped her once more. She glanced back at Melissa and said with simple conviction, "I can't do this. I want out."

Melissa heaved a sigh and reached for her hand. "All right. I'll make those inquiries. But at least think about what I said. It's a shame you had to come all this way for nothing, and I know I'll miss you. But—" She poked Joanna's arm. "Before you leave, you have to see some of this place. It's amazing. Tell me when you have some free time, and I'll check out a cruiser and take you into the canyons."

Joanna smiled for the first time, and allowed herself to relax a little. If Melissa said she would help, then she could count on her to do so. "That sounds terrific. I'll have to look at Ambassador Kromon's schedule." Then she remembered and groaned.

"What's the matter?"

"Oh, I'm not supposed to go outside the perimeter."

"Why?"

"Alex thinks it's too dangerous."

"Oh, star pits!" scoffed Melissa. "I've been out of the settlement dozens of times on my own and nothing even remotely threatening has happened."

"I didn't say I *wouldn't* go, and I certainly don't plan on asking him for permission. How do we get through the perimeter with all the new security procedures going into effect?"

Melissa grinned and waved a hand unconcernedly. "Leave it to me. We'll pick up—"

"Hello, ladies."

They turned as one, startled by the interruption, to see Mark Oberan and Jason Asteril standing immediately behind them. The expression that appeared on the faces of both men as they were treated to the full frontal impact of Melissa was identical and, from Joanna's perspective, downright comical. She rolled her eyes. Even hardened warriors, it seemed, could make blithering idiots of themselves over an attractive woman. Jason tore his fascinated and admiring gaze away from Melissa long enough to raise a questioning eyebrow at Joanna. She hastily performed the introductions and watched with amusement as Melissa turned on the full strength of her considerable charm. The poor fools didn't stand a chance. Not when Melissa was so clearly thrilled with these two attractive specimens of Mariltar manhood and determined to bewitch, bemuse and seduce. Joanna wondered idly which one would fall prey to Melissa first.

After exchanging a few comments with Melissa, the men reluctantly excused themselves and went off to find their own table.

Melissa was ecstatic and fairly bouncing in her seat with excitement as she watched them go. "If even half the men in the Mariltar fleet look like that, this place is going to be pure heaven."

Joanna snorted, unimpressed. "Well, they do. I think it's sort of obscene, myself. You'd think they'd chosen them for their looks and not their warrior skills. You're—"

"There's another one headed this way," Melissa hissed. "And if that's commander's insignia I see, this one's your husband. You're crazy, woman! If he were mine, I'd let him do whatever he wanted to me, and then I'd go back for seconds!"

Joanna's mouth dropped open in sheer outrage at such a complete defection of loyalty. Torn between trying to think of something suitably scathing to say, and the overwhelming desire to turn and look for her husband, she was saved the necessity of making the choice by the arrival of Alex at their table. He introduced himself to Melissa and spoke with her briefly while his hands clasped and caressed Joanna's shoulders. She barely restrained herself from pulling away. He couldn't have proclaimed his possession of her any louder than if he had shouted it, she thought, fuming.

As he turned to leave to join Mark and Jason, he glanced at Joanna sharply and asked softly, "Are you all right?"

She flushed with the memory of what had happened the last time they had been together. "Of course."

He studied her intently a moment longer before nodding and strolling off.

SHORTLY AFTER, the two women rose to return to their respective work assignments. Watching through narrowed eyes, Alex tapped thoughtfully on the tabletop and wondered out loud, "Why do I get an extremely uneasy feeling about that pair? Does either of you know anything about Melissa?"

Jason picked up his utensil, preparing to attack a plate of steaming vialor noodles. "I glanced at her file this morning. She's head of the children's scholastic program and is very well respected in academic circles."

"Any connection to Joanna?"

"None that was mentioned. They were in the Neutral Realm for a brief period together."

"Your instincts are probably not misplaced, Alex," Mark said quietly. "We interrupted a very intense discussion. They were plotting something."

"Mmm," Alex grunted as he surveyed a suddenly unappetizing bowl of his favorite soup. "Keep an eye on her—on both of them."

Chapter 13

ALEX PAUSED in the open doorway. The sight of the slender figure standing on the steps leading to the beach brought a deep feeling of relief. She was here, home early for once! And if he had anything to say about it, they would finally spend some time together and clear up that last little misunderstanding, although he still had no real clue as to what had caused it. The resulting coolness and extreme politeness of her manner on the few and very brief occasions they had spent together since were beginning to get on his nerves.

The last several days had been extremely hectic as more colonists and two more ambassadors arrived, straining the resources of the settlement. Ambassador Kromon's team had been completed, and Joanna's days had become very long as the team continued to prioritize their tasks, and spent countless hours arguing and trying to compromise on even the simplest issues. He knew from Kromon's reports that Joanna found her negotiating skills stretched to the limit as cultures and viewpoints clashed, and he saw that she often arrived home exhausted, unable to do more than find something quick to eat and crawl into bed.

He, too, was working long hours. As he had done on the *Astran*, he left before Joanna was awake in the morning. Some evenings, he was home before her, but deeply involved in discussions over the information console and, while he acknowledged her presence, they had rarely been able to exchange more than a few words.

She never knew how often he went to sit on the bed beside her, aching with desire, to watch her sleep. He longed to stroke a hand over an exposed shoulder, to sweep away the light cover, to explore her secret places, to plunge himself inside her while she was drugged from sleep, warm and sweetly yielding. But he always forced himself to leave again without waking her, promising himself that one day soon he would fully satisfy all his yearnings, and learn all the secrets of her womanhood.

Now, he savored the moment as he watched her, anticipating the evening ahead. The breeze was warm, inviting, heavy with a sweet scent. It played with the bright strands of her hair, and toyed with the hem of her skirt. She stood with her face tilted to the sky, her stance relaxed. He almost hated to disturb her. But he also refused to waste another moment of the time he had with her. He moved forward.

"I'm delighted you're home early tonight, too." He had startled her. He saw the slight telltale jerk of her shoulders, although she didn't turn around and didn't acknowledge him. So, she was still at that game? His hands curved around her shoulders and he held her lightly, feeling the tiny tremors she couldn't hide. "Want to take a walk by the lake?"

"All right." The answer came more quickly than he had expected. She stepped forward, moving out from under his touch.

Down on the coarse rose-colored sand, instead of turning toward the settlement, Alex steered her in the other direction. Soon the last of the living units was left behind, and the only sounds were the soft swish of water, the rustle of trees and, far in the distance, the sound of some creature squealing faintly.

They walked in silence, enjoying the calm after a hectic day, neither one willing to speak and risk breaking what seemed to be tentative truce. The squealing was becoming louder and, as they rounded a curve in the beach, they saw a creature struggling frantically in the water near a rock. Joanna stopped abruptly to watch closely.

"Poor thing!" Alex heard her mutter to herself. "It looks like it's trapped."

Before he realized her purpose, she had slipped off her shoes and started to wade into the lake.

"What are you doing?" he called after her. "Come back!"

Joanna stopped, knee deep in the lake, and looked around. The expression on her face raised his blood pressure a few notches. It wasn't the first time she had looked at him like he was a complete idiot, and it was a distinctly unpleasant feeling for a man whose actions were rarely questioned. "It's trapped! I'm going to see if I can help it." The condescending tone of her voice was no improvement either.

"No, you're not! Joanna, it could be dangerous. Come back immediately!" He didn't bother to soften the commanding edge to the order. Her intentions were admirable if clearly misguided, and he wanted and expected to be obeyed.

She hesitated. The creature squealed pathetically once more and thrashed helplessly, beating itself against the rock. He watched in utter disbelief as she made her decision, turned her back on him and continued to wade in knee-deep water toward the rock.

"Joanna!" Alex roared. This time she didn't even turn her head. How dare she so deliberately defy him? Muttering angrily to himself, he began yanking off his boots. Cor's blood, but she would learn that when he delivered an order he expected her to listen!

He caught up with her just as she arrived at the rock, and reached out, intending to throw her over his shoulder and carry her back to the beach. His action was frozen by the distressed face she turned to him.

"It's really trapped. What can we do?"

He sighed resignedly, amazed to realize that his anger had diminished considerably in the face of her absolute belief that he was there to help. "I'll hold it. You see if you can free it," he said grudgingly.

He cautiously reached his arms around the creature and lifted it up, careful to avoid the small head with a sharp beak-like mouth. The creature immediately stopped struggling and went quiet in his arms. It's claw was caught in a web of vines under the surface of the water. Joanna bent down and started to tug at them, then seemed to realize that she was making the situation worse.

"I'll need to cut these. Do you have something sharp on you?"

"There's a laserray in the pocket of my breeches. Set it on medium strength, and be careful!"

She reached behind him and dug into his pocket to find the tool. In doing so, her breasts brushed against his arm. That soft, cushioned pressure combined with the squirming of her fingers against his buttocks produced a fire of sensation in Alex's groin, and he started muttering again under his breath.

"What did you say?" Joanna asked, finally locating the slender laser tool and pulling it out.

"Nothing! Just hurry up, will you? This thing's heavy."

The laserray cut through most of the vines quickly. One thick vine resisted, and Joanna asked Alex to lift the creature higher while she increased the strength of the laser slightly and attacked the vine again. The vine gave way. The creature, sensing freedom, started struggling again and, with a renewed surge of strength, pushed itself out of Alex's arms and scrambled onto the top of the rock.

Taken by surprise, Alex stumbled backwards, lost his balance and went sprawling in the water. A string of colorful curses expressed his irritation, and he looked up just as Joanna dissolved into giggles which quickly became helpless gales of laughter. Fascinated, Alex stared at her, forgetting his own ridiculous predicament and irritation. His lips twitched as he listened to her laugh, delighting in the sound.

"Oh!" she finally gasped. "I'm sorry! The expression on your face was just s-s-so f-funny!" And she leant back against the rock howling uncontrollably again.

Alex struggled to his feet. "I'm glad you find this so amusing," he growled with mock ferocity. "I suggest we get back on the beach before something else happens."

He grabbed her arm and led her giggling still back to the shore. There she collapsed on her back in the sand, and announced breathlessly that she needed to rest. As Alex sat down beside her, he realized with some surprise that his anger had almost completely evaporated, although some irritation still lingered over her refusal to listen. Used to being obeyed instantly, he was pondering this unique and rather baffling response when his thoughts were interrupted.

"Oh! Alex, look! How beautiful!"

Her tone was filled with such wonder, that his eyes were drawn to her face first and he found he couldn't look away. The red-gold hair fanned out behind her head and was undoubtedly getting covered with sand. But that appeared to be of no concern. Her face was unshadowed by the wariness and unhappiness she so often displayed in his presence, and the beautiful profile was highlighted by the luminescence from the water. His eyes hungrily traced every curve and hollow, desperate to memorize exactly how she appeared at this moment.

"Look!" she insisted urgently. He tore his gaze away and followed the direction of her pointing finger to see the creature circling overhead. Transformed from a soggy, shapeless mass, its bulk was now revealed to be mostly a huge wing span in a rainbow of shimmering colors, which dwarfed the small beaked head. A long, thin tail floated elegantly behind it. It cried harshly once, then disappeared over the lake.

Awed by what they had seen, Joanna and Alex lay quietly. Darkness swept rapidly across the sky. The planet's moons became brighter, more visible. Joanna slowly stretched up a hand, as if convinced that one was close enough to touch. Alex chuckled and began pointing out various features visible on the moons and planetoids in orbit around them.

The temperature dropped sharply with the onset of darkness. Joanna sat up abruptly, briskly rubbing her arms.

"Time to head back?" Alex inquired lazily.

"Umm." She picked up her shoes and stood up. As she slid her feet into them, she ducked her head and murmured shyly, "Thank you for helping me."

"Yes, well, the next time I'll expect you to listen to me! You could have put yourself in a great deal of danger," Alex grunted, sounding harsher than he'd intended. He knew immediately he'd made a mistake. She fairly bristled.

"I can take care of myself," she shot back. "It may have escaped your notice, but I'm a grown woman and perfectly capable of making intelligent decisions."

He looked at her warily as he rose to his feet and reached for his boots. He seriously doubted she *was* capable of protecting herself against some of the dangers that threatened on Treaine, but he wasn't about to make an issue of it right now. The comfortable mood was broken and he had unwittingly put her on the defensive again. She stood watching him, tense and fuming, as he began to pull on his boots.

"Actually," he said, trying for a little humor as he balanced precariously on one foot, "I'm *fully* aware that you are a grown woman, rather painfully so, I might—" He never saw the finger that reached out and poked him hard in the chest. He staggered back struggling to keep his balance, then fell to the sand with an outraged shout.

Joanna hesitated only a moment before she turned and fled down the beach but, in that instant, he saw anger turn to gleeful amusement. She had just declared war, but what she didn't know, he thought, as he hastily finished pulling on his boots, was that he was the master at this particular game and he would have his revenge.

It didn't take him long to catch up with her. Hampered by laughter and a wet skirt that kept binding itself about her knees and making her stumble, she had barely made it around the curve of the beach with the lights of the settlement in sight, when he grabbed an arm. He whirled her around, flung her over his shoulder, and set off jogging easily, despite his burden, in the direction of their living unit.

Between gasps for breath, she was begging him to put her down when he obligingly slowed to a walk and said loudly and calmly over her pleas, "Good evening, Ambassadors."

"Ambassadors? What ambassadors?" she squeaked in dismay. She wriggled frantically on his shoulder. He clamped an arm more firmly around her thighs to keep her in place and nodded politely at Ambassadors Kromon and Soron but continued walking. They were standing by the lake and watching with interest, neither making any attempt to hide their amusement.

Joanna gave a mortified groan and hissed, "Alex, put me down right now! How am I ever going to face him in the morning?"

"I'll put you down when we're inside and not before," he replied cheerfully, "and I'm sure Ambassador Kromon will be a perfect gentleman and won't mention a word about this."

He walked up the steps into their garden, ignoring her protests. He wasn't about to let her go now. The time of reckoning had arrived, and he wasn't going to take no for an answer. Completely focused on his goal, he slid the doors to the unit open, then stopped abruptly and cursed under his breath. Regretfully, he let her down from his shoulder. She followed the direction of his gaze to see the blinking light on the console demanding a response.

"I have to get that." Alex sighed, his hand lingering on her back. "But—" he continued huskily as his gaze swept over her, his voice full of promise, causing her to visibly tremble, "—*we* have some business to finish as well. I'll be quick."

As he turned to the console, he threw over his shoulder, "Bring me a towel, please?"

When she returned with his towel, he was deep in discussion about a security issue. He had already removed his boots and was in the process of stripping off his wet shirt. He took the towel and gave her a smile and a look that clearly flustered her. She went scurrying back to the refuge of the sleeping chamber.

It was some time later before she emerged again. He kept half an ear on the discussion as he watched her head for the utility area in search of something to eat. Her hair hung clean and damp past her shoulders. She wore a short, long-sleeved tunic, and he wondered with more than a passing interest if she wore anything underneath. She sneaked a glance in his direction. Her eyes widened and she looked as if she might bolt for the sleeping chamber again. His own clothes were a wet soggy pile beside him and he was sitting at the console stark naked. The towel, draped over one thigh, did absolutely nothing to hide anything. He caught her eye, raising an eyebrow in challenge, then grinned to himself as she sniffed and sailed by him into the utility area having obviously decided to accept his challenge.

Turning back to the discussion with his security team, Alex didn't hear her come up behind him and was surprised when she set a bowl of soup none to gently in front of him. He was less interested in the food than in the length of bare leg revealed by the short tunic. Watching the highly erotic sway of her hips as she walked away, he missed a question being asked and had to ask for it to be repeated.

The session dragged on. The security teams were investigating the entertainment houses and, as Ambassador Soron's wife had intimated to Joanna on the first day, had discovered some highly unsavory activities. Decisions were being made on how to deal with them. With few common laws yet established on Treaine, Alex had the authority to shut down the worst offenders. Several, with more minor offenses, were being referred to the Ambassadors' Council for disciplinary action, and others would be allowed to continue with their present activities until additional laws were in place.

A particularly ugly case had come up that day.

Two hours later, Alex walked into the sleeping chamber to discover Joanna fast asleep. He propped himself up on one elbow beside her to watch her sleep. One hand reached out to stroke her hair away from her face and play with the silky strands. Unable to resist this time, he allowed his hand to brush further down her body over the curve of a breast and across the swell of her bottom. When she didn't stir, he sighed heavily and rolled away from her.

Sleep was slow in coming that night.

Chapter 14

THE BUSY pace of their lives only intensified in the next several days. Alex finally delegated a routine security meeting of his officers to Jason's care one evening, hoping to spend a few hours with Joanna. Despite the late hour, their living unit was empty.

Disappointed, he was looking disinterestedly over a selection of food prepared by the mechaide and pondering the advisability of calling her office to order her home, when he happened to glance outside. His missing wife was sitting on the steps leading down to the beach. Her very posture attested to exhaustion. She was hunched over, knees drawn up pillowing her head and hiding her face, completely immobile. Choosing a couple of food dishes at random, he tossed them into the heater, and pulled out a flask of Mariltar ambrosia.

He glanced toward the steps again. Her position hadn't changed.

Becoming concerned, he was just about to go to the door and call to her, when she rose slowly and stiffly to her feet and started to wander back to the unit, her head bowed, her shoulders slumped. She walked inside, answered his greeting with a decided lack of enthusiasm, and dropped into her favorite chair with a heavy sigh.

Alex studied her carefully. Obviously something was amiss, but her rigidly held body and blank, almost frozen expression didn't invite conversation. Just then, she caught him staring, scowled fiercely and turned her head away.

Behind him, the food heater chirped softly and he reached to pull the meal out. "Are you hungry?"

"What?"

"Are you hungry?"

She shook her head and hunched her shoulder. Her hair slid forward to hide her face.

Alex was completely at a loss. What in Sagar's name was he supposed to say next? And just what was *this* attitude all about? Even though they had seen very little of each other over the last few days, they had always managed a few cordial words. None of his experience in commanding an elite warrior force had prepared him for one small woman whose disposition at this particular moment, it seemed, was to behave like he didn't exist.

He felt a spurt of annoyance. He wasn't a mind reader and couldn't think of a single thing that had happened in the last few days that would prompt her to treat him like this. If this was a new attempt to undermine the marriage partnership, he was going to put an end to it immediately.

Pushing the food aside, he leaned forward on the counter and said more harshly than he'd intended, "Would you care to tell me what's bothering you?"

"Nothing's bothering me." The tone was as cold as the drift of early morning mist over the lake.

Alex lost his patience. "Balls of Sortor, Joanna!" His hand slammed down on the surface of the counter, making her jump. "I'm not in the mood for games. And I'm growing very tired of going through mental contortions to try to understand what's going on inside that beautiful head of yours. Now, please tell me why you're behaving this way."

She flew to her feet and faced him, eyes flashing with anger, fists clenched at her sides. "I don't have to explain myself to you, and if you're tired of my behavior, I think you know the solution I'd suggest."

They stared at each other. She was breathing fast and hard, her face pale, her eyes brilliant and enormous. Alex felt a fist squeeze his gut. Something was very wrong and, despite her words, he was beginning to think it had nothing to do with them.

"Joanna," he said more gently, "what's the matter?"

Her eyes flickered, and dropped away from his. Her head moved in denial. "Nothing." But the anger had gone out of her tone.

He moved around the curve of the counter to stand in front of her, saw her wince when he took her chin in his hand to raise her face to his. "Joanna?"

To his dismay, the green eyes filled with tears. In the next instant, she had wrenched her face out of his grasp. "Leave me alone! Just leave me alone," she choked out and fled the room.

Alex's dark brows drew together in a perplexed frown. He started to go after her then hesitated. Maybe she needed some time to herself to work out whatever it was that was troubling her. Her message had certainly been loud and clear. On the other hand, why did he have such an overwhelming sense of urgency to follow her? The instinct that had never failed him in times of critical need was prodding him sharply.

What did he do now? This indecisiveness was an entirely new experience for him. He was used to knowing exactly how to deal with something and make quick decisions.

"Blood of Cor," he muttered furiously. He didn't like this uncertain feeling at all. And, furthermore, what had happened to the quiet, relaxing evening he had hoped for?

Irritation building, he whirled and strode after her. He *was* going to get to this bottom of this. She *was* going to talk to him. He *deserved* an explanation.

He arrived at the entrance to the sleeping chamber and came to an abrupt halt. She was curled up on the bed, her face buried in a pillow, tremors shaking her slender body. Moving cautiously, he sat down beside her, and touched her shoulder lightly, only to have her reject him once again. She hunched away from him and curled up even more tightly.

"Joanna, come here!" he persisted softly, and lifted her onto his lap. She was tense and resistant, and continued to cry silently, her body shaking with the force of her emotions. He pulled the pillow away, and she immediately turned her face into his shoulder, quickly soaking his shirt. He held her gently, stroking her back and head with soothing motions. The still unfamiliar feelings of protectiveness welled up inside of him and he wished he could absorb some of her distress.

Gradually the storm subsided, and the tremors racked her body less often until she lay quietly in his arms, occasionally hiccuping and sniffling.

"Here, blow your nose!" He reached over and grabbed a small cloth off the nearest table. He continued to hold her, and she seemed content to rest on his lap with her head against his shoulder.

Finally she said softly, "I'm sorry. It...it was a r-rough day."

"Tell me about it. It might help," Alex said quietly, smoothing the damp hair back from her face. Her nose and eyes were reddened from crying, and wet spiky lashes fanned her cheeks giving her an oddly vulnerable appearance.

She was silent for so long, that he almost repeated the request. But then she gave a deep sigh and said, "We're negotiating a settlement for the orphans of Taragon and—" Tears filled her voice again, and she stopped abruptly.

Alex's arms tightened. Taragon! Of course! He should have remembered what Ambassador Kromon had told him that morning. How could he have forgotten? The team had just entered into the most difficult and delicate negotiations thus far, and Joanna was leading this particular session. She moved restlessly, and he loosened his hold. Under control again, she asked, "Have you heard what the people of Taragon do with their children?"

"I know that they put them into institutions from birth. Most of the children don't know who their natural parents are."

He knew more than that. Taragon was the most primitive and war-like of the nations in the Crestar System. Since the Conflicts had begun generations ago, Taragon had almost completely abandoned its simple mining operations. All the adults served the war machine in some capacity, some often away for years in far flung assignments. Taragon's children were usually separated from their parents at birth and herded into crowded institutions where they were given little individual attention and taught the warrior crafts as soon as they could walk. Those who didn't attain certain achievement levels were almost completely abandoned.

Alex knew that the Taragon nation was the one of the biggest challenges facing the peace accord. Taragon, however, had a strong motive to be integrated into the peace process. The planet was completely devastated and its people were on the verge of starvation. It wouldn't survive without the Coalition.

"What's the issue?" he asked gently.

Joanna sniffed. "Some of the Taragon adults are trying to identify and claim their children so they can start to live as a family. The Coalition has promised and will provide extensive counseling to assist with the process. But there will be so many children left in those horrible institutions. The images we've seen are so awful, so heart-wrenching, e-especially of the babies. They don't get any emotional support at all."

She paused to blow her nose again. "I've proposed that other families in the Crestar System be allowed to take these children into their homes. The Taragon negotiator rejected the proposal out of hand. He said that Taragon could not possibly allow its past and its future to be corrupted and lost by the customs of other nations."

She lifted her shoulders in a gesture of helplessness. "The team is really divided. Alex, if we can't protect and nurture the children, what good is any of this? It's the children, most of all, that need to learn about peace and caring and tolerance. What sort of future does the Coalition's Vision have if we can't even give them those values?"

Alex tightened his arms around her, his heart aching at the raw pain he heard in her voice. He couldn't tell her that there were children in the settlement who had suffered a possibly worse fate in the entertainment houses. As hardened as Alex was to the terrible things civilized races could do to one another, he had been shocked and revolted by some of the reports from his teams. "Have you asked

Ambassador Kromon to take this issue before the Ambassador's Council?"

Joanna nodded. "Yes, but he said we had to get closer to a resolution before he would. It's such an emotional topic. The team was starting to work well together before this came up. Today was awful! Everyone was angry and shouting."

"Perhaps it's time for a break. You've all been working non-stop since we arrived. Some time off might allow things to cool down, give you all time to think and an opportunity to come up with a fresh perspective."

"I wouldn't object to that." She gave a huge yawn and burrowed against his chest. She had apparently decided to trust him, at least for now. Her eyelids drooped tiredly and he realized how emotionally exhausted she must be. In a few minutes, she was fast asleep.

Alex continued to hold her for a while longer, wondering anew at the surge of fierce protectiveness he felt toward this woman. Thus far, they had found no indication of a Soron attempt to sabotage the peace initiative. In fact, Ambassador Soron had established himself to be one of the more reasonable voices on the Ambassador's Council. Nor had there been a shred of evidence that Joanna might be a target. Two days ago, against Jason's advice, he had ordered the security team to minimize its monitoring activities of her. She spent most of each day surrounded by the negotiating team anyway. He could control her physical safety to an extent but, short of ordering her to quit her position, he couldn't protect her against the emotional pain and stress she encountered in her work. That was not to say that it *hadn't* crossed his mind once or twice to demand that she substantially reduce her commitment to the negotiating team to take up the duties of an ambassador's wife.

But, for once in his life, he was reluctant to face the conflict he knew such a demand would provoke.

Eventually, he reluctantly eased her into bed and went off to report the conversation to Ambassador Kromon.

Chapter 15

IT WAS LATER than usual when Joanna awoke the next morning. She sat up in bed slightly disoriented from a deep, exhausted sleep and panicked when she saw the time. She was going to be late for the first negotiation session of the day. As she threw back the cover, she saw with a small sense of shock that she was still dressed in the short, loose-fitting casual outfit she had put on after work the day before. For the life of her, she couldn't remember what had happened after that emotional outburst in Alex's arms.

She was smoothing a crease in her clothing and puzzling over the memory gap, when Alex startled her by strolling into the room. What was he doing here? He was never home this late in the day.

He smiled. "Good! You're up. I was just coming to wake you. You don't need to hurry. Your first session has been delayed."

He sat down next to her. His eyes swept over her from head to toe taking in her tousled hair and bare legs. Everywhere his gaze rested, Joanna felt as if he had physically touched her, and she gave an involuntary shiver.

"How are you feeling?" he asked huskily reaching over to lightly stroke her cheek.

"Fine. J-just a little tired," she responded, her stomach doing somersaults.

"Hmm." The blue eyes were brilliant this morning. He was clothed in a close fitting exercise suit that emphasized the powerful muscles of his arms and legs. He fairly radiated energy and excellent health, and made her want to crawl back into bed and cover her head. He captured her hand. "You were exhibiting some symptoms of stress last night. I want you to start working more rest *and* more recreation into your schedule. You can't keep up this pace, Joanna. I spoke with Ambassador Kromon and he told me you take on more than anyone else on the team. He knows the Taragon matter is extremely stressful for everyone, but he wants to see some progress before he'll authorize some time off for the whole team."

He moved his hands on either side of her and leaned forward, forcing her back into the pillows.

"And in case you missed it," he said softly, his chiseled lips hovering over hers, his breath fanning her face, "that is *not* a request. It's an order."

Watching in anticipation and fascination as his face came even closer, Joanna waited for the familiar surge of irritation at his determination to control her life. It never came. Her defenses were nonexistent this morning. His lips finally came down to rest on hers, and she closed her eyes and gave herself up to the fiery sensations racing through her body.

He ravished her mouth, nibbling at her lips and thrusting his tongue past the soft barrier to glide over her teeth and tongue. He lowered his body to press against hers, and she delighted in its strength and hardness. Her hands gripped his shoulders. Her hips moved restlessly, seeking greater contact. She felt him shift slightly, and then his hand was running down her body and back up again, grazing over her hip, the curve of her waist and over her breast before moving to pull urgently at the fastenings of her clothes.

The feel of his hand against the bare flesh of her breast caused her to moan helplessly and arch up against him. He gently tugged at a nipple and stroked and cupped the swell of her breast before running his hand back down her body. He pushed insistently at her thighs to part her legs. In a tiny corner of her mind a shred of resistance still lingered and a fleeting rational thought told her she would regret this later. But when his fingers stroked through the curls at the base of her belly and wriggled down between her tightly closed legs, she ceased to think at all as unbearably pleasurable sensations flamed through her body. Her legs fell apart.

He probed and stroked the sensitive petals of flesh, and slowly eased a finger into her. "Ah, Meira," he whispered, touching his tongue to the edge of her ear, "you feel so incredibly good, better than all my dreams."

Joanna shuddered and moaned against his neck, lost in a storm of sensation. His thumb tormented the nub of flesh that was her pleasure core. His finger, moving inside her, created a friction that had her digging her nails into his shoulders, and tossing her head on the pillow. Another finger joined the first, stretching her, sending a burning, tingling burst of erotic sensation arcing through her body. She felt her control slip and dug her fingers more deeply into his shoulders to anchor herself, afraid of falling, afraid to let go.

"Relax, Meira," he whispered in her ear. "Relax and let it take you."

His thumb continued to roll over her hardened nub, teasing to the point of discomfort that was also unbearable pleasure. Then she ceased to think at all as his fingers twisted inside her, and a final thrust pushed her into a violent climax. He gathered her close, holding her tightly as she whimpered against his shoulder and the last of her tremors subsided.

When he pulled a little away from her, she closed her eyes and turned her face away embarrassed by her easy surrender and the intensity of her reaction. But she couldn't close her ears and the promise he whispered in her ear left her shaking. "We'll finish this tonight, Meira."

He stood up to leave, but turned back, remembering something. "Don't forget, the Ambassador's Reception is this evening." Then he leaned over her, turned her face and kissed her deeply again.

DRESSED IN A wrap, Joanna was putting the finishing touches to her appearance when Alex walked into the sleeping chamber early that evening. She avoided looking at him as he pulled off his clothes and inquired how her day had gone. There had been no progress on the Taragon issue and, after a few hours, a more subdued team than the day before had agreed to set the matter aside for a time to give it more thought and try to arrive at additional solutions for discussion.

Alex had finished undressing and was standing naked, with arms folded, listening attentively to her description of the day's events. He nodded his approval at the outcome, and went off to the bath chamber. As he disappeared through the archway, Joanna watched covertly in the mirror, admiring the broad, muscled back and tight contours of his buttocks.

She cupped her chin in her hands and stared at herself in the mirror. When had she crossed the line from being totally resistant to this marriage partnership to wanting him so much? He had helped her immeasurably yesterday just by listening to her pour out her grief over the day's events. The burden that had crushed her spirit had felt incredibly lighter and she had been filled with a fresh conviction that it would be possible to find the right solution for Taragon. Despite the lack of progress today, she still felt that way. But the episode this morning had caused her to be distracted all day wondering what it would be like to make love with him and anticipating the night ahead. She was torn between wishing they didn't have to attend the reception, relief that they did because the inevitable could be postponed, and nervousness since this was the first occasion on which she was expected to act in an official capacity.

She sighed and picked up some ornate gold combs to sweep her hair off her face. She had curled it earlier, and now it cascaded past her shoulders in a riotous tumble. She tweaked some short strands to softly frame her face and rose to put on a simple, but elegant, cream-colored gown with a long, body molding skirt made up of a multitude of tiny knife-edged pleats. High-necked and demure in the front, the gown left the whole of her back bare to well below the indent of her waist. Joanna felt more than a little uncomfortable in it, but her wardrobe was limited and she didn't really have anything else that was suitable for such a formal occasion. Although she chose not to wear any jewelry, she was pleased with the whole effect.

Alex's expression when he entered the great room some time later to join her was both immensely satisfying and nerve-wracking. He stopped short and allowed his eyes to devour her hungrily. His slow smile and the fire in eyes that had darkened to deep sapphire left no doubt in her mind as to what he was thinking.

Tonight there would be no excuses. She would be his.

With surprising tentativeness, he reached out to touch her shoulders, then tipped her face up to look into her eyes. "I don't know what to say. You take my breath away," he murmured.

For the space of several heartbeats, time was frozen as they stared at each other. Then Joanna smiled tremulously, pulled away to hide the wave of color that washed across her face and walked to the door. "Shall we go?" she tossed back over her shoulder. The expression she caught on his face made her want to break into nervous giggles.

Mouth agape in shock, Alex had just been hit with the full impact of the backless gown.

She arched an innocent eyebrow. "What's the matter?"

He shook his head rather dazedly. "Nothing!"

But as he came to take her arm, he growled into her ear, "*You* are not leaving my sight this evening, Meira. You're enough to start the war again all on your own!"

Chapter 16

WITH THE INTRODUCTIONS finally over, the ambassadors and their wives were free to leave the receiving area at the entrance to the huge reception hall. The building was part of the new construction and had just been completed. Not far from the Marketplace, it faced out onto the lake, commanding a spectacular view through a towering wall of glass.

Kara and Joanna walked into the main hall, followed closely by their husbands. The two women, who hadn't seen each other since the day of Alex and Joanna's arrival on Treaine, had their heads together and were deep in discussion about Kara's pregnancy when Melissa appeared out of nowhere and pounced.

"God, I thought you people were going to be out there the whole evening! I'm starving! Let's go get something to eat." She glanced at the men and said carelessly, "You don't mind do you?"

Melissa made friends easily and had little regard for protocol. While Kara was obviously included in her invitation, the men just as obviously weren't. Despite having just confided a desperate need to eat and rest, Kara nevertheless hesitated and looked at her husband, seeking his approval. He encouraged her with a gentle smile and a nod.

To Alex's deep chagrin, Joanna didn't follow suit, but merely said casually, "I'll see you later," flipped a hand at him, and followed the others.

As the three women, each attractive in distinctly different ways, walked across the room, many admiring glances followed their progress. Alex was experiencing a conflict of emotions, some of them entirely unwelcome. He had planned to keep Joanna close to him tonight, and leave as soon as possible to fulfill the promise of that morning. Now he realized with something approaching dismay that those plans were to be frustrated.

His pride and admiration over his wife's appearance were tempered by other strong feelings, one of which was unquestionably anger as he saw several men openly ogling her. The other emotion was completely alien to him but he suspected with growing uneasiness that it might be jealousy. There was no other explanation for the primitive urge welling inside of him to smash his fist into some faces.

The loud clearing of a throat broke through his distraction, and he glanced at his companion. Ambassador Soron was observing him with sympathy and amusement, a knowing look on his face. Despite their past conflicts, the two men had discovered some common ground and a similar mind-set in the work they were accomplishing with the Ambassadors' Council. A mutual respect was slowly developing between them along with a somewhat tentative friendship. Although Alex could never let himself forget that the Soron might be a threat to the peace initiative despite a lack of evidence, he found himself liking the other man nonetheless.

"You have something to say?" His tone was dangerous. He was in no mood to be humored.

The Soron grinned. "Marriage seems to bring a whole different perspective to relationships, doesn't it, my friend? Before I took Kara as my marriage partner, it didn't particularly matter to me when other men lusted after my women. With Kara it's different. I selfishly want to keep her to myself and sometimes feel like isolating her entirely. The first time I saw another man look at her with more than a little interest, I wanted to sink a diralm blade in his neck!"

Alex was surprised at having his feelings put into words, and shocked when he realized he did feel such a strong possessiveness. "They look at her like they're stripping off her clothes," he complained, completely forgetting that he had done just that the first time he had seen her.

The ambassador laughed. "Have some sympathy, my friend," he said. "If you were in their place, you'd be doing exactly the same. Just remember, you alone have that delightful privilege, and there is not a man in this room who would actually dare touch her. Allow them their fantasies, because that's all they have."

As their wives disappeared into an adjacent hall where a vast array of ethnic food was attractively displayed, the Soron turned serious. "I feel I should warn you, Alex. Cerata is here tonight."

Alex shrugged. "No need for a warning. It was over between us long ago."

"Maybe for you," the ambassador countered, "but she was deeply disappointed when you rejected her as a mate. I think her feelings for you are perhaps stronger than you realize."

"Then I'm sorry for that. I've chosen my mate and, contrary to our rather antiquated custom, have no desire for another woman in my life. Your sister is charming and beautiful, and there will, no doubt, be many men ready and willing to console her."

"Perhaps. I'm more concerned for you than her. She can be very determined."

It was Alex's turn to be amused. "I'm well able to take care of myself." He changed the subject abruptly. "Shall we find Ambassador Kromon? I'd like to see if there has been a resolution on this morning's issue."

THE WOMEN filled their plates from the wide selection of food representing the nine nations of the Crestar System, and made their way to the tables on the raised platform which ran around the perimeter of the room. It afforded them an excellent view of the lake and also allowed them to observe the people milling around the vast hall.

Joanna sank thankfully into her seat. She had been delighted to see acquaintances from the Earth colony, but her head was reeling from all the introductions, and she knew she would never remember most of the names. She was also tired from standing for so long, and could only imagine what Kara was feeling so near to giving birth. They were happily attacking their food and comparing notes about various people they had met, when Melissa paused suddenly and said with her mouth full, "Oh, Lord. What's *she* doing here?"

Kara and Joanna followed the direction of her gaze. A dazzling Soron beauty was poised dramatically at the entrance to the hall surrounded by an escort of admirers.

Kara grimaced. "My husband's sister. She arrived just this morning. Do you know her well?"

"No, but I know *of* her." Melissa spoke her mind as always, conveniently disregarding the fact that a member of her subject's family sat at the same table. "I've heard some *very* strange things about her. And I mean *weird*, abnormal, bizarre stuff. But I'm more concerned about *why* she came back. Rumor has it that she used to be Alex's lover and wants him back. Was in a tearing rage in fact when he chose Joanna. I just don't want to see Joanna get hurt."

Both women glanced at Joanna. Melissa, seeming to realize belatedly how her words must have sounded, stretched out a hand and patted her arm comfortingly. "I'm sorry, Joanna. It was over between her and Alex some time ago, and I'm sure Alex isn't interested any more, otherwise he would have chosen her, wouldn't he? Anyway, she's hardly any competition for an ambassador's wife. She's a promiscuous witch who'll open her legs for anything with the right equipment."

Joanna was staring at her in horrified fascination. "Melissa, where do you get all this? How do you *know* those things?"

Her friend waved a hand airily. "I'm on the receiving end of a very efficient and highly accurate grapevine. But trust me, Joanna, don't tangle with her. She'll gobble you alive."

"*Melissa!*" Joanna slid a glance at Kara. She was, Joanna was relieved to see, looking somewhat amused rather than offended.

"Oops, sorry again." Melissa sounded anything but. "All right. I'll shut up. I just thought you ought to be warned."

Joanna turned her head away, pretending indifference, but her heart was pounding hard. She desperately needed to collect her thoughts. So *that* was the beautiful Cerata. She stared disinterestedly at the exotic selection of food on her plate. She had definitely lost her appetite, but Melissa's words had given her something to think about. Alex may not have considered Cerata appropriate marriage material, but that didn't mean he wouldn't seek to continue a liaison with her. Especially since he wasn't getting any satisfaction from his wife. Alex, Joanna suspected, had a large and probably very adventurous sexual appetite.

So why did she feel as if her heart had just been wrenched out of her chest?

Unwillingly, her eyes were drawn to the glittering creature who was as tall and striking as her brother. And she suddenly felt plain and uninteresting by comparison. Cerata was dressed in a rainbow of floating, swirling scarves which did more to reveal than conceal a sleek, voluptuous body. How could any man resist her? Her laughing vivaciousness certainly held the male population surrounding her enthralled. Joanna was reminded of the gorgeous loralite—a creature similar to the arachnids found on Earth. She had seen one once in an exhibition in the Neutral Realm, and had admired the delicate, glittering creature until someone had told her it tortured its prey before consuming it.

Across the crowded room, the glances of Joanna and the Soron suddenly locked. Joanna was shocked by the venom and hatred she saw briefly exposed on the other woman's face. Something ice-cold and smothering wrapped itself tightly around her causing her to fight frantically for breath. The sensation was gone in the next instant, and Cerata acknowledged her with a graceful bow of her lovely head and a dazzling smile, leaving Joanna to wonder if she had imagined that malignant stare.

"*Joanna!*"

Slightly dazed, she focused on the concerned faces of Kara and

Melissa.

"Are you all right? Your face is as white as your dress."

She nodded. "I-I'm fine. It was just a momentary dizzy spell." She followed the direction of Melissa's stare to her hands and was dismayed to see them trembling. She quickly put down her eating utensil and hid her hands in her lap. Her scowl dared Melissa to pursue the subject.

After finishing their meal, the women rose to circulate among the other guests, stopping to speak with old acquaintances and trying to remember names of others they passed. Kara and Melissa, having been on Treaine longer and not confined as Joanna was to negotiation sessions, knew more people and prompted Joanna when she was at a loss. Kara soon became separated from them, drawn into a group of Soron women wanting to talk about the imminent arrival of their ambassador's child.

Joanna had caught glimpses of Alex earlier in the crowded hall, but now he was nowhere in evidence and she was beginning to feel disgruntled. What had happened to his promise to not let her out of his sight? To her disappointment, he hadn't reacted at all to the challenge she had thrown out earlier when she had accepted Melissa's invitation without consulting with him, and now *he* had disappeared altogether. And all of a sudden, *that* Soron woman was also conspicuously absent.

The captains of the Mariltar fleet had all approached them at some point or another to exchange a few words and flirt with Melissa. Jason stayed the briefest time of all, and Melissa's face bore a perplexed look as he strolled off in the direction of an attractive woman dressed in the uniform of a Mariltar pilot.

Concerned as she was about Alex's whereabouts, Joanna nevertheless felt some amusement at Melissa's expression. Could Melissa have finally met a man she couldn't twist around her finger? Jason certainly hadn't paid much attention to her and, in fact, had only spoken as many words as politeness dictated before leaving.

Melissa caught sight of Joanna's expression. "What?" she asked with some belligerence. "Oh, all right. I haven't figured him out yet. But I will. Do you mind if I desert you for a while?" She grinned wickedly and added, "I have some hunting to do." She wandered off in the direction Jason had taken.

Left on her own, Joanna's need to find Alex, or at least assure herself as to where he was and what he was doing—and with whom— became more urgent. After scanning both halls and still not seeing him, she decided to look outside.

A door led her out onto a wide platform overlooking the lake where a number of people were strolling about or gathered into small groups. Joanna wandered around, briefly stopping to exchange a few words here and there. She rounded a corner into an area which was darker and deserted. About to turn back, she noticed a couple a short distance away on the beach. They were standing close together, apparently absorbed in discussion. She recognized Cerata immediately as her filmy garment floated in the breeze and caught the light of the moons. In the next instant, she knew without a doubt that her companion was Alex.

Her whole body tensed and she started to tremble. Unable to help herself she continued to watch, and then wished she hadn't. The Soron woman suddenly threw her arms around Alex's neck. In the faint light, Joanna watched their bodies merge into one and their lips meet in a kiss.

She didn't wait to see more, but whirled and blindly found her way back to the hall, fighting back tears of disappointment and anger. The festive atmosphere of the evening had fallen flat and now became something to be endured. She saw Melissa and Jason talking together and started to make her way across the room toward them. Part way there, Ambassador Soron and Kara stopped her to say they were leaving. Seizing the opportunity and not caring what Alex might think, she begged a ride home with them, then went to tell Jason and Melissa.

AS SHE WATCHED Joanna leave, Melissa's brow wrinkled thoughtfully. Jason, aware that he had lost her attention and curious as to the cause asked lightly, "Anything the matter?"

Melissa shrugged and shook her head, causing strands of silky blonde hair not confined in an outrageous and elaborate arrangement to float around her face. "No, not really. Where do you suppose Alex is?"

"I don't know. I haven't seen him for a while."

"I suppose it's also coincidental *that* woman isn't anywhere to be seen either," she muttered.

"What woman?" Jason was confused, but increasingly fascinated by this attractive creature who had pursued him and almost rudely managed to maneuver him away from a casual flirtation.

"The Soron, of course!" Her tone was impatient and derisive.

"Oh, Cerata?" Now it was Jason's brow that creased in a thoughtful frown. Before he could respond further, a beeping sounded from his wrist communicator. Other Mariltar security officers were receiving the same signal and, seconds later, Alex entered the room with Cerata clinging to his arm. He left her at the door with a few brief words and headed for Jason.

"There's a security issue," Jason hurriedly explained to Melissa. "I have to go, but—" he smiled, "—let's continue our, ah, very interesting discussion another time."

As Alex reached them, he asked distractedly, "Where's Joanna?"

"She already left with Ambassador Soron and his wife."

If Alex was surprised at this piece of news, it didn't show. Jason saw his own concerns reflected in his commanding officer's face. The brief message that had been relayed from the Control Center was extremely disturbing. Something large and unidentified had made an attempt to breach the perimeter, then had vanished without a trace.

The men spent the remainder of the night at the Security Control Center monitoring the security team's progress, and discussing additional protective measures. It didn't appear as if the perimeter had been in any real danger of being penetrated but, as the night wore on, an even greater worry became evident in the tense faces in the Center.

They were having absolutely no success in determining what had caused the alarm.

IT TOOK JOANNA a long time to fall asleep that night. Body tense and ears constantly straining, she listened for Alex to come in. As it grew later, increasingly lurid images of Alex and Cerata tangled in passionate love-making tormented her mind.

She rolled over and viciously punched her pillow. He needn't think he could come crawling into her bed and expect her to welcome him with open arms and legs, she thought angrily. She flopped over on her back again and stared at the play of pale shadows across the ceiling. But he did think that, she reminded herself miserably, and she had no doubt that he would eventually lose patience with her and force the issue. And the worst part was, she didn't know if she would be able to resist him.

The depth of her feelings came as a surprise. She was furious that what she had observed that evening had affected her so much. After all, he *had* warned her about other women. But still she had let herself be seduced by his charm and the brilliant eyes that sent messages that muddled her mind and made her forget all her best intentions.

Her resolve to leave Treaine was strengthened. She would return to her former responsibilities in the Neutral Realm and put this whole bizarre episode behind her. She was also desperately aware that for her plan to be successful, she would have to avoid Alex as much as possible in the meantime.

And the knowledge opened a great icy void in her that refused to close.

Chapter 17

SEVERAL DAYS later, Alex watched Joanna's image fade from the screen of the information console as she abruptly cut him off. He slammed his hands down on the table in front of him in sheer frustration, then surged to his feet and started to pace restlessly around the room muttering to himself.

In another part of the Security Control Center's briefing room, Jason stopped what he was doing and turned to watch Alex. "Is something wrong?"

Alex glanced at him. "What did you say?"

"I asked if there's a problem."

"A problem? Should there be?"

Jason shrugged, tilted his chair back and planted his boots on the table in front of him. Straight-faced, he said, "Oh, I don't know. The fact that you're beating up the equipment and talking to yourself doesn't have any particular significance, I suppose."

Alex stopped abruptly and scowled ferociously. He fisted his hands by his sides, struggling to bring himself under control. He lost the battle. "She's driving me crazy!" he exploded suddenly. "I don't understand her! Just when I thought we were starting to work things out, she's turned to ice again. She's working longer hours than before and only comes back to our unit to sleep. I hardly ever see her, and when she *is* home she goes out of her way to avoid me. She finally has a free day tomorrow, and she tells me she's already made plans—for the whole day—and can't even spare me a couple of hours!"

Jason's attempt to hide a grin wasn't entirely successful. "It's difficult to imagine any woman deliberately avoiding you, Alex. But, then again, no other woman has ever had this particular affect on you— that I've observed, anyway. What happened to change things?" His tone was carefully neutral.

"Cor's blood, I wish I knew! I'm not even sure exactly *when* things changed." Alex started to pace and mutter again, then suddenly stopped short and stared at Jason suspiciously. "What do you mean 'this particular affect'?" He waved his hand. "No, don't answer that. I don't want to know."

He stalked to the window. The view of the cheerful bustle in the

Marketplace did nothing to improve his mood. His thoughts moved rapidly over the last few days, sorting, analyzing and discarding the significance of every moment, every brief interaction with his wife. "The reception! The day after the reception, I started getting this cold, don't-come-near-me attitude from her again." Swinging around, he was in time to see Jason lean back in his chair and roll his eyes at the ceiling. Jason knew something—or thought he did and, knowing Jason, was probably debating whether or not he should get involved. He had limited his comments thus far about the state of friend's marital affairs to his opinion that Alex was particularly obtuse when it came to understanding his own wife. And Alex, despite the fact that he had asked for it, hadn't taken *that* comment particularly well.

"Well?"

Jason looked at him warily. "Well, what?"

"You obviously have something to say. So, say it."

Jason sighed. "Just don't bite my head off again. Maybe you should consider a session with Advisor Barok. He—"

"Balls of Sortor, I don't need a marriage counselor, Jason. I want to know what *you* think."

Jason sighed again, this time with resignation and swung his legs to the floor. "Alex, you spent quite a bit of time with Cerata that evening. I saw you together. Others saw you together. Did you ever consider that Joanna might have seen you together and drawn some conclusions? It's none of my business what you and Cerata were doing all the time you were absent from the hall, but Joanna doesn't strike me as the type of woman who would be tolerant of a shared arrangement. You have to remember that particular custom may not be embraced by her culture."

Alex stared at Jason. Could Joanna have seen him with Cerata? He wondered why it should matter if she had, except...there had been that embrace, promptly broken off, but still perhaps open to interpretation by anyone happening to observe it. He considered Jason's words. Would Joanna really care if he entered into an arrangement with another woman, assuming he even wanted to?

He finally said with uncharacteristic defensiveness, "Cerata and I spent some time talking, that's all. I discouraged her from thinking there could ever be anything between us again. Nothing happened to speak of. *And*, just for the record, Joanna is the *only* woman I want and need in my life right now. Although," he muttered under his breath and quite dishonestly, "I'm beginning to think the woman is more trouble than she's worth."

Jason smirked. "You needn't justify your actions to me. Tell her, not me. You know, she was gone from the hall for a while, and when she came back, she looked a little peculiar. Melissa was quite concerned about her, and wondered if something might have happened."

Alex remembered something else. He had spent the rest of that night right here in the Control Center catching brief naps as they had tried to track whatever it was that had attempted to breach the perimeter. He hadn't had a chance to tell Joanna that, and wondered if it could also be an explanation for Joanna's recent behavior since he hadn't yet fulfilled the promise he had made to her.

But if that was the case, why didn't she just say something, he thought disgustedly. He couldn't read her mind! In fact, quite the opposite. He never knew what to expect from her. One thing was clear. He wasn't going to put up with her attitude any longer, and they were going to have an honest discussion about recent events. He swung around and went to the console, rapidly finding the information he needed.

"What are you doing?" Jason asked curiously.

Alex frowned at Joanna's schedule on the screen. "I'm going to have a talk with my wife whether she wants to or not. Her last negotiation session is over early today, but I'll have to cancel our Lon match."

Even then, he'd have to take a chance at finding her in her office, since he didn't want to give her any advance notice. It also wouldn't give him much time. Alex had planned to join a scouting trip with one of his security teams, which was scheduled to leave just after darkness fell. He considered dropping out of the expedition, but rejected the idea almost instantly. He had commanded Mariltar warriors since he was barely out of his teens. One small woman shouldn't be giving him this much trouble. This course of slow, patient seduction he had decided upon definitely wasn't working.

Perhaps it was time to try something different.

DEEP IN CONCENTRATION, Joanna was unaware when someone entered her work station. She jumped when hands came down on her shoulders and two large thumbs caressed her neck in little feather strokes. She twisted around to find Alex standing just behind her.

"Alex! Y-you startled me!" She saw him reach over to touch a pad on the wall she hadn't previously noticed. "What are you doing?" A soft whirring sound answered her. The transparent walls of her small work space were quickly hidden by mechanized screens, creating complete privacy.

Alex propped himself against the table and folded his arms. If his proximity and actions weren't enough to make her nervous, the expression on his face made her stomach do a somersault. This unexpected visit definitely boded no good.

"We need to talk." The tone of his voice did nothing to ease the sudden cramp in her stomach.

"I-I'm very busy right now. Can't it wait?" she asked.

"Until when?" he raised an eyebrow sardonically. "There hasn't been a single opportunity in the last few days at our unit."

Joanna was starting to feel slightly sick. She really wasn't prepared for this confrontation. And why did he have to stand so close to her? "Well, um, maybe this evening? I can try to leave early." It would at least give her time to rethink all the different versions of the conversations she had had with him in her mind.

He shook his head. "No, it won't work. I'm leaving on a scouting trip, and will be gone most of the night. It has to be now."

Anger began to surface. Why did *he* always have to be the one in control? She resented the interruption, because she did need to finish a proposal for Ambassador Kromon. In her present mood, his excuse merely made her skeptical, and it crossed her mind that he might be covering up plans to spend the night with Cerata—again. She still didn't know why he hadn't returned to their unit the other night, but could make a very good guess!

She hid her feelings by shrugging carelessly and saying grudgingly, "All right! I suppose I can take a minute or two. What do you want to talk about?"

She was aware that her attitude was starting to annoy him. His dark brows almost met in a fierce frown that hovered above the bridge of his aristocratic nose. He studied her for so long without speaking, his expression cold and forbidding, that she began to squirm uncomfortably.

Finally he said, "Let's start with why you've been avoiding me ever since the reception."

"I don't know what you're talking about." Joanna denied the charge instantly. "I've been busy. Everyone on the team has. We all knew there were going to be long hours involved when we signed up." Before she could stop herself, she added spitefully, "What I didn't know was that I'd have all these other *responsibilities* as well that you seem to expect."

"*Enough!*" Alex roared. His hands came down forcefully on the arms of her chair, and he lowered his face until they were nose to nose, causing her to shrink back into her seat. Clearly struggling to control his temper, Alex bit out slowly and distinctly, "I thought we had gone beyond this, Joanna. Let me remind you that your position as my marriage partner takes far greater priority than your position as a Senior Negotiator. In fact, I have a strong recollection of telling you that you could continue in your position only as long as it didn't interfere with your duties as my wife. I've tried to indulge you, but my patience is at an end. Either you find more time for the duties of our marriage partnership, or I will speak with Ambassador Kromon about finding another negotiator."

Shocked, Joanna could only stare at him, struggling to find her voice to respond. To her relief, he backed off and paced to the end of the small cubicle, before coming back to stand in front of her.

He folded his arms and pinned her with a thoughtful gaze. "Furthermore, I think it's time for complete honesty between us. You *were* forced into this marriage partnership, but since we've been on Treaine, I don't think I'm wrong in believing that you have reached a certain acceptance of the arrangement. You certainly cannot deny that there is an extremely strong attraction between us. I've enjoyed the time we've spent together, brief as it has been, and I think you have, too. We seemed to have regressed recently, and the reception seems to be the event that produced the change."

He leaned forward again and said softly, "What happened that night, Joanna? Why have you been avoiding me?"

Joanna chewed nervously on her lower lip. She wasn't about to tell him that she had seen him with Cerata. He would wonder why it mattered so much and she didn't understand it herself. "Nothing! Nothing happened!"

"Are you upset because I didn't come back to the unit and make love to you?" The darkened sapphire eyes caressed and compelled an honest answer. She looked away, swallowed against the dryness in her throat and gave a tiny shake of her head, justifying her less than honest response by telling herself she really hadn't known what she'd wanted that night.

"Joanna!" Strong fingers on her chin turned her head. "I want to know what's bothering you. Something has happened to cause this attitude. Tell me!"

Her will to resist was fading fast. Those seductive blue eyes were mesmerizing. Still, she made one last attempt. "I don't know what you expect me to say, Alex."

He reared back and thrust his hand through his hair in frustration. "All right! Let's try something else. Did you see or hear anything that night that upset you for some reason?"

"No, I don't think so," she said cautiously. He seemed grimly determined to have a particular answer and warning signals were sounding crazily in her head.

Alex sighed, "I had to marry a negotiator!" He paced to the end of the room again, turned and said abruptly, "Did you see Cerata and me together?"

Joanna shrugged, pretending unconcern, although her mind was in a turmoil. The signals had become great clanging bells. He *did* know! "I don't remember. Probably. I saw you with a lot of people that evening. Why does *that* matter?" She knew she was failing miserably in maintaining a facade of cool indifference. Her voice was strained and her body tensed tightly as a coiled spring in her seat.

Alex said carefully, "Maybe it doesn't." Then he added with shocking bluntness, "But would it matter if you saw her kissing me?"

Joanna looked down at her lap, twisting her hands together and gave up. She muttered under her breath.

"What did you say?" She felt Alex's hand under her chin again forcing it up.

She avoided his eyes, but his insistent, "Joanna, look at me," brought her gaze back around. Already tense and highly emotional, the unexpected look of compassion in his eyes almost undid her. All of a sudden, she didn't want to fight him anymore. Why not let him have what he wanted? In all honesty, she wanted him too, didn't she? She didn't make commitments lightly, and had had brief love affairs with only two other men. It had taken some time to recover from both relationships. Yet her feelings for Alex were more complicated and far stronger than she remembered having for the other two. Her greatest fear was that when the time came to leave, and leave she would, it would break her heart to walk away.

Her musings were interrupted by Alex, who had watched the play of expressions across her face with interest. He shook her gently. "Joanna, what did you say?"

"I said, it looked more like a body meld to me!" she snapped.

His reaction took her by surprise. He threw back his head and laughed. "So, you did see us!"

Irritated by his laughter, Joanna said tightly, "I don't see what this has to do with anything. You can kiss whomever you want, and sleep with whomever you want." Ignoring the silent decision made just moments earlier, she added crossly, "I don't care. Just so long as you don't sleep with me!"

Still amused, Alex said, "You evidently didn't see my response. Just so there is no misunderstanding, Cerata and I were lovers once, a long time ago. But she understands now that I do not have any desire to resume the relationship. *And,*" he continued pulling her up out the chair and into his arms, "I think you *do* care. This erratic and irrational behavior seems to be a clear indication of strong emotions, and may I remind you that you were far from indifferent to me the morning of the reception."

Joanna blushed at the memory and hid her face in his shoulder, trying not to tremble. She felt his hands move caressingly down her back. Then they were cupping her bottom and pulling her hard against him, providing her with undoubted proof of his desire for her.

He sighed into her ear. "What am I going to do with you?" Then he added huskily, "Maybe I should just keep you in bed for a week. Come to think of it, that's an excellent idea."

She squeaked in protest and tried to wriggle away, but stopped immediately at his growl of warning, "Don't do that, or your team is going to have more to talk about than they already do!"

He turned her face up. "I wish I wasn't going to be gone this evening, and I'd change my plans if I could. But make some time for me—for us—tomorrow. Please?" he cajoled.

All resistance gone, Joanna closed her eyes and nodded, desperately wanting him to kiss her. Instead, she felt his face brush gently against the top of her head before he released her. Only after he was gone did she realize that she still didn't know where he spent that night.

Chapter 18

"THIS IS SO glorious." Joanna rolled over onto her stomach and breathed the musty, earthy aroma underneath her nose. Cradling her head on her arms, she closed her eyes reveling in the still warmth of the day. The tension of the last few days seemed to seep from every pore, and she wriggled with pleasure, drowsiness starting to overcome her.

"I love this place," Melissa agreed contentedly leaning back on her arms, and looking about her.

The women had left their cruiser an hour's walk away, and hiked through massive trees and thickening undergrowth, following a faint trail recorded in old settlement logs, to reach the large meadow. It was an idyllic spot. They were surrounded by towering cliffs on three sides and forest on the other. The cliffs were covered with a wild tangle of exotic plant species. Large and small leafed, the plants bore flowers of every description, size and color. A waterfall tumbled out of a narrow cavern part way up one of the cliff sides and splashed into a wide pool at its base. From where they sat, the pool had no visible outlet into the meadow.

Melissa pushed herself forward and started pulling off her shirt.

Joanna opened an eye, and looked at her friend. "What are you doing?"

Melissa grinned. "Getting naked—well, not entirely." She proceeded to remove the rest of her clothes, leaving on only a very skimpy pair of underpants.

Joanna rolled over and sat up. "Aren't you afraid other people might be around?"

"No," Melissa said carelessly. "I've been out here a dozen times and I've never seen anyone else." She tossed her clothes in the direction of the multi-purpose pack they had left several yards away, and sank back into the soft, spongy ground covering. "Go ahead," she encouraged with a wicked grin. "There's no one here."

Joanna hesitated, tempted to follow suit, but decided she didn't have Melissa's confidence of complete privacy. She contented herself with removing her sturdy shoes and socks, then rose to her feet and wandered over to the pool. Sitting down, she dipped her feet in the water, surprised to discover how warm it was. Peering past the blurred outline of her feet, she tried to make out the bottom of the pool, but the lavender waters darkened considerably a short distance under the surface giving up no clues.

The shadowed waters moved in odd patterns as she gently swirled her feet and tried to sort through her confused emotions. So far, with one huge exception, Treaine was everything she had hoped it would be and more. She sighed as she thought of Alex. She had no doubt that this time, the end of the day would bring them together in that massive bed to do more than just share it in sleep. She quivered and closed her eyes. Just the thought of what might happen had a throbbing heat building between her legs and her insides turning to liquid.

Resolutely turning her thoughts away from Alex, she got to her feet. She had to talk to Melissa about finding a way back to the Neutral Realm.

MELISSA TURNED her head as Joanna plopped down beside her and groaned silently. *That look* was back on her face again. She knew what had caused it. If Joanna and Alex didn't work things out soon, she thought, she would be sorely tempted to stick her nose in where it wasn't wanted and talk to Alex herself. Melissa hated to see Joanna so torn apart by the difficult emotions born of this rocky relationship.

She turned her thoughts to her own frustrating lack of progress with Jason. The harder she tried to entice him, the less he seemed to notice. She had never run into a man she desired more strongly with each encounter, yet who appeared so supremely indifferent to her charms. She glanced at Joanna again and grimaced at the pain she saw on the lovely face. What a pair! Both of them twisted into knots by a Mariltar male.

Groaning dramatically, she rolled over, propped her chin on her hands and said, "All right, tell me!"

Clearly startled at having her thoughts interrupted, Joanna hesitated. But once she started to talk, she couldn't stop. She poured out her soul describing what she had seen at the reception, what she had thought, and Alex's visit to her work station the previous day.

Melissa mentally shook her head. God, these two were so blind! "Have you decided what you're going to do?"

Joanna stared up at the sky. Two of the moons were glowing faintly through the lavender haze. "Yes, I'm going to sleep with him."

Melissa's relief at hearing that piece of news was short-lived at hearing Joanna declare, "But I still want to leave. I hate this marriage partnership. The terms of it are completely unacceptable to me. I can't be what he wants me to be, Melissa."

Melissa repressed the urge to point out that she hadn't tried very hard. She was convinced that if Joanna turned more of her energies to accepting the marriage partnership than resisting it, she and Alex might forge a powerful foundation for a relationship. She turned to look down at her friend. Joanna, however, was in no mood to hear that. Her heart sank at Joanna's next words.

"Have you had any luck in locating a vessel returning to the Neutral Realm?"

She hadn't. In fact, she hadn't made any inquiries at all thinking she would wait a while to see how things worked out. But Joanna didn't need to know that. "I'm working on it," she assured her. "I have a date with a trader coming in next week. He has a regular route to the Neutral Realm and maybe he'll have some ideas."

Joanna nodded, apparently satisfied that at least something was being done. She turned over on her stomach.

Suddenly, she giggled.

"That's funny?" Melissa asked, mystified.

"No, not that. I just thought of the look on that security guard's face, when we passed through the perimeter this morning. The poor man didn't stand a chance against you!"

Melissa laughed. "I was exceptionally good, wasn't I?" She hadn't wanted to take the slightest chance of being turned back and had made a supreme effort to be at her most dramatic and charming. And befuddled, dazzled and thoroughly confused, the young guard at the perimeter checkpoint had let them through with barely a protest. Melissa heaved a sigh of satisfaction and sat up. "Is it time to eat yet?"

Chapter 19

THE SECURITY Control Center was unusually crowded and active. All the captains were there, except for Bavin Moresol who was out on a reconnaissance mission. Jason, Sebastian and Mark with several of their men were busy analyzing and discussing the results of the previous night's expedition. Eric and Justin with a smaller group were checking records in another part of the room.

His attention attracted by a sudden lessening of noise from the other part of the room, Jason glanced up. Eric was leaning over a console watched intently by others in his group. "Is there a problem?" Jason demanded.

Eric looked around. "You'd better come see for yourself. I can't quite believe what I'm seeing, and I've double checked it."

Jason got up and walked over to the group. Curious, the others followed. Someone had been checking the perimeter entry and exit records for the morning. Joanna's and Melissa's names were prominently displayed under the exit log.

Icy fear clutched at Jason's gut. He swore loudly and viciously. "Let's hope that someone's made a mistake," he said grimly, knowing how unlikely that was, but unable to believe that security procedures, so carefully crafted and analyzed for soundness, had failed completely. "Mark, verify this information with the guard who was on duty. Justin, trace their wrist communicator signals, and locate them. Someone, find out what vehicle they used. How by the balls of Sortor did they get past the guard?"

In seconds the information came back. The guard's description identified Joanna and Melissa without a doubt. Neither woman was wearing her wrist communicator. Both signals tracked to their respective living units. The vehicle's signal, however, was located about a half hour's distance outside the settlement.

"Where's Alex?" Jason asked.

Sebastian had already checked, and reported, "He's in a council meeting."

"All right. Sebastian and Justin, you're with me. Choose one man each. We're going after them. Mark, the guard is your man. Pull him off duty and find out what happened!"

Mark nodded grim faced, deferring to Jason's seniority. Every man in the room was aware the situation was critical. Security measures had failed on several counts, demanding immediate attention and resolution. The fact that they had failed with the Mariltar ambassador's wife, a woman for whose safety they were personally responsible, made the situation doubly serious. Jason knew that each man was aware if Joanna was not recovered safely, they would have a crisis of extreme proportions on their hands.

Swearing under his breath, Jason planted his hands on the table and stared blindly out the panel of glass in front of him trying to calm himself and order his thoughts. Knowing what he alone in the room knew, his fear was that there was more to the situation than a breakdown of their security measures. He couldn't believe that all of their controls could fail at the same time. Something else was at work here. Had Joanna been lured from the settlement? Had something or someone been able to disable the perimeter checkpoint long enough to get the women through?

Melissa! His amusement over Alex's dilemma the previous day had quickly faded when Melissa's face intruded on his mind as it had an annoying habit of doing lately. There was another one who was nothing but trouble! As much as he tried to ignore her, she was starting to wriggle her way into his consciousness at unexpected moments. What was it about these Earth women that got men so distracted they couldn't think clearly? And what was this pain that slashed fiercely at him at the thought of her in danger? He pushed it firmly aside. Joanna had to be his primary concern. This might, after all, be nothing more than an unauthorized expedition. He straightened and turned. "Eric, stay here on the monitor! Have a back-up team ready in case we need it."

"Shall I alert Alex?"

In the process of checking his survival belt, Jason paused. Alex was going to explode like a Gargan over this one. Jason had observed the full force of his anger twice. He had a momentary pang of sympathy for the small woman who would bear the brunt of it this time if this *was* nothing more than an unauthorized trip. But they were all going to feel its heat. None of them were going to come out of this unscathed.

"No, not yet. I'll tell you when." He pulled on his jacket and scowled. "Let's go! Hurry it up, men!"

IT DIDN'T TAKE long to find the cruiser. Mark had reported nothing useful from the guard, so the group spread out to determine in which direction the women had headed after leaving the cruiser. Within seconds their tracking equipment had picked up a trail. Jason left two men with the vehicles and the others set off. Unsure of what they might find or how long it would take to track the women, each man was absorbed in his own thoughts and there was little discussion in the party.

Finally, they broke through the trees and came out at the edge of the meadow. Jason saw Melissa and Joanna immediately. Sitting close together, facing away from the forest toward the waterfall, their laughter floated back to the group at the forest's edge.

His deep relief at finding them safe and unharmed was short-lived as he allowed his anger to build. The scanners the men were using showed no indication of anything unusual or other large sentient forms in the area.

"Stay here!" Jason ordered his men. He had a few things to say to the women that didn't require an audience.

He started across the meadow. Part way there he paused. What *was* Melissa wearing? Or rather, what was she *not* wearing? Her long blonde hair partially covered her back but, as he drew closer, he saw that she was indeed almost naked. He smiled grimly to himself. This was going to prove interesting!

The noise of the waterfall masked his approach. Standing immediately behind them, he said casually, "Hello, ladies."

Their reactions were eminently satisfying. Joanna jumped and twisted around so fast she lost her balance and went sprawling. Giving a shriek of surprise, Melissa curled up in tight ball hugging her knees to protect her nakedness.

"Ouch," Joanna sat up rubbing her neck and glared. "Jason, what are you doing here?"

He folded his arms and said in a deceptively soft tone, "What am I doing here? What am *I* doing here?" He strolled around in front to face them ignoring Melissa's desperate wriggles. "Well, let me see," he began in a conversational tone which changed quickly to anger, leaving no doubt as to his feelings. "It seems I was very inconveniently interrupted a short while ago at the Security Control Center when a report came in that an unauthorized and unescorted exit from the perimeter had taken place several hours earlier. If *that* wasn't bad enough, it seems that one of the two parties involved was the wife of a High Lord of Mariltar, for whose personal safety and protection the captains of Seventh Fleet are directly responsible. *Furthermore,* neither individual was wearing a wrist communicator *and* had failed to go through proper channels to be assigned the use of a vehicle."

He directed a cold stare in Melissa's direction and raised an eyebrow. "Getting a little chilly, Melissa?" Melissa, he decided, didn't appear to be suitably contrite.

In spite of his obvious displeasure and the list of indiscretions he had cited, she had quickly recovered her composure and now faced him defiantly. Her eyes sparkled with challenge. Her tone was filled with amusement as she replied, "Uh, oh. It *does* seem a few degrees colder around here." She glanced sideways at Joanna who *was* looking worried and grinned. "I think we might be in trouble."

Jason struggled to keep his temper under control. "You have no idea of the possible danger you could have been in, do you?" he asked.

"Oh, come on, Jason," Melissa said smiling unconcernedly. "What danger? I've been here by myself dozens of times. It's a lovely, tranquil spot. The only thing possibly representing a threat around here are the thorns on that plant." Her arm waved in the direction of the nearest cliff and then hurriedly returned to shield herself. "Stop glowering and sit down and have something to eat! If there's anything left, that is," she added, peering doubtfully in the direction of the bag they had brought with them.

Jason decided not to argue. Both women needed to understand the seriousness of the position in which they had placed themselves today. Alex would deal with Joanna and he only hoped he wouldn't be too hard on her. His commander, who demanded exceptional performance from his subordinates but was always fair-minded, nevertheless, seemed to loose some of his control and objectivity when it came to Joanna. And he would have few things to say to Melissa when he got her somewhere private and wasn't increasingly distracted by her lack of clothing. His main purpose for now was to get them safely back within the perimeter.

"Get dressed!" he said abruptly. "We're leaving."

Melissa, looking like she was about to argue again, opened her mouth, but was forestalled by Joanna who had noticed the other men at the edge of the meadow.

"It probably is time to head back, Melissa," she said with a warning jerk of her head.

"Oh, all right," Melissa grumbled. She smiled winningly and said, "Hand me my clothes please, Jason?"

Jason didn't move. "Get them yourself!"

"I'll get them." Joanna rose to her feet.

"No!" Jason snapped out. "She can get them herself."

Joanna sank back on her heels, a shocked expression on her face. Jason ignored her, his whole attention was concentrated on Melissa.

"Fine!" Melissa said with a toss of her head. Her arms dropped away and she rose regally to her feet. The skimpy underpants concealed very little. When she reached her clothes a few steps away, she turned defiantly to face him. He glowered back, folded his arms, and deliberately followed her every move as she dressed.

Chapter 20

JOANNA ROLLED her eyes and went to pick up their bag. Was she the only one embarrassed by this whole ridiculous scene? Something was going on between those two that was more than just conflict over the present situation, and she definitely felt like the odd man out.

Try as she would, she couldn't keep thoughts of Alex out of her mind. If the normally good-natured Jason was this upset with them, she dared not think about Alex's reaction. She took a deep breath and gazed around the meadow. Well, no matter how angry Alex might be, it would be worth it. This place in all its spectacular beauty was a definite balm to the spirit.

"All set!" Melissa sang cheerfully. They started off across the meadow with Jason close behind.

When they reached the forest, the other men met them with friendly enough greetings, but at an impatient signal from Jason, the group arranged itself protectively around the women. Little more was said as the party started down the trail, forced to go single file at first because of the thick undergrowth.

As the path widened out, Melissa came abreast of Joanna. "Don't you feel a little like we're being sent to the school director's office for a beating?" she hissed, loud enough for Jason, who was walking in front of them, to hear.

"Melissa!" Joanna teased in a shocked whisper, giggling. "Is that how you treat your students?"

"I wish I could," Melissa said fervently. "Some of those little beasts certainly deserve it." She turned serious. "You're not going to get in too much trouble with Alex, are you?"

Joanna shrugged trying to convey unconcern. The same question had been paramount in her mind. "I don't know."

"I'm sorry. I should never have persuaded you to come. You did say he had forbidden you to go beyond the perimeter."

"You didn't have to persuade me. I wanted to," Joanna replied. "I'd been looking forward to this for days, and it was worth it." She paused, then said with more confidence than she felt, "It'll be all right."

They walked in silence for a while until Melissa jerked on Joanna's arm. "I have to pee!"

"Can't it wait? Why didn't you go back in the meadow?" Joanna whispered, feeling an overwhelming urge to giggle again. God, she was so tense, she was becoming hysterical!

"Well, I guess you could say I had other things on my mind! Besides there are some things I will not do in front of an audience. It's urgent. What should I do?" she asked plaintively.

"Tell *him!*" Joanna said gesturing at Jason, and then called to Jason herself when Melissa groaned.

The whole group came to a halt. Faced with Jason's frown, Melissa stuttered, "I, uh, uh..." She glanced at the other men, hung her head, and mumbled, "I need to go."

Clearly impatient at the delay, Jason looked around and pointed at a large tree several yards off the trail. "Over there, and be quick about it!"

Melissa went off meekly. Joanna put her hand up to her mouth to cover a smile. The urge to laugh was becoming even stronger. She peeked surreptitiously at the rest of the group and her shoulders started to shake. Most had amused expressions on their faces except for Jason, who was still scowling and swinging his arms as he paced impatiently.

Her amusement changed to concern upon hearing a yelp from the direction of the tree. "Melissa," she called starting forward. "Are you all right?"

Jason put out an arm to stop her, a frown creasing his forehead.

"Yes, damn it! I'll be right out!" Melissa emerged a few seconds later rubbing her bottom.

"What happened?" Joanna asked.

"Nothing! Just a little scratch."

"Where? Is it bleeding?" demanded Jason.

Melissa glowered at him. "Well, I don't know. It's in a spot I rarely get to look at. Can we go now?"

It was the last straw. Joanna doubled over with laughter. Throwing a disgusted look at her, Jason approached Melissa. "We need to take a look, and treat it if necessary. Some of these plants are extremely toxic."

Melissa backed up, bumping into a grinning Sebastian. "Oh, no! You're not touching me and you're not 'taking a look'. This is all your fault anyway. You told me to use that tree. *I* would have gone over there." She waved an arm vaguely.

Jason had clearly had enough. "Sagar's sacred crystals," he swore through gritted teeth. "Joanna, get over here! Look and tell me if the surface of her skin is broken. Everyone else turn your backs."

Brushing away tears of laughter, and trying to control her giggles, Joanna obediently approached Melissa.

"It's not funny," Melissa hissed. "I could use some support here."

Glaring at the backs of the men, she pushed the back of her shorts down. Joanna looked. A red, angry line was running down one buttock.

"Her skin is broken, and looks inflamed," she reported soberly to Jason.

With a muttered curse, Jason demanded the medical kit from Sebastian then, before anyone else could move, took Melissa's arm and yanked her off behind another tree. A string of protests from Melissa could be heard, accompanied by indistinguishable sounds from Jason. Finally, there was a loud 'ouch'. Minutes later the two emerged, Jason with a smug expression of satisfaction on his face, and Melissa looking slightly bemused.

As they started off again, Melissa complained loudly to Joanna, "The man's a blasted, insensitive gorilla. I don't know why I ever thought I was attracted to him! You should have *seen* that disgusting thing he poked me with. It looked like—"

The vivid image Melissa's words conjured up in Joanna's mind was too much, and she exploded into giggles again, leaving her friend to subside into sulky silence.

The rest of the trip went uneventfully until they were within several hundred meters of the vehicles. Joanna had ceased trying to cajole Melissa out of her strange mood. She was becoming increasingly aware of an odd sensation. The skin at her nape was prickling with awareness. Her heart had begun to pound uncomfortably. It felt like a dozen pairs of eyes—unfriendly eyes—were observing her.

She glanced back at the men behind her. They still had their scanners out and appeared undisturbed by anything. As she turned her head, a movement in the trees caught her eye. She looked more closely. A shadow moved from behind a trunk. It loomed menacingly. She opened her mouth to call out an alarm but, with a suddenness that stole her breath, a blast of frigid air surrounded her. In the next instant, she had crashed to the ground. Pain shot up her leg. Her chest burned as her lungs fought to expand.

"*Joanna!*"

She felt hands on her, helping her to a sitting position. She wanted to tell them to leave her alone. She was dizzy. Spots danced in front of her eyes. Then, just as suddenly as it had appeared, the awful pressure in her chest was gone, and she drew in great gulps of air.

"Joanna, what happened?" Melissa's worried face swam into

focus. "Are you hurt?"

She looked up at the circle of concerned faces around her, then beyond them. The forest was normal. The shadow was gone. The only thing that remained of the whole bizarre experience was a sharp pain radiating up her leg.

She shook her head a little dazedly. "I-I'm fine, I think." She almost blurted out what she thought she had seen but noticed Jason glance inquiringly at Mark. Mark's response was to glance at his scanner, then give a brief negative shake of his head. She must have imagined the whole thing, she thought bleakly. But what about those awful sensations?

She allowed Melissa to help her to her feet, and then gasped with pain as she tried to put weight on her foot.

"You *are* hurt," Jason said with rough impatience. "Sit back down. Sebastian?"

Melissa removed her shoe and sock. Sebastian came forward and conducted a brief examination of her foot, then strapped a small, cool pouch to it bringing immediate relief.

"Better?" Melissa asked.

She nodded.

Sebastian adjusted the pouch. "You've strained some tendons. This will keep the inflammation down and eliminate the pain, but you shouldn't walk on it right away," he said. He looked up at Jason. "We'll have to carry her the rest of the way."

Jason nodded resignedly. "At least the vehicles aren't much further."

Sebastian helped Joanna carefully to her feet, cautioning her not to put any weight on her damaged foot. Justin came forward to help and, with the two men supporting her, the party made its way more slowly to the vehicles.

Once there, Jason ordered both women into his cruiser, while the rest of the men divided up between the other vehicles. As they started off, Jason reported to Eric at the Security Control Center, giving brief details of the search and Joanna's accident.

Joanna shivered when she heard him say, "Send a report to Alex immediately. Interrupt the council meeting if necessary."

The rest of the short trip back to the settlement was accomplished in silence. Within minutes of entering the settlement, the cruiser was drawing up in front of Joanna's unit. As Jason got out to help her to her door, Melissa made a move to go with her.

"Stay where you are!" Jason snapped. "You and I have a few

things to talk about."

Melissa sank meekly back in her seat, the stunned expression on her face making it evident she was unused to being treated with such curtness by an attractive male. Joanna pulled a sympathetic face. Despite her own concerns, she was worried for her friend. Jason's obvious displeasure over their expedition and the determination in his steely expression didn't bode well for Melissa. Her foot felt normal again, but she allowed Jason to partially support her to the door, and breathed a sigh of relief when the door finally closed behind him.

She sensed without looking that Alex wasn't there, and was grateful that she didn't have to face him immediately.

Chapter 21

"JAAASON?" Melissa purred.

Jason opened one eye and looked into the beautiful face hanging over his. Long blonde hair fell in a shining cascade over her shoulder and onto his bare chest, tickling his neck.

He had hauled her, with little ceremony and no explanation, back to his quarters where a shouting match had ensued. Jason had accused her of being highly irresponsible and selfish, and she had countered with colorful descriptions of what she thought of him. When they both paused for breath, anger and irritation shifted subtly. Sexual awareness flared powerfully. They had simultaneously reached out for one another. Within minutes they had ended up in Jason's sleeping chamber, tearing off each others' clothes and had fallen onto the bed, where a passionate, thoroughly satisfying love making session had followed.

"Hmmm?" Jason responded, closing his eye again.

"Are all Mariltar men such exciting lovers?" Her fingernail was drawing patterns on his chest, causing immensely pleasurable sensations and reactions in other parts of his body again.

He smiled at the very Melissa-like compliment and answered lazily without opening his eyes, "That's a personal opinion, my dear, although I've heard we do have a reputation for keeping our women well satisfied." He stretched. "You, however, are never going to have a chance to personally discover the answer."

He felt Melissa pause in the middle of drawing a circle, and cracked open an eye curiously. She had an arrested expression on her face. Then, clearly coming to some sort of a decision, she nodded, gave him a blinding smile that stole his breath and continued leisurely with the pattern. In another instant, a small frown crossed her face. "Jason, Alex is going to be very angry with Joanna, isn't he? I feel kind of guilty, because I *did* talk her into going with me. She wasn't supposed to go outside the perimeter."

Jason opened both eyes this time to study her face. "You *should* feel guilty and, make no mistake, *I'm* still angry with you. Both of you flagrantly ignored security regulations." He chose his words carefully as he continued, "Alex isn't going to be happy with her, to put it mildly. If there's one thing he won't tolerate, it's deliberate disregard for his wishes and this involved her personal safety which is doubly serious."

To his disappointment, Melissa stopped what she was doing and fell back beside him, staring up at the ceiling. "Well then, maybe he needs to stop running his marriage like a warrior vessel and treat it more like what it's supposed to be, an equal partnership!" she said angrily. "If he quit ordering her around, and asked for her opinion every now and then, he might get better results."

It was Jason's turn to prop himself on one elbow and lean over Melissa. "Alex has been incredibly patient with her," he defended his friend. "I've never seen him indulge anyone the way he indulges her. It takes two to make a relationship work, and I'm not sure that Joanna has fully accepted the arrangement. But I do know this. Alex will never let her go. She'll make it easier on herself if she starts demonstrating a little more flexibility with some of what he wants from her." He studied Melissa's worried expression, and said gently, "I don't think he'll be too hard on her. He really does care about her, more than I think he realizes." He kissed her softly on her lips, and then repeated the action more slowly as she reached her arms around his neck.

"Why are we talking about someone else when there are more interesting things to do?" he said. "I want you to explain to me *exactly* what a gorilla is."

He moved his body to cover hers.

Melissa wriggled delightedly underneath him. "Ooh. Are you going to be angry with me again? Oh, oh, you are, aren't you?" And it was a long time before she mentioned Joanna and Alex again.

Chapter 22

ALEX TOOK A deep breath before reaching out to splay his hand against the scanner activating the door mechanism. He had stayed away as long as he could, trying to bring his churning emotions under control. Earlier, he had listened to Eric's report with concern, disbelief, and quickly mounting rage. It was bad enough that she had defied him, but that she could so carelessly put her life in danger was beyond his understanding. She had gone too far this time, and he had had enough!

The anger he had so carefully brought under control was simmering again, close to eruption, by the time he had searched the unit, unable to find her in any of the rooms. As he stalked furiously back through the great room, a solid splash of color outside caught his eye. She was kneeling in the far corner of the garden, her hands busy with a large flowering shrub.

The soft ground cover masked his approach, but he saw her start and tense as his shadow fell over her and he said with far more calmness than he felt, "Hello, Joanna."

She swiveled her head to look at him, and returned his greeting hesitantly. Then, clearly uneasy and uncertain, returned to trimming the branches of the shrub that had invaded the corner.

Alex studied her in silence. Her hair tumbled untidily around her shoulders. Her face was glowing with a sheen of perspiration from the warm air and was devoid of cosmetics. The dark turquoise matching shorts and tunic set she was wearing barely covered the tops of her thighs.

She looked incredibly young and innocently beautiful, and desire surged within him, fierce and powerful and almost uncontrollable. He barely restrained the primitive urge to push her down against the soft, spongy earth and plunge himself into her body.

He clenched his fists. There were critical matters to resolve. Her lack of apparent concern, and the fact that she offered no immediate explanation for the morning's activities only fueled his anger, but he cautioned himself to move slowly. His position and rank normally assured unquestioning execution of his every command. Nobody had ever dared to defy him to the extent she had, and would have faced harsh and swift disciplinary measures if they had. He had no idea of how to deal with his beautiful wife, but was determined to make her understand and respect his authority.

THE LONGER ALEX loomed silently over her, the more nervous Joanna became. The quick glance at his shadowed face moments earlier had failed to reveal his mood. She tried to convince herself that he hadn't sounded too angry.

Her hands moved instinctively over the fragile branches, separating and removing while thoughts tumbled chaotically through her head. Had she pushed him too far this time? All thoughts of seduction had flown from her mind the moment she knew she and Melissa had been discovered. Upon her return to their living unit, she had showered and changed and then found herself pacing agitatedly, rehearsing what she was going to tell Alex. Finally, desperate to soothe her nerves, she had grabbed up some garden tools and gone outside to work. Now, she couldn't remember a word of what she had planned to say to him, but she was determined to not let him intimidate her. She jumped when he spoke.

"That plant's not poisonous, I hope."

It was the last thing she expected him to say, and she deliberately chose to interpret it in the worst possible way. He obviously believed her to be a brainless idiot. She replied with infuriating and condescending logic, "I assumed it wouldn't be since it's planted here but, of course, I also checked in the data bank." She caught a glimpse of his absent nod. He seemed undisturbed by her tone. The observation increased her nervousness rather than reassured her.

"Did you enjoy yourself this morning?"

Her hands slowed in the delicate task of separating a small branch from the main trunk of the shrub, and she glanced at him sideways still unable to clearly see his face. "Um, yes. Melissa's always fun to be with." As soon as the words were out of her mouth, she regretted them remembering that he had asked her to spend the day with him but, once again, there was no obvious reaction.

"How's your foot?"

"Fine, thank you."

"I thought I had made it clear that you were not to go outside the perimeter. I assume you remember that discussion." His tone hadn't changed but the words put a knot in her stomach.

And it wasn't a discussion, Joanna thought resentfully. She remembered it as more of an order. She answered defensively, her voice rising slightly, "Of course I do."

"And you chose to defy me anyway?"

Joanna froze. The words hung heavy with challenge in the air between them.

She ran her tongue over dry lips and swallowed hard. "You told me not to go out without an escort. Melissa has traveled outside the perimeter dozens of times and hasn't ever had any trouble. I thought she more than fulfilled the requirement."

"Is that so?" The calm, even tone had gone. His voice had lowered to become soft and infinitely dangerous, finally responding to her deliberate provocation.

Joanna felt her stomach cramp more heavily. Instinct warned her she was approaching hazardous territory. But her own temper was starting to boil. How dare he make her feel like a recalcitrant child? She decided to brazen it out. Resting the laserray in her lap, she turned, still in a kneeling position, to confront him, trying to get a better view of his face. She raised a hand to push the hair off her forehead and felt the grittiness of dirt against her skin. Impatiently, she rubbed at it.

He had moved slightly or else the light had changed, but his features were now clearly revealed. As soon as she saw them, she realized how badly she had misjudged what his reaction might be. The pulse at his temple beat slowly and almost blackly. His eyes had darkened to the same color.

He was furious.

Her courage almost deserted her, but what, after all, could he do to her? "I'm sorry if you're upset, but I'm not a child. I've told you, I'm perfectly capable of making my own decisions."

Arms folded, Alex studied her. She had never seen such a cold expression on his face. "I don't think you do clearly understand your position or the risks and responsibilities associated with it, or else you've chosen to ignore them. But, irregardless, I expect you to respect my wishes."

Joanna heard anger and impatience in his voice. More than that, he wasn't even trying to understand her viewpoint as usual. Nerves stretched to the limit, her temper exploded. She picked up the tool and took a vicious swipe at the bush, accidentally severing a limb she had so carefully pruned moments before.

In frustration, she threw down the tool and jumped up. "Your *wishes* are delivered as orders," she shouted angrily, "and I refuse to be dictated to. I am *not* one of your subordinates. I *will* make my own decisions about where I go and what I do, and I'll damn well decide myself what I want to do with my free time. *You*," she stabbed her finger at him for emphasis, "can just...just go to *hell*!"

With deep satisfaction, she saw a stunned, disbelieving look cross his face. Probably no one had ever talked to him like that before. Well, she wasn't sorry she had. As far as she was concerned, he deserved it *and* more. She turned on her heel and stalked off. He caught up with her as she reached the door leading into the main room of their unit, and jerked her around to face him.

"No, you're not one of my subordinates," he agreed, his voice icy. "If *anyone* under my command ever *dared* to so blatantly disregard one of my orders as you have done, they would be terminated from their position instantly."

Joanna felt her face redden. "Sounds like a wonderful solution to me," she snapped. "Let's end this marriage partnership. Then neither of us would have to endure this misery any longer."

Alex glared at her. Then, abruptly, he seemed to come to a decision. His face cleared, his eyes lightened and he said silkily, "Oh no, my dear. That would be too easy, wouldn't it? And I *do* have a reputation for always taking the most challenging path. There are other, ah, choices, other methods to ensuring a lesson is learned, and the consequences of one's actions are clearly understood." He held out his hand. "Come inside with me, please."

Puzzled and confused by this sudden change in demeanor, Joanna reluctantly put her hand in his and allowed him to lead her inside to one of the comfortable sitting areas. He let go of her hand and immediately started to remove his tight-fitting, lightweight jacket. "Wh-What are you doing?"

He was silent, considering her through narrowed eyes. Starting to roll up a sleeve of his shirt, he said casually, "Since we've already determined that I can't discipline you as I would one of my subordinates, and that termination of this marriage partnership is not an option, I've chosen another method. Perhaps the palm of my hand against that enticing little bottom of yours will get your attention. I will not tolerate deliberate disobedience, Joanna."

Her eyes widened in shock and her mouth fell open as his meaning sank in. "Y-you can't be serious!" she squeaked.

"No?" His tone was almost pleasant. He started on the other sleeve. "But that's been the problem from the beginning, hasn't it? You haven't taken me or this marriage partnership very seriously. Well, things are about to change, and you are going to find out *just* how serious I am."

He finished rolling his sleeve and reached for her. She stumbled back a few paces and turned to run, but it was too late. His hand caught her in an iron grip and twisted her around. He took her with him as he dropped onto the couch. Before she could react further, she found herself face down across his lap and staring at the rough weave in the rug on floor. A steel band clamped across her waist and arms, controlling her frantic wriggles to escape.

The first blow hurt, and produced an involuntary yelp. The ones that followed merely stung, but seemed to go on for an eternity. When he finally hauled her into a sitting position on his lap, she was thoroughly humiliated and spitting with fury. She swung at him with a free arm, but he caught it easily and pressed her back against the pillows, holding her lower body immobile with his and her arms stretched above her head.

Her chest heaved with rage and the effort to draw air into her lungs. She felt the heat in her face as she struggled silently and ineffectually against him.

"*Joanna!*" The warning note in his voice caused her to still. "I didn't particularly enjoy doing that," he said through clenched teeth as he leaned over her, his face a hand's breadth from hers, "but I enjoy even less being made to look a fool. *Especially* by my wife, who should be setting an example! *I'm* responsible for security on this planet, but that authority is made to look particularly ineffective when my own wife flagrantly ignores measures put in place to protect everyone, not to mention deliberately puts her own life in danger."

Joanna stared at him, appalled at the sudden realization of the position she had put him in. She hadn't given a thought as to how her behavior might reflect on his professional duties, and was shocked at her insensitivity. The tenseness left her body and she collapsed under him. Turning her head away, she whispered, "Oh God, Alex. I'm so sorry."

She felt his hand touch her cheek and turn her face back to him. His brows drew together thoughtfully as he watched a tear slip out of her eye and make its way down her cheek. He touched a finger to it and then used the wetness to rub at the same spot on her forehead where she knew she had smeared dirt earlier. It was an incredibly tender gesture.

His eyes raised to hers again. Misunderstanding and conflict melted away as if they had never been. Slowly, he bent his head and lightly kissed her mouth. He drew back to study her face again. She felt the last of her resistance fade, and lay quietly with eyes half closed and lips slightly parted, waiting to see what he would do next. Desire, fierce and raw and intense shone from his eyes. His grip on her body tightened.

Then he pulled away suddenly and she could have screamed with frustration. Her body ached with a need that shocked her by its strength and sudden appearance. But he rose to his feet, then bent and gathered her into his arms. She turned her face shyly into his shoulder as he strode toward the sleeping chamber, knowing without a doubt that this time there would be no turning back.

And she wanted it, needed it. Wanted him.

He put her down gently on the bed and knelt beside her. Keeping his body apart from hers, he bent his head slowly and touched his lips to hers again.

Joanna's body was tingling all over, aching for more. She hesitantly brought her arms up around his neck and caressed the back of his head and neck, running her fingers through his thick, dark hair, encouraged by his low groan of pleasure. When she thought she wouldn't be able to stand it anymore, he began to stroke her body, starting at her shoulder and moving down between her breasts, continuing on across her belly to sweep down her hips and legs. Everywhere he touched, and even through her clothes, her skin felt as if it were being licked by flames. Her breasts and sensitive inner thighs, craving his attention the most, remained untouched.

He slid off her shoes, and his hands began the journey back up her body. This time he paused to tug at her clothing. After a few fruitless moments, he finally muttered in frustration, "How, by the fires of Pormiam, does this thing come off."

Face tucked into his neck, Joanna choked back nervous laughter. "I-it just pulls off."

"Ah!" He grasped the shoulders of the tunic and slowly pulled it down her arms and over her chest. The provocative bit of gossamer fabric she had donned earlier in an effort to give herself false courage hid nothing. She knew her breasts were clearly exposed to his hungry gaze. He sucked in a deep breath and impatiently finished stripping off the tunic and attached shorts. The fragile undergarment was removed more carefully until she lay naked beside him.

"Meira, you are so lovely," he whispered in her ear, capturing an earlobe with his teeth. His hands were busy again, sliding over her skin, touching her everywhere except where she most needed to be touched. He was driving her wild with a burning need for so much more. Then he was turning her over on her belly, and caressing every curve and hollow of her back with his hands. Only this time, he was following his hands with his lips, pushing aside her hair and tonguing her nape, discovering every sensitive spot along her spine, at the base of her buttocks, behind her knees and at the arch of her feet.

She was mindless with pleasure when he finally turned her over again, and captured her hand to press it against the front of his breeches. She almost cried out when she felt the hard, thick ridge of his erection through the thin cloth, but he was urging her to help him with his clothes, then left her briefly to impatiently finish the task himself.

When he returned, he lowered his head to one breast and at last took a nipple in his mouth. She writhed and arched against him as he thoroughly explored her with his tongue and lips before shifting his attention to the other breast. His hand moved down her body, stroking, kneading, leaving a trail of fire and inserted itself between her legs. A finger gently separated the folds of her sensitive flesh and with a sure knowledge sought out and found the small, hard button of sensation. With a slow circular motion he massaged her. Moaning helplessly, she pushed against him wanting, needing more. She felt herself teetering on the verge of release again and again, but he always pulled her back until, with a startling suddenness, he pulled himself over her and positioned himself between her legs.

He drew her knees up spreading her wide, and reached down to guide himself to her opening. She felt his thickness stretching her as he pushed into her slightly. But then he pulled back only to repeat the teasing action several times. Joanna was crazy with need. Her nails raked his back desperately and, in final surrender, she whimpered, "Aaalex...please."

"Please what, Meira?" he whispered nibbling the side of her neck. "What do you want?"

"Pl-please—I need you inside me," she begged.

The deep grunt of satisfaction that issued from his throat was primitive, wholly male. He surged into her slowly and steadily, watching her face intently. She couldn't have looked away even if she had wanted to. He bent to trail kisses across her face and groaned as he sheathed himself fully inside her. "Ah, Meira. I've waited so long for this." He breathed hard against her neck and she sensed his struggle to hold on to his control. "You feel so incredible. Are you all right?"

She hid her face in his shoulder. The discomfort caused by his initial invasion rapidly faded as he rocked his hips gently and her body adjusted to his bulk. She moaned with pleasure and her hands gripped his hips urging him to move. The sleek, muscled body tensed and gathered momentum as he thrust harder into her softness. His eyes glittered fiercely above her. He seemed incapable of holding back now, lost in his own storm of pleasure. And she reveled in his possession of her body, the hard, hungry thrusts that had become almost rough. He dipped his head and closed his mouth around one sensitive nipple. She felt the wave swell and grow, spreading out from her core, bringing with it a shattering release. As she felt her muscles contract and tighten around him, Alex stroked into her one last time, then groaned and collapsed against her.

His breathing sounded harsh in her ear, as his final shudders subsided. Then he rolled over on his side taking her with him. He was still lodged deep inside her and she wanted to keep him there. He rubbed his face in her hair and spread a large hand over her bottom to pull her closer still.

She drew a deep, trembling breath. A deep contentment swept over her. Her cheek rested on his chest and his heart thudded loudly beneath her ear. Her eyelids were drooping with drowsiness, but she struggled against sleep, wanting to savor this most amazing feeling for as long as possible.

The chimes of the information console announcing a caller in the main room intruded. Alex swore under his breath but didn't move. The chimes came again. He reached up to the panel over their heads and silenced the console.

"You're not going to answer it?" Joanna asked sleepily.

He shifted until he was looking into her face. "No, I am not. There are other ways to get in touch with me if it's an emergency." Gently, he stroked the tangled hair back off her face. "Was I too rough?" he questioned softly. "I didn't hurt you, did I?"

She shook her head shyly, and veiled her eyes. She wasn't ready to express her feelings, didn't want to talk about what had just happened. He shifted against her, drawing her closer still and sighed. Reaching above his head again, he pushed another button on the panel. Soft, haunting music filled the room.

Joanna stirred. "It's lovely," she murmured, "Mariltar?"

"Yes," Alex confirmed absently, continuing to stroke her hair. "I like your Earth music as well. I enjoyed listening to the selection you were playing the other day."

They lay in silence as the music floated and soared around them in harmony with the rapidly changing colors outside. The sky darkened swiftly from lavender to deep purple and the moons appeared, shining more brilliantly than usual.

Joanna started to wriggle restlessly, growing uncomfortable with her position and with a thought that kept niggling at her mind. Her movements produced an instant affect on Alex. He started to swell inside her again. He rolled her over on her back and captured her face in his hands, bending his head to kiss her. How could he be ready again so soon? Joanna wondered. And, as his hips started a gentle thrusting motion, and liquid fire raced through her body, she wondered at *her* readiness. But then she had never experienced such intense, mind-numbing pleasure before. Her previous explorations into sexual activities had always been somewhat disappointing and had left her wondering what all the fuss was about.

The waves of pleasure started to build, but the thought was still there, more insistent than before. She tore her mouth away from Alex's, and pushed slightly at his chest.

"A-Alex?"

"What, Meira?" he demanded gently, frowning a little at her troubled face.

"I-I don't want to get pregnant," she whispered. She saw the surprise in his face and knew he was wondering why she wasn't on some form of birth control.

But he bent to kiss her again and murmured reassuringly, "It's all right. My sterilization implants won't wear off for another several months."

He resumed the gentle thrusting, gradually increasing the pace and strength of the motions. This time was different, slower, but the climax she achieved was no less intense, nor was his obvious pleasure. When the last spasms had died away, he slipped out of her body and sat up, pulling the cover up over her.

"It's getting late. Are you hungry?"

Joanna repressed the urge to giggle. Food was the last thing on her mind, but she nodded in the affirmative anyway. He demanded that she stay where she was, and rolled out of bed. Admiring the view he presented as he walked naked to the archway, she suddenly noticed with shock the red streaks down his back and vaguely remembered raking her nails across his skin in the throes of ecstasy. Embarrassed, she buried her face in the pillow. God, she had completely lost control, not once, but twice.

She rolled over again smiling. But he had made her feel so incredibly good! She had never been loved so thoroughly or so well before. Stretching luxuriously, she jumped out of bed and headed for the bath chamber.

Chapter 23

WHEN ALEX reappeared a short while later, she was immersed in the large bath, up to her chin in bubbles, her hair piled in wild disarray on top of her head.

"You have a hard time listening to anything I say, don't you," he scolded in mock seriousness, stalking over to the bath, and depositing the plate of food and two goblets of a pale blue liquid on the ledge. "Move over!"

He settled in beside her, then reached behind them and touched the computer panel. The lights dimmed and the ceiling panels above them slid noiselessly open to the night sky. Chilly air rushed in through the opening. Joanna looked up in awe to see, immediately overhead, the largest of the moons shining directly into the room.

She sneezed suddenly.

"Too cold?"

"No, the bubbles just tickled my nose."

Alex chuckled. "How about some music." He touched another button, and the same haunting music that had played in the sleeping chamber echoed softly around the room. "And a massage." He caught her completely off guard and she squealed and jumped when the bath began to vibrate and pulses of water caught her in a sensitive spot. He grinned knowingly and gave her a wicked leer. Wrinkling her nose at him, she adjusted her position carefully, and leaned her head back with a sigh of pleasure.

Alex picked up the plate and offered it to her, a pleased expression crossing his face at her exclamation of surprise. "Where did all this come from?"

"I ordered it from the Marketplace earlier today." As they ate, he explained the various delicacies he had selected. The food was delicious, rich and varied in taste. When they had both had enough to eat, he put his arm around her waist and held her close against his side as they sipped at the ambrosia. Joanna broke the comfortable silence a few minutes later.

"Alex?"

"Hmm?" he murmured lazily above her head.

She almost forgot what she wanted to tell him. The pale blue liquid swirling in her goblet fascinated her. It was creating the most exquisite patterns. Ignoring the danger of the topic, she asked dreamily, "Why isn't anyone allowed to go outside the perimeter without an escort? I know you said your teams had to explore the area to make sure it was secure, but hasn't that been done by now?"

Beside her, she felt Alex tense. Too sated with pleasure to feel much concern, she was nevertheless vaguely aware of his exasperation when he said, "Don't you ever pay attention to your security bulletins?"

"What security bulletins?" She tipped her head up.

His reply was slow in coming. He seemed to be momentarily distracted by something in the vicinity of her chest. "The ones you're required to review every time you sign on to an information console."

"Oh! Oh, I never look at those," Joanna confessed carelessly. "I never have the time."

Alex groaned. "That would explain a lot! If you *had* been paying attention, you would know that something tried to breach the perimeter the night of the reception. We haven't been able to identify it or its intent, and *that's* why no one is supposed to go outside the perimeter without authorization or an escort right now. *You're* not supposed to go outside unescorted at *any* time for reasons we've already talked about. And I don't ever want to catch you without your wrist communicator outside of this unit again!"

He shook his head, clearly frustrated. "I don't know whether to be angry at you all over again, or relieved that you weren't out there deliberately putting your life in jeopardy. And why wasn't Melissa aware of any of this, or did she simply choose to disregard it as well?"

He brought his face closer to hers and held her gaze with his brilliant eyes. "More importantly, would you have gone if you had known?"

"N-No, I don't think so," Joanna stammered. Her eyes widened as she finally realized the extent of the jeopardy they might have been in.

"Hmmm." Alex drew back a little, still holding her gaze. "I certainly hope not. Well, there's a security issue revealed right there," he pondered. "Chances are you two are not the only ones ignoring the bulletins. We'll have to code them and lock the screen so no one can bypass without reviewing and acknowledging them first."

"What do you think this...this thing is?"

"We don't know." Alex shrugged. "It's puzzling. It disappeared without a trace, and we haven't any clues at all. We searched the records of Treaine and have found no similar unexplained occurrences. It could be something that was transported here recently, or it could be something that was already here and was never recorded. We just don't know yet."

Joanna stared up at the moon, which for some peculiar reason seemed to want to change shape. Its edges blurred and wavered. Shadows danced across its surface. She blinked. Something tugged at her memory, something she knew she should tell him, but she couldn't remember. She was beginning to feel distinctly lightheaded. "Are we safe inside the p-perimeter?"

Alex nodded. "It's an extremely strong barrier. Whatever it was didn't come close to penetrating even the outer field."

Frowning, Joanna concentrated on remembering another question she knew she needed to ask him.

"Will tha-, uh, very nice guard tha- let us th-through be in tw-twouble?"

Even to her own ears, there was a distinct slur to her words. Alex peered at her closely, before smiling slightly and saying, "I think, Meira, the ambrosia is having far too strong of an affect on you, and you haven't even drunk that much. You've had enough." He took the goblet out of her hand and set it down. "Are you all right?"

"Oh, yeth." She leaned her head back against his shoulder and gave him a brilliant smile. He blinked and his expression changed subtly. The arm around her waist tightened.   "W-will he?"

"Will he what? Oh—yes, of course. He'll be disciplined."

Joanna shook her head vehemently, causing some of her hair to tumble loose. The beautiful spinning patterns in front of her eyes enthralled her. She concentrated hard. She had to make him understand something. "No, y-you can't. W-wasn't his fault, Alex." She giggled and hiccupped. Clapping a hand over her mouth, she hiccupped again and said, "Mel—we were awfully persuasive. He didn't weally have— have...?"

Puzzled, she stared at him. What had she meant to say? God, was she making any sense at all? She was feeling wonderfully disembodied and relaxed. Alex didn't seem to be paying much attention to her anyway. His eyes were fixed on her chest again, and his hand was stroking up the inside of her leg producing an absolutely delicious sensation. Impatiently, she grabbed his hand. "*Alex!*"

"What?" He looked up, a slightly dazed expression in his eyes, then seemed to remember they were supposed to be having a conversation. "The man failed miserably in his duties, Meira. However strong the persuasion, he failed to follow the most basic procedures and must be disciplined."

Deciding that he wasn't really getting the point, Joanna threw a leg over him and straddled his thighs. She didn't care that now her chest was completely bared to his gaze. Grabbing his face in her hands, she shook his head back and forth. "No—no—no. Y-you mustn't punish him. Was *our* fault." She leaned forward until her lips were grazing his, wriggled until she felt the thickness of his arousal nudging the inside of her thigh and breathed, "Please?"

To her deep satisfaction, Alex groaned and gave in. "All right! I'll talk to Mark in the morning and tell him to reduce the penalty. But I will not allow it to eliminated entirely, otherwise we could risk a discipline—"

"Promise?" Joanna interrupted.

"Yes! I promise. Now, Meira," he growled, "be quiet. We have other things to attend to."

His lips nibbled their way across her neck, causing her to moan with pleasure, while his hands captured her hips and lifted her up, bringing her down to sheath the hard length of him. Floating pleasantly on waves of sensation, Joanna simply allowed herself to follow where he led but, when it was over, she collapsed against him feeling suddenly exhausted. The dizzying affects of the ambrosia were wearing off, and all she wanted to do was close her eyes and sleep.

She didn't object when Alex helped her out of the bath, and dried her off, then swung her up in his arms and carried her through to the sleeping chamber to deposit her on the bed. She was slipping into unconsciousness within seconds of her head touching the pillow, and was only vaguely aware when he joined her a few minutes later to curve his body around hers.

Chapter 24

WHEN THE computer's programmed greeting spoke softly into the quiet of the room the following morning, and then repeated at two minute intervals, it was Alex's hand that reached out eventually to silence it.

He sat down on the side of the bed and shook her shoulder. "Joanna!"

Her eyes fluttered open and then closed. He was fully dressed and looked disgustingly healthy and far too energetic.

"Joanna." His voice was more insistent.

She opened her eyes reluctantly and drew her brows together in a small frown. Pushing herself up on her elbows, she looked at him sideways, then collapsed back on her stomach with a heartfelt moan and pulled the pillow over her head. She simply couldn't deal with Alex this morning. "I don't feel well. Go away!"

Surprisingly, it seemed to work. She was conscious of his weight lifting from the bed and peeked out from under the pillow a few seconds later to check that he was gone. She truly didn't feel well. In fact, she decided, she must have her very first hangover, and wondered miserably how long it would take this dreadful queasiness in her stomach and pounding head to disappear.

Unfortunately, her condition didn't inhibit her thoughts. All the memories of the previous evening came rushing back and her face, still buried under the pillow, started to burn. The more she remembered of all the little details of their lovemaking, the hotter she grew, until it felt like her whole body was on fire with embarrassment. God, the things he had done to her, and the way she had responded! She would never be able to face him again.

She wasn't allowed to wallow in her embarrassment for very long before she felt Alex's weight settle on the bed again. He tugged at the pillow and she tightened her grip.

"Joanna!" He sounded exasperated, and suddenly the pillow was gone, yanked away despite her desperate efforts. "Sit up and drink this. It'll help. What time does Ambassador Kromon expect you this morning?"

The question got the desired action with a swiftness that must have startled him. Joanna rolled over and shot up looking at the time on the computer display in panic. Ambassador Kromon? Oh, God! She couldn't be late for this morning's session. They were voting on an important proposal. She relaxed a little when she saw she still had time to get ready, and then became aware that the cover had dropped to her waist and Alex's interested gaze was focused on her naked breasts. She snatched the cover up protectively, earning a sigh of regret from her husband.

"Here!" He held out a cup containing a thick ghastly green liquid. When she wrinkled her nose and pushed his hand away, he said somewhat impatiently, "Just drink it. It tastes better than it looks, and it's the best remedy I know of for a hangover."

She eyed him suspiciously and hesitantly took the cup. He didn't look like he was going to go away. Her stomach was heaving and she was afraid she was going to disgrace herself in front of him. She quickly gulped the liquid down. The taste wasn't bad but the texture almost made her gag, and she gave an involuntary shudder as she set the cup down.

Alex reached out to cup her chin and examine her face. "You look tired. Why don't you stay in bed and rest a while longer?"

Tired? She felt exhausted and wasn't sure how she was going to be able to handle the difficult day ahead. She didn't know what time she had finally slept, but it seemed like she had just closed her eyes. She shook her head.

"I can't," she said. "We're taking up the Taragon orphan issue again today. It's too important to me to miss."

"Come here!" He lifted her, still clutching the cover, onto his lap and hugged her tightly, making her feel immeasurably better. He kissed her forehead, then stared into her eyes as he said softly, "I want you know that last night was very, *very* special for me. I hope it was for you as well."

She blushed and hid her face in his shoulder.

"Listen to me. I know you have a difficult session today, but you can't let yourself get too emotionally involved with this issue. It won't help anybody. Hear what the others have to say, and listen for any of their ideas that you can use. You're a good negotiator, Joanna. Don't let your personal feelings get in the way."

Resentment flashed briefly that he was telling *her* how to do her job. But reluctantly she admitted to herself that he might be right. Her emotions on the subject *were* too strong. She had to find a way to back off and look at it more objectively. She allowed herself the comfort of his arms for a few minutes longer, then pushed away. "I really do need to get dressed now."

"Are you sure you're feeling up to this?" He studied her intently, concern evident in his eyes.

She nodded with more confidence than she felt, and was relieved when he seemed to accept that. She watched as he left the room. A dreamy smile crept across her face and she stretched with abandon. Embarrassment gone, she thought about how his hands on her body had made her feel. She had never been loved so thoroughly or so well. The concoction he had just given her had done its work. She was feeling a lot better, with only a lingering tiredness and slight soreness between her thighs as physical reminders of the previous evening.

She bounced out of bed. Today *would* go well. Fired with fresh determination and energy, she was convinced of it.

Chapter 25

WHAM!

The first puck slammed into the wall outside the grid, the force of the impact absorbed by the padded walls, and plunged to the floor. The second hit the ceiling then joined its mate on the ground.

"Great Sagar, Alex!" Jason threw his glove up in the air in disgust. "If you were concentrating any less, you'd be lying asleep on the floor. That score is pathetic."

The men were playing a regularly scheduled Lon match, a game that required great skill and concentration. It had taken them three years of playing together to reach level four, in a game where the sixth level represented complete mastery. Today, they hadn't advanced beyond level one.

Breathing hard and pulling off his glove, Alex shrugged and grinned, feeling surprisingly undisturbed by Jason's criticism.

"Your playing isn't much better, my friend. I've been distracted by that silly look that keeps crossing your face at odd moments."

Startled, Jason's hand involuntarily rose to his face and wiped across the lower half of it. Then he laughed. "It shows that much, huh? There's a beguiling little sorceress with blonde hair and gray eyes who's taken possession of my mind...and a few other things," he added thoughtfully.

"Melissa? I thought you weren't going to get involved with her?"

"I wasn't, but things changed with that whole fiasco yesterday. I swear that woman truly is a sorceress. One minute I'm ready to throw her into a lockup because I'm convinced that's the only way to get her attention and teach her the error of her ways, and the next minute I'm in bed with her."

They walked into the empty shower facilities to strip and clean up.

"And there's more." Jason groaned as he thought about it. "In a moment of pure insanity, I asked her to move in with me."

Alex stopped scrubbing to stare at his friend. "She agreed?"

"Yes, without hesitation."

"And now you're having second thoughts?"

"Yes—no—I don't know! Sagar's sacred crystals, Alex, I don't know that I'm ready for this. I've never spent more than three or four consecutive days with a woman before, let alone contemplated something more permanent like this. I do know that *this* woman has been driving me crazy ever since I laid eyes on her."

Alex pulled on his shirt in silence feeling some sympathy for Jason. It seemed that his friend was going through an experience similar to his. Alex had never allowed his emotions to become involved in his relationships with women before. While he knew that family obligations would require him to take a partner and have a family one day, the nature of his responsibilities had kept him constantly on the move and, more often than not, placed him in highly dangerous circumstances. Those conditions were not conducive to forming strong attachments.

He hadn't really sorted through all his feelings for Joanna yet. Used to being in control and having his orders obeyed without question, she exasperated and angered him by defying even what he considered to be simple requests. He had been shocked by the utterly debilitating fear that had all but paralyzed him the previous day upon learning she had put herself in danger by venturing outside the perimeter. The rage which quickly followed after Eric had assured him she was unharmed and on her way back had only been brought under control with a great deal of effort.

Anger, helplessness and sheer frustration over her refusal to conform to his wishes and his own inability to control her actions had driven him to deliver the punishment he had yesterday. He had had no desire to hurt her, only a determination to seize her attention and impress upon her just how serious he was.

The lesson had had unexpected results. Highly satisfying results, in fact! But he wasn't convinced that it had delivered the message he intended. She aroused physical passions in him which surpassed any he had previously experienced. Still fresh in his mind was the memory of the deep contentment and fierce possessiveness that had swept over him as they lay together after making love for the first time. He had never felt that way about anyone before. All he could think was that she was finally his. And somehow they would solve this problem of her annoying tendency toward independence and unpredictable actions.

A thump on his back brought him back to the present. Jason was looking at him inquiringly, and Alex realized he had asked a question. He shook his head distractedly and said, "I'm sorry. What did you say?"

"I asked how things went with you and Joanna yesterday."

Alex's lips curved as he remembered again how things had gone. But the whole experience was too recent, too extraordinary to share even with the man he was closer to and trusted more than any other. He answered with deliberate casualness, "Oh, we worked a few things out."

As they left the facility, Jason commented, "Melissa thought she might have to pick up the pieces after you got through with Joanna."

Alex snorted. "Just tell Melissa to mind her own business!"

"I would if I thought it would do any good. She's very protective of Joanna." Jason nodded to a passing acquaintance, then said with barely concealed curiosity. "There's something else I've been meaning to ask you about. I heard an unlikely rumor this morning, but discovered it wasn't a rumor at all. Did you really ask Mark to reduce his man's punishment? What made you change your mind?"

"I didn't. It was changed for me. I had second thoughts about it this morning, but couldn't very well back off a promise," he said in a disgruntled tone.

To Alex's disgust, Jason gave a shout of laughter. "She *made* you promise? I would give a geela to know how she extracted that." He punched Alex's arm lightly. "Then again, maybe it wouldn't take very much of a guess at all."

"Yes, well Melissa was at the root of this particular problem. Just keep that lady of yours under control, Jason." Alex warned, wincing inwardly at his own inability to influence his wife's behavior.

"I'm thinking of issuing a directive to all the unattached males of the Seventh Fleet," Jason mused. "A warning to avoid Earth women, at least until their senior commanding officers have reached some level of understanding of what exactly they're dealing with, and how they should handle it!"

His laughter rang mockingly in Alex's ears long after he had disappeared down a narrow pathway.

WHEN ALEX WALKED into their unit in the early evening, he was surprised and pleased to find Joanna home already. The screen on the information console was filled with Melissa's image. Joanna glanced around and smiled shyly as he passed, the color on her cheeks heightening at his warm look.

He prepared a cup of seeka, then sat down to relax and wait for her to end her conversation. Snatches of their discussion drifted over to him. They were exploring various educational options for the Taragon orphans, and he was relieved to know that today's session appeared to have advanced far enough that methods of implementation were under consideration.

His attention was caught and he looked up when he heard his name mentioned. Melissa had started to grill Joanna about his reaction to the previous day's excursion. Joanna sneaked a look in his direction, saw that he was making no pretense about not eavesdropping, and frowned at Melissa.

"What's the matter?" Melissa asked plaintively. "Oh! I take it you're no longer alone. Well, tell him to go away again so we can talk about him."

"Melissa." Amused, Alex rose to his feet and walked over to stand behind Joanna. "You can talk about me anytime you want, even in front of me if you want to." His brought his hands to rest on Joanna's shoulders and started to massage them lightly. She quivered under his touch sending a surge of satisfaction through him.

"Oh, I know that," Melissa responded airily. "It just isn't as much fun when you're around. I couldn't do as good a job of ripping you to shreds and assassinating your character. Anyway, I've got to go. I've got a date. Talk to you later, Joanna."

Alex came around to lean back on the console as Joanna closed out the screen. He had a faint smile on his face.

"Why are you looking at me like that?" Joanna demanded defensively.

Shrugging, he smiled more broadly and said, "I'm just imagining how you might have responded to her questions, that's all."

Joanna's face glowed and she scowled. She rose to her feet and moved away to stare out the window.

Alex followed. "It sounds like you made some good progress today on the Taragon issue."

"Yes," she sighed and rested her forehead against the cool panel of glass, staring out at the lake. "It actually went far better today than I had dared hope. The whole group came back to the table with the realization that compromises need to be made on all sides if we are to have any success with the project at all. Even the Taragon negotiator indicated, without making any promises, that he might be willing to reconsider his position on adoption outside of Taragon if enough of an assurance is provided that the children's heritage will be preserved. There's a long way to go, but at least we're exploring some ways that might make adoption by other nations more acceptable to the Taragon people."

"Excellent!" He hesitated. She was obviously tired, but he wanted it to be her choice. "Ambassador Soron and his wife are having an informal gathering this evening. Would you like to go?"

He couldn't read the look she gave him, but it was followed by a nod of agreement. Alex felt a sting of disappointment. He had hoped to spend the evening alone with her and continue where they had left off the previous night. Perhaps they could leave early, he thought, as he watched her go off to change her clothes.

Chapter 26

A SMALL GROUP had already gathered by the time Alex and Joanna arrived at the neighboring unit. Kara greeted Joanna warmly and took her off to introduce her. She was acquainted with several people, and only vaguely recalled meeting the others at the Ambassadors' Reception. Some were already helping themselves to an attractive array of food covering a table set up to one side of the room. Kara told her proudly that she had prepared many of the dishes herself and that they were either Liarte or Soron in origin.

Alex was soon back at her side and taking her elbow to direct her over to the food table. They filled their plates and joined another couple to eat. Keeping one ear on the conversation, Joanna glanced curiously around the room.

Its size and configuration were similar to the great room in their unit, but there the likeness ended. The room's furnishings were a stark, unrelenting white, a showcase for the large, bold, brightly colored pieces of art scattered around and on the floor, tables and walls. Each piece was distinctive, with its own unique style and character. Several pieces of furniture, too, seemed very oddly shaped and Joanna wondered at their functionality.

She was suddenly seized with an overwhelming impulse to brighten the bland interior of their unit. She had, up until now, ruthlessly repressed any desire to retrieve more of her belongings from storage, but these peculiar and unwelcome urges had become more frequent lately and certainly stronger. Time after time, she had had to remind herself that, if all went as planned, she would be gone very soon.

She turned her head at the sound of Alex's laughter. His handsome head was cocked attentively as he listened to his companion's story, but his eyes caught and held hers. The heated expression in them turned her insides to liquid and held a promise she couldn't possibly misinterpret. She desperately tried to recall just why it was so important that she leave.

Just then, a small flurry of activity surrounding some late arrivals thankfully provided an excuse to break eye contact with him. Melissa was walking into the room and Joanna stared. She had never seen her friend dressed so simply and elegantly. She had forgone her usual multi-colored apparel, and tonight was wearing a short, plain, body-hugging black dress while her hair was swept back smoothly from her face, and allowed to fall freely down her back.

Melissa looked up, caught her eye and grinned, giving a saucy wave. Joanna smiled back and her curious gaze traveled beyond Melissa to her escort. Her eyes widened with shock. What was her friend doing with Jason? Then Ambassador Soron moved in front of the two, blocking her gaze momentarily. When he stepped aside, she tried to catch Melissa's attention again, but Melissa was looking beyond her, a peculiar expression on her face.

Joanna turned and received another, this time wholly unpleasant, shock. Cerata was bending over Alex's shoulder not quite touching him, although she might as well have been. Her entire posture bespoke a deep intimacy. And from just where, Joanna fumed, a feeling suspiciously close to possessiveness welling inside her, had *she* materialized? And why did her husband have to look like he was enjoying the attention so much? She caught a whiff of a strong, rather overpowering scent and wrinkled her nose. When she focused on Alex again, she saw with disgust that he was watching her closely, an amused expression on his face. His eyebrow lifted slowly in clear challenge and she restrained herself just in time from poking out her tongue.

He rose smoothly to his feet, forcing Cerata to move back, and took four steps to stand directly in front of her. "Cerata," he said, turning slightly in the beautiful Soron's direction, but never taking his eyes off Joanna, "I don't believe you've met my wife, Joanna."

The woman literally oozed to his side. "We haven't been formally introduced." Eyes as cold and gray as the lake mists inspected Joanna thoroughly. "I'm very pleased to make your acquaintance at last. You're very lovely. I can see why Alex made the decision he did." The words and tone were gracious, the smile warm and charming. But the eyes sent their own message, and Joanna didn't mistake it's meaning. Melissa was right. No matter what Alex thought or said, this woman still wanted him and, in Joanna's mind, she was a formidable rival.

A none to gentle nudge in her ribs from Alex reminded her she had yet to respond. She hastily stammered out a polite, stilted greeting, and watched Cerata's lips curl slightly with contempt before she nodded and turned dismissively away. Somehow in doing so, she linked her arm with Alex's and not even his apologetic look as he was borne off could squelch the cold despair welling up inside Joanna.

It was some time later, and several people had already left when she finally caught up with Melissa at the buffet table. Melissa took a bite out of a large tart, and grinned at her. "What happened to the witch?"

"I don't know, and I don't care," Joanna snapped. She was in a foul mood, and desperately wishing she could leave. Cerata and Alex had both disappeared earlier. When she had finally noticed Alex again in the corner of the large room deep in conversation with Ambassador Soron, Cerata was nowhere to be seen.

"My, my. Touchy, aren't we? What was Alex trying to do? Make you best of friends?"

Joanna snorted. "There is something truly sinister and repellent about that woman. I don't understand why men are attracted to that type."

Melissa laughed. "It's because they all have a kinky streak in them."

Joanna sighed and glared at Alex's unsuspecting back. Jason had moved over to join the small group of men. "Speaking of kinky, what are you doing with *him?* I thought the two of you were going to come to blows yesterday."

Melissa's smile could only be described as smug. "A lot's happened since yesterday!" She glanced around the room and nodded to a door leading outside. "Let's see if we can find some privacy."

As they settled themselves in the chairs outside, Melissa filled Joanna in on what had happened between her and Jason after they had left Joanna at her unit. "He's asked me to move in with him," she said dreamily leaning back in her chair and gazing up at the glowing moons.

"And what did you say?" Joanna asked, anticipating the answer. To her knowledge, Melissa's numerous affairs had never resulted in cohabitation with anyone. Her friend's brief reply shocked her.

"I said I would."

"Don't you think it's too soon?"

"Probably! But what the hell. No one's ever ordered me around before. I kind of like it."

Joanna frowned and shook her head in bewilderment. Before she could pursue the subject, Melissa demanded an answer to the question she had posed earlier when Alex's interruption had prevented a response. She followed the demand with a soft admission. "I was worried about you, you know? Was he very angry?"

Joanna considered her reply carefully, before saying noncommittally, "I suppose he was."

"You seem comfortable together this evening. I assume it wasn't too bad? No shouting? Or threats of a penal colony because you didn't obey your lord and master?"

Joanna looked away and let the tranquility of the evening wash over her. She breathed deeply of the mysterious aromas of the night, and savored the soft touch of the breeze on her face. Melissa's questions had opened the deep well of confusion swirling in her. At some point in the last twenty-four hours, the overwhelming urge to escape the marriage partnership had died to a whimper, only to be resurrected full force at the sight of Alex with Cerata. Why hadn't he chosen her? Cerata was obviously in her element in this type of social setting, and would have made a perfect hostess and ambassador's partner. It was also just as obvious the two had shared a special connection.

"Joanna?"

She started at Melissa's sharp tone. "I'm sorry. What did you say?"

"I seem to be sitting here having a conversation with myself. I asked what happened between you and Alex yesterday."

Joanna groaned silently, torn between telling Melissa to mind her own business and confessing everything. The struggle was brief. Melissa would extract all the details sooner or later anyway. "He didn't really shout at all. We strongly disagreed about my ability to make my own decisions, and he decided to exercise his male physical superiority. By the way, did you know about the security bulletins?"

"What security bulletins? Don't change the subject again! What do you mean by male physical superiority?"

"He, um, spanked me. I tried to hit him in retaliation. He kissed me, and...we, um, ended up in bed."

She sneaked a look at Melissa's face and almost laughed out loud. It was a study in outrage, interest and delight.

"Well, damnit, I'm glad you two finally figured out what a bed is for. But what do you mean, he spanked you? He really hit you?"

"He spanked me." She shrugged nonchalantly trying to hide her embarrassment. "It didn't hurt—well, not much, anyway."

"Hmmm. As interesting as that sounds, I think I'll leave that one alone—for now." She leaned forward eagerly. "Tell me about the bed part. I want all—"

She was interrupted as Kara stuck her head through the open door and exclaimed, "There you both are! Everyone else has left. Can I join you or is this a private discussion?"

"Of course," Melissa waved her hand. "We're just talking about men."

"Oh, good! My favorite subject," Kara sighed, easing her bulk down into the seat next to Joanna. "Our three are in there earnestly talking about some completely boring game as if it were the most exciting thing in the whole system. I couldn't take it any more!"

A short while later the laughter and noise they were making drew their respective partners outside. Joanna and Kara were leaning together giggling helplessly at something Melissa was saying. As soon as the men appeared, Melissa fell silent.

Ambassador Soron regarded his wife fondly. "Is this a joke we can share?"

"Oh," she said sitting up carefully. "We were just discussing the cultural event and deciding how everyone was going to participate."

The men glanced at each other, puzzled.

"What cultural event?" Jason asked, shrugging at the brow Alex raised in silent query.

Melissa ignored the question, and waved a hand at Ambassador Soron. "You," she announced, "are going to be playing the neeje. And Joanna was just about to tell us what Alex is especially good at."

Joanna was still trying to contain her laughter. "Well," she said pretending to think hard, "he warbles."

"Warbles?" Ambassador Soron and Jason spoke in unison, looking at Alex in amazement. The promise of revenge was evident in the gaze he turned on Joanna, but before he could counter or defend himself, a giggling Kara demanded to know what Jason could do.

"Jason and I don't know each other very well, yet," Melissa sent a sultry look in Jason's direction. "But what he does *really* well, I don't think he'd be allowed to do in public."

"*Melissa!*"

Melissa continued hurriedly, ignoring the threat in Jason's voice and gathering frown on his face, "But he's got grace and a nice swivel action to his hips. I think we can sign him up for a dance routine."

"Oh, yes. And dress him in one those whatchamacallits, those ah— those things we saw at the Marketplace the other day," Joanna contributed.

"Oh! Oh, yes. Thanks for reminding me. I'd forgotten all about those," Melissa exclaimed with delight. "The blue feathers, I think," she added thoughtfully.

Kara jumped in. "So, now we have a musician, a singer, and a dancer. I'd say we've made a good start."

"And just what are you ladies going to be contributing?" her husband asked.

"We're organizing it. That's enough! We don't have to do anything else. Oooh!" Kara clutched her belly, then grabbed Joanna's hand and held it against the bulge. "Do you feel her?"

"Wow!" Joanna said in awe looking up and catching Alex's eye. A strange expression crossed his face. The baby moved more strongly, causing a visible ripple across Kara's belly.

"What's that little knobby thing I feel?"

"Her hand, her foot, her little bottom. Take your pick." Kara was smug in her contentment.

Alex unfolded his arms and straightened up. "I think it's time for us to go. Thank you both for your hospitality."

"We should leave as well." Jason held out his hand to Melissa. In the activity surrounding the good-byes and promises from Melissa and Joanna to get back together with Kara soon, Melissa suddenly spoke up in a serious tone of voice. "You know, we joked about a cultural event here this evening, but I think we should seriously consider organizing one. Nothing will bring this community together better than something like that if it's done well."

"I agree," Joanna chimed in.

"All right, Kara you're in charge—well, for the next few days anyway." Seriousness gone, Melissa looked pointedly at Kara's now quiet stomach.

Ambassador Soron frowned. "I don't think you should be taking this on just now," he objected to his wife.

"I would love to try it," Kara said, waving a hand dismissively. "I need something more to keep me busy."

As the group moved toward the door still arguing and discussing the concept, Alex's hand closed around Joanna's arm pulling her back.

"We're walking back along the beach," he announced to the rest of the group. They said their good-byes, and turned toward the lake.

JOANNA AND ALEX walked in silence for the few minutes it took them to reach the beach. The sand glowed a lovely, soft iridescent pink in the moonlight.

He took her hand and teased, "Warbling—how did you come up with that one?"

"I heard you when you were dressing the other morning. It was a very nice warble." She giggled softly, her mood still buoyant.

"You women need to learn more respect! I suppose I should be grateful. I came off lightly compared to Jason. I thought he was going strangle Melissa!"

"If they're planning to cohabit, he'd better get used to her outspokenness. Melissa doesn't hold back, but her intent is never malicious."

"Hmmm."

The way back to their unit took longer along the beach, but by mutual and silent consent, they walked slowly.

Still a short distance away from the steps leading into their garden, Alex stopped her and gently but firmly drew Joanna back against his chest, folding his arms across her front. He leaned his chin on the top of her head. "Joanna," he started to speak, and hesitated. "When you said last night that you didn't want to get pregnant, did you mean not at all, or just not right away?"

Imperceptibly, Joanna stiffened at the question and closed her eyes to think about how to respond. The events of the last twenty-four hours had definitely made her life more complicated, and she didn't want to think too far into the future. She was still deeply convinced that the marriage would never work which made having a child with Alex not even a remote possibility. "I-I suppose I always thought I'd have a family some day," she answered and paused, nervous of how he might interpret her next words. "But I'm not ready for that kind of commitment, not now when there's still so much to be done to establish this colony's course. Children need attention and love to thrive, and I believe both parents should be deeply involved in raising them."

She knew that this latter opinion was probably not too far different from his own. He had told her not too long ago that his own parents were devoted to their four children, and the Mariltar culture in general cherished their young and were strongly committed to stable family units. She was more concerned that he might decide he wanted a child immediately. When he didn't respond, but only tightened his arms around her and drew her more closely against him, she wished she could see his face. This subject could have the potential of being yet another area of conflict between them, and she wondered uneasily if she could trust him with preventative measures. Perhaps she should pay a visit to the Medical Quarter and take care of the matter herself. Then she realized with a feeling approaching panic that she had just accepted that their sexual relationship had a future.

A flash of color across the lake caught her eye. Glad for the distraction, she freed an arm and pointed. "Look, Alex. It's that creature we saw the other day."

"It's a gromorion," Alex said idly. "A type of bird with some reptile characteristics. It's one of the few creatures native to Treaine."

With relief, she decided he didn't seem to be harboring any ill feelings about her negative response and allowed herself to relax a little. They following the shimmering, colorful creature's flight across the lake. It dipped and soared in intricate patterns as if it were aware it had an audience, before it disappeared over the forest.

"How does it get through the perimeter?" Joanna asked curiously.

"It's small enough. Much larger, and it would be repelled."

"Oh, what's that?" Joanna was looking in the direction in which the creature had disappeared. A thick, dense black cloud shot with blue and yellow flashes of light appeared to be boiling out of the forest. In a few seconds it had blotted out one of the moons and was advancing rapidly toward them.

Alex straightened hurriedly and tugged at her arm. "Let's go. It's a storm, and it looks like a powerful one."

"Can't we stay and watch for a few minutes? It's so beautiful."

"No!" His tone surprised her with its sharpness. "It's coming too quickly. Come on. Run!"

They joined hands and raced down the beach. Hard, stinging rain hit as they reached the steps to the garden, and they were drenched in the few seconds it took to reach the door. With the door safely closed, they turned to look behind them. The force of the rain was driving plants in the garden against the ground. The downpour was so heavy, it had obscured the view of the lake.

"My God!" Joanna breathed in awe, glad they weren't out in it. She glanced at Alex and smiled at his drenched appearance, and then saw the look on his face change to one of intense sexual awareness as he ran his eyes over her body. Her own thin garments were clinging to her like a second skin.

The next instant, she found herself dragged into his arms. He kissed her passionately and started walking her backwards toward the sleeping chamber.

She tore her mouth away from his long enough to protest, "We're dripping all over. We'll ruin the—"

"I don't care," he said huskily, recapturing her lips. His hands were busy sliding up and down her body, even as they guided her through to the other room.

Once there, he let her go abruptly, and stood back. "Take off your clothes!"

She stared in shock and automatically started to refuse, but the pounding rage of the storm outside encouraged some primitive emotion, and the shivers of excitement he had already generated in her body made her throw caution to the winds. She bent her head so she wouldn't have to look at him, and slowly started removing her tunic, followed by the thin undervest. Her nipples, already sensitized from his touch, tightened and tingled even more as cool air brushed over them. Her excitement rose, knowing that he was closely following her every move.

She kicked off her shoes and pushed down her trousers and underpants together, almost losing her nerve. Completely naked, she forced herself to raise her gaze to his. What she saw in his face, made her catch her breath.

"You're so exquisite, Meira," he said softly and tenderly, reaching out to run his hands down her arms, and then back up along the sides of waist, and still further to cradle and weigh her breasts. She wondered about the meaning of the name he said so gently and was using more frequently, and then forgot about it as he bent and kissed her again.

He pulled back a few seconds later to remove his own clothes and, for the first time, she allowed herself to closely examine his magnificent, naked maleness, wondering at the hard sculpted perfection of his body, marred here and there by faint ridges of scars which even advanced medical technology couldn't erase.

It was a warrior's body. A lover's body. And he was fully erect, pulsing with desire, ready for her. He caught her hands and drew her close, and closer still, until she felt every ridge and hollow of his body pressed against her breasts and belly.

He bent his head and with agonizing slowness explored her face with his lips, before settling on her mouth again. His tongue thrust into her mouth arousing sensations that made her head spin and her knees buckle. She would have fallen, if he hadn't captured her bottom in both hands, holding her tightly against him, rubbing her against his hardness. He backed her up against the bed, and guided her down onto it, careful not to crush her with his weight.

The fury of the storm outside had calmed to a whimper before the raging passion in the room was satiated, and its occupants fell asleep still intimately joined.

Chapter 27

THE FRANTIC PACE slowed in the next few weeks. More colonists arrived, but in fewer numbers, and were easily accommodated as parts of the new city were completed daily.

Joanna's schedule had become lighter. She was arriving home earlier and taking more time off. Alex's, by contrast, had become fuller. A large number of issues, referred to the Ambassadors' Council by negotiating teams and other groups for discussion, resolution or approval had become bottlenecked.

The Taragon project had become a perpetual battle fought in skirmishes. Joanna's team was making progress, but it was a painfully slow process. For every agreement and concession won in their attempt to craft an acceptable adoption program, there were enormous barriers thrown up unexpectedly that had to be torn down, or seemingly impossible bridges that had to be built in order to continue. It remained their most difficult and emotionally draining assignment, and Ambassador Kromon frequently ordered them to set it aside and work on other issues.

The security sweep of the planet had been completed, and no clues had been discovered to shed any light on the incident which had occurred the night of the Ambassador's Reception. Several parties, appropriately escorted, had been allowed to venture beyond the perimeter to explore the spectacular natural beauty Treaine offered.

Melissa had been out several times accompanied by Jason to hike various established trails surrounding the settlement. Alex had reluctantly allowed Joanna to go along on one such occasion, but only after a loud argument which had resulted in her stony silence until, exasperated, he had given in.

Even after he had given his consent, she remained cool toward him for the rest of the evening and had gone off to bed earlier than usual. He was confused and irritated by his own hesitation in allowing her to travel outside the settlement, knowing she would be well protected. But he was unhappy at letting her outside the security of the perimeter when he couldn't be with her, and his own schedule required him to be in a council session for most of the day in question.

The concept of a cultural evening had burgeoned and caught fire.

In fact, the response had been so enthusiastic, that a number of events were now planned, each one to be organized and hosted by the nation or colony who had responsibility for the event. Kara was thus relieved of what had quickly become an enormous task as her husband had foreseen.

The baby arrived precisely on schedule and, two days later, Alex and Joanna went to visit the proud parents and the first child born of the Coalition's Vision. The baby had inherited predominantly Soron physical characteristics, including the six digits on each hand and foot. Only the slight greenish cast to her skin betrayed her Liarte heritage as well.

As Alex watched his wife on her knees in front of Kara exclaiming in wonder and delight over the tiny features of the baby cradled in sleep on her mother's lap, he felt a sharp stab of intense longing. A vision of Joanna holding their own child imprinted itself clearly in his mind.

Alex's and Joanna's lovemaking was different that night, slow and gentle and almost hesitant. Afterwards, as Alex held his sleeping wife and listened to her deep, regular breathing, he reflected on the last few weeks and tried to sort out the feelings he had for the woman he held in his arms. He couldn't recall a time when he had been happier or more contented, except perhaps as a child, before the Conflicts had called him into the duties of manhood, before he had quite left off the last vestiges of childhood.

As busy as his schedule was, he frequently thought about Joanna during the day, and anxiously looked forward to the evening when they were always able to spend a few hours together. He enjoyed the stimulating conversations they shared, and her intense curiosity about everything. She often peppered him with questions about where he had been, what he had seen and what he had done, and he reveled in the role of teacher.

On the other hand, her independent spirit and resistance to accommodating many simple, reasonable requests continued to annoy him, and were the basis for many arguments. But he was learning to compromise, and discovered that some things just weren't that important after all.

More often than not their arguments resulted in passionate lovemaking. Sex between them was wholly fulfilling and extremely pleasurable. In fact, he often felt that he was in a constant state of arousal when he was with her, knowing what they could be doing in a short while.

While she never initiated their lovemaking, she had never refused his advances, except once on the first day of her monthly bleeding. When, on occasion, she put up a token resistance, the barriers fell quickly under his skilled onslaught. He ached to try some of the pleasure enhancing techniques he had learned on his extensive travels, but warned himself to go slowly in the face of her obvious inexperience.

It was at times like this, when she slept and he should have felt the deepest contentment, that the doubts beset him. The niggling suspicion that Joanna hadn't completely accepted her position or was comfortable in her role as his wife intruded on his mind. Like a writhing noil vine, it temporarily smothered his happiness, and left him feeling helpless, because he didn't know what else he could do or how he should deal with it.

Outside of their bed, she never touched him and never demonstrated any sign of affection. Their conversations usually avoided any personal discussions and exploration of their feelings. Once or twice when he had tried to bring up the subject, she had abruptly changed it and, like a coward, he had allowed her to, afraid to force her to discuss her feelings when he wasn't sure of the response.

He had swallowed his disappointment over the fact that she didn't want a child immediately, but allowed himself to be encouraged by her stated intent to some day have a family. Their living unit remained devoid of any personal touches. He kept telling himself that she was busy, and simply didn't have time, but he knew she had containers of personal belongings that remained unopened. Wanting her to make the first move, he hadn't bothered to bring out some of the artifacts he had collected over a number of years.

He sighed and stroked her silky hair, trying to assure himself that his doubts were unwarranted. Time was on their side and they had plenty of it. The vision of Joanna holding their child crossed his mind again and, smiling, he turned his face into her hair breathing deeply of the delicate, fresh scent, and slept.

Chapter 28

SEVERAL DAYS later, Joanna and Melissa were exploring booths in a section of the Marketplace they hadn't previously visited. Melissa's attention had been caught by a display of gaudy jewelry, and she was soon involved in what appeared to be a lengthy haggling process with the vendor over the price of a particularly ornate and garish necklace. Growing restless and bored, Joanna was looking idly around when she noticed some brightly colored fabrics at a narrow entrance opposite the jeweler's booth. Her interest piqued, she wandered over to examine them.

Reaching the entrance to the store, she stared in delight at its interior. The brightly lit room was narrow and long. So long, in fact, she couldn't determine its end from where she stood. Wound around bolts, fabrics in a rainbow of colors and a variety of textures and weights were stacked from floor to ceiling against the walls on either side and piled high down the middle of the room.

Joanna hesitated. She reached out to wistfully finger a fragile gauze, and a wave of intense longing swept over her. It seemed an eternity since she had indulged her creative passions, and the feelings that she had suppressed at Ambassador Soron's gathering weeks earlier suddenly bloomed again even more strongly.

She glanced once more at Melissa who was still loudly occupied. A quick look certainly wouldn't hurt anything and her feet seemed to have a mind of their own anyway. But as she crossed the threshold from the warmth of the open air Marketplace to the cool interior of the store, a faintly panicked voice in her mind urged her back. A chill briefly whispered over the back of her neck. Vaguely concerned, she looked carefully around again.

The booth was deserted. The brightly colored aisles waited serenely, a treasure trove begging for discovery.

Impatiently, she shook her head. Ever since the trip to the meadow, these strange sensations were becoming more frequent. And they occurred at such odd times. It had crossed her mind more than once to tell Alex but, each time she tried to formulate her concerns, they sounded so insubstantial, so bizarre, so crazy in her own mind, she hadn't yet been able to verbalize them. Their relationship was strained and fragile enough as it was and admitting to hallucinations would be too embarrassing.

She reached the end of the aisle and paused in delight in front of a heavy cream-colored brocade. Its rough texture was shot through at irregular intervals with a pale green thread which shimmered and changed shades as the light touched its folds. Humming softly to herself, Joanna fell into pleasurable reverie, imagining how it might look in her living unit.

The sound was faint and barely disturbed her concentration. It came again, more loudly this time, a scuffling accompanied by a tiny whimper. She looked up startled, expecting to see the vendor, but the aisle remained deserted.

"Hello, is anybody there?" Silence greeted her question. The whisper of warning that had been knocking in the back of her mind became a shout. Suddenly, realizing how isolated she was at the far end of the empty store, she moved hurriedly around the corner and bumped into a short, fat little woman coming from the other direction.

"Oh, star prisms!" the woman exclaimed, clutching her hands to a large bosom and falling back. "You gave me such a start. I didn't realize anyone was here. I'm so sorry! I had to go out for a few minutes. How can I help you?"

Relief swept over Joanna in a wave. The sense of threat along with the warning voice in her mind vanished. Even so, all her instincts prompted her to leave the booth. She crushed them ruthlessly. She really had to get a grip on herself. Quickly, before she could change her mind, she explained to the vendor what she wanted. Delighted, and chattering exuberantly, the woman led her over to a nearby shelving unit and pressed a button on the wall. A panel slid silently aside revealing a computer.

"Various dimensions for all the living units of the colony are entered into the data banks," the vendor explained. "Your finger identification is all that's needed to access yours. The computer will lead you through a series of design steps and figure quantity once you've decided what you want to do. Let me know if you need some help."

She disappeared through an opening in the bolts of fabric.

Left to herself again, Joanna stared after the woman, sorely tempted once more to just leave. The sensation of being watched stole over her again but, this time, it was strangely non-threatening. Reassured by the noises she heard coming from the direction in which the vendor had disappeared, she set to work on the computer.

"There you are!"

Melissa's distinctly peeved voice at her shoulder a short while later made her jump. Twisting around to look at her friend, Joanna's eyes were drawn immediately to the chunky necklace over which Melissa had been haggling earlier. The garish piece perfectly coordinated with the fuchsia and burnt orange of Melissa's tunic. Before Joanna had a chance to comment, Melissa scolded, "I wish you'd tell me where you're going. I hate it when you wander off like that. I've been looking all over for you."

"Sorry," Joanna said guiltily. "I just meant to look quickly."

"That's what you always say," Melissa replied with airy exaggeration. She stared over Joanna's shoulder at the computer screen. "Very nice. Are we finally to be treated to a new look at the Mariltar ambassador's residence?"

The screen was filled with a three dimensional image of the great room in Joanna's unit. The heavy brocade she had admired was draped at the windows, softening the blank walls of glass, lending comfort and elegance to the room. She had been experimenting with colors and textures in other parts of the room, and on the furniture.

"No, I'm just playing."

Melissa groaned with exasperation, grabbed Joanna's shoulders and shook her lightly. "When are you going to accept reality? You love your job! You and Alex may not see eye to eye on everything, but then how many marriage partners do? I haven't heard you talk about leaving Treaine in several weeks, and I've given up trying to find a vessel for you. No one is willing to test the power of the Mariltar nation. Anyway, since you and your Mariltar lord have decided to behave like adults and indulge yourselves in the multiple pleasures of the marriage bed, you've been positively glowing. You're a stubborn idiot, Joanna Chase—Mariltar—whatever." She threw up her hands in disgust.

Leaning forward on her elbows, Joanna cupped her face in her hands and stared blindly at the screen. Briefly, she squeezed her eyes shut. Melissa didn't know just how hard she was fighting her feelings for Alex. Because every time she surrendered to his passionate love-making, his warm caresses that drove her wild with wanting, his husky voice that was seduction personified, the cold pit inside her yawned even wider.

It was becoming more and more difficult to avoid stroking the soft hair behind his ears as he worked at the information console in the evening, to resist running her hands over the hard planes of his chest when he emerged damp from his bath in the morning, to not climb onto his lap and curl up in the comfort of his arms at the end of a long, hard day, to keep her hands away from...down there, when they itched to touch and stroke the hard, erect length of him and give him as much pleasure as he gave her.

And he had been remarkably patient, she conceded. Her official duties, thus far, had been light and easily fulfilled. But she was also aware that other ambassadors' wives did far more, and she feared it was only a matter of time before Alex began demanding she play a greater official role. Although today, she realized with surprise, even that thought didn't make her as nervous as it once had. Then again, there were those awful words he had spoken to her the day after the mating ceremony, the words she could never forget and never accept. How could she allow herself to feel so strongly for a man who expected her to share him with other women?

Melissa was right though, she mused. She *would* stay on Treaine for a while longer, not because of Alex, but because she really had become an indispensable part of Ambassador Kromon's negotiating team, and she couldn't in good conscience abandon the group at such a critical stage. She would continue to resist yielding to Alex entirely and, when the opportunity came, she would leave. Even if it broke her heart.

"All right, I'll do it!"

"You will? Well, miracle of miracles!" Melissa rolled her eyes. "Progress! Slow and painful. But progress!"

Joanna laughed and turned her attention to the screen. "What do you think? Do you like this." She changed a color and design. "Or this?" A different shade of the same design appeared.

Absorbed in experimenting, the women barely paid attention to the occasional activity around them. When Joanna finally made a decision and was discussing delivery and installation of the products with the vendor, Melissa wandered away to wait for her.

She wore a puzzled expression on her face when Joanna joined her minutes later.

"What's wrong?"

"I don't know. I heard a peculiar sound, but I don't see anything."

"Well, I'm glad it's not just me that's a candidate for therapy. I heard something too, before you came in. And then I felt as if I was being watched. It was awfully strange."

"It's probably nothing." Melissa shrugged it off. "Ready to go?"

They had almost reached the entrance to the store when Joanna suddenly clutched Melissa's arm. "What was that?"

"What was what?"

"I thought I saw a movement." Joanna was staring at the wall of fabric bolts.

"Joanna! There's nothing there. We're going to be puddles of mindless idiocy in another minute. Let's go!"

As Melissa grabbed her arm to urge her down the aisle, a small whimper made both women freeze.

"There *is* something there."

Joanna glanced to the back to the store. The vendor was nowhere in sight. "Melissa, what are you doing?"

Melissa was pulling out a bolt. Instead of solid wall behind the fabric, they saw a cavity. And in the cavity, a very small, very dirty creature was cowering. It was shivering violently, its face hidden in filthy hands.

"Oh, my God! It's a child." Joanna whispered. She glanced around again, looking for the vendor, but still didn't see her. Looking back at the child, she felt a tremendous surge of compassion and protectiveness at the sight of the pitiful creature. As frightened as it obviously was, it wasn't making any move to disappear into the dark cavity.

"We won't hurt you," she crooned reassuringly, holding out her hand. "Do you want to come out of there?"

"Joanna, don't!" Melissa said sharply. "It could be diseased or dangerous or both. We should tell security."

At her sharp tone, the child curled itself up more tightly and started to whimper.

"Shhh!" Joanna soothed and glared at Melissa. Melissa, a resigned look on her face, raised her hands and backed off. Joanna spoke gently to the child, trying to coax it closer to the opening. She heard Melissa muttering that she thought it would be an extremely good idea to locate a security person, but ignored her. The child was scared enough as it was. A figure of authority would likely make him bolt.

Just as Melissa impatiently announced her intention to contact Jason on her wrist communicator, the creature launched itself through the opening and into Joanna's arms. It burrowed itself tightly against her chest. With it came an overpowering, extremely obnoxious odor.

"Give me your jacket!"

"Excuse me?"

"Give me your jacket. I need it to cover him."

"No, that child is filthy!"

"Melissa!" Joanna hissed angrily.

"Oh, all right." Melissa reluctantly removed her fuchsia and orange striped jacket and spread it over the tattered bundle in Joanna's arms.

"What are you going to do now?"

"*We* are going to take him home, feed him, clean him up and try and find out where he belongs."

"Joanna, you're crazy. I think we need to call in a professional team. Anyway, maybe he belongs here." If Melissa had any hope at all, it must have been quickly crushed as the vendor, walking down the aisle to see why they were still there, caught sight of the child. She backed off, her hands held up in front of her and a look of horror on her face, babbling in a language they didn't understand. The child, made aware of another presence, clutched frantically at Joanna with surprising strength.

"See how scared he is? He comes with us. *Then* we'll decide what to do," Joanna declared firmly.

Melissa rolled her eyes and muttered darkly, "I still think this situation requires professional handling, Joanna. I hope you aren't going to regret this."

"I know," Joanna said softly. "But he seems to trust us. Let's just get him to my unit, and then we'll call in whomever we have to." There was a growing urgency in her to leave this place and, for the life of her, she couldn't explain this strange compulsion to keep the child with her. Her heart was torn with compassion for his plight, but she knew Melissa was right, knew that others were better equipped to help.

"All right!" Melissa sighed. "When we get to your place, I'll get in touch with Jason, and see if he's had any reports of a missing child."

AS THEY MADE their way out of the booth and turned down a narrow deserted alley to avoid the crowded Marketplace, the child, covered from neck to ankle in the wildly colorful jacket, walked meekly between them. And in a shadowed doorway three booths away, a thin figure gathered his robes more closely around himself and watched with pleased satisfaction as the trio disappeared.

It had been so easy. Everyone had played their parts to perfection. He took tremendous enjoyment in these games, didn't care when they didn't always go according to plan because he knew the next time would bring greater challenge, greater pleasure.

And he always won in the end.

But this particular game had been an exquisite ecstasy far more powerful than any sexual release. He had toyed with her, seen her awareness of his presence, although she had never identified him, and laughed at the failure of the mighty Mariltar nation to protect her.

The game wasn't over and an urgency was growing in him to end it.

Very soon, she would be his.

Chapter 29

THEY REACHED Joanna's living unit without incident, and Joanna took the quiet child straight through to the bath chamber, claiming she was unable to tolerate the smell any longer. Melissa had just opened a communication line to Jason, when a high pitched scream suddenly ripped into the room. Fearful for her friend, Melissa tore into the bath chamber and stopped short.

Joanna was kneeling on the floor by the bath tightly holding the squirming child, still clad in most of its tattered garments. Tears were streaming down her face. When she saw Melissa, she shook her head and silently motioned her out of the room.

Unwilling to leave, Melissa mouthed, "What happened?"

Joanna shook her head again and motioned her out of the room even more frantically.

Jason was pacing nervously when she returned to the console. "What is going on?" he barked.

"I don't know, but I think you'd better get here as soon as you can. And bring Alex!"

It wasn't long before the men arrived but, to Melissa, the wait seemed like hours. Banished again from the bath chamber by Joanna, she had stood outside straining her ears to hear the reassuring noises and gentle murmurings from within. Alex looked none to pleased at being summoned out of a council session. Irritably, he demanded an explanation. Melissa launched into a confused description of the morning's events, in the middle of which Joanna came into the room carrying a small shape completely covered up by a towel.

Alex started toward her. "Joanna, what by the balls of Sortor are you—"

At the sound of his voice, the shape twisted sharply in Joanna's arms, the towel fell away from its head and a terrified face was turned toward the small group. As the child caught sight of the newcomers, it started to scream hysterically and frantically clawed at Joanna trying to free itself. Pandemonium erupted. Melissa, Jason and Alex all jumped to help subdue the child. Joanna was shouting to leave them alone and let her deal with it. The child continued to struggle and scream piercingly.

Finally, Jason had it held tightly face down against the floor. Alex rushed off and came back with a small cylinder which he pressed behind the child's ear. Instantly, the struggling ceased, the little body went limp, and Jason released his hold.

Joanna stared with shock at the undernourished, battered, naked child. "Oh my God," she whispered. "What did you do to her?"

"I just put her to sleep," Alex said, clearly irritated at the implication that he might have hurt the child.

As Joanna moved to cover the body and pick it up, Alex stopped her. "You're hurt," he said sharply staring at the blood trickling down her neck from the scratches the child had inflicted.

"It's nothing," she responded absently, putting a hand up to touch her neck and looking at the blood on her fingers with detachment.

"It needs to be dealt with." Without giving her a chance to object, Alex jerked her to her feet and pulled her off toward their sleeping chamber.

"I'll call a doctor," Jason said. "This child is not in good condition."

Melissa nodded, picked up the creature, who weighed hardly anything, and set it down on a nearby couch.

WHEN ALEX AND Joanna emerged a few minutes later, Melissa and Jason were standing over the child quietly discussing it. As Joanna knelt by the couch to examine the sleeping face, Melissa said gently, "Jason hasn't had any reports of missing children, Joanna."

Joanna shook her head in sorrow. "How could anyone abandon a child? Where is she from?"

"Oh, I thought you knew," Melissa said in surprise. "She's from the Merlon nation."

"Ambassador Kromon's world?" It was Joanna's turn to be surprised as she looked at the rough, almost scaly texture of the child's skin, the beautiful delicate features and the tiny pointed ears set well back on the hairless head.

"Yes, their children are all born sexless. When they reach sexual maturity after about fifteen years, they go through a sort of metamorphosis, shedding the skin you see and developing their male or female identity and genitalia."

That would explain her confusion when she had undressed the child, Joanna thought. She had originally believed the child a boy, but lack of obvious sex organs had made her change her mind. She wondered why she hadn't realized before who and what the child was, as now she vaguely remembered seeing one in the company of its parents when she lived in the Neutral Realm.

A soft chime made her start. "Who's that?"

"I called a doctor," Jason reminded her. "The child has obviously been abused and needs to be examined and treated."

Joanna shut her eyes tightly to hold back tears at hearing the confirmation of what she had suspected but hadn't wanted to acknowledge previously. She nodded. Seeing her obvious distress, Alex coaxed her to her feet.

"She'll sleep through the examination. Come wait outside with me."

He led her out into the warmth of the day and down to the beach, where she sat down on the sand, leaning against his chest, and stared blankly out across the water. They were still sitting that way in silence a little while later when Melissa plopped herself down beside them. She looked sideways at Joanna and then into Alex's questioning face and drew a deep breath.

"It's not good, Joanna," she said softly, and proceeded to briefly describe the terrible sexual torment the child had suffered, leaving out the worst of the details the doctor had guessed at from the state of the child's body. Her voice, filled with an agonized sadness, trailed away as Joanna turned her face into Alex's shoulder and wept.

When Joanna had herself under control again, Melissa informed her, "The doctor wants to take her to the Medical Quarter for treatment."

"Oh, no!" Joanna whispered. "Can't she stay with us? She needs someone to hold her and...and care for her. I-I think she trusts me."

"She needs medical attention, Meira. She'll be well taken care of." Alex tipped her face up. His eyes held deep concern.

"No, please," Joanna begged. "Can't we keep her, just for tonight?" Tears threatened in her voice again.

Melissa sighed, rose to her feet, brushed off the sand and, ignoring Alex's frown of disapproval, said, "I'll go see what the doctor says."

Joanna pulled out of Alex's arms to follow her. And in the end, the doctor was powerless against Joanna's and Melissa's combined pleas. He agreed it probably wouldn't hurt to leave the child with Joanna overnight given the bond that seemed to have formed between the two. He left some instructions about nourishment and a fresh supply of the drug Alex had used earlier, then checked the scratches on Joanna's neck.

As he was leaving, he warned Alex and Joanna that the child's behavior might be unpredictable and that she should be sent to the Medical Quarter immediately if she became uncontrollable. Melissa and Jason left not long after to speak with Ambassador Kromon and initiate a search for the child's parents.

Chapter 30

NATURE SEEMED determined to impress that evening. Darkness was preceded by a dazzling display of color and light. A giant invisible hand slashed and swirled every shade of rose and purple imaginable in broad sweeps across the canvas of the sky and threw in bursts of shooting stars for good measure. Out on the lake, a thousand tiny lights danced and sparkled as flower dust swirled in clouds, absorbing the bright glow of the moons.

Beyond a brief look, Joanna ignored the display. When Alex tried to persuade her to come outside and watch, she resisted and remained kneeling beside the couch keeping a vigil. She was rewarded when the eyes finally fluttered open and a shy smile lit the delicate face. The look changed quickly to terror when Alex appeared beside her. The terrible screaming started again, and Joanna quickly grabbed her and held her tightly, rocking back and forth and crooning. When the child finally calmed sufficiently, Joanna looked around for Alex. He was preparing food in the kitchen out of the child's range of vision.

"Why is she so afraid of you?"

"I would guess after what she's been through that her fear might be associated with anyone of the male sex."

The child had tensed at hearing his voice, but Joanna immediately began to talk soothingly again, reassuring her, without knowing if her words were being understood, that no one was going to hurt her.

Alex approached cautiously again, but the screaming didn't resume although the child clutched Joanna tightly and warily watched him. He set a bowl of thinnish liquid down on the table near them. "See if she'll eat."

It seemed the child's hunger was greater than her fear of Alex. She perked up and looked longingly in the direction of the food which was just out of her reach, now ignoring Alex who had retreated a few paces. She did, however, refuse to leave the shelter of Joanna's arms, and Joanna finally took the bowl and spooned the liquid into the eager mouth. Once fed, she snuggled against her benefactress and seemed content to stay there, listening to Joanna hum softly to her and tracing the design on the front of Joanna's dress with her finger.

It was growing late. Joanna was beginning to develop a cramp from sitting for so long in one position with the child's weight, small as it was, in her lap. She looked over to where Alex was busy on the information console about to suggest that they settle the Merlon for the night, when the child suddenly erupted from her lap. Leaving her towel covering behind, she raced to the far corner of the main room and, before Joanna and Alex could guess her intent, squatted and relieved herself. After she was finished, she didn't seem to know what to do with herself, and shrank back into the corner, hiding her face and making no attempt to avoid the mess she had made.

Joanna fought to hide her shock that this small creature had apparently no familiarity or was unused to even the basic conveniences of a civilized world. She snatched up the towel and hurried over to her, wrapping her in it quickly. As she bore her off to the sleeping chamber, her eyes sought Alex's in some embarrassment and silently pleaded with him to understand.

"I'll clean it up," he said roughly, waving her on. "Just take care of her."

Joanna washed the child off again and explained how the various fixtures in the bath chamber worked, hoping that if her words weren't understood her demonstrations would be. Other than the screaming and whimpering, she had yet to hear a recognizable word. She found a shirt of her own which covered the small body from shoulder to toe, and led the now quiet creature into the sleeping chamber.

THE CHILD WAS falling asleep on a bed of blankets and pillows, lulled by the soft sounds of Earth music, when Alex entered the sleeping chamber a short while later. He stood quietly for a few moments, his eyes fixed on the woman bending protectively over the small shape, then went to prepare for bed in the adjoining room.

As he pulled on a pair of thin, loose pants in which to sleep, in deference to the child's presence, he reflected ruefully that he couldn't remember the last time he had worn anything to bed. But then, he seemed to be making a number of adjustments to his behavior and life these days, and not necessarily willingly either. And just what *was* he going to do with his wife, he mused. It seemed she felt this overpowering urge to become personally involved in rescuing every helpless creature that crossed her path. Concerned about the emotional toll on her, he nevertheless felt a surge of pride in her determination and ability to care so deeply.

He was in bed when Joanna finally rose to her feet. She glanced once in his direction, and then walked toward the bathroom rubbing her shoulder, tiredness evident in every slow step. She was in there for so long, he was about to go check on her when she finally emerged wearing a silky, clinging garment that raised his blood pressure a few notches. He saw at once, however, that she had been crying and his heart ached for her.

"Joanna, come here!" The tenderness in his voice was enough to start the tears again, and she closed the remaining distance between them at a run and all but threw herself on the bed. She crawled into his arms, in much the same way the child had done with her.

"Talk about your feelings, Meira. Don't hold them inside," he encouraged her.

He heard her gulp and felt her struggle to control herself, then the words burst forth in an anguished torrent.

"I just can't *believe* how *anyone* can abuse a child like that. She's just a baby, Alex. Those terrible things that were done to her— it...it's s-s-so sick, so perverted."

"I know, I know," he soothed, rubbing her tense shoulders.

"You'll find the person responsible and punish him, won't you?"

He hesitated, amazed at her naive confidence, and then decided to be completely honest with her.

"Joanna, it's probably not just one person who is responsible. There are...places, established when Treaine was purely a trading colony, that are located off the Marketplace and cater to, ah, different kinds of needs. I think she may have escaped from one of those. We've identified and closed down several of the worst ones, but we're not sure we know about all of them."

"Oh, my God," she whispered in horror. "You mean there may be more children like her?"

"I don't know. I hope not." Privately, he thought it would be a miracle if the Merlon child *were* the only one. "Our best chance, obviously, is if she can talk, give details of where she was held and describe her master or mistress." His lips brushed her forehead. "Go to sleep, Meira. We'll talk of this more tomorrow."

HE STOOD IN darkness.

There was no light inside the living unit but, with his eyes closed, he saw the room as if it were lit with the brightness of day. Excitement clutched at him.

It was time.

RISE!

The child stood and groggily wandered from her pallet to the bath chamber. She returned within seconds, a drug pellet clutched in one hand. Moving shakily but quietly, she went to stand beside the warrior who lay unconscious in the deepest phase of sleep. This was where the exquisite challenge, the danger lay. The warrior could wake at any moment.

The child bent. Her hand stretched out.

There was a movement. But it was the woman next to the warrior who sat up. He saw her lips move. He couldn't hear what she said and it didn't matter anyway.

It was too late. He would have to take a chance.

COME TO ME!

The child straightened slowly and turned. The pellet dropped forgotten from her hand and rolled unseen under the bed platform.

COME TO ME!

All his formidable powers were thrown into the silent command. He only wanted one. The other was just a tool, plucked from a horrible fate and easily manipulated, just as the women had been when they had been drawn to that particular section of the Marketplace today. With deep satisfaction, he saw the child all but run to the door. And the woman followed. She never spared a glance for the sleeping warrior.

YES, COME TO ME!

He *would* succeed. His eyes flew open. The child hurtled through the door. The woman ran after her, calling out, begging for her to stop. Within a few more steps, she would be his, and he would have the key to that which he desired above all else.

At first, he didn't recognize the ripple, didn't want to acknowledge it. And then it became a great tide, shattering his concentration, stealing his power, breaking the link.

Through a red haze he saw the warrior appear at the door, saw the woman and child both stop and turn back at his shout. His silent scream of agony and rage absorbed the last of his energy and he sank to the ground defeated.

The bond between the woman and the warrior was far stronger than he had estimated, had been led to believe.

Mariltar would pay even more dearly for making him wait.

"*JOANNA!* WAIT! Come back here."

Even the stern command, delivered in an uncompromising tone, didn't make her pause. She had to get to the child. She was terrified, she could tell. Alex's first shout had stopped them both and broken the strange trance-like state the child appeared to have been in, but now she huddled in misery on the cold ground as an impossibly thick mist rolled out of the shadowed darkness and seemed to devour her.

Joanna dropped to her knees and reached for her. But, caught in the grip of a terror so great, the small creature appeared not to recognize her, and threw her off with superhuman strength. Joanna's head smashed against the wall of the building, rendering her helpless momentarily as a wave of blackness descended.

"*Joanna?*"

She felt Alex's hand touch her face and roused herself to murmur, "I'm all right. The child?"

"She's here. I have to get you both back inside. Can you walk? I don't want to leave you here with this mist coming in. I can barely see the light in the unit as it is."

Joanna rolled her head. It ached unbearably and, as she looked over Alex's shoulder at the dense gray blanket that had suddenly surrounded them, she thought she saw red pinpoints of fire flaring brightly before they faded away.

Alex turned away to pick up the child who struggled briefly before seeming to collapse in his arms. He reached down and wrapped an arm around Joanna's shoulders, supporting her as she stumbled to her feet. Dizziness overwhelmed her, but she gritted her teeth and allowed herself to be led back into the bedchamber.

She watched from the bed as Alex administered enough drug to send the child into a deep sleep. At least her head had stopped spinning and she no longer saw red spots. Alex, nevertheless, insisted on examining her thoroughly and administering the same drug given to the child to relieve the lingering pain and help her sleep.

Early the next morning, to her disgust, Joanna discovered that her husband had no intention of stopping there. He demanded that she take the day off and, when she refused, talked to Ambassador Kromon himself and excused her. Then he packed both her and the curiously subdued child into a land cruiser and took them over to the Medical Quarter, where he waited patiently while she settled the child as best she could, making numerous promises to visit as often as possible.

From there, he took her back to their unit, marched her protesting into their sleeping chamber, stripped off her clothes and commanded her to stay in bed.

Actually, Joanna thought, smiling secretly as a heavy lassitude swiftly overcame her, this didn't feel so bad, especially after only three—three and a half maximum—hours of sleep. It didn't feel so bad either, this time, to have Alex take charge, though his dictatorial manner was a continued irritant and definitely needed to be adjusted....

Chapter 31

NOW WITH two major projects outside of her work schedule, Joanna found her time with her husband in short supply again. Melissa had bullied her into not only participating in the Earth cultural evening, but helping to organize it as well. She was also trying to spend some time each day with the Merlon child.

With intensive treatment, the child was making good progress. After the first few days, she had stopped screaming every time she caught sight of someone of the male gender, and eventually allowed male medical personnel within an arm's length distance of her, although she still wouldn't tolerate any one of them touching her.

Then, one day, she started to talk and, once started, she couldn't seem to stop. Joanna was visiting her the day it happened. Her name was Ariad. She had only vague recollections of another home and people who had been kind to her. But she couldn't describe either place or people. Nor did she know how old she was.

It was the story that poured from her lips as Joanna held her in her lap that horrified and saddened her listeners, prepared as they were for what they thought had happened to her. In a child's language, she described her torment and identified her tormentors. She had lived in an entertainment house that turned out to be one that had recently been shut down by the security team. But it seemed that Ariad had been one of three children kept to satisfy certain tastes. While the story was incomplete, Jason and his team were later able to piece together the missing parts.

When the master of the house became aware that the security team was closing in on his operation, he had tried to eliminate the children, knowing his punishment would be more severe if he were caught with them. With the rest of the occupants in the house in a panic, Ariad had managed somehow to escape. She didn't know what had happened to the other children. She had discovered the tunnels in the fabric booth quite by chance, and had survived for three weeks by stealing food when she could in the quietest hours of the night when activity in the Marketplace slowed.

On the day Joanna had appeared in the booth, she hadn't eaten in two days. Driven by hunger and an immediate and compelling attraction to both women, she had overcome fear and caution and thrown herself on the mercy of complete strangers.

The people running the entertainment house had already been sentenced to a penal colony on the far side of the Crestar System. But when an additional investigation revealed that the other two children had not survived, Alex assured Joanna that their penalty would be the most severe allowed under the terms of the peace accord.

ALEX WAS STARTING to complain that once again Joanna was taking on too much, and he wasn't seeing enough of her. One evening he came home and stopped short just inside the door, amazed at the sight that greeted him. For a moment, he thought had walked into the wrong unit. The entire room had been transformed. The original predominantly beige color scheme had given way to various shades of cream and green, enhanced by different textures and designs. The panel of windows was softened by flowing drapes. The affect was simple, welcoming and elegant.

Elation swept through him. Finally! Another sign that she was beginning to accept the marriage partnership.

As he advanced into the room, taking in all the changes, he noticed Joanna perched precariously on a chair in the corner, stretching to adjust the drape of the material over the window. She was so intent on what she was doing that she hadn't heard him come in. Even as he watched, she struggled to keep her balance. Convinced she was going to fall, he swore under his breath, and leapt across the room to assist her, knocking over a small table in his haste. Startled by the noise, Joanna twisted around and this time did lose her balance. Alex reached her just as she fell.

Cradling her in his arms as he knelt on the floor and assured that she was all right, he started to scold, "What am I going to do with you? Sometimes I think you don't have any sense at all in that beautiful head of yours. You could have been hurt!"

"I was doing perfectly well until you came barging in making all that noise," she snapped back.

Whatever response he might have given was lost as his gaze swept over her heaving chest and bared legs where her skirt had been pulled up to the tops of her thighs. His eyes and pulse at his temple darkened.

Belatedly, she reached to yank her skirt down, but he caught her wrist and bent his head to whisper against her lips, "I like what you've done in here." He deepened the kiss, drawing forth the tiny moan that always excited him unbearably. When he broke off the contact and raised his head slightly, she whispered back, "You don't mind?"

Alex trailed his lips across her cheek to her ear and delicately probed it with his tongue, then gently and slowly nuzzled the sensitive side of her neck. "Not at all," he murmured, as his hands became busy exploring the bared length of her leg.

Joanna made a weak attempt to push his hands away and wriggle out of his grasp. "Alex, stop it! I need to finish this before I leave for rehearsal."

"No you don't. You don't *need* to go rehearsal either. What you *need*—" he said, and trailed his fingers up the inside of her thighs, pushed her clothing aside and probed a sensitive spot, "—is to spend some time with your husband who is feeling very neglected."

He heard her choke back a laugh at the deliberately plaintive note in his voice and set about with fresh determination to convince her that nothing else but him required her attention at that particular moment. Much later, when they were ensconced more comfortably on one of the newly covered couches, Alex asked her idly how Ariad was doing.

"Much better. She improves every day. It's amazing!" She twisted her head around to look at his face. "Did I tell you that Ambassador Kromon and his wife have taken an interest in her and have been visiting her as well? Since Jason hasn't been able to locate her parents, Ambassador Kromon told me this morning that he and his wife are thinking of trying to adopt her."

"That shouldn't be too difficult a process for them. You're all right with that?" Alex was relieved when Joanna nodded. They had once discussed what would happen to the child when she was well enough to leave the Medical Quarter, and Joanna had made it clear that she wanted her if there were no better alternatives. Reluctant to take on a partly grown child, Alex had argued vehemently against the idea, but had known in the end he would give in since it meant so much to his wife.

Just then the information console chimed to life and Melissa's questioning voice filled the room. "Joanna, are you there? If you are, you're late! You're supposed to be here and I need you, damnit. Joanna?"

As Joanna sat up guiltily to respond, Alex covered her mouth with his hand, and pulled her back against his chest. "Go away Melissa! We're busy! Joanna can't make i—" The rest of his words were lost as Joanna freed herself and shoved a pillow in his face. Melissa was forgotten for a moment in the ensuing struggle, which ended with

Joanna pinned underneath Alex, her arms stretched over her head and held in his iron grip. She was giggling, trying to catch her breath.

Before she could summon the words, Melissa said in a distinctly peeved tone, "Oh, *I* get it! Busy, huh? Can't you two *be busy* at a more convenient time? You'd better show up for the next rehearsal, Joanna, or we'll have to have a serious talk about your priorities!"

The console went silent.

The outraged expression on Alex's face made Joanna collapse with helpless laughter, which quickly turned to squeals and then sighs of pleasure as Alex decided she needed to be taught a lesson, and went about it in his own unique way.

Chapter 32

NINE DAYS OF raging weather kept the population of Treaine mostly indoors, except at the Marketplace which was protected by the dome. Having shown its beauty, warmth and tranquility to the new arrivals, it was as if the planet had decided to test their resolve. Howling winds swept down the pathways of the settlement, carrying debris, tearing at vegetation and knocking over those unwary enough to be caught in the strongest gusts. The winds' constant mournful wailing, sounding uncannily like a human lost in the depths of agonizing sorrow, could be heard even through well insulated walls and wore on more than a few nerves. Fierce rains, sometimes mixed with pellets of ice, pounded on roofs. The temperature had dropped dramatically. Thick black cloud cover blotted out light making it difficult to distinguish between night and day.

Except for those who lived and worked under the shelter of the dome, everyone stayed in their own units and tried to continue with their assigned tasks as best they could, communicating through their information consoles. Food and supplies were delivered by unsophisticated robots through small, narrow subterranean tunnels, which connected living units with the Marketplace, and were generally only used for emergencies.

On the third day of the storm, the winds calmed to occasional fitful gusts, although the rain continued to lash the saturated community. Joanna awoke to find Alex fastening up a padded protective suit. Clearly, he was planning on going out despite the directive to remain indoors.

She propped herself up on an elbow to watch as he pulled on boots and gloves. He glanced up to catch her gaze and gave her a smile that sent a current of warmth flowing through her lower belly, and set her heart to pounding a little faster.

"Sorry, I didn't mean to wake you," he said.

"You didn't. Where are you going?" she asked curiously.

"One of the hydroponic towers was damaged yesterday, hit by a slide of earth and trees. It's in danger of falling, and needs to be braced until permanent repairs can be made. I'm going to see if I can help."

"Oh. Can't the construction robots handle it?" The five

hydroponic towers housed most of the settlement's food supply. Built of thick, transparent material, the massive structures rose above the surrounding buildings, separating the old settlement from the new city. The maze of tubes and grids inside supported intensive crop production. Only three of the towers were fully in use as the community had not yet grown to a size to require all five. Still, it would be a disaster if one were lost.

Alex shook his head in answer to her question. "No, the robots aren't very reliable working in these weather conditions. The Ambassadors' Council has asked for volunteers." He strolled over to the bed, leaned over and planted a kiss on her forehead. "It shouldn't take too long. We've had excellent response. The winds are going to pick up again by late afternoon, so it's critical that we're finished by then."

Watching him walk out the room, Joanna suppressed a small shiver of fear. It sounded dangerous. She got little accomplished that day, her mind distracted by worry over Alex and wondering how the rescue effort was going.

She was sipping a freshly brewed cup of tea, and staring out the window when she heard him come in. The winds had started to gust strongly again an hour or so before, and the terrible howling seemed worse than ever, tugging at her nerves, and feeding the fearful mood she couldn't seem to shake. She had to prevent herself from rushing to greet him, but saw with relief that he was all right. With only a brief acknowledgment, he disappeared immediately into the sleeping chamber.

A few minutes later he was back.

"Joanna, I need your help."

She turned in surprise. "What can I do?"

"Come with me." His brief uncommunicative statement sounded impatient. He disappeared again.

Bemused, she followed him into the sleeping chamber. He was standing barefoot by the bed tugging at his saturated clothing with one hand. The other arm hung stiffly by his side.

"Oh, you're hurt!"

He shrugged. "It's nothing. A bruised shoulder. I need to get out of these wet clothes, and treat it with that."

He gestured to some type of medical device lying on the bed. "Will you help?"

"Of course. What do you want me to do?"

"Help me off with my clothes."

Joanna swallowed. "A-all right."

Nervously she moved toward him, and finished unfastening the front of the protective suit. It hadn't protected him that well, she thought distractedly, but as she started to pull it off his uninjured shoulder and he turned slightly to help her, she understood why. The suit had been ripped across the back of his shoulders allowing the rain to enter.

As she started to work on the other arm, she gave a shocked gasp as the extent of his injury became evident. He had suffered a tremendous blow. The skin was unbroken but already discolored, and she guessed by his cautious movements that he was in pain.

"Alex, what happened?" She couldn't keep the tension and concern from her voice.

He raised a questioning eyebrow. "I wasn't paying attention, and got hit by a falling grid."

He seemed disinclined to elaborate, and she said impatiently, "And? How bad is this?"

"My shoulder was dislocated. It's all right. I just spent the last hour in the Medical Quarter undergoing treatment. I should probably have stayed longer but the winds are rising again and I wanted to get home to you. I didn't want to leave you on your own any longer." He gestured again to the equipment on the bed. "This will work just as well."

A warmth bloomed in her chest and gradually spread to her whole body. He had been concerned about *her*, thinking about her when he had been putting himself in harm's way. "Did you save the tower?"

"Yes, it should be all right until the foundation and braces can be permanently repaired. Why are you stopping?"

She had pulled the suit down to his waist. Unsure of what to do next, and disturbed by a growing feeling of intimacy, she had backed off.

"Joanna, I am not going to go about in wet clothes, and I can't do this by myself. I need your help!"

She thought he could have handled that part of it very well on his own but, gritting her teeth, she approached him again and jerked at the fastening that held the suit up around his waist. With a few hard yanks, it was lying around his feet and she held it while he stepped out.

"I can't lie down until I'm dried off." There was a suspicious tremor in his voice, but his face was expressionless when Joanna glanced sharply at him.

"I'll get a towel." She all but ran into the bath chamber, her heart pounding. She took several deep breaths trying to quell the excited trembling of her body. Damn the man and her own reactions! Even though her mind rebelled, her body betrayed her every time! It was getting so she melted into a quivering, helpless puddle whenever he slanted those blue eyes at her.

Unfortunately, he hadn't moved by the she returned and, from the look on his face, obviously expected her continued services. She gently dried off his shoulder and injured arm, but the growing belief that he was using her unnecessarily, caused Joanna to scrub roughly at the rest of his body. She avoided his groin area entirely and averted her eyes, but he made no comment.

He settled himself face down on the bed, then asked her to attach the equipment. She carefully followed his instructions as he walked her through the steps and soon the machine was pulsing against his shoulder. His sigh of relief was a clear indication that the injury was bothering him more than he had admitted to her.

Joanna asked cautiously, "Is there anything else I can do?"

"Mmm. You can rub my back."

It wasn't what she had had in mind, and she hesitated, inclined to refuse. But the thought of what he had been through that day changed her mind, and she settled herself next him and began to run her hands over his back. She enjoyed the silky feel of his skin and the contrasting hardness of his muscles. He mumbled something she didn't hear.

"What did you say?"

"I said, lower please."

She slid her hands lower, to the small of his back, rubbing along the hard plane just above the swell of his buttocks.

"Mmm. That feels good. Lower!"

Joanna paused, then cautiously moved onto the top of his firm buttocks.

"Lower!" His voice came again, deeper and gruffer, and he shifted his hips slightly against the bed.

"Oh!" Joanna sprang to her feet, now convinced that her ministrations were being required for a purpose other than to soothe aching muscles. "Y-you are impossible!" she spluttered.

Unrepentant, Alex turned his head and grinned at her. "That was very, ah, soothing," he said. "Can you do one more thing?"

What now, Joanna wondered. If he asked her to touch him—anywhere—one more time, she would downright refuse. Her emotions were in a turmoil but, truthfully, she would have liked to curl up next to his warm, naked body and continue touching until...She jerked her thoughts back as he asked her to bring him something to eat, and went off gladly to do this latest bidding.

MELISSA GRUMBLED to Joanna two days later that she really hadn't bargained for such a long isolation period with Jason when she had moved in with him. But when Joanna inquired in some alarm if things were all right between them, she responded cheerfully that they were enjoying themselves so thoroughly, it was going to be hard to return to their previous routine.

Fresh from an energetic lovemaking session with Alex, her body still tingling and throbbing, Joanna had to silently agree with that sentiment. The enforced isolation, far from driving them apart with its constant intimacies, had brought them closer together as they discovered common interests, shared thoughts and experiences and realized that they simply enjoyed being in each other's company.

Later that morning, after a conference with her team had been cut short because everyone seemed unusually distracted and found it difficult to focus, Joanna wandered into the great room. She was feeling bored and extremely restless. Alex was at the information console on a non-visual conference with Jason and Mark Oberan as he reviewed some data on the screen. By mutual consent, they had agreed that she would use the slightly less sophisticated console in the sleeping chamber so that he could access a more complete database from the console in the main room.

Alex was exchanging some laughing comments with the two captains when he caught sight of Joanna and abruptly sobered. Too distracted to pay much attention, she meandered through the room fluffing a pillow, tweaking a drape and straightening a table. She came to the panel of glass and stood staring through the gloom at the lake, wishing she could go for a long walk on the beach. Alex had tried to get her to participate in part of his vigorous exercise routine in the morning but, so far, she had resisted, less than enthusiastic about pushing her body so hard.

She could barely see the lake through the sheets of rain coming down, and she wondered idly why the water level never seemed to rise in spite of the unceasing torrential downpour. Alex had assured her the ugly weather was expected to last for only two more days, but the way she felt at the moment, that seemed like an eternity.

Turning around again, her eyes came to rest on her husband sitting at the console still talking with Jason and Mark. He was turned sideways to her, and her gaze skimmed over his bare upper body and down across the loose, thin black pants he was wearing. She found them incredibly sexy.

Her interest suddenly was piqued as an idea formed and a little imp of mischief dared her to act on it. It was time to pay him back for what he had put her through the other day when he had required her to undress him. It seemed safe enough. The conversation with Jason and Mark sounded as if it might continue for a while.

Silently she walked up behind him. He jumped in surprise when she lightly touched his head and gently stroked the hair behind his ears. She must have caused him to miss what Mark was saying because he asked him to repeat it. Even as he continued to talk, he rubbed his head back against her hands encouraging her to continue. She moved her hands onto his shoulders. His injury had healed quickly and he claimed he had no more discomfort. With feather touches she stroked the sleek, hard muscles and, from the tensing of his body, knew she had shocked him. She had never voluntarily tried anything like this before. A wave of excitement rolled down her spine as she debated how far she should go. When her hands slid down the side of his neck and across his chest, pausing to tease his nipples, he groaned out loud.

He was clearly trying desperately to concentrate on the conversation and savor the rising tide of pleasure she was causing at the same time. His breathing had quickened and she could feel his heart pounding under her exploring fingers. If he was wondering what she was going to do next, he didn't have long to anticipate. Having thoroughly explored his chest, she walked her fingers with tantalizing slowness down to the waist of his pants and toyed with the drawstring holding them up. Joanna watched the growing bulge in his lap with delight and fascination. But she had gone too far, and Alex couldn't control himself any longer.

Abruptly he sat up straight causing her hands to fall away. He snapped out a command to Mark to do what he thought best under the circumstances and for them both to report to him the following day, then closed the channel. Joanna warily backed off a few paces, taken by surprise at the sudden end to his conference. He surged to his feet, and turned to face her, the look on his face impossible to misinterpret. Deciding to brazen it out, she turned and started in the direction of the utility area, asking innocently if he would like something to eat.

His response was emphatic and left no doubt that she had aroused the sleeping beast. "Oh no, Meira. *You* are going to finish what you started, and give me a very good reason why I just cut short a conference."

He stalked her across the room, his face filled with determination and desire, ignoring her half-laughing, half-serious protests and excuses, and finally cornered her. He snatched her up, tossed her across his shoulder with ease, and bore her off to their bed, where he did make her finish what she had started to the deep satisfaction of them both.

Chapter 33

TWO DAYS LATER, the angry black clouds disappeared, the howling winds ceased abruptly, the day brought warmth and light and the populace of Treaine ventured out to survey the damage. The settlement and the new construction had held up well despite the horrendous pounding from the elements. The engineers had designed to withstand the worst of the storms in Treaine's recorded history. Broken branches and felled trees littered the area, but the cleanup crews were fast and efficient and, within a day of the storm's passing, very little evidence of it's fury and power remained except for some bedraggled plants.

Joanna was awakened one morning by Alex singing lustily and badly off key as he dressed. Through a fog of growing consciousness, she wondered what was going on since he rarely disturbed her before he left their living unit for the day. She peeked at the time on the computer. It was still a whole hour before she normally got up. She groaned and rolled over on her stomach covering her head with her pillow. She heard Alex chuckle and then the pillow was removed.

"I thought you liked my, ah, warbling. Come on, it's time to get up."

"No, it's not. Go away!"

"Hmmm. I think we need to start with an attitude adjustment." He attacked her ribs and waist, tickling her unmercifully until she was squirming and, between giggles and trying to catch her breath, begging him to stop. He caught her up in his arms and gave her a hard kiss on her mouth, which immediately softened as his tongue started to explore. He smelled clean and fresh from the shower, and she felt her head start to spin, and the familiar warm rush of sensation between her thighs. She folded her arms around his neck and wriggled against him.

He groaned and pushed her back with great reluctance. "No. No time. Next step is to get you dressed."

"Alex, tell me what you're up to. I don't have to go to work this early."

"It's a surprise, and you're not going to work today."

"What?" She stared at him open-mouthed.

He grinned and pushed gently on her chin, closing her mouth. "It's all right. Ambassador Kromon knows."

Joanna frowned, still wary about this change in routine. "So, what are you up to?"

"It's a surprise," he insisted. "Trust me!"

He strode over to the wall housing the storage units, and opened the panel concealing her clothes. Going through them rapidly, he chose comfortable, casual trousers, shirt and light jacket and, apparently surrendering to some compelling male fantasy, a completely impractical gauzy, black undergarment. He dropped them all in a pile on the bed, told her she had fifteen minutes to get ready, and left whistling cheerfully.

What *was* he up to, Joanna thought, picking up the fragile garment and staring at it in puzzlement. She certainly wasn't going to wear *that* under the other clothes he had chosen. Intrigued by this side of Alex she had never seen before, she hopped out of bed and dressed rapidly, pulling on socks and sturdy shoes to go along with the casual outfit. Cosmetics applied sparingly as usual and hair brushed back and caught with combs, she was ready within the time allotment Alex had given her.

It was still dark when they left their unit with Joanna none the wiser about what was happening. Alex steered her in the direction of the Marketplace, keeping up a cheerful monologue about something that had occurred the previous day. Barely listening, Joanna shivered in the predawn chill, and was grateful when he noticed and wrapped an arm around her, hugging her to his side.

The Marketplace was already bustling despite the early hour, and the air was redolent with tantalizing food smells. Joanna was hungry. "Are we going to eat breakfast?" she inquired looking longingly at some of the booths they were passing.

"We certainly are," came the cheerful response. "Here we are!" He stopped in front of a large table where Jason and Melissa were already seated. Melissa was actually cuddled in Jason's lap, her head resting on his shoulder, eyes closed apparently in sleep.

"I see you had more luck with yours than I did with mine," Jason greeted them, grinning.

"Barely." Alex chuckled. "Melissa isn't an early riser either, hmm?"

Melissa slitted her eyes open and glared at him balefully. "Early riser? It's not even the crack of dawn, and it's cold," she grumbled. "*And* I have no idea why I'm up this early. Do *you?*" This last was directed to Joanna.

"Not a clue."

But this was definitely starting to get interesting, Joanna decided. Just then, she caught sight of Ambassador Soron and Kara making their way toward their table and, following close behind them, came Mark Oberan and a woman Joanna had seen him with several times in the Marketplace.

Mark introduced her as Elana Derra, a junior communications officer under Sebastian Asteril's command. Introductions completed, the women were invited to sit down while the men went off to select their breakfast. Ambassador Soron adjusted the carrying pouch which held their sleeping infant snuggled against his chest, and warned his wife, "Just remember, they don't know what we're doing today."

Melissa pounced as soon as the men were out of earshot. "How did you find out what this is all about? And just what are we doing today?"

Kara shrugged, and said smugly, "I just told him I couldn't possibly go somewhere for the whole day with an infant without knowing what to expect. When I started to go through the list of supplies the baby might need, he gave in."

"So." Melissa leaned forward on her forearms and waved her hand. "Continue!"

"No, I gave my word I wouldn't tell you." She paused and looked at the group. "I'm excited though. I've wanted to do this ever since we arrived."

Melissa groaned and dropped her head on her arms. "I can't *stand* this," she wailed.

Joanna laughed and leaned over to pat her back consolingly. "You'll live."

A food server approached their table with a selection of hot beverages. After the women had made their choices, Kara glanced behind them to make sure the men weren't within hearing distance and said, "It really is extraordinary of them to plan something like this, *and* to make it a surprise for us. It must have taken some organization."

"Oh," Joanna exclaimed. A vague recollection of the day she had heard Alex talking with Mark and Jason was surfacing in her memory. She hadn't paid any attention at the time, but she did remember that he seemed to change the subject rather abruptly when he noticed her enter the room.

"What?" Melissa perked up. "*Do* you know something?"

Joanna thought hard, but couldn't remember anything specific and shook her head regretfully. "I think Alex may have been planning something several days ago, but I didn't really hear any details. We'll know soon enough."

The men returned with laden plates. Melissa rolled her eyes at the food Jason set in front of her. "I've lived with the man for two months, and he *still* doesn't know that I hate solid food for breakfast."

"Is she usually this obnoxious in the morning?" Alex asked curiously.

"Yes," Jason said cheerfully. "I usually just ignore her before mid-morning." He patted Melissa's shoulder. "Eat up, my heart. You'll be grateful for it later."

"Well that sounds really promising." Melissa picked up a bread roll and examined it doubtfully. "They're going to starve us the rest of the day."

Mark laughed. "Any other guesses, ladies?"

Chapter 34

THE SKIES WERE beginning to lighten and the mists were rising from the lake when they finished eating. If any of the women had come close to guessing the activity for the day, the men had done a skillful job of denying it. Melissa had eaten everything Jason had carefully selected for her, and was in a considerably better mood. She kept up a steady stream of chatter, amusing the whole group with her dry wit, as they walked back through the Marketplace. Mark directed them down a narrow alleyway between an entertainment house and a food booth, and they came out on the other side to see two land cruisers waiting for them.

The cruisers started off slowly, maneuvering carefully through a busy section of the settlement, past the hydroponic towers where a huge mound of earth and twisted, broken trees, pushed close up against the base of one, gave mute testament to the near disaster. They cruised through part of the new city, where Melissa pointed out a section of living units for Earth colonists to Joanna. Both women had expected to be living there upon their completion until fate had dictated otherwise.

They came to a perimeter gate unfamiliar to Joanna, and were cleared in seconds. Jason set the controls, giving the cruiser to the automatic navigator, and the vehicles entered the forest following an ancient trail hardened and widened by generations of use.

On either side of the trail, the forest growth was heavy, almost impenetrable. Thick vines slithered down massive trunks, and reached grasping claw-like fingers high above the trail. Thriving, despite the lack of light, tall pale fronds raised up like wraiths, in a battle for space with the poisonous, weeping leaves of the swaying calo tree.

Occasionally, a ray of light penetrated the thick canopy high above their heads, but it only added to the eerie, gloomy atmosphere of the forest. It was damp and cold. And over the slight hum of the vehicles, a hissing, whispering sound could be heard of the forest in constant motion even though there was no breeze.

Joanna shivered, and moved closer to Alex, pressing against his warmth. This place was such an incredible contrast to the forest west of the city, which had been filled with color and light.

Suddenly, Melissa gave a shriek making Joanna jump in fright.

Melissa clapped her hands over her mouth, as if surprised by the noise, and turned a wide-eyed gaze on Joanna. "I know where we're going!"

She checked the coordinates Jason had entered into the control panel, and looked back at Joanna. Her face was filled with excitement. "We're going to the ancient city," she said with conviction. "The City of Sarach." She turned to Jason and demanded, "Aren't we?"

Both men were grinning, pleased by her excited reaction. At Jason's nod, Melissa launched herself at him, throwing her arms around his neck and covering his face with kisses. The land cruiser rocked wildly.

"Steady." Jason laughed, disentangling himself to check the controls.

Melissa grinned at Joanna. "My begging must finally have worn him down." She continued enthusiastically, "I've wanted to see this place ever since I heard about Treaine and knew I was coming here. This was the most ancient civilization in the whole of the Crestar System, but there is no known record of what happened to it and why it vanished so abruptly. The records that do exist speak of a race whose technologies were far in advance of others of their time. They were great healers, but the records also indicate they were practitioners of mystical rites. Oh, I wish we knew more. Have any of your men explored the ruins?"

Jason shook his head. "No, we scanned the area when we performed the security sweep, but no one has actually entered it since we've been here. I'm not aware of anyone from the original settlement venturing this far either."

Leaning into Alex's shoulder, Joanna watched the forest flashing by. It seemed to become darker and gloomier the further they went. She had been as interested as Melissa to explore the ancient ruins, and they had spoken of it often, wondering about the mysteries that shrouded the race of people who had once called this planet home. But in contrast to Melissa's mood which became more animated and passionate as she continued to talk about her research on the City of Sarach, Joanna had started to feel a sense of foreboding, as if something dark and infinitely dangerous and monstrous were hovering over her. She tried to shake the feeling off and concentrate on what Melissa was saying, even though she had heard most of it before. But as the forest grew thicker, noisier and murkier, the sense of threat deepened.

"What's the matter, Meira?" Alex spoke softly into her ear. Joanna started and looked at him questioningly. Surely she hadn't betrayed any of her thoughts. The man seemed to be able to read her mind sometimes.

"You're very quiet. You don't seem to be enjoying this as much as I thought you would." Alex stroked the hair at her neck gently and ran his fingers through it. The action was comforting.

Joanna looked away. "No, I'm looking forward to it. This...this forest disturbs me a little, that's all."

"It's not a place I'd choose to come to for spiritual renewal," Alex agreed, "but it has a certain fascination and beauty. We should be there soon."

SENSING AN OBSTACLE ahead, the land cruiser slowed and Jason took the controls to navigate carefully over a fallen tree. A short while later, the path took a sharp turn. Abruptly the forest ended and the vehicles came to a halt. They were in a wide clearing bounded on three sides by forest. Directly in front of them, a massive stone and metal portal rose out of the bare earth and soared into the sky.

Rivaling the trees in height, a center stone column, separating two metal gates, tapered up to a pinnacle and bore intricate carvings of unfamiliar signs and symbols. The walls that stretched away on either side of the gate were also of stone, thick blocks held together with no visible mortar. Each of the solid metal gates bore a simpler symbol of an inverted triangle, with its lower point slightly skewed to the inside. Each triangle was circled by star symbols, which gleamed brightly golden in the morning light.

"My Lord," Melissa breathed. "It's awesome."

She scrambled out of the land cruiser, but paused at Jason's sharp command to wait. He was using the scanning equipment on the vehicle to make a standard security sweep of the area. "Mark, any problems?"

"No. My equipment doesn't show anything unusual."

"All right. Everybody stay together, at least until we see what's inside. Make sure your wrist communicators are functioning properly."

"How do we get through the gates?" Joanna asked Alex.

"I don't know," Alex responded looking at the daunting barrier in front of them. "We may have to find another way."

Talking excitedly, the party started toward the portal. When they were within a short distance, a bright, blinding white light flashed briefly from the mid-point of the center column. Slowly, soundlessly the doors slid open, and disappeared into the stone walls on either side.

Joanna felt as if something cold and damp was crawling across the bare skin of her neck. She shivered violently and reached up to brush it off. There was nothing there. Her breathing became labored, and she began to feel as if she were suffocating. What was the matter with her? She glanced furtively around at the others. Everyone else was behaving normally and arguing good naturedly about which path to take.

The open gates revealed two parallel corridors, which they could see turned sharply after a short distance and went off in opposite directions. At Jason's insistence, the party agreed to stay together and decided to explore the corridor which led to the left first.

The corridor was short, ending in a small, unremarkable, windowless chamber. Large doors were set into the opposite wall and, once again, as if on silent command, they slid open as the party approached.

Framed in the opening was the City of Sarach.

Seemingly perfectly preserved, and breathtaking in its beauty of softly rounded architectural style and warm earthen colors, the city stretched away before them, dropping down from the wide platform on which they now stood to follow the slope and curve of a narrow valley.

It was a spectacular but very eerie sight, Joanna decided. As well preserved as the city appeared to be, it should have been bustling with activity. Instead, silence wandered the pathways and not even a whisper of a breeze stirred the stillness of the shrubbery protecting the base of the platform.

Up on the top of the ridge sloping into the valley, the stone wall offered formidable protection on all sides causing Mark to question what the city was protecting itself from. Something compelled Joanna to turn her head to look behind them and to the right in the direction the second corridor had taken. She gasped and stumbled back in astonishment, bumping into Alex and stepping on his foot.

"Joanna!" He grabbed her shoulders to steady her then followed her gaze.

Like a malignant growth set into the wall of the hillside, a large black box of a building thrust itself out into the valley without visible support from beneath. From where they stood and from the city, it held a position of dominance, its ugliness contrasting strangely with the grace and warmth of the valley's other structures. Its looming darkness presented a vague sense of threat.

"That's where I'm going," Melissa announced. "Come on, Joanna. Let's go see what it is."

She yanked on Joanna's arm and steered her back into the small chamber, ignoring Joanna's obvious reluctance and without waiting to see what anyone else had to say. They were half way through the corridor before Jason and Alex caught up with them. The others had, apparently, decided to explore the city.

The second corridor was very similar to the first, as was the entrance. The door leading from the small chamber, however, slid open to reveal a cavernous room in the shape of a hexagon. Three carved columns were planted in the center of the room, lit mysteriously from underneath.

Also of a smooth, shining black material, five of the room's walls were covered by intricate carvings. The sixth, facing out onto the valley, appeared to have been left plain but, upon closer inspection, was discovered to be a window providing a clear and magnified view of the City of Sarach.

Melissa's delighted exclamations filled the room as she went from wall to wall. She insisted on needing more time when Alex suggested it was time to leave to explore more of the city. Despite her reservations, Joanna offered to stay with her, and the men extracted a promise that they wouldn't leave the room until the rest of the party returned.

MELISSA HAD become engrossed in the carvings running down the wooden columns in the center of the room. Growing bored with staring out the window trying to catch glimpses of the rest of the party, Joanna wandered off to examine more of the room. What had it been used for? Rituals? A meeting room? Some kind of religious ceremony?

She was running her hand over a peculiar design in the center of one wall, when she felt a slight give under her fingers and then a chill draft sweep her shoulders and neck. She turned. A narrow fissure had appeared in the design. She pressed harder and the fissure opened further until it was the width of a narrow door. Joanna glanced back over her shoulder. Melissa was still studying the columns and mumbling to herself as she tried to decipher the meaning of the symbols.

Joanna examined the cavity again and opened her mouth to call to Melissa, but closed it again without making a sound. All of her earlier apprehensions were welling up again. She felt a tugging and, without knowing quite how she got there, found herself inside the opening. As her eyes grew accustomed to the dimness, relieved only by the narrow band of light from the opening, she saw a steep, winding staircase leading down into blackness.

Fear!

It boiled out of the pit and slammed into her with a force that left her breathless.

Her mind screamed at her to get out of there, but some invisible force compelled her to step forward for a better view.

Absolute terror! Dark and smothering, it swelled like an evil, noxious cloud and threatened to overwhelm her, weakening her legs, causing her to stumble, and fall to her knees. Her hands reached out for support and found...nothing!

Fighting a numbing helplessness, she reached deep within herself and found the strength and will to throw her body backwards onto solid ground, where she lay curled tightly in a fetal position. A growing noise was rising from the pit below her and her mind was assailed with a thousand tortured screams. She covered her ears trying to block them out. Vivid images of souls in indescribable agony flashed across her vision, puncturing the darkness.

Vaguely through the screams, she heard her name being shouted. And then she was out in the light, cradled in Alex's strong arms. He was shaking her and speaking urgently, and she realized suddenly that *she* was screaming, and stopped abruptly.

Trembling and exhausted, she turned her face into her husband's shoulder, catching a glimpse as she did so of Melissa's frightened face and Jason's concerned one hovering over her. As Alex continued to soothe her, Jason rose to his feet and crossed the short distance to the opening. Just as he reached it, the door snapped shut with incredible swiftness.

He pulled out his scanner and spent several minutes examining the wall. When he returned to the group, his face wore a troubled expression. Alex raised a questioning brow and Jason handed him the scanner. Alex's forehead creased in puzzlement as he read the survey results. As if anticipating his question, Jason shrugged and said, "I scanned it three times. The readings were the same each time."

"What's the matter?" Melissa asked curiously.

"Malfunctioning equipment, most likely," Jason answered. Then he added with determined cheerfulness, "I, for one, am getting ravenous. It's time to move on to the next stop on our tour, which does include lunch, ladies."

"Oh good!" Melissa jumped up, taking her cue. "They're not going to starve us after all."

The two started out of the room, good-naturedly needling each other. Alex lifted Joanna's chin with a finger and examined her face. Worry dimmed the brilliance of the sapphire eyes. "Do you want to go home? We were planning to go to your meadow for lunch, but we don't have to if you don't feel up to it."

"Oh, no. I'd love to go the meadow. I-I'm fine, Alex. Really!" In fact, she couldn't think of a place she'd rather go just then.

As Alex helped her to her feet, and she brushed herself off, she wondered if she was losing her mind. The room appeared normal and all the violent feelings she had experienced had vanished as if they had never happened, except for the lingering memory and sense of something truly terrible and evil. She glanced back over her shoulder as they left the room. For a moment, she thought she saw the opening in the wall but, when she looked again, the beautifully carved panels were unbroken.

Chapter 35

SERENE AND beautiful under a lavender sky, the meadow basked in
the warmth of mid-day. It appeared untouched by the storm that had
pounded the settlement with so little mercy. Joanna drew a deep breath
and felt her body and mind relax as the tensions and fears of the
morning dissipated. They had finished lunch, a gourmet's delight of
beautifully prepared and presented exotic foods. There had been so
much variety, but Joanna had only sampled a small amount, her
appetite impaired by the events of the morning.

Now she and Kara lay stretched out on a mat playing with the
baby lying between them. Joanna's finger was held firmly in a tiny fist,
and she was teasingly trying to tug it away while she cooed at the little
face lit up with smiles. Kara watched her daughter lovingly as she
squirmed and kicked with excitement under Joanna's attention. Their
husbands sat close by talking quietly, but observing the scene
indulgently. Jason and Melissa had disappeared soon after the meal,
claiming there were parts of the meadow they hadn't explored yet, and
now were nowhere to be seen. Mark and Elana, heads close together
and absorbed in each other, sat some distance away near the waterfall.

Under Joanna's fascinated gaze, the tiny face suddenly split into a
huge yawn, the baby's eyelids drooped and within seconds she was fast
asleep. "Does she always fall asleep so quickly?"

Kara laughed as she gently laid a soft cover over the little body.
"Never at night. This only happens when she's been unusually
stimulated, or when it's inconvenient for her to be sleeping."

Joanna sat up and gently tugged her finger free. The little fist
promptly wound up stuffed in the baby's mouth.

"She's so beautiful. You're so lucky!" she said, a wistful note in
her voice.

Kara fussed with her daughter's cover, then looked up at Joanna.
"Are you planning to have one?" she asked hesitantly.

Intensely aware of Alex sitting within hearing distance, and
realizing he had fallen silent and was probably listening, Joanna didn't
answer immediately as she stared off into the distance. A strangely
peaceful feeling was suffusing her body. Then she turned her face back
to Kara, smiled and said quietly, "Some day, when I'm not so busy and

can spend more time with the child." She astonished herself with her answer. Where had that come from? Was she really thinking in terms of having Alex's child? As she examined her feelings, the certainty grew in her that she did want her husband's child.

Unquestionably.

Desperately.

She also knew something else.

She loved him!

And she could never let him know. It would give him complete power over her.

Joanna turned her head, seeking him, and looked straight into his eyes. She was startled to find him so close. The look on his face caused the now familiar quivering to start in her belly. She couldn't look away.

He held her gaze, his eyes a smoky, dark, passion-filled blue, then rose slowly to his feet and held out his hand. "Let's walk!"

It was a softly spoken command, and she couldn't refuse. Hand in hand and in silence they wandered across the meadow, heading away from where Mark and Elana sat engrossed in each other. It soon became evident to Joanna that Alex had a definite destination in mind. His pace quickened as they approached a stand of thin trees swaying gently in a light breeze. Long tentacle-like branches bore large, silver colored flowers crowned with delicate sprays of black and orange.

As they drew closer, Joanna felt a flutter of nervous anticipation. Alex had a purpose, she knew, and she wasn't sure what to expect. Trying to calm herself, she concentrated on absorbing every detail of the lush growth on the cliff to one side of them. Her glance passed over a jutting razor-edged rock and then came quickly back. A deep shadow, where there shouldn't have been one, creased the foliage behind the rock .

Curious, she tugged on his hand and pointed out the spot. "Can we go look?"

He nodded, appearing resigned to the delay but willing to indulge her. The shadow proved to be a surprise. It was no shadow at all, but a narrow crevice in the cliff face which opened up into an equally narrow tunnel with a glimpse of light at the other end.

Without hesitation, Joanna stepped into the tunnel, anxious to see what was on the other side. She was promptly jerked roughly backwards.

"Ouch!" she complained rubbing her bruised arm and glaring at the cause of it. "What did you do that for?"

Alex shook his head, clearly exasperated. Without apology, he said, "When are you ever going to learn to approach new surroundings with the proper caution. *I'll* go first. After, and only after, I've performed a scan, and it registers negative, *and* given you permission, may you follow."

Childishly, she stuck her tongue out at his retreating back, and then instantly composed her features when he chose that precise moment to turn around and check on her. He quirked an eyebrow at her, but decided to otherwise ignore her gesture, and continued on to the end of the short tunnel. After a few minutes, he called for her to join him.

Joanna exclaimed in delight at the sight that greeted her. A smaller meadow stretched away in front of them, and this one was bounded on all sides by steep cliffs covered with dense plant growth in varying shades of green, brown and gray. Here too, there was a profusion and variety of blooms, but nature's artist had chosen to paint selectively with white and gray and silver creating a magical, mystical feel of an enchanted place. And in the very center of the meadow stood the artist's masterpiece, a tall tree spreading a beautiful canopy of crimson blossoms.

On impulse, Joanna danced a few steps away from Alex and twirled around, hair flying and filled with light, arms lifted in abandon. "Oh, it's so magnificent!"

She saw Alex smile in agreement although he had barely glanced at natural beauty before him. His eyes had remained fixed on her and she saw a curious mixture of worry and desire on his face. He followed her further into the meadow. As they drew closer to it, he pointed and said, "That must be the famed saralin tree. Only a few of them exist on this planet. I've heard they can live to be very old and will flower continuously. Legend has it that they have special healing properties, but only for a fortunate few."

Joanna wondered what he meant by that, but her attention was distracted by a flash of bright colors as a gromorion burst from a clump of bushes, and circled above them uttering sharp, harsh little cries. Finally, as if satisfied with the scolding it had delivered, it performed one last swoop over their heads, and flew over the rise of the cliff.

She laughed in delight as she watched it go. The creature had barely vanished before Joanna felt Alex's fingers on her chin, insistently turning her face toward him. The brief flash of desire she had seen earlier was gone, and worry was strongly evident.

He looked deep into her eyes and asked, "Can you talk about this morning?"

She didn't want to. She wanted to enjoy this magical place, and didn't want to have to think about the ugliness and inexplicable events that had happened earlier. But Alex's face was filled with patience and tenderness and she owed him an explanation.

She found herself whispering, "I don't know what happened, Alex. That forest, that...that *place* terrified me. It just seemed so cold, so—" She looked away and shook her head, struggling for words to describe what had chilled her very soul that morning. "So evil. I didn't want to go through the opening in that panel, but it was as if something—someone—*pushed* me. And I know there was no one else near. Melissa was across the room. I almost fell into that black pit, or whatever it was. There was nothing there. And...and then I heard screaming—awful, awful screaming, and saw such clear images of people in absolute agony. But I knew none of it was real, that it was all happening inside my mind. And I couldn't control it anyway. I was so afraid!"

She looked up at him, needing, wanting his comfort and reassurance, feeling a return of some of the despair and pain she had experienced that morning. "Something terrible happened in that place, Alex. I know it did. Or else I'm losing my mind."

"No, Joanna. You're not losing your mind. You may be more sensitive than the rest of us to the atmosphere of the city. Kara also felt uncomfortable there, and she wasn't even in that building. It may have something to do with what happened to the population of City of Sarach. There is no known record explaining why its people vanished so abruptly."

He hesitated then said with some reluctance, "When Jason went back to examine the opening where we found you, it closed before he could reach it. He couldn't discover how to open it again, and when he scanned the wall, the readings registered solid granite. It was as if the opening never existed, and yet we all saw it, and you were inside it."

He pulled her closer, rubbing his hands up and down her back comfortingly. He continued speaking confidently, "You should know that Jason called for a team to investigate. They're there right now. We'll know soon what happened this morning, and perhaps even solve the mystery of the City of Sarach." He compelled her to look at him again, his expression intense and serious. "Joanna, don't ever, ever be afraid to tell me what you're feeling. If you experience feelings anything like you did this morning, you are to let me know immediately. Understand?" She nodded, avoiding his eyes, feeling somewhat embarrassed by her reactions now that it was all over. He hugged her close and kissed her lightly on her forehead. When she allowed herself to relax against him, his lips moved softly down the side of her face and captured her mouth. Moving slowly and gently until he felt her begin to respond, he nibbled and sucked and suddenly thrust his tongue into her mouth, exploring and tasting. Joanna's knees buckled, and she sagged against him. Without knowing how she got there, she found herself lying on the ground staring up at a hazy lavender sky. Alex was lying next to her, propped up on one elbow. To her disappointment, he had stopped kissing her, but then she saw the look in his eyes.

"No, we can't!" Her voice came out as a squeak.

"Can't what?"

"Can't do *that* here."

He chuckled huskily. "Why not? No one's around."

His finger traced around the shape of one breast. A fastening was released from its binding on her shirt, and then another.

"But someone might come."

Another fastening fell to his determined fingers. "If they do, they'll be polite and go away again."

"Ale—"

Her protest was lost as his mouth covered hers again. When he pulled away, she had lost any desire to resist him. With eyes half closed, she watched as he slowly unfastened the rest of her shirt and then carefully pulled the two sides apart.

"You didn't wear it!" His voice was disappointed.

"Wear what? Oh!"

She remembered the impractical undergarment he had selected so early that morning, and smiled. "I would have been horribly uncomfortable all day in that thing."

"Mmmm." It seemed to be forgotten already as he undid the straps of the plainer undervest she was wearing with tantalizing slowness. Grasping the top of the garment, he pulled it down to her waist. A satisfied expression crossed his face as her breasts bounced free of their confinement.

"You have beautiful breasts, Meira," he murmured, his voice deep and molten with need. She watched as his finger reached out and slowly traced a circle around the edge of the dark pink crest of one breast. He looked fascinated as the soft skin instantly tightened, drawing into her nipple. His tongue moistened his lips. Anticipation filled his face. He leaned over and touched the tip of tongue to the hardened nub, then drew back and looked at her expectantly. A smile filled with promise had her holding her breath as he bent his head again and drew her nipple fully into his mouth, probing with his tongue and sucking hard. She moaned and arched her back, clutching at his shoulders.

After a few minutes, he switched his attention to the other breast. She was beginning to writhe and nudge her body up against him, desperate for more satisfying contact and long past caring about any possible witnesses. Grabbing his hand, she moved it suggestively down her body, stopping short of the juncture of her thighs. She left his hand there, and brought her own back up to wiggle underneath his shirt and tease his nipples.

ALEX REGRETFULLY left the enchantment of her perfectly rounded breasts, and trailed kisses up her chest to lick at the hollow of her throat. At the same time, he moved his hand lower, and pressed hard between her legs through her clothing. She bucked her hips, and squirmed even more frantically.

"Aaalex, please." It was a whispered plea, and he lost his little remaining control. Suddenly impatient, he brought his hand up to make short work of the rest of her clothing.

Pain exploded against the bridge of his nose. He rolled over on his back clutching it, convinced it was broken. Swearing loudly and at length until the pain subsided, he finally turned an annoyed eye on his wife and demanded, "Balls of Sortor, Joanna! What did you do that for?"

"Shhh." She was sitting up absently rubbing her forehead, which seemed to be what had connected with his nose, apparently unaware of the pain she had caused him. For a moment, he forgot his discomfort, distracted by the sight of her breasts swinging free and displayed to their best advantage in natural light.

She turned to him. "Didn't you hear that?"

"Hear what?" he questioned irritably.

"Someone called my name."

Alex sat up and looked around. "Joanna, there's no—"

"Shhhh," she said again. Her brow furrowed, her head bowed, and eyes closed, she stared at the ground in concentration. "I heard it again."

Alex looked hard at his wife, and then carefully around the meadow again. The scene was as tranquil and as undisturbed as when they had first arrived. Frowning he looked back at Joanna, and then reached out to touch her face, wondering if she was becoming delirious and having some sort of a delayed reaction from the events of the morning. The green eyes opened and looked at him in confusion and puzzlement. Then her gaze drifted beyond his shoulder and her eyes widened in amazement.

"Oh my God! Alex, look!" she whispered.

He turned his head. A rush of adrenaline heightened his senses as his warrior instincts warned him of imminent danger.

Beneath the saralin tree, where moments before there had been nothing but a carpet of crimson petals, there now lay a giant shaggy creature. Bluish hair covered its body, except for three fingered almost human-like hands which lay folded and relaxed in front of it. The face was also devoid of hair and had no visible mouth or nose. Only a pair of huge dark eyes, fathomless mesmerizing pools, stared out at them from dead white skin. The head bore a pair of large ears pricked at attention and, sprouting from the points, were long tassels that fell forward partly obscuring the face.

"Alex." Joanna tugged insistently at his arm. "What is it?"

Alex shook his head. "I don't know, Meira."

"I keep hearing my name."

"Just sit quietly for now. Don't move."

The creature hadn't altered its position, but continued to stare in their direction, its eyes unblinking. It didn't *appear* threatening, but Alex had no idea what he was up against. Surreptitiously, he checked the weapon in his belt, then manipulated his wrist communicator and touched the emergency signal. He carefully monitored the creature for any signs of alarm at his actions.

His signal was acknowledged immediately. "Understood. How do we reach you?"

"Follow the west cliff wall south. You'll find a narrow, hidden tunnel behind a jutting rock." Alex mentally berated himself for not checking in with his officers earlier to inform them of his and Joanna's whereabouts. Wrist communicators and scanners would locate their position instantly, but the tunnel was easily missed, and precious time could be lost searching for it.

He took his eyes off the creature long enough to glance over at Joanna to see how she was faring. For once, she had followed his instructions and was sitting still, her clothes still in disarray, her chest bared, with an expression of intense curiosity and concentration on her face. In contrast to her fearful reaction to the morning's events, she seemed to display little concern over this latest development.

"Cover yourself!" he barked harshly, unreasonably irritated by her posture, and sudden lack of modesty in the face of an alien presence.

Startled, she glanced at him then down at herself, and hurriedly pulled her clothes back together. "It's communicating with me," she said softly, awe in her voice.

"What?"

"It's communicating with me," she said again, explaining the look of concentration. "I can hear its voice. It's so beautiful. Can't you hear it? It says it's waited a long time for us." She paused, then said in a puzzled tone, "It wants to convey a warning to me— us," she amended hurriedly.

Alex was skeptical and unconvinced. And he had had enough of the bizarre incidents which seemed to be centered around Joanna today. He started to speak, but paused as her features took on the look of intense concentration again. Then her face relaxed and she laughed delightedly.

Leaning into him, she said, "It says you're too protective, a non-believer. Your warrior instincts are too strong, and you doubt anything that doesn't have a logical explanation. Your mind is a strong barrier. Put those doubts aside, and you'll be able to hear the message as well."

How by the blood of Cor was he supposed to do that when every instinct in his body told him to get his wife out of there? And just what sort of control was this creature exercising over his wife's mind?

Just then his wrist communicator spoke softly, "Alex, we're right behind you. We see it."

The creature gave no appearance of alarm. In fact, it hadn't moved at all but continued to gaze serenely in their direction. A thin blanket of crimson petals now covered its back and head, lending it a slightly comical appearance.

"Do we know what we're dealing with?" Alex demanded.

A rustle of footsteps sounded, and then Mark and Jason were standing protectively on either side of them, although no weapons were yet in evidence.

"Well?" Alex asked impatiently when a short silence had passed and no one had volunteered an explanation.

Mark shook his head. "I'm not sure," he said slowly. "When I was a small child, my great grandmother told me stories and described a creature exactly like this. I always thought it was a child's fantasy until I was working an assignment in the Hrebir System and ran into a traveler who claimed to have briefly glimpsed a creature of the same description. I was intrigued, so I researched it further, and found a number of similar stories and some written records, but nothing that could really be termed hard evidence. The name they're referred to as is Multak. They've never been known to harm anyone. To the contrary, in fact, they're generally considered to be benevolent beings, and seeing one is thought to be a good omen."

The creature's ears twitched and it shook itself in great, slow, gentle motions dislodging some of the crimson petals. It settled back and continued to stare at them.

"A *Multak?*" Alex said incredulously. "I would agree with your first conclusion that it's a mythical creature, a product of fertile imagination. Nothing I've ever heard would lead me to believe that it actually exists."

"Apparently it does," Joanna contradicted quietly.

Jason spoke for the first time. His voice sounded strange. "Why are you so convinced, Joanna?"

"Because it just confirmed that it is what Mark says it is."

"It's communicating with her telepathically," Alex said by way of further explanation, skepticism still heavy in his voice.

"If it is, then we have two compelling characteristics of a Multak," Jason said, his voice tight with suppressed excitement.

"What do you mean, two?"

"My scanner shows there is absolutely nothing, sentient or otherwise, beneath that tree. The legends say that Multaks have no solid form, and only rarely choose to reveal themselves. They know no boundaries and can cross time and space with no need for a physical transport device. It is said they can penetrate any security barrier without being detected."

"It seems we have another student of legends," Alex commented dryly. "Why does my scanner show a definite life form under that tree?"

Jason ignored the question and pointed out, "This may very well be the cause of the attempted perimeter breach, and why we were unsuccessful in determining the cause."

"If so, then why did we know there had been an attempted breach?"

It was Joanna who answered Alex's question. "It was deliberate. The Multak wanted you to impose stronger security precautions and be on greater alert. It sensed extreme danger both from without and within that night."

"What does that mean?" Alex spoke sharply. "We found nothing else out of the ordinary that night."

Joanna shivered at the reply and then said carefully, her voice trembling, "The threat was neutralized because of the security alert. But it's still out there, growing stronger by the day, and will come again. Soon, we'll know its power."

Alex shook his head in disbelief. He was impatient to be done with this bizarre situation, and unwilling to place any credence in the warning of a creature that existed only in myth, even though his eyes told him otherwise. Unfortunately, his officers seemed to think it deserved more attention.

"Joanna." Jason's voice was urgent. "Ask for an explanation!"

Into the stillness of the meadow came a sound as soft as a whisper at first. It grew in volume and strength, until the prophetic words danced and swirled in deep crests and waves, resonating around the group of four.

> *"When fire flies from the golden orb, and the trees of Heribon weep the tears of the dying, then the pathways of the ancient lost souls must be trod, else the life of an unborn shall be forfeit. Strength grows from darkness and despair, agony and grief, conquering fear and evil and nurturing life. A noble and great cause would perish at the hands of a trusted friend, but rise again on the wings of a dawning star with the gift of a respected enemy. The prophecy was born generations ago, the path established, the gift bestowed. Fulfillment cannot be denied."*

As the last of the words faded into an echo, Joanna reluctantly opened her eyes, feeling a deep sense of loss. She had heard the beautiful melodic sounds, been mesmerized by the words, but had not understood the message.

She looked up.

The ground beneath the tree was bare, the creature gone. She sighed with disappointment and turned to Alex.

He took her arm, and said amazement in his voice, "It's gone. It seemed to just fade away." Then more firmly he added, "It's time to go before something else happens. We have enough to investigate from this day's events, I think."

As they walked out of the meadow, cautiously keeping their scanners active, he continued to discuss with Mark and Jason the possible ramifications of the message. It was a riddle, and he ordered it to be thoroughly analyzed as soon as they returned. He also wanted a full report on Multaks to be made available to him immediately.

The rest of the group was anxiously waiting for them, and had a barrage of questions which Joanna gratefully let the others handle. She was feeling strangely relaxed and contented. When she bumped up against Alex by mistake, a shock of sexual awareness ran through her body. It must have reflected in her face as well, because the look he shot back at her made her quiver with excitement.

The next second, he was bending over her, murmuring in her ear, "I haven't forgotten what we were about when we were so rudely interrupted, Meira. And we will finish it as soon as we're alone again."

The firm declaration weakened her knees, and sent heat to her face. As they started down the path on the way back to the vehicles, every fiber of her being tingled with the awareness of his gaze at her back, while wild images of what would come later tortured her mind, try as she might to banish them. She made the mistake of looking back at him at one point, only to find his eyes fixed on the vicinity of her swaying hips. She stumbled at the blatant look of desire on his face.

When he threw his arm out to steady her, she hissed, "Stop looking at me like that!"

"Like what?" His question was posed with innocence, but his confident grin told her he knew exactly what kind of affect he was having on her. She threw him a look of disgust, and quickened her pace to catch up with Melissa who was still grilling Jason excitedly about what had occurred in the meadow.

The respite from Alex was brief. They arrived back at the vehicles, and he touched her more than was necessary as he assisted her into her seat. She squeaked with surprise when she sat down only to discover his arm curved tightly around her waist, his hand brushing against the side of her breast. The glare she sent him only caused him to wiggle his eyebrows fiercely and suggestively as he settled himself beside her. Her own squirmings to avoid his hand were useless. She finally gave up and leaned into him, feeling his breath stir the hair on the top of her head, and desperately wished for the trip to be over.

It was, soon enough. She fled ahead of him to their living unit, as he lingered for a moment to say good-bye to Jason and Melissa, but he caught up with her in the entrance. Before the door had even closed, he hungrily captured her lips and began tearing urgently at her clothes.

The sexual tension that had been building between them most of the afternoon exploded, and her hands just as urgently plucked at his shirt and then at the waist of his breeches. She murmured a protest as he laid her down on the cold, hard surface of the entryway, but he ignored her as he hurriedly shed the rest of his clothes.

The chill of the floor was banished by the warmth of his body and his mouth against her breast. His tongue probed and his lips suckled as he picked up where he had left off earlier that day. Suddenly, his pace slowed, urgency turned to languor as his mouth traveled down over her soft belly. He nuzzled the nest of curls at the apex of her thighs and tugged gently with his lips. Joanna tensed, suspicious of his intent. Her sexual inexperience had not led her this far before, and her thighs refused to part under his insistent hands.

But his mouth continued to work its magic, and a huskily whispered plea put up a strong offense against her resistance. "Joanna, open your legs. Please. Let me..."

Heat and unbearable pleasure raced through her as his tongue found the sensitive, throbbing core of sensation. With vague awareness, she knew her muscles and will had failed her, and she felt him spreading her legs more widely apart, then wider still. She didn't care any longer. She was past thinking about anything but the mounting intensity of the sensations he was causing. His tongue stroked the sensitive flesh, and his lips nibbled at the plump folds, sending her into a squirming frenzy. She felt his fingers exploring and finally thrusting into her, and she screamed with the violent climax which shook and shuddered through her body.

Her muscles were still spasming when he pulled himself over her and hung poised at her entrance.

"Look at me, Meira." The demand was said softly against her parted mouth followed by the touch of his lips, and she tasted her own essence. Still feeling deep ripples of pleasure and anticipating, needing him inside her, she opened her eyes reluctantly, hesitant to expose her deepest feelings. For a moment, she gazed at him blindly, before allowing her lids to sink closed again.

He pushed against her, beginning the journey inside, and his voice came more insistently, "Meira, look at me."

This time when her eyes opened, he held her face between his hands and his eyes mesmerized her with their smoky passion. With infinite slowness, he pushed into her, filling and stretching her until he was completely sheathed in her body.

Then his control broke, and he pulled back to plunge again and again, fast and hard, stroke upon stroke building to a crest and causing her to cry out as she peaked again, before he achieved his own explosive release.

He collapsed against her, nuzzling her neck and holding most of the weight of his body off her with his arms. "You've cast a spell over me, Meira," he complained. "I can't get enough of you."

Joanna smiled uncertainly at his accusing but tender tone, wondering at truth of it. She became aware of her position and their location and wriggled uncomfortably beneath him. "Ouch, I think my back's broken."

He lifted his head and grinned at her. "I have a cure for that."

Without further ado, he scooped her up into his arms and carried her off to deposit her in the bath. After starting the water, he left without explanation. Joanna watched disappointed and feeling somewhat abandoned, but he returned moments later. This time, she didn't look away as he crossed the room, entirely comfortable in his nakedness. She examined his body minutely, her eyes lingering with fascination and interest on his manhood, and then was jerked back to awareness when she realized he had come to a stop by the bath and was waiting. She blushed and looked away. The water moved around her as he slid in beside her. Her chin was grasped in his strong fingers and her face was turned toward him.

"Joanna, you can look as long and as much as you like. Don't ever be embarrassed by your passions. I relish whatever you want to do to me and with me."

He gave her a hard kiss, then turned her around and grunted. She felt the soft touch of his lips along her spine. "You're going to have bruises, Meira. I'm sorry." He pushed her forward until her head was pillowed on her arms on the side of the bath, and gently rubbed up and down her back until her muscles relaxed. Then he pulled her onto his lap. She sighed in contentment and leaned her head into his neck, suddenly tired. It had been an amazing day, she reflected and there were parts she would just as soon forget about.

Her thoughts drifted, until a nudge from Alex brought her back to the present.

His amused voice sounded above her head. "Are you falling asleep on me? Bedtime for you, young woman."

In short order, he had her out of the bath, dried off and tucked into bed. She refused any food, claiming she was too tired to eat and was still full from lunch. His putting her to bed was getting to be a habit, she thought drowsily as she snuggled into the pillow, but one to which she had no immediate objections.

Her last thought before sleep claimed her was of a dead white face surrounded by a shag of bluish hair. And, even though the face had no mouth, it seemed to smile.

Chapter 36

SHE WAS LATE.

Horribly late!

And Melissa was going to kill her! She had missed other rehearsals recently, and had promised on pain of death to attend this one since the Earth colonists' scheduled cultural evening was only two days away. But the last major piece of the Taragon project had finally fallen into place today, and she had spent the last few hours hammering out the minute details with two other senior negotiators so they could present a completed proposal for the Ambassadors' Council tomorrow.

She had contacted Melissa earlier to let her know she wouldn't be on time, but the hours had flown as the team had become absorbed in the final details, determined to reach closure, and she hadn't realized just how late it had grown.

She hurried down a short flight of steps leading into the Marketplace. She had never been out this late on her own before, and a twinge of uneasiness hit her as she remembered Alex's warning and demand that she have an escort after dark.

But the Marketplace was bustling with activity as usual. Nothing could possibly happen to her with so many people around, she reassured herself. Besides, she thought she glimpsed the dull but distinctive uniforms of Mariltar security several booths away.

Unexpectedly, the strange words of the Multak, spoken so many weeks ago, swept with startling clarity and perfect recall through her mind. Despite an exhaustive investigation and intense computer analysis, the message the creature had delivered remained enigmatic and apparently without foundation.

Alex had all but shrugged that bizarre incident off. Her warrior husband, well-traveled and well-acquainted with unusual and unexplained phenomenon, had been unable to reach a satisfactory conclusion about the creature or its message and, therefore, had chosen to largely ignore it. Or, at least, had seemed to. Yet Melissa had complained loudly only yesterday that security was unreasonably tight and, once again, rigorous procedures were back in place for expeditions outside of the perimeter.

As Joanna continued weaving her way through the busy

Marketplace, enticing food smells assailed her nostrils and made her mouth water. She remembered that she hadn't eaten since the early morning. Now she was starving and feeling slightly queasy because of it. She glanced longingly at the food booths she was passing, but she simply didn't have the time to stop for something to eat.

A narrow alley between two booths caught her attention. If she took that path, it would cut about five minutes off her walk to the rehearsal hall. She hesitated. It was dark and quiet in contrast to the well lit, busy Marketplace. But she would be through it in no time, she thought.

Several steps into the narrow alley, she knew she had made a terrible mistake.

It was too late.

The same choking, smothering sensation of foulness and terror she had experienced once before rushed upon her, surrounded her, pressed her helplessly into the ground. She opened her mouth to scream, but heard no sound. The biting needle of pain on her neck, just under her ear, felt like the sting of an insect, only she knew with utter despair it wasn't. She felt her communicator being dragged roughly from her wrist and heard the sharp crack as it was smashed against the wall above her.

Just before darkness claimed her, she thought sorrowfully that Alex was going to be really angry with her this time.

ALEX PACED THE main room of their living unit restlessly.

Where was she?

Rehearsals should have ended some time ago. He would be glad when this business was over. All of it! He had had little enough time with her recently. She was his wife, and he wanted her with him performing the appropriate duties of her rank and position, not to mention the more intimate duties of being his wife. He didn't want to have to be fit into her busy schedule. She had missed two official functions in the last month because of the Taragon project and, when she wasn't working on that, she was involved with these blasted rehearsals.

They hadn't made love in a week because she was too tired and had been feeling slightly unwell. But still she refused to take the time to visit the Medical Quarter.

By the balls of Sortor, things were going to change, Alex vowed. He had been remarkably patient and indulgent, but he had had enough! With the Taragon project almost ready for implementation, and Earth's cultural evening only several days away, it was an appropriate time to put some stricter parameters on his wife's schedule. She wasn't going to like it, but he almost relished the coming confrontation and the opportunity to express the frustrations that had been building recently. A twinge of misgiving disturbed his well-ordered thought process as he thought of how stubborn and very independent she could be, but he shook it off impatiently.

Where was she?

He wandered over to the glass panels for what seemed like the hundredth time that evening to stare out at the water. Absently, he noted that the largest moon glowed a soft yellow color in the deep purple of the night sky and was ringed by a halo of dancing red light.

"*When fire flies from the golden orb...*"

Where had he heard that? He pushed the thought aside impatiently and glanced at the computer display again. His patience snapped. That was it! No matter what her reaction was, he was ordering her home immediately. He signaled her on his wrist communicator and frowned when he didn't receive a response. Glancing at the display, he saw that the signal hadn't been completed, which meant that her communicator was turned off or she wasn't wearing it. Anger rushed through him, the strength of it surprising him. No one had ever taken him to the heights and lows of emotion like she did.

He strode over to the console and opened a communication line to the rehearsal hall. There was no response. A spasm of concern wormed its way into the anger. Hurriedly, he entered the code for Jason's living unit. Jason responded immediately.

"Jason, is Melissa home yet?"

"Yes," he sounded surprised at the question. "She just walked in the door."

"Is Joanna with her?"

"No. Just a moment." Jason turned away. Alex heard muffled voices, and then Melissa's concerned face appeared on the screen.

"I haven't seen her today, Alex. She was supposed to come to rehearsal. In fact, she promised she would, but she never made it. She sent a message earlier to let me know she was wrapping up some details for the Taragon project, and she probably just got tied up. Have you tried her work station?"

Fear had stabbed through him at Melissa's initial words, but it quickly abated at her question. Of course she was at her office.

"No, I haven't yet because I thought she was with you. I'll try there immediately. Sorry to have disturbed you."

Jason's face reappeared on the screen. "I'll stand by until you reach her, Alex. She'll need an escort."

His voice sounded a little tense although his features were composed. Alex opened another line without bothering to reply. He planned to go get her himself.

There was no response. He entered an urgent signal into the transmission. Still, there was no response. And all of a sudden the fear was back.

Fear for Joanna. Something was dreadfully wrong and a wave of unfamiliar helplessness swept over him.

"She's not responding." His voice surprised him with its calmness, when he felt like he was shattering into a thousand pieces with fear. It was an alien emotion and one he didn't quite know how to deal with.

Through the numbness that descended upon him, he heard Jason tell him something he already knew. "Her communicator's dead. I'll pull in a team to trace her movements. Do you want to meet me at the Control Center or wait there?"

Alex feared he would go crazy waiting alone in the living unit he shared with Joanna and said curtly, "I'm coming to the Control Center."

"I'll send an escort for you."

"Why? Blood of Cor, let's not overreact here." He was utterly astounded. What had gotten into Jason?

"Look at the moon, Alex. It appears exactly as the prophecy described, yellow with a ring of fire. There is no record of such a phenomenon in Treaine's recorded history. It may be coincidental but, under the circumstances and until we know what we're dealing with, I think an escort is necessary. It *is* my prerogative to make that decision. Don't make things more complicated than they already are, Alex. Wait for the escort!"

Swearing viciously, Alex reluctantly agreed. The fragment of memory that had teased him now writhed insistently, prompted by Jason's words. Alex resumed his restless pacing of the floor frantically trying to remember the rest of the prophecy, angry with himself for being distracted by it. There were more compelling explanations for Joanna's disappearance than meaningless words uttered by an overgrown non-sentient being.

Eventually, he found himself staring, once again, out the glass panels at the fiery moon. And, with shattering clarity, he remembered the still unexplained events that had led up to that strange encounter and Joanna's moments of uncontrollable panic. Cold terror, deep and numbing, and unlike anything he had ever felt before, rushed through him momentarily paralyzing thought and motion.

Was it coincidence that Joanna had disappeared on a night when the largest moon had turned to fire, or was she involved and a part somehow of the Multak's prophecy? And why hadn't they been able to unravel its mystery? And did any of this have anything to do with the as yet unfounded rumors of a Soron conspiracy to destroy the peace accord?

His chaotic thoughts were interrupted by the arrival of his escort. When he arrived at the Control Center, it was jumping with noise and activity. Sympathetic glances were directed his way, but everyone busily continued with their tasks and avoided meeting his eyes. Jason motioned him through immediately to the private briefing chamber. Inside the room, he stopped short in surprise when a white-faced Melissa rose to greet him. The Control Center had restricted access for security team members only, but Jason had obviously thought it necessary to make an exception.

For a brief moment, he forgot his own concerns at the sight of her drawn face. Wordlessly, she walked over to him and hugged him, and he sensed how close she was to losing control. He patted her back awkwardly, and found himself saying with conviction, "We *will* find her. You must not doubt that."

Yes, he thought bleakly. He had no doubt that his elite warrior force *would* find her. But what would she have suffered in the meantime? He shook himself mentally. He was becoming more convinced with each passing moment that she was in mortal danger. His sense of urgency was accelerating rapidly.

Jason pushed the control to close the door and the noise from the other room was shut out. He immediately launched into a report of what they had determined thus far. "We've traced her as far as the Marketplace, Alex. She left her office about an hour before you contacted us. She was alone and on her way to the rehearsal hall according to her two team members. Several people have placed her at the Marketplace also heading in the direction of the hall but that's where her trail disappears. The Marketplace was the last location in which she was seen. I have investigators out scouring the area, looking for traces, talking to people, scanning the entertainment houses and booths. She hasn't passed through the perimeter, we do know that much. So she's still in the settlement somewhere."

He nodded in the direction of the glass wall enclosing one side of the room. "You've seen the moon?"

"Of course. You mentioned that before. Do you really think it has significance? I prefer we deal in known facts rather than in the indecipherable babble of a mythical creature."

"I certainly don't think we should discount it. Sebastian is gathering a team composed of representatives from all the nations and any appropriate disciplines from the general population. We have to make another effort to decipher the Multak's meaning. I've also sent Mark and a couple of his men to the meadow to look for the creature. Is there anything you can think of that might help us, anything unusual that's happened, her attitude, what she's been doing recently, with whom she's been associating?"

Stuffing his hands into his pockets, Alex wandered over to the glass wall. He stared blindly out at the waters of the lake, barely noticing that the reflected red and yellow lights of the moon above made the lake itself appear to be on fire. He felt so helpless! He functioned at his best under intense pressure, as he had proven time and time again. But now, when he needed them most, all his skills, all his experience failed him. All he could think of was Joanna. Where was she? What was she going through?

"Alex?" Jason spoke sharply, reminding him that a response was required.

He ran his hands in frustration through his dark hair, and shook his head. "Nothing, there's nothing. She was spending most of her time on the Taragon project and going to those blasted rehearsals when she could. She didn't have time for anything else."

Including him.

He added as an afterthought, "She seemed particularly tired the last few days, and complained of not feeling very well. Maybe she went to the Medical Quarter?"

A spark of hope had lightened his voice, but was quickly dashed when Jason replied, "No, it was one of the first places we checked."

Jason was standing at the console scrolling through the reports, now coming in rapidly. Alex moved over to stand beside him. Every report was negative. Joanna had vanished without a trace.

Melissa was becoming more and more agitated. Unable to sit quietly any longer, she jumped up and began pacing, smacking her hands together unconsciously. Distracted by her behavior, Alex gave an impatient exclamation and swung around from the console. "*Melissa*. If you can't sit quietly, you're going to have to leave. You're—" The words died on his lips at the sight of her distraught face. This was more than anxiety over a missing friend. Melissa knew something.

She gave him a haunted look and burst out, "Have any vessels left Treaine this evening?"

Her question startled both men. Jason responded automatically, "Two, why?"

"Why aren't you communicating with them?"

Jason shook his head puzzled. "Why would we? Joanna's disappearance doesn't concern them. The gate scans are proof that she didn't pass through the perimeter."

"Is it possible she could have left another way?"

Jason and Alex glanced at each other. "What are you getting at, Melissa?" Alex asked roughly, urgently.

She avoided his eyes, and turned her head away, twisting her fingers together.

"Melissa!" His voice held warning and impatience.

She glanced at him quickly, and then at Jason as if for assistance. None was forthcoming. "I don't want to tell you this," she whispered, "because it probably has nothing to do with Joanna's disappearance."

In an instant, Alex was in front of her, grabbing her arms hard enough to hurt. "If there's the smallest chance it does, you have to tell us." He was impatient, wondering how she could possibly withhold information under the circumstances. Her next words made him wish she had.

"She...she never really accepted the terms of your marriage partnership," Melissa said softly, so softly, he had to strain to hear. "In the beginning, she talked of leaving, of going back to the Neutral Realm. She wanted me to help her find transport. I never did," she said hastily, "because she seemed to be settling in all right, and you and she became closer. She hadn't talked about it for a long time, but Joanna can be stubborn and something might have happened to— I just thought I should mention it—but it probably has nothing to do with her disappearance. Forget it!" she finished miserably.

Alex was paralyzed by her words. All warmth and emotion drained out of him. His face felt like it was carved in ice. A laserray had sliced his heart in two and left it shredded, bleeding and exposed. His confidence that Joanna had finally accepted the marriage partnership and the trust that had built up over the last few months crumbled away to nothing. A few months ago, he would have shrugged Melissa's words off with anger and gone about finding and retrieving what was his. And then he would have taken steps to ensure that he never lost it again. But Joanna had crept into his heart, had become a part of his very soul. The depth of emotion he felt for her was beyond his ability to describe. He had never felt this way about anyone before and knew he never would again. If she died, the rest of his life would be meaningless and, if she left him, he would become an empty shell without purpose.

Vaguely, he was aware of Jason snapping out a demand for a recheck of the gate scanners and, because there was an infinitesimally small possibility she could have circumvented the perimeter, ordering the two departed vessels, under a provision of the peace accord, to return to Treaine's dock.

Melissa had sunk back into her chair. Under Alex's cold and emotionless stare, she shivered and curled tightly into herself, as if trying to make herself as inconspicuous as possible. A crack opened in the protective barrier he had thrown up. It wasn't her fault, after all. He had demanded she tell what she knew, but still he couldn't bring himself to reassure her. The crack was widening, and he knew a storm was waiting on the other side. Waiting to sweep him away. And when it burst through, he wasn't sure he would survive.

Tense and deathly still, Alex forced his eyes away from Melissa to stare out at the lake, struggling to suppress his betrayed emotions and raw pain. Physical wounds had never brought the agony he was experiencing now. When he thought he had himself sufficiently under control, he turned, and the mantle of authority which had been lacking earlier, was once again upon him. He had become the cool-headed decision maker, the supreme leader of an elite corps of warriors. Ignoring Melissa, he strode over to join Jason and together they began exploring and rejecting an endless number of strategies. Additional investigations were launched and countless orders given.

Security officers came and went. The night wore on. The halo of fire around the yellow moon flared strongly and brightly, and then abruptly disappeared leaving behind a landscape bathed in cold mists and fearful secrets.

The first vessel returned and was searched, its records and port system examined minutely. Within an hour, it had been released. Melissa had fallen into an exhausted and restless sleep by the time the second vessel arrived and was searched. The results were equally unrewarding. Jason rose tiredly to his feet and rolled his shoulders to work the kinks out. He walked over and paused by Melissa's chair. Crouching down, he moved her arm to a more comfortable position, and then rested his head briefly on her lap. Watching, Alex felt a wave of unbearable longing crash through him, followed by pure helplessness and a growing rage against the whoever or whatever had caused Joanna's disappearance. Because deep inside, despite Melissa's words that had opened up the well of grief, he knew that Joanna had not left of her own free will.

"Alex, go home and get some rest! Everything's being done that can be done. We're going to find her." Jason stood in front of him, calmly reassuring, filled with determination and energy, which belied the tiredness lining his face.

After a fruitless night of searching, Alex wasn't sure how strongly he believed that any more, but couldn't have accepted anything less at that particular moment.

Chapter 37

SHE WAS FLOATING, lighter than a feather on an errant breeze. It was a wonderfully pleasant sensation being cradled in this pillow of air and rocked gently back and forth. As her mind slowly returned to consciousness, she tried to resist, wanting to remain in the warm and comforting cocoon, wanting the moment to last. Her eyelids reluctantly fluttered open.

Deep, stygian blackness surrounded her. She could see nothing. The floating sensation persisted. She could feel no support underneath her. Tentatively she tried to move her arms. It took tremendous effort.

Panic started to thread its way through her mind, destroying the contentment she had felt moments before. She must still be sleeping, she thought, still be in the grip of a dream which was rapidly becoming a nightmare. She pinched herself, the effort exhausting her. The pain was real. This was no dream!

She thrust out with her arms and legs, desperate to feel something solid. The sensation was akin to moving through a very dense liquid substance. The warmth she had felt upon waking was rapidly dissipating. Icy coldness pressed in close around her. Desperation grew with fear.

Her eyes frantically searched the darkness, seeking the faintest indication of light. Like a suffocating blanket, silence enfolded her, all the more terrifying because she couldn't hear herself take a breath, couldn't hear her own body's movements.

Slowly, memory returned. She remembered wrapping up the last few details of the Taragon project, and hurrying to keep her commitment to Melissa. She remembered turning into the narrow alley in the Marketplace to save a few minutes of time, and she remembered with utter clarity the helpless feeling of dread when she realized she had made a mistake.

Panic surged through her again. Powerless to fight it, she opened her mouth to scream.

"Helllp meeee."

The words were clear and loud in her mind, driven by her will. If any sound issued from her mouth, it was immediately absorbed into the surrounding blackness, destined never to be heard.

But warmth was returning, and Joanna allowed herself to be seduced by its comfort and drawn back into oblivion.

THE NEXT TIME she awoke, a thin shaft of yellow light pierced the darkness some distance away. It hurt her eyes and it took several seconds for her to adjust to the brightness. This time she lay on solid ground. It was cold against her back. Her body ached unbearably, but she found she could move normally. The light illuminated several containers, but did little to relieve the blackness beyond.

Slowly, painfully, Joanna pushed herself up on her knees, and then stumbled to her feet. Her tongue was thick in her mouth craving moisture, her bladder painfully full. Hardly daring to hope, she moved in the direction of the light. The tip of her shoe caught a loose, unseen object on the ground, and sent it clattering over the floor. The noise it made was frighteningly loud and echoed in the silence.

She moved into the column of light and peered into the containers. One small, brightly colored bowl contained water, another several hard squares of a food substance and yet another a reddish colored mush. The last and largest container was empty.

The water was gulped down quickly taking the edge off but not quenching her thirst completely. She tentatively tried one of the hard biscuits. Finding it almost tasteless, she finished eating the rest of them before reaching for the bowl with the red slop. She stuck her finger in it and lifted it to her mouth. The taste was foul, the texture unpleasant. Where it had touched her finger and tongue, she felt a stinging sensation which gradually faded away. She shuddered and pushed the bowl away.

Having temporarily taken the edge off her thirst and hunger, she was urgently reminded of another need. Hastily, she picked up the empty container and tried to step back outside the column of light. She was unable to do so. The yellow shaft had become a prison, an impenetrable barrier to the void beyond. Whimpering with distress, she huddled on the floor, convinced she was being watched, determined not to beg. Finally, she could wait no longer and made use of the container, humiliated and embarrassed by the length of time it took her to finish.

She waited. After a while, when nothing happened, she pushed herself to her feet and paced around the small space, working the stiffness out of her muscles. Every now and then, a faint wave of nausea distracted her.

Thoughts tumbled through her head as she sought answers to her predicament. Alex had warned her that there was danger on Treaine, that the peace accord had enemies, that she, as his wife, could be a prime target. She had scarcely heeded him, had scoffed at his warnings, determined to maintain her independence. She had, in fact, not given any thought to requesting an escort to the rehearsal hall, even though darkness had long since fallen.

Alex! She wondered bleakly if she would ever see him again, and then shivered at the thought. She wondered how long she had been gone, and if he had even missed her yet. She wondered how he would feel when he discovered she was missing.

Tears pooled in her eyes, but she squeezed them shut and clenched her hands together not allowing them to fall. How she had grown to love him! Despite her strongest resistance, he had swept away all the barriers and stolen her heart. She hadn't had a chance to tell him, she thought miserably. She hadn't told him that she wanted his child, that she would try to accept the conditions of the marriage partnership. Now, he might never know.

Resolutely, she shook off the latter thought, disgusted with herself for preparing to give up so easily. They were feeding her, weren't they? They must mean to keep her alive.

Abruptly, the column of light disappeared. She was lifted and surrounded by the same icy cold floating sensation she had experienced earlier. Gradually it warmed and her mind became numb. Sleep overtook her moments later.

Chapter 38

THE DAYS PASSED with agonizing slowness. The population of Treaine rallied around, offering complete cooperation and whatever assistance they could. It was widely recognized that Joanna's disappearance could cause an irreparable breach in the peace process if she were not returned safely. More than that, she had unknowingly gained a reputation throughout the settlement as a champion and protector of the young and vulnerable. The depth of her compassion was admired and honored, and her work and unswerving devotion to what she believed was right and just to understand and improve other lives so different from her own was respected.

Alex feared he was going mad. His heart, like his bed, was cold and empty. A great void surrounded him and he felt completely powerless. His days were a travesty of trying to keep busy and focused. His nights were far worse. Sleep was elusive, and only came for short restless stretches when he was completely exhausted. He would have avoided it entirely if he could have because he suffered from nightmares— nightmares of Joanna terrified and in pain, crying for help which he was unable to give.

He wanted her back, but his reasons for it varied from hour to hour. She was his marriage partner and, by Mariltar law, was bound to him for the rest of his life or hers, whether she liked it or not. Despite her inexperience, she brought the greatest sense of fulfillment of any lover he had ever had. He would not allow anyone else to have her, nor did he want anyone else. He enjoyed her mind and her company more than any other woman he had known. He couldn't imagine the rest of his life without her and...he loved her.

He had finally recognized and named the emotion that had brought such delight at her increasingly uninhibited responses to his lovemaking, such contentment on the rare occasions they spent simply talking and such pain at her assumed betrayal.

He had thought she was beginning to accept her circumstances even though she continued to avoid most of her duties by offering excuses he couldn't really contest. He had hoped she was beginning to experience and share some of the same feelings he had. In the deepest recesses of his soul he continued to believe she hadn't disappeared of her own accord, but the vulnerability of his emotions often introduced a strong thread of doubt.

Close to dawn on the fifth day, his tortured mind had just drifted off into sleep when the console chimed and his wrist communicator beeped simultaneously. Struggling through a fog of disorientation when normally he would have been instantly alert, he responded, his voice harsh with tiredness. "Yes?"

"Alex, we intercepted a message you may want to see." Eric's voice contained barely controlled excitement.

"I'm on my way!"

When he stepped into the private meeting room of the Control Center minutes later, he found Mark and Eric huddled around the information console in heated discussion.

"What do you have?" he asked quietly.

Both men glanced around.

"See for yourself," Eric answered, clearly trying to mask his shock at his commander's appearance. In the three days since Alex had last seen him, he knew that insufficient sleep, indifference to proper sustenance and worry had left their mark. His face was haggard and drawn, the blue of his eyes and the pulse at his temple dulled and almost lifeless.

Alex approached the console, hardly daring to hope. It was a few moments before the characters on the screen began to register on his mind. His gaze sharpened, he focused more intently and sank into a chair, swearing softly and violently.

Several minutes later, having read the message several times, he raised his head. "Who knows about this?"

"Just us." The reassurance came quickly from Eric. "It was a scrambled transmission. We weren't even sure it *was* a message, but we've been investigating every possible electronically-transmitted sound relay. It took several hours to unscramble the code. We pulled it in here, when some of its aspects were becoming apparent. We still don't know where it originated, or its destination."

"Have you notified Jason?"

"He's on his way."

Alex nodded absently, and refocused on the screen. The message was stark and clear. The wife of the High Lord of Mariltar was barter for certain conditions to be placed in the peace accord. Her life was forfeit if the conditions were not met. The conditions were outrageous. The declaration of war couldn't have been clearer.

Alex was so intent on the message, he was unaware that Jason had arrived until a touch on his shoulder made him start.

"Soron?"

"It appears so."

Unspoken and unacknowledged until now, the nation of the still unknown author of the message was finally identified out loud. The four men in the room stared at each other, aware that the peace accord, off to such a promising start, was about to be rent in a million small pieces and the genesis of the Vision obliterated without a trace before it could be fully birthed.

Once more, Alex considered the damning words. His sources had been right all along. But he had allowed himself to grow careless, to let down his guard, because he hadn't wanted to believe, because he had grown to respect and admire the Soron accomplishments on Treaine.

And now his carelessness, his lack of faith in his own instincts could mean Joanna's life.

Rage rose sour and hot within him. He should have listened to the instincts that had never failed him before, should have taken greater care to protect what was his. His voice was cold and deadly when he spoke again, "Bring me Ambassador Soron. Now!"

It was clearly the last order his officers expected to hear. After a split second of surprised hesitation, Mark and Eric turned to leave the room. They paused only briefly when Alex added, "And do it discreetly. His visit should not appear to be anything other than just that."

ROUSED FROM SLEEP, Ambassador Soron had responded quickly and good-naturedly to the Mariltar officers' order, barely disguised as a request, that he accompany them to the Control Center. If he wondered at their lack of friendliness, and the circuitous route they took to avoid more traveled pathways, he made no comment.

It was obvious he was little prepared, however, for the cold hostility in Alex Mariltar's gaze when they finally faced each other in the private briefing chamber. Sudden awareness of how vulnerable he was flared in his face and Alex knew with a dark satisfaction that he was remembering their all too recent enmity. He remained silent, watching the Soron's gaze flick quickly to assess the posture of the fifth man in the room. Jason was clearly agitated, and the look he directed at the Soron was also none too friendly.

Despite his visible discomfort, the ambassador turned back to Alex and asked calmly, "You requested a meeting?"

"Leave us!" Alex said curtly, dismissing all three of his officers.

Once again, he knew the order was unexpected. Mark and Eric reluctantly followed Jason who strode quickly and angrily from the room.

Mariltar and Soron faced each other in wary silence. Alex's eyes bored into the other man, searching for answers, trying to read the secrets of his soul.

The Soron shifted uncomfortably and broke the silence by taking the initiative. "There *is* a good reason why I was aroused from my rest at such an early hour, is there not?"

Alex moved aside, and gestured to the screen of the information console which had been effectively obscured by his body. "Please!"

The ambassador raised an eyebrow inquiringly and moved forward after a brief hesitation. Alex shifted position to keep his face in full view. He wasn't sure what he expected, but the Soron's reaction startled him. His face paled to a deathly white and his features froze into an expression of incredulity and horror. He put out a shaking hand and groped blindly for support, unable to tear his gaze away from the message.

Aching with impatience and nerves stretched to breaking, Alex waited. Finally, after an agonizing delay during which the message was read and re-read, the ambassador straightened and faced him. "Do you think *I* had something to do with this?"

Alex's response was prompt and emphatic. "No! No, I don't. I asked you here because I need your help."

"How can you be so sure?" the other man persisted.

"Because I consider myself a good judge of character. Because I believe we've developed a friendship over the last few months. Because I believe you are as deeply committed to the Coalition's Vision as I am, and because," he finished softly, "if I'm wrong, we'll all be plunged into a raging, bloody inferno, from which, this time, there may be no deliverance."

"You have a greater conviction than I, my friend." The Soron fell into contemplation once again, then roused himself to say quietly, "If it helps, I believe she is all right—for now. You will need all your skills and resources to bring her safely through this."

"What can you tell me about this message?"

Clasping his hands behind his back, the ambassador hesitated an agonizingly long moment before beginning. "There is an ancient clan on Soron, unknown to outsiders, protected by our customs. It goes by the name of Tam. The Tam have a history that is longer than the memories passed from generation to generation. They play an integral part in all our spiritual ceremonies, and their elders are consulted on every major political decision. It is said they have great mystical powers, but no one outside the clan has ever witnessed such an event."

He closed his eyes briefly before continuing, "Before the great Conflicts, a branch of the Tam clan split away to concentrate on strengthening their powers. But power corrupted, and soon the whispers began of unexplained disappearances, torture and human sacrifice. The elders of the Tam clan were asked to intervene, but they couldn't or wouldn't, and soon those corrupt powers were being used to control some of our leaders."

He walked over to stand face to face with Alex. "Soron never wanted war with Mariltar. It was the Tam rebels that incited the first act of aggression with Mariltar, and their greed that drove us to attack other nations. We were powerless against them at first, not really comprehending their hold over us. Finally, there came a Tam elder who was not afraid to fight back and use the ancient powers against them. In the end, they were destroyed, but we were still fighting a war."

Turning to look at the console, he shuddered, "We *thought* they had been destroyed, but that transmission has the mark of a rebel Tam. It's beginning again."

"No!" Alex said fiercely. "It will *not* begin again. There must be *someone* who has information. Go back to your Tam elders. Find out who sent this message and for whom it was intended."

The Soron shook his head sadly. "I doubt it was intended for anyone. It was meant to be intercepted and interpreted as a act of war by the Soron nation. What they did not know was that a Soron would betray them by revealing their existence. That will give you the advantage—for a while. I will find out what I can."

He moved toward the door. Alex's voice made him pause.

"Gan! What you've revealed to me today, I may not be able to hold in confidence. Joanna's life is a stake. What will happen to you, your family, your clan?"

The answer came with a resigned shrug. "Perhaps nothing, or perhaps we will be outcast from Soron society. It is a small enough price to pay to prevent another Conflict. Do what you must to recover your wife, as I would do if our positions were reversed."

The door hissed closed behind him.

Chapter 39

TIME HAD LOST all meaning for Joanna.

She had no clear sense of how long she had been confined in the prison of darkness. There were no clues to tell her whether it was day or night. During periods of wakefulness, she tried to occupy herself by reliving happy memories and dreaming of a future with Alex. Those dreams, more often than not, now included a child with his father's mark upon his temple, or sometimes a daughter with her father's sparkling blue eyes.

But the dreams weren't enough. Claustrophobia seemed to press upon her more quickly and the feeling of helplessness in the smothering restriction of the invisible blanket which encased her grew stronger with the passage of time. There was a pattern of sorts to relieve the boredom and the fear which often tore at her in the endless darkness.

The column of yellow light had become a friend. It always brought its inadequate supply of water and barely edible food, and freed her from the terrifying floating confinement. In her dark, soundless world, it seemed as if the light appeared at irregular intervals, sometimes very shortly after she had eaten, and sometimes many hours later when hunger was tearing a hole in her belly. She had learned to eat when food was offered and managed to choke down every pitiful morsel.

More recently, other images and sounds had added to her torment. The wailing screams from the City of Sarach sometimes echoed eerily through her mind until she thought she would go mad. Images from childhood nightmares came colorfully and horrifyingly to life in hallucinations that reached out for her and plucked at her sanity. She began to despair that she would ever leave this place, that she had entered a living hell.

But always, when she thought her own screams would burst forth and drown out those in her mind, when her nerves had reached breaking point, when she couldn't recall the pleasant memories to chase away the despair of the present no matter how hard she tried, the warm comforting arms of sleep would descend upon her and sweep her away into blessed oblivion.

One day, she woke with a start and knew immediately that

something was different. Total blackness still surrounded her. Her heart was pounding, and she forced herself to breathe deeply and slowly to calm herself.

There! She heard a sound. It came again, louder this time. It was the tinkle of a woman's light laughter, obscenely out of place in this hell. Something else was different. She could move freely, the invisible bonds, released only with the advent of the column of light, were gone. Nonetheless, she lay still, her eyes closed. There was more laughter and now voices, and she didn't know if they belonged to an enemy or a friend.

Very close now, the laughter was abruptly silenced and a malevolent hiss whipped through the air and wrapped around Joanna.

"What is this? She appears no different than the day we brought her here." The voice, a woman's voice, rose shrilly in outrage and disappointment. "You promised she would be near death, would even welcome it, by the time I returned. Why isn't she? Have your methods failed? Are your powers too weak? She was supposed to suffer before she died. You prom—"

"Silence!" The word thundered and cracked, echoing as if released in a great cavern. Joanna shuddered, more terrified by the sound of it than by the words the woman had spoken.

"How dare you question my powers or my methods. I promised you nothing!"

"There must be a body. Time runs swiftly. Kill her now, and deliver her to the settlement." The other voice was whining now, uncertain, and held an overtone of panic.

"There *will* be a body to display for your Mariltar lover, but only when I am done with her. Her mind fascinates me. She is far stronger than I had counted on, stronger than any other, a contradiction to the weakness of her race. It is almost as if something or someone protects and shields her. I must have more time to study her, to try other methods to probe her mind and draw forth her spirit and energy. This *is* the one who will feed and strengthen my powers, and allow me to finally achieve the dominion sphere."

"Please, Or Ton. I cannot wait much longer. Word comes that the settlement is being torn apart with suspicion and old hatreds. I must go to him before our people are at war again, before it is too late."

"Then go, woman. Your impatience weakens you. Use your powers wisely and bind him to you. Mariltar will fall all the more easily and, once Mariltar falls and we have harnessed the great skills of her warriors, we will control the Crestar System."

The words trailed into a sibilant whisper, echoing in the great void. And faintly through the looming, threatening darkness came the promise. "The body will be delivered in two days."

Chapter 40

JASON SURVEYED the tense, silent group in front of him. He had called a meeting of the captains on Bavin Moresol's vessel to finalize the strategy for Joanna's rescue. After endless, grueling days of waiting, then sorting through the confusing amount of information Ambassador Soron had finally been able to provide, the biggest break had come when a security team had brought word on Mark Oberan's shift of a strange phenomenon occurring in the southern forest. The giant trees were wilting and dying. The massive trunks were bending like saplings in a strong wind and the trailing branches were shriveling and shedding foliage.

Several hours later, as he was about to go off his shift, a memory had surfaced in Mark's tired mind. Suddenly energized, he had searched the records, which had been minutely examined many times over, and finally put together a piece of the puzzle.

"*When the trees of Heribon weep the tears of the dying...*" The southern forest was given a name. And through Heribon ran the pathway of the ancients, the gateway to the City of Sarach. Although never identified by name in Soron records, the bits and pieces of description were too strikingly similar to be coincidence. It appeared the City of Sarach had harbored the rebel clan in its catacombs for countless years. Joanna had been right under their noses the whole time.

The discovery had come none to soon. It had been almost three weeks since she had disappeared. Tension within the settlement had been increasing by the day as word had leaked out that the Sorons might be responsible. Several confrontations had been broken up in the entertainment houses and Marketplace, and everyone was treading warily as suspicion grew.

The ambassadors had been highly visible in the community, both separately and as a group, urging calm and cooperation, but the security team was uneasily aware that any incident small or large could shatter the hard-won peace.

Jason lowered his eyes to collect his thoughts. As he contemplated his hands lying on the table in front of him, he sent a silent plea to his ancestors for guidance. What he was about to do went against all his training, and could be construed as rebellion against the allegiance to which he had been pledged from birth.

He raised his eyes and surveyed the faces of the five men around the table.

"We have one last matter to settle. The vote must be unanimous or we abandon the plan. If we vote to employ it, be cognizant that, at the very least, your careers will be at stake even if we are successful with the rescue attempt. If the rescue fails, our careers are surely doomed and our lives, and perhaps those of our families, will be changed irrevocably."

He paused and rubbed his sweating palms together. "I vote that Alex Mariltar be excluded from this mission." His throat tightened as he spoke the words, and he almost choked. Every instinct in his body cried out that the decision was the right one, but still his heart raced and the taste in his mouth was bitter at the betrayal he was forced to propose.

"Agreed." The single word from Mark Oberan brought his attention to the group. Without hesitation, the remaining four gave their consent.

Jason's shoulders sagged briefly with relief. Eric grinned without humor. "If you hadn't made the proposal, Jason, one of us would have. Alex cannot be objective enough. He cares about Joanna too deeply, and might take risks that would endanger us all and accomplish nothing."

"Now that that's settled," Sebastian spoke up somewhat impatiently, "what's the plan for approaching Alex? I doubt he's just going to meekly accept our decision."

"We don't tell him." Jason rose to his feet. "He has a meeting with Ambassador Soron in a half hour to review some final details which we've already covered. His drink will be drugged. He'll sleep it off in a locked room in an entertainment house, and with Great Sagar's mercy, our mission will be successfully completed by the time he returns to consciousness."

Eric pursed his lips and whistled silently, then shrugged resignedly. "Facing Alex when all this is over is going to be the worst part of this whole mission. We may as well get started."

The six made their preparations for the most part in silence, each painfully cognizant that they were about to embark on one of the most dangerous undertakings of their lives. Fearless and aggressive when facing a known and predictable enemy, there was a deep awareness and some apprehension that the information they were using to penetrate the rebel Tams' stronghold came from a source considered to be a deadly foe in the not too distant past.

"A noble and great cause would perish at the hands of an trusted friend, but rise again on the wings of a dawning star with the gift of respected enemy." The words ran incessantly through Jason's mind, mocking his ability to decipher their meaning. Was the Soron a trusted friend or a respected enemy? He would know soon enough, and only hoped that he would live to share the knowledge.

Time was critical and, to avoid detection as long as possible, they would be porting from the vessel to the planet, a risky undertaking in and of itself. But the portal would place them squarely within the catacombs of the rock which ran underneath and behind the temple, tunnels which their scanners had told them didn't exist, but that the Soron information insisted did. A miscalculation, and any one or all of them could die before the mission was barely begun.

It had been decided that only the six would go, as the group of Tam within the bowels of the temple was reportedly not large. It was less difficult to employ anti-detection proximity devices with a small group of men, and backup would be provided, if necessary, from small hover craft and a contingent of ground forces.

Ambassador Soron had warned that all their careful preparations might be worthless since the powers of the Tam were legendary amongst the Soron people and might easily uncover any attempt at invasion.

Their preparations completed, they waited only for word from the surface. When it came, their faces grave and unreadable, already concentrating on the task ahead, they clasped hands briefly and moved into position.

Chapter 41

PAIN SLICED THROUGH her head, tearing at her temples. A single agonizing scream of unbearable intensity and volume pierced her ears and jerked her from sleep. Her body felt as if it were on fire, tormented by relentless burning pinpoints everywhere. Harsh light streamed into her face, scorching her eyeballs even through closed lids. She forced her eyes open and looked straight into the face of purgatory. The disembodied face hovering over her was pure evil, and surely not human. Fire glowed from black rimmed, fathomless eyes. Deep grooves shadowed the features, melting them together, the head was hairless and only holes remained where once there had been ears.

"Good! Very good!" The deep resonant tones filled with menace came from the mouth stretched into the semblance of a smile. "It's working. She's weakening. We came close to shattering the shield around her consciousness. It shouldn't be too much longer."

Through the intense burning sensation, Joanna struggled with a myriad of thoughts, knowing she had to calm her mind to retreat into the oblivion that had never failed her before. This time it didn't work, although the pain lessened somewhat.

There was a violent curse and a woman's voice questioning anxiously, "What has happened?"

"The shield around her has strengthened. I wasn't quick enough. I'll have to—"

Another sound penetrated, even as the pain increased again and then miraculously disappeared altogether. The harsh alarm of a warning system echoed in the chamber.

"We've been breached! But how—it's not possible!" The woman's tone was shocked and disbelieving.

"Incompetents!" The snarl was deadly. "Guard her!"

Hope rising fiercely within her, Joanna flexed her limbs and found them free of restraints. She slitted her eyes open again, fighting against the intensity of the light, but could see nothing within the range of her vision. She appeared to be lying on a solid surface, but had no way of knowing what her elevation was. Deciding to take a chance, she braced and then threw herself to one side. But she was weaker than she knew, and though she tried to bring her legs into position to take the brunt of what turned out to be a short fall, they buckled underneath her and she collapsed to the ground.

A mocking face swam in front of her eyes. The light dimmed allowing her a clearer view.

"Well, well. That was a weak attempt if ever I saw one. I cannot imagine what he sees in you." Contempt laced the voice, and Joanna finally recognized her tormentor.

"Cerata!" she whispered hoarsely, the sound of her own voice after so long startling her.

The expression on the face became sneering. "You've managed to deceive my master with your tricks, but now you're mine. And I'm not interested in mind games. Alex Mariltar belonged to me until you appeared, and he will be mine again, because you will be *dead* before the end of the day."

The last few words were spat out. Loathing and jealousy twisted the beautiful features. A six-digit hand reached out like a claw, twisted in Joanna's hair and, with surprising strength, jerked her to her feet.

Cerata pulled her roughly outside the column of light. Instead of the black void Joanna expected, the cavernous room which they were in was dimly lit. Unrelenting in her purpose, Cerata forced Joanna toward the center of the room until she stood on the brink of a large pit containing a rippling pool of foul smelling liquid.

"Don't worry," Cerata whispered maliciously close to her ear. "It eats at the flesh slowly, but you'll only have an hour or so to endure before you lose consciousness."

She released Joanna, and backed away slowly. Now there was a weapon in her hand.

Joanna stared in horrified fascination at the pool, before tearing her gaze away to look at Cerata. Her knees trembled with weakness, and she called upon her last remaining reserves of strength. "Why are you doing this? Alex will never take you back. He told me it was over between you."

"Hah! And you believed him? What a gullible fool you are! Even if you weren't dead, he would have come back to me eventually because I can give him what you cannot. Indescribable pleasure! Not tepid embraces and weak responses. My power is unparalleled and stronger than the last time we shared a bed. He will beg for more when he has me again."

The last part of the boast was shouted in triumph as the speaker convinced herself that it would be so. The echo fell into eerie silence as the alarm stopped abruptly.

"*Cerata!*" Pain and shock filled the masculine voice that spoke the name.

Both women turned in the direction of the sound, but Cerata's weapon remained trained on Joanna with deadly intent. Bavin Moresol stood a few yards away, his face pale and tense, his gaze fixed on Cerata, a weapon dangling limply in his hand.

"I love you," he said hoarsely. "I don't believe that all those times we spent together meant nothing to you. You swore you loved *me*, that you had forgotten Alex." His tone became increasingly helpless as the reality of her betrayal appeared to sink in.

The chilling sound of Cerata's laughter echoed in the chamber. "You're as big a fool as she is," the answer whipped back at him. "I *never* loved you. I only used you, and you were a willing tool." Not content to leave it at that, she went on to cruelly taunt him. "Alex Mariltar is twice the man you'll ever be, and *knows* instinctively how to please a woman. If you're here to rescue *her* you've also failed at that. Now you can watch her die."

"Don't do this," he pleaded, making another attempt. "Come away with me. We can make a life together far from all this. The House of Mariltar will release me from my bond and..." His voice trailed away as the maniacal, mocking laughter crushed the life out of hope. Making a visible effort, the young warrior jerked his gaze from Cerata to look at Joanna.

"Move away from the pool, Joanna."

"Stay where you are!" The evil, glowing stare turned back to Bavin. It was painfully evident from the fleeting expression of shock and horror on his face that he was wondering how he could ever have been so deceived. "Make one move, and you die as well."

"And what do you hope to accomplish?" The young warrior's posture changed subtly. A flicker of his eyes and a minute movement of his head signaled Joanna, even as his attention seemed to remain centered on Cerata. "Conflict again? Perhaps, this time, Soron destroyed? Your family dead? Alex will *never* take you back. He loves Joanna, will loathe the instrument of her death, and will surely never rest until he has revenge. Forget Alex Mariltar, my love. You and I can make a good life elsewhere."

His stance appeared relaxed, with legs spread and weapon dangling loosely from one hand, but even at this distance Joanna sensed the tense alertness in his body. He was primed for action. Frozen briefly in place by his words, it took another slight movement of his head to force her to take a few steps. But precious time had been lost.

Momentarily distracted by the same words, Cerata now swung her enraged gaze back. "Enough! This ends here!" The words were a maddened shriek. The weapon shifted threateningly.

Pandemonium broke loose.

Joanna heard her name shouted even as she saw Cerata bring the weapon around to fire at her. Bavin Moresol threw himself across the space that separated them. At the same time, he lifted his own weapon and fired in Cerata's direction. From several different directions in the room, movement erupted as other men burst into the area.

The echoes died away and silence filled the great cavern. Joanna moaned and sank slowly to her knees, staring horrified at Bavin's still body. Cerata lay crumpled a short distance away. Too weak to pull herself up again, she crawled over to where the young warrior lay.

The youngest of Alex Mariltar's captains was dead, a dreadful, gaping, gurgling hole in his chest. The choice had been made between the woman he thought he had loved, and the woman he was sworn to protect. He had made the ultimate sacrifice.

"Joanna?" She felt a gentle touch on her shoulder. Dazed and in shock she looked up into Jason's concerned face. "Can you walk?"

She shook her head slowly. "I-I don't think so." She began to tremble violently, her stomach heaved and she covered her mouth, desperately hoping she wouldn't be sick. Swiftly, he turned her away from the body, knelt beside her and began pulling a thin body-warmer out of a small hip pack. His gaze roamed over her, examining her closely. She was horribly and embarrassingly aware of how dirty and weak she was.

But when his eyes lifted, she saw only compassion and some relief. "We'll have you out of here soon," he promised wrapping the cover around her and supporting her with his body.

She leaned gratefully against him. "Jason?" she whispered urgently.

"Shhh. Don't talk, Joanna. Save your strength."

"No, please. I-I don't want Alex to see me like this," she begged, close to tears. She didn't think she could bear to face him for another, more compelling, reason. Two people close to him were dead and, dazed and in shock from witnessing the event, she blamed herself.

She felt some small relief when Jason said distractedly, "He's not here, Joanna. He couldn't come with the ground support team. He'll meet us back at the settlement."

Later, when all her fears and doubts beset her again, she was remember those words and wonder if he hadn't cared enough to be a part of rescue attempt himself.

Despite the body-warmer, she continued to tremble violently in Jason's arms. She watched saddened as Mark and Sebastian readied Bavin's body to be carried out of the temple. It appeared that rather than risk porting back to the vessel, they would walk out and meet the ground support. The other two captains walked up a few minutes later after completing a thorough scan of the chamber.

Joanna was vaguely aware of Eric's intent look and the questioning gaze he directed at Jason. Jason responded with a brief nod. "Are we secure?" he questioned out loud.

"As secure as we ever can be in a place like this. Great Sagar, but I've never been in *any* place with such a foul feel to it," Justin grumbled.

"I'm not entirely convinced we've flushed out all the Tam," Eric added grimly. "The scanners show no sentients left but us, but despite Ambassador Soron's reports we have little enough information about these reputed powers. As sophisticated as our equipment is, it may not be completely effective."

Jason nodded. "Once we're out of here, we'll exercise our authority to engage the final phase. Let's go!"

He raised Joanna to her feet as Eric moved closer to help support her. She glanced back over her shoulder as they started off.

"Cerata?"

"She's dead, Joanna."

"You can't leave her here," she objected weakly. "Her brother will want her body to observe proper Soron funeral rites."

The men were already heavily burdened, and her words fell on less than enthusiastic ears. Jason rubbed the back of his neck tiredly and sighed. "Balls of Sortor, I'd completely forgotten about the relationship. You're right, of course, Joanna."

"I'll take her." Justin walked over and quickly wrapped a cover around the body before lifting it easily across his shoulder. The party moved quickly, Jason and Eric supporting Joanna between them. The journey through the maze of tunnels seemed endless to her, desperate as she was for a glimpse of natural light and fresh air. Finally, they burst through the concealed opening into the reception room of the temple and, shortly thereafter, were outside being surrounded by the ground team.

A medical officer immediately assumed charge of Joanna. She was carried to a cruiser, where she gratefully sank into a seat and rested her head against the back. The light hurt her eyes, accustomed as they had been to such long periods of darkness. She tried not to think about the coming confrontation with Alex.

The cruisers were a fair distance away from the city, when she heard a heavy rumbling. Curiosity flared briefly, then died. The effort required was too great, and she had so little energy.

Chapter 42

"HOW IS SHE?"

The question was posed to the man and woman wearing senior doctor insignia on their clothing. Dominating a room filled with equipment, a large viewing screen allowed them to observe the patient in the next room. She appeared to be asleep.

It was the woman who responded to Ambassador Mariltar's question.

"She's weak, malnourished and dehydrated, but not severely. They gave her just enough food and water to sustain her. She'll recover her physical health quickly. Her mental state is highly puzzling..." The doctor paused, and then continued hastily aware of how that statement must have sounded, "It's remarkably good, actually, considering what she's been through. She was completely unaware that she had been held captive for three weeks. She was under the impression that she had been gone for only a few days."

The man continued, "She has few memories of what occurred. They didn't harm her physically. From what we can determine, they followed the pattern Ambassador Soron described and tried various mind probe methods." He shook his head. "She must be extremely strong. They don't appear to have succeeded in whatever they were after. She seems to have spent an extraordinary amount of time simply sleeping or unconscious. We want to keep her under observation for forty-eight hours, but then she can be released."

Alex listened in silence, his eyes glued to the still figure. Relief weakened his knees as the meaning of the doctors' words sank in. She was going to be all right!

"I'd like to go in and see her—in private."

"Of course."

A touch of a button caused the screen to blank out. The equipment continued to murmur and whisper, monitoring Joanna's physical and mental state.

As Alex reached for the door control, the doctor spoke again. "Ambassador, were you aware that your wife is pregnant?"

He stiffened in utter shock. It was several seconds before he could find his voice to respond. Hoarsely, he said, "I thought you said they hadn't harmed her physically?"

Dismayed, the doctor stammered, "Th-they didn't. She's six weeks along. The child is yours."

Alex stared at the two doctors, completely taken aback. "You're sure?" he asked without thinking, and then mentally kicked himself for sounding like a fool. The two wore barely concealed expressions of curiosity on their faces.

The woman smiled slightly, reassuringly. "We ran all the tests. Despite what she's been through, the child is healthy, and he is unquestionably yours."

He frowned and shook his head dazedly. He must have miscalculated. He'd known his sterilization implants were running out, but he had missed those blasted tests and never had rescheduled. Somehow it just hadn't seemed important. "You said "he--"?"

"The child is a boy."

"Does she know—about the child?"

"If she does, she hasn't said anything. Because of the timing, we didn't want to raise the issue with her until we had talked with you. If she doesn't know, we thought you might like to tell her."

Alex absently nodded his thanks and contemplated the door in front of him. A myriad of emotions tore at him. Love for the woman who was his wife and now soon to be the mother of his son. Deep uncertainty and concern over how Joanna would receive the news. And a tiny seed of excitement that was burgeoning and growing rapidly, mixed with not a little nervousness, over the prospect of impending fatherhood. There was still much to be settled between them. The wound that Melissa had opened with the suggestion that Joanna might have left him, still oozed and bled, fed by the vulnerability of emotions he had never experienced before and the realization that his love for her knew no boundaries. This new development was certain to add complications.

He sighed and squared his shoulders, for once in his life, tempted to turn and run. But there was nothing to be gained by delaying the inevitable, and he wanted so badly to see her, to touch her velvet skin, to bury his face in the fresh, familiar scent of her hair, to fold her in his arms and never let her go. Even if she couldn't return his feelings, he was prepared to settle for whatever he could get.

The door hissed closed behind him. Treading softly, he approached the elevated medical platform, and leaned over the tubular cocoon to study her. Forewarned by Jason, the sight of her, nevertheless, struck like a blow to his chest and drove the air from his lungs. She was so painfully slender, her body barely lending shape to the thin cover over her. Her skin had lost its healthy glow and her eyes were sunken in wide bruised circles.

His throat tightened, and he reached out a hand that was less than steady to brush away a strand of hair which lay across one cheek. Her lashes quivered and the beautiful eyes, color dulled, fluttered open.

"Alex!" Her voice was sleepy, but for a second he thought he heard a note of gladness. Then he knew he had been mistaken. In his vulnerable emotional state, he interpreted the strange expression that crossed her face as one of distaste for his touch. She didn't want him. He removed his hand and drew back slightly. "How are you feeling?"

"All right." She rolled her head impatiently, and amended, "I don't seem to have much energy. When will they let me leave?"

"In about two days. They want to keep you for observation, and continue some treatment. Do you need anything?"

She shook her head. They fell into awkward silence, each avoiding the other's eyes. He felt extraordinarily uncertain, not knowing what else to do or say, yet bursting with things that desperately needed to be said, wanting to reach out and fill his empty, aching arms.

She had said 'leave', Alex thought bleakly, not 'go home'. How could he tell her about the baby? The simple fact was, he couldn't. Not just yet. He wanted to ask a hundred questions about what she had been through, what she had felt in those lonely hours, and reassure her that she would never experience anything like that again. He wanted to snatch her out of the cocoon in which she was lying, into the cradle of his arms and never let her go.

The questions remained unasked, the actions unfulfilled. Her face was still turned away. She looked as if she were about to fall asleep.

HAD HE BEEN ill, Joanna wondered? He looked terrible. His face was thinner, almost gaunt, and drawn into forbidding lines. She shuddered imperceptibly, and all her fears that, this time, he wouldn't forgive her came rushing back. Despairingly, she wished that he would shout at her, accuse her, punish her, anything but this cold silence. She wanted to tell him how devastated she was by Bavin's death, how sorry she was that Cerata had died, despite what she had done. She wanted to tell him how much she had missed him, how much she needed him right now and how she longed to burrow against the safe haven of his body. Turning her head, she forced herself to look into his face, but the rigid expression froze the words on her tongue.

Dispassionately, abruptly, he leaned forward and lightly brushed his lips against her forehead. "You're tired. You need to sleep. I'll see you tomorrow."

No, she screamed silently at his retreating back. *Don't go! I've had enough sleep to last a lifetime. I need you!* But the door had already closed with finality behind him.

The pain in her chest was unbearable. Her body shook with violent trembling, and the tears that hadn't fallen during her ordeal now gushed forth uncontrollably. The cocoon prevented her from curling up to comfort herself, but she turned her head to one side in an attempt to hide her face as an attendant rushed into the room. Her muffled entreaties to be left alone were ineffective, and relief only came with the pinch of a drug pellet against her neck.

JOANNA OPENED HER eyes and lay quietly, savoring a moment of deep contentment. She was in her own bed and, through the windows in front of her, could see the moons, their brightness paling with the sweep of light across the sky.

She turned her head and became aware of Alex's steady, deep breathing next to her. In an instant, contentment had fled to be replaced with apprehension. She had been allowed to come home late yesterday, feeling much stronger after a concentrated course of treatment, although still with a curious lack of energy. Matters hadn't improved between her and Alex. If anything, they had become worse. They didn't seem to be able to communicate. He had helped her to bed the previous evening, yet had avoided touching her as much as possible, or so it had seemed.

Unconsciously, Joanna sighed heavily. Light was quickly filling the room and soon he would be gone about the day's business. Or would he? She didn't know any more. Perhaps he didn't follow the same routine. So much seemed to have changed in the three weeks she had been gone. It was still slightly disorienting to her that so much time had passed when her own instincts insisted it had only been a few days.

She watched the light patterns dancing across the ceiling and all of a sudden felt her stomach lurch. The nausea was back. She closed her eyes and lay still, hoping it would go away quickly. Within seconds, she knew she was in trouble. Throwing back the cover, she rolled out of bed and stumbled across the room. Alex caught her before she reached the archway and carried her the rest of the way. Tender hands held back her hair and supported her as she emptied the meager contents of her stomach. When she weakly indicated she was finished, he wiped her face gently with a cool cloth, then picked her up again.

He seemed loathe to let her go now that he finally had taken her back in his arms. He settled on the bed, cradling her on his lap. Making soothing noises against the top of her head, he rubbed her back and neck until the tremors that shook her body eased. Joanna closed her eyes and relaxed against him allowing herself a brief fantasy of feeling safe, secure and cherished.

It ended all too soon.

"Joanna?" His breath was warm against her ear, sending tingles down her spine. "Do you feel better? We need to talk, Meira."

Ignoring her murmur of muffled protest as she burrowed her face against his bare chest, he forced her chin up to look into her eyes. "Yes!" he said firmly. "There are things that need to be said between us, but first..."

He slid her off his lap, and settled her against a mound of pillows. Pulling on a pair of loose-fitting lounging trousers, he ordered her not to move, and left the room.

Apprehension and relief battled in Joanna's mind. He sounded like himself again this morning, she thought. His face had lost that look of cold detachment, and he was ordering her around. She thought she was ready to talk. No matter what the outcome, anything would be better than the silences and awkwardness of the last few days.

Back within minutes, he bore a plate of the broken bread chips she liked so well from the Marketplace, and a goblet of the liquid nourishment he had accustomed her to drinking in the morning. Touched by his thoughtfulness, she nevertheless refused his offerings saying, "I don't think I should so soon. I'll just get sick again."

"Try," he insisted. "It might make you feel better."

Doubtfully she took the goblet. After a few tentative sips, she decided she did feel a little more energized and the feeling of nausea faded.

Alex took her free hand in his and gently ran his thumb over the back of it. A thoughtful frown creased his brow. Her hands still bore some faint yellow bruises as did other parts of her body. Finally he said awkwardly, "Why do you think you were sick just now?"

Puzzled, she stammered, "I-I don't know. I assume it was just a lingering reaction from the last few weeks."

"It's more than that." He pinned her with an unwavering gaze. This morning, his eyes were an expressionless pale blue, giving nothing away. "Do you remember when you had your last monthly bleeding?"

She felt her cheeks pinken. Even more puzzled, she thought hard. "I don't remember," she whispered, mentally counting back over the weeks. The significance of his questions created a dawning awareness. She thought of the nausea that had plagued her off and on, the growing tenderness in her breasts, the lack of energy. She raised questioning, startled eyes to Alex's face.

He smiled slightly, but his expression became wary and watchful. "The doctors say you are about six weeks pregnant." He studied her face intently, as if looking for clues to her feelings.

"Oh! But you—"

"Miscalculated," he said ruefully.

"A baby?" she said wonderingly, her hands going unconsciously to her stomach and smoothing over the still flat surface. "Is it all right?"

"The doctors assured me it is perfectly healthy. Do you want to know what it is?" She nodded hesitantly and he said softly, "We're going to have a son."

"Oh!" Thoughts turned inward to the tiny being growing inside of her, Joanna felt a surge of uncontrollable emotion. It was so intense she burst into tears. Shocked at her own reaction, she nonetheless found she couldn't stop crying and gave up, leaning into Alex and rubbing her wet face into the rough hair on his chest.

EQUALLY, IF NOT more so, stunned by the unexpectedness and intensity of her response, Alex could do little more than hold her and wonder what it meant. He had just allowed himself to relax a little, having convinced himself that things were going quite well and that she had accepted the news with surprising calmness. Now he didn't know what to think. Becoming concerned after listening to several minutes of gut-wrenching crying, he attempted to claim her attention. "Joann—?"

Her hand rose to clutch his arm, and he heard a muffled sound through the cries against his chest.

"What is it, Meira?"

"I c-c-can't stop," she wailed. "I'm s-sorry! I d-don't know why I'm c-crying."

For the first time in weeks, a grin lifted the corners of his mouth, and understanding lifted a heavy burden off his shoulders. Hadn't the doctors warned him about the possibility of sudden mood swings? Cautiously, he sought confirmation of what he suspected. "I know you didn't want a child right away. Are you upset that you're pregnant?"

A vigorous shaking of her head and more abuse of his chest was accompanied by another wail. "N-no! I don't know! I'm s-so s-sorry,

Alex. I j-just didn't think!"

They weren't talking the baby any more, he realized, but what were they talking about? Deciding his chest was soaked enough, he yanked impatiently on the bed cover, the closest thing available, and freed enough of it to dry his chest and roughly scrub at her face. Her loud sobs had died to whimpers and hiccups, though tears still streamed down her face. "Joanna, what are you talking about?"

"B-Bavin and Cerata. Y-you m-must hate me for what happened to them."

"Oh, Joanna." He folded her tightly in his arms and rocked her back and forth. "Is that what you've been thinking? That I've been blaming you for all that's happened? Oh, Meira. It wasn't your fault. How could you possibly think that?"

But she didn't know the whole story, he realized, and he would never forgive himself for not forcing himself to reveal it to her sooner. "You might have made it easier for Cerata and her clan when you didn't take an escort that night, but they would have found another way sooner or later. We're sure now they tried several times before. All those unexplained, bizarre incidents that involved you are definitely suspect. They were determined to start the Conflicts again, and might have succeeded with your torture and death. Cerata wanted you dead for her own reasons. But if their plan hadn't worked, they would have chosen another way. They had too much to lose with peace in the Crestar System."

He went on to tell her about Ambassador Soron's role, what they had learned about the Tam and the days of fruitless searching.

Joanna listened quietly and when he was finished, she said sadly, "He told her he loved her, you know. But she laughed at him and threw his love back in his face. She was so cruel." She shuddered. "How could someone so beautiful be so evil?"

"Cerata always hungered for power. The Tam could give her all she wanted and more. Once she became a part of that group, there was no turning back. She simply chose the wrong path. Ambassador Soron had no idea that she had become a part of that clan, only that she had changed somehow in the last few years."

"Did you love her?"

"No, Meira. I never loved her." He made the simple statement with great firmness and sincerity, hoping to finally convince her and drive the last doubt she had about that long ago relationship from her mind. "You still haven't told me how you feel about this baby." He was testing her, he knew, but wanted to hear her feelings, no matter what they were, so he could reach an understanding of where they stood.

She shrugged. "I don't know. I'm getting used the idea. It doesn't seem real."

How was he supposed to interpret *that* response, he wondered in exasperation. Joanna shifted in his arms. Curling up more tightly and hiding her face in his neck, she added an afterthought. "But as long as *he* understands from the very beginning that his mother will not be ordered around by the men of the House of Mariltar, I suppose it's all right!"

Lightheaded with relief, Alex playfully growled a warning in her ear and gently pinched her bottom making her squirm and squeal in protest, before laying her back against the pillows. His eyes devoured her beloved features, and one hand stroked the hair back from her face.

"Old habits are hard to break, *Meira*, so here's another *order* for you. You are to stay here and rest and eat. The doctors have provided a long list of foods that are nourishing for you and the baby. I have a few things to attend to today, but I will be back here frequently to check on you." His mouth hovered inches away from hers. "Will you behave yourself?"

He suspected she probably had little energy or inclination to do anything else, but his stubborn wife was still reluctant to show submission. Her rebellious hesitation brought another growl of warning.

"All right, all right," she said hastily.

He rewarded her with a soft touch of his lips to hers. He deepened the kiss, making her moan as his tongue enticed the soft barriers to open and plundered the lush, velvet contours of her mouth. Several minutes later, wholly satisfied with her sweet response, he tore himself away, and rose, stretching, to prepare himself for the day.

Chapter 43

SEVERAL WEEKS later, Joanna stood staring out at the lake, and thought she was going to go out of her mind with boredom. She had recovered quickly, remembering little of her ordeal. Occasionally, she woke at night with a vague recollection of feeling smothered, helpless and deeply afraid, but Alex's steady, quiet breathing beside her always reassured her and sent her back to sleep quickly.

At first, she had enjoyed the enforced relaxation. It had been a while since she had taken any extended leisure time and, after the stress of the last several months, it felt good to wake up in the morning knowing she wasn't accountable to anyone but herself for her time that day. Idleness was not in her nature, however, and she soon became restless.

Ambassador Soron and his family came to visit. They were leaving Treaine to accompany Cerata's body back to Soron for the ritual funeral festivities, and would be gone for several months. With great dignity and sadness, the ambassador apologized to Joanna for the harm his family had caused her. Having learned from Alex that the Soron had put himself and his family at great risk in the attempt to find her, Joanna put her heart into reassuring him that she held him completely blameless for Cerata's actions, and offered her sincere sympathies for the loss of his sister.

It was from the ambassador that she learned the fate of the temple, and the source of the sound she had heard that day. The governing body of the Soron nation with the concurrence of the Coalition had ordered that the Tam be shown no mercy. The two dozen clansmen discovered in the tunnels that day had fought to the death. The Mariltar security forces had found the tunnels underneath the temple to be extensive. Mindful of their earlier experience when the detection devices had failed, they decided to take no chances and had blown up the structure, perhaps burying forever the secrets of the City of Sarach.

Her relationship with Alex had become a puzzle to her. Beyond insisting, as the doctors did, that she rest for several days, he informed her that she was free to pursue whatever activities she wished. The only exception was that he refused to allow her to return to the negotiating table, claiming that she wasn't fully recovered. He was attentive to her every need and indulged her in ways he never had before.

But they hadn't made love since her return.

"I DON'T UNDERSTAND it," Joanna burst out in frustration to Melissa later that day. "He's constantly touching me, and kissing and cuddling, but we never go beyond that. He treats me like I'm a fragile star prism that will shatter if dropped!"

Melissa stretched, enjoying the play of the warm breeze over her bare legs and arms. After a morning spent pursuing her favorite activity in the Marketplace, they were relaxing beneath the shelter of a whispering torg tree outside of Jason's living unit.

She eyed Joanna's now barely rounded belly and said jokingly, "Maybe there's an unspoken taboo against Mariltar men making love to their pregnant wives. Want me to ask Jason?"

In the next second, she wished she could have recalled the words spoken so unthinkingly. Joanna's reaction dismayed and alarmed her, as her face tightened with the effort to hold back tears and she said softly, "I was thinking that maybe he just doesn't find me attractive any more. And now that I'm on the way to fulfilling the most important requirement of being a good Mariltar wife, maybe he doesn't find it necessary to continue those particular attentions. Perhaps he's even looking elsewhere."

Melissa forbore to point out that he would hardly be cuddling and kissing her if he found her so unattractive and asked instead, "Have you tried to, um, seduce him?"

"Yes, sort of." Joanna hung her head. The memory clearly embarrassed her. "I'm telling you, he wasn't interested."

"Hmmm," Melissa mumbled unhelpfully. She tended to doubt that Joanna had tried very hard, and wondered if these two were ever going to stop hurting each other and just acknowledge their true feelings, of which everyone but Joanna and Alex seemed to be clearly aware. Joanna was one of the most insightful and tolerant people she knew, which was what made her such a strong negotiator, but she had an incredible blind spot when it came to Alex. She longed to give both of them a good shaking and force a confrontation to clear the air, but Jason had told her to stay out of their affairs and, for once, she was trying to conform to his wishes.

"Give him time," she compromised. "You went through a horrible ordeal. He was frantic with worry the whole time you were gone and--"

"He was?" Joanna interrupted.

"Oh, Joanna. Of course he was. I don't think he slept at all the first three days. He probably just wants to make sure that you're completely recovered. You've got the baby to consider now too, you know."

Joanna hunched her shoulders and stared up at the swaying tree. "I don't think that's it. You probably misread anger for worry. I can't imagine Alex being frantic over anything. Anyway, I feel fine and I don't see how a little activity in bed can possibly do any harm!" She stared suspiciously as Melissa gave a muffled snort. "What's so funny about that?"

"Absolutely nothing. But this is certainly a major change in attitude. Three months ago, you swore you'd never sleep with him."

Joanna wrinkled her nose in disgust at the reminder, and chose to ignore the comment. "He also won't let me go back to work yet," she complained. "I'm just about out of my mind with boredom, and will probably throw a screaming fit if I ever see another holographic adventure game."

"What you need—" Melissa declared, leaning back and closing her eyes, "—is a change of scenery. I'm planning a trip to the Earth substation near Merlon. You can come with me if you like." This mysterious message delivered, her lips quivered as she tried to control a grin in anticipation of Joanna's response.

Astonished, Joanna stared at her. "The substation near Merlon? Whatever for?"

"Oh, I don't know. I just thought it was the best place to find everything I'm looking for."

"And what are you looking for that's so special you have to take a five day trip?"

"All the trappings and accessories for a full-blown wedding ceremony!"

Joanna's response was immensely satisfying. "What?" she shrieked, and threw a well-aimed pillow at Melissa. "You've been keeping that news from me all day? How could you? When was this decision made anyway?"

"I asked him last night. He had to think about it for a few minutes but, with a little persuasion, he decided it was the right thing to do," Melissa said smugly. "His only insistence was that we use the Mariltar mating ceremony. Other than that, I can do anything I want, and I want it to be celebrated Earth-style."

Joanna threw her a skeptical look. "You've never been a traditionalist, Melissa."

"No, but that's what I want for my wedding day. So, will you come?"

"Of course!" Then she added with less certainty, "If Alex will let me."

Melissa waved a hand nonchalantly. "We'll work on him. He has to agree."

Joanna got up and hugged her. "I'm so happy for you," she said somewhat wistfully. "You and Jason do belong together."

"Just as you and Alex do," Melissa said with conviction. "Are you leaving already?"

"Yes, another doctor's appointment. I'll ask Alex about the trip tonight."

Melissa watched her go. "You won't be the only one to ask," she muttered to herself. Jason, she was determined, was going to get involved in this whether he liked it or not. Perhaps a few more days spent without the company of his wife would have Alex Mariltar on his knees and confessing his deepest feelings when she returned.

JOANNA LEFT THE Medical Quarter and hesitated at the intersection of several main pathways. Making a decision, she turned and hurried in a direction opposite to one she would have taken to go home. Several minutes later, her heart beating faster with excitement and some nervousness at the thought of Alex's certain displeasure over what she was about to do, she ran lightly up the familiar steps to the office space assigned to Ambassador Kromon and his team.

With a considerable amount of prompting on her part, the doctors had reluctantly told her today that her health seemed to be completely restored, the baby was doing well, and there was no medical reason why she shouldn't return to work. Their attitude confirmed a suspicion she had had for several days and convinced her that they had probably been under direction from Alex to delay giving their consent as long as possible.

The seed of anger that had germinated at the thought had fully sprouted by the time she reached the top of the stairs. No one was going to control her life like that! She would make her own decisions about what to do with her time.

Kromon wasn't in the office, but her fellow negotiators crowded around pleased to see her. The few minutes she had planned to spend, to declare her intent of returning to work, lengthened into several hours as they updated her on completed projects and drew her into discussions of their current work. The Tarragon project into which she had put so much of her time and expended so much emotion had been accepted unconditionally by the Ambassador's Council, the Coalition and the leadership of Tarragon and was in the first phase of being implemented.

When she finally left, it was late. Darkness was sliding rapidly across the sky, and she knew she'd be lucky to get home before Alex did. Energized by the last few hours, she was more determined than ever to convince Alex that returning to the negotiating table was the best thing for her.

UNFORTUNATELY, HER timing couldn't have been worse. When she walked in the door, he was pacing the floor impatiently, unreasonably irritated that she hadn't been home. His day had not gone smoothly. The Mariltar security contingent had gathered early in the day to memorialize one of their own, a promising young captain whose life had been cut short in the line of duty. Afterwards, Alex had spent some time with Bavin Moresol's family who had traveled the great distance for the ceremony. The group of seven had been as close as brothers, and he found the occasion difficult and deeply wearing on his emotions. He wished Joanna could have been at his side to help ease some of the pain, but he had made the decision not to subject her to it, not entirely convinced that she didn't still blame herself in some way for Bavin's death.

He was envious of Jason's and Melissa's support of one another and their obvious happiness, which even the sadness of the memorial service couldn't dim. Melissa had expressed surprise at Joanna's absence. Privately, she had told Alex she thought Joanna was strong enough to bear up under the demands of the occasion, and that Alex had been wrong not to at least give her the choice. But she reluctantly agreed not to speak of it when she saw Joanna later. Alex saw the doubt reflected in her eyes and the gnawing uncertainty about whether he had made the right decision returned even stronger than before. Impatiently, he pushed it aside. He had never questioned his own judgment before.

The day didn't get any better. A serious security issue had arisen when a new trader to the settlement was discovered to be smuggling shlil dust, a dangerous hallucinogen derived from small sponge plants harvested from deep underground caverns in the neighboring star system. It had been outlawed in the Crestar System for many years. The trader had maintained that he was merely passing through with the substance, but further investigation had revealed that the drug had found its way to at least one of the more disreputable entertainment houses. Resources had to be freed up to trace the path of the hallucinogen and ensure that any supplies were destroyed. Since the settlement's abilities to prosecute serious criminal activities were limited, arrangements were made to transfer the trader on Eric Stromi's vessel to the nearest substation.

The Ambassadors' Council meeting that followed had become deadlocked on an issue that should have easily been resolved in Alex's opinion. But without the calm reasoning of Ambassador Soron to act as a buffer, the council had been unable to reach a decision and had tabled the discussion for another day.

He had been looking forward to a restful evening with his wife but, by the time Joanna finally walked into their unit, his mood had worsened considerably. Joanna, fresh from her meeting with her fellow negotiators and filled with enthusiasm, didn't wait to inform him of her intent.

He greeted her announcement with stony silence, unable to believe what he was hearing, and feeling a resurgence of fear that, once again, she was slipping away from him, that she was telling him that she could not now or ever belong in the world he wanted for them. He couldn't help himself. His voice was ice-cold when he responded. "I will not discuss this, Joanna. You are not going back to work and that is final! You will be taking up more public duties as my wife, and that should be enough to keep you busy until the child is born."

"But—"

"No! I told you I will not discuss this." He knew his tone was unreasonably harsh. He saw any desire to argue further shrivel and die. She fought to hold back the tears that surfaced so easily these days, inclined her head and walked past him with great dignity to shut herself in their sleeping chamber.

She pretended to be sleeping when he went to check on her later, but he saw from the way her hand clenched the edge of the pillow that she was aware of his presence. Over the course of the next few days, while not completely ignoring him, she maintained a facade of coolness and disinterest. Having been subjected to this treatment once before Alex, who was equally determined not to give in on this particular issue, decided to let her indulge in her moodiness, believing it couldn't last for too long.

Chapter 44

ON THE DAY the Merlon cultural evening was scheduled to take place, Joanna met Melissa at the Marketplace for lunch. She had barely sat down, when a familiar laugh, carrying through the mid-day hum and bustle, caught her attention. Several booths away, Alex, turned with his profile to her, was enjoying a break for the mid-day meal. He wasn't alone.

The woman leaning toward him and claiming his full attention was extraordinarily attractive. Short, black hair smoothly framed and molded a face that was distinguished by exotic slanting dark eyes set above high sculptured cheekbones. Her hand, stretched across the table, frequently touched his. The two seemed completely oblivious to everyone else around them.

Joanna desperately tried to concentrate on Melissa's chatter and tried not to be too obvious about stealing glances at her husband and his companion. It had been a long while since she had seen him so relaxed and enjoying himself so much.

Finally, unable to bear the suspense any longer, she interrupted Melissa in mid-sentence. "Who's that with Alex?"

Melissa followed the direction of her gaze. "That must be Arna Teln, the new captain who replaced Bavin Moresol. Jason was talking about her this morning. She just arrived yesterday. Alex didn't tell you?"

"N-no." Joanna faltered, reluctant to admit that she and Alex were barely talking.

"Is something the matter?" Melissa asked curiously seeing Joanna's obvious discomfort.

Joanna shrugged. "Nothing. Not really. I'm just surprised that Bavin's replacement is a woman, that's all. I had just assumed for some reason that the personal guard assigned to Alex would all be men."

"Well, don't forget they pledge allegiance to you and your children as well. Jason tells me she has outstanding credentials, and won many service recognitions in the Conflicts. I also understand that she and Alex have a close friendship that goes back quite far. There's some history between their families as well."

"Really?" Joanna kept her tone deliberately casual, uncaring.

"Um. It's quite interesting. But you should ask your husband, my dear. What *I* want to know is have you talked to him about the trip yet? I want to leave by the end of the week."

Joanna glanced over at the cozy scene again, took a deep breath, and lied. "Yes. I'm going with you."

"Wonderful," Melissa squealed and clapped her hands, as excited as a child. "This will be so much fun!"

Joanna barely paid attention as Melissa, wrapped up in her own plans for the future talked enthusiastically about what she wanted to accomplish on the trip. She deliberately avoided looking in Alex's direction again. By the time she and Melissa were ready to leave, and her glance was drawn involuntarily again in that direction, the table was empty.

LATER THAT afternoon, a package was delivered to Joanna. The message on the communicator chip from Alex was brief and formal, the tone stiff and containing little warmth. "Please wear this tonight. I regret I am unable to accompany you to the Hall, but will meet you there. Mark and Eric will escort you."

With trembling fingers, Joanna opened the small tubular package. Inside lay a delicate, shimmering prism the color of her eyes. She carefully lifted it out of its confinement by the slender coppery thread to which it was attached and held it up to look at it. The prism seemed to glow with a life of its own.

Without warning, an overwhelming wave of grief washed over her. This was the first gift she had ever received from Alex. And it came too late. The beautiful, fragile jewel slipped forgotten from her fingers to fall into the cushioned safety of the couch as Joanna's thoughts turned bleakly and with growing determination to the realization that an end had to be reached in this situation with Alex, no matter the outcome. She couldn't go on like this. Tonight must be the night to confront him and offer an ultimatum.

She was cool and withdrawn when Mark and Eric arrived to escort her later that evening. They declared her elegant and stunning in the simple, unadorned black she wore and she acknowledged their compliments politely but without enthusiasm. They did their best to entertain her on the way to the Hall, but she couldn't bring herself to smile, nor did their lighthearted antics come close to penetrating, even for a moment, the wall of sadness that encased her.

The cultural events of the evening were over and the guests were beginning to sample the tempting food delicacies laid out for them by the time Alex appeared, his new captain by his side. From across the room, Joanna felt his eyes on her. She allowed her gaze to meet his briefly and saw his attention shift slightly lower seeking, she knew, the gift he had bestowed on her earlier. Even at this distance, she saw the brilliance of his eyes dull and his expression become shuttered as he found no evidence of it around her throat.

Joanna watched out of the corner of her eye as he started to make his way across the room, stopping every now and again to introduce the woman at his side and share laughter with various acquaintances. Although he wasn't on a direct path, it became obvious he was heading in her direction. She lost her nerve.

Mumbling an excuse to Melissa, she fled to the closest door leading outside. Gulping in great breaths of the chill night air, she wrapped her arms tightly around herself to try and still the violent trembling of her body. So much for courage and determination, she thought miserably.

Tonight the sky was filled with darting streaks and swirls of phosphorescence green, and the moons had dimmed and retreated as if recognizing that even their magnificence couldn't compete. Joanna allowed herself to be mesmerized and soothed by the display. The gentle night noises were a welcome relief in her present mood after the fast paced activity of the Merlon entertainers and the strain of socializing, which was the last thing she wanted to be doing.

There was a light touch on her bare arm, and she knew without turning who stood there.

"You didn't wear it!" His tone was filled with what could have been disappointment, but she chose to interpret it as accusatory.

She shook her head, unable to speak and not yet ready to turn around and face him.

His sigh whispered softly past her cheek and disappeared into the mists rolling in from the lake. "Joanna, what's the matter? Why can't we even talk to one another anymore?"

She was silent, struggling to suppress tears, willing her voice to be steady. Finally she said quietly and firmly, "I can't *be* what you want me to be, Alex."

"So it would seem." His own tone came across as forbiddingly cold and inflexible.

She was afraid to turn and face him, afraid of what she would see in his face, afraid she would break down completely and give in to what to he wanted, and in doing so, destroy her soul. "You've put me in a prison, and I don't know that I can live this way. I need some time. I-I want to leave Treaine. I have to, *need* to go away for..." Her throat closed against the heaviness of unshed tears. She couldn't complete her thoughts. Everything she wanted to say was coming out all wrong. Her voice trailed off as she fought to control herself and not reveal her emotions. She took several deep breaths and opened her mouth again to tell him that she wanted to go away with Melissa, to put some distance between them, so that she could try, once and for all, to try to come to terms with what he expected of her, but his voice, quiet and emotionless, stopped her.

"I can't fight you anymore, Joanna. If this marriage partnership is so abhorrent to you, I'll arrange a formal release from your responsibilities. I cannot allow a complete severance for the sake of the child, but the release will allow you to go your own way. All I ask is that you allow me to be there for the birth of my son, and to have some influence on his upbringing."

The words, so horribly unexpected, so terribly out of character for Alex, froze her completely and shattered any slight hope she had that they could still work things out. He had paused, as if waiting for a response, then she heard him say quietly, "I'll arrange for a quorum in the morning. Mark and Eric will escort you home tonight."

That which she would have welcomed several months ago, now tore at her soul and shattered her spirit. Her heart was pounding so loudly in her ears that she didn't hear him leave and, when she turned around seconds later to beg him to keep her on any terms, only a mist-filled emptiness stretched before her.

Later, she didn't remember clearly how she got through the rest of evening. She vaguely recalled returning to the Hall and must have gone through the right motions and said the right words because no one commented on her behavior, or asked her why her heart was breaking, or asked why Alex seemed to have disappeared.

He didn't return home that night, and Joanna tossed and turned restlessly in the big bed. She finally fell into an exhausted slumber as light was rapidly filling the room with the promise of the new day, only to be awakened what seemed to be minutes later by the insistent chiming of the computer letting her know someone was at the door.

She buried her head under the pillow, willing the noise to go away, but it continued, seeming to become more frantic and persistent in its tone. Finally, she stumbled out of bed, grabbed a wrap, and headed for the door, determined to get rid of whomever it was in a hurry. She made the mistake of releasing the door mechanism and stumbled back as Melissa stalked unceremoniously into the room.

"You look like hell," she declared rudely, surveying Joanna's rumpled and weary state.

"Go away, Melissa," Joanna said tiredly. "I need to sleep."

"Maybe. But it seems to me you desperately need something entirely different. What the hell is going on between you and Alex? Jason tells me he's called a quorum this morning and that it has something to do with you and him. What does it mean?"

"It means that he's releasing me from this marriage partnership." The brave smile she tried to paste on her face failed miserably. "Just what I always wanted, right?"

She blinked at the stream of colorful words that issued from her friend's mouth, wondering inanely where Melissa could possibly have picked them up. Exhaustion made her feel strangely detached, and she made no objection when Melissa grabbed her arm and hauled her back into the sleeping chamber. She found herself shoved onto the bed as an angry finger was shaken in her face.

"Just stay here! You two are obviously incapable of acting like adults around each other. I *am* going to interfere, and I *am* going to get this whole miserable farce of a marriage straightened out."

Before Joanna could respond, Melissa, blond hair flying, had stamped furiously out of the room and was gone.

ALEX STARED in frustration around the table as he furiously debated in his mind what his next course of action should be. His marriage had fallen apart. Last night, his deepest fears had become reality. He had been willing to compromise, had finally accepted that she needed her work, had been ready to tell her that he wouldn't stand in her way any more. But before he could, she had told him that she didn't want him, couldn't even tolerate being with him it seemed. And he loved her too much to hold her. The agony he had felt when he had told her he would release her still churned within him, and he wondered dispassionately if it would ever ease.

And now, as he looked at each of his captains in turn, he knew he had what amounted to mutiny on his hands. Not a single one of his captains had agreed to his request to formalize a separation. The five men had refused their consent and Arna Teln had cautiously withheld her vote, not fully understanding the circumstances.

The door to the room slid open with a bang and Melissa marched in. Magnificent in her fury, she was dressed for battle in a wild array of clashing colors. Her beautiful, long blond hair was drawn up high on the back of her head and swirled freely around her angry face. Her entrance brought the occupants of the room to their feet in shock. Jason opened his mouth, looked at Alex, then curiously pressed his lips grimly together again. With a gesture, he sent the other captains back to their seats.

Melissa ignored them and went to stand within inches of Alex. Unflinchingly, she glared up into his face and demanded, "Do you love her?"

"What?"

"You heard me. Do you love her?"

"That's none of your business," Alex snapped, wondering why Jason didn't escort this crazy woman from the room.

"It is my business when you're about to ruin my friend's life and drive her into insanity," Melissa declared sweepingly.

"You're wrong, Melissa," Alex said tiredly, backing away a step, only to find himself closely pursued. "It's what she wanted."

"Maybe in the beginning, but not anymore, not for a long time. She loves you. Do. You. Love. Her?" The words were practically spat out, demanding an answer.

Alex studied her carefully and saw the conviction written in her face. A seed of hope sprouted and grew strongly within him. A great weight was lifting. He responded with quiet dignity, "More than my life."

"Then tell her that, you brainless idiot—"

Jason's hands slammed down on the table. "Melissa!" he roared warningly.

She barely paused. "And when you're done convincing her of it, you'd better be ready to work out some compromises if you want that woman by your side for the rest of your life."

She stopped abruptly, satisfied she had accomplished her purpose, and meekly walked to where Jason stood, his face filled with wrath and admiration. Silence filled the room. Everyone held their breath.

Alex's lips twitched. "This meeting is adjourned, ladies, gentlemen." He moved hastily to the door, then turned back and directed a parting shot at Jason. "I don't think she can help it. Don't be too angry with her."

Chapter 45

JOANNA WANDERED slowly along the shore. She loved this time of day, when the early breezes were just coming to life and scattering the last remnants of the mists. Feeling strangely relaxed, the thought that she might, even now, be released from her bond with Alex didn't weigh too heavily on her. She wondered curiously what Melissa was up to and then even that thought had dissolved, leaving her mind empty.

She had almost reached the spot where she and Alex had first seen the gromorion when a shimmering cloud of light caught her attention. She waited quietly, expectantly, and within seconds the cloud had reached her and taken shape in front of her. She smiled and sank to her knees.

"It's you," she said softly.

"Yes, lady." The gentle whisper of sound embraced her with warmth, reminding her of another time not so long ago when she had experienced the same feeling.

"It was you," she gasped in wonder. "You were with me in the Temple. You protected me from those people."

"I only added strength to your own abilities." A pause, and then, "Your husband comes, lady. Open your heart and mind to what he has to say."

A slight crunch of sand followed the words, and Joanna rose to her feet and turned slowly, hardly daring to hope. Alex stood before her. The expression on his face made her want to weep. Something had driven the coldness from his eyes and swept the veil from his emotions. Love and tenderness and caring shone from his face. He stretched out a hand in invitation and spoke the words she had longed to hear.

"I love you, Joanna. More than I thought I could ever love anyone. Please stay with me and share my life."

Her hand reached out and was enclosed tightly in his. "I love you, too, Alex," she whispered.

He looked deeply into her eyes and read the undeniable truth. Then she was crushed in his embrace. Their hunger and passion for each other had been too long denied and, without thought or caring, they tore at each other's clothes and sank to the beach to satisfy temporarily an explosive need.

Later, much later, Joanna lifted her head from his chest and glanced around. "Where did it go?'

"I think it's purpose was accomplished, Meira."

She sighed, and dropped her head back down on its hard, throbbing pillow. "What does that mean?"

"It wanted to make sure the prophecy was—"

"No." She laid a finger against his lips. "What does 'Meira' mean?"

"I thought you knew," Alex said in surprise. He kissed her finger, then her forehead gently. "It means, ' deeply beloved'."

"Oh. I do love you," she said, raising up on one elbow to look in his face.

"I know that, now." His expression turned serious. "Joanna, we *will* work out our differences. Be patient with me. We still have so much to learn about one another. And I admit I haven't made much of an effort thus far to understand your culture. I'm used to having my requests— orders as you call them—carried out without question, and I suppose I'll continue to expect that to a certain extent." He sighed. "I know you want to return to the negotiating table, and I can accept that now. I understand it's important to you and I know you're very good at it. I just wish it didn't consume so much of your time." The pulse at his temple beat more darkly and his mouth tilted in a grin. "But I will try to listen and understand your point of view, if you promise never to ignore me again."

It was a huge admission for him and the concession was all the sweeter. Joanna laughed suddenly and tickled his ribs. "You'd better," she threatened, "or this baby's career path will be determined at birth, because he'll be counseling at all our fights. And I promise not to ignore you again—for more than a day, anyway."

Her laughter increased as she continued to torment his ribs.

Far, far across the lake, a shimmering cloud spun and dipped before disappearing into the forest.

The End

Anne Clarke

TRIPS TO the library, from a very young age, are treasured memories in Anne Clarke's mind. Reading and writing have always been twin passions and stories of futuristic worlds hold a special fascination for her. Also a lover of exotic places, she has traveled on three continents. Those travels have helped inspire the creation of distant and futuristic worlds.

Although now firmly grounded with a banking career, marriage and two young sons in Portland, Oregon, she dreams of the day she can expose her sons to some of the experiences she had growing up in Africa even as she dreams of other more imaginary worlds.

Printed in the United States
1059800005B

9 780759 905344